HER MAGIC TOUCH
Hell Yeah! Book 3

SABLE HUNTER

This is a work of fiction. Names, characters, places and incidents are either the product of the author's imagination or used fictitiously, and any resemblance to actual persons, living or dead, business establishments, events or locales is entirely coincidental.

Copyright © Pending Sable Hunter

All rights reserved.

www.sablehunter.com

ISBN-13: 978-1475120349
ISBN-10: 1475120346

Six brothers. One Dynasty—
TEBOW RANCH.
Meet the McCoy brothers and their friends— men who love as hard as they play.
Texas Cowboys – nothing hotter.
HELL YEAH!

Take a moment to check out Sable's current and upcoming projects.
Visit her on:
Website: http://www.sablehunter.com
Facebook: https://www.facebook.com/authorsablehunter
Email: sablehunter@rocketmail.com

Check out all of Sable's books on Amazon
http://www.amazon.com/author/sablehunter

Cover and Technical Advising by Barb Caruso
http://www.addedtouches.com

CONTENT

1	Chapter One	1
2	Chapter Two	29
3	Chapter Three	55
4	Chapter Four	83
5	Chapter Five	103
6	Chapter Six	125
7	Chapter Seven	149
8	Chapter Eight	177
9	Chapter Nine	195
10	Chapter Ten	225
11	Chapter Eleven	251
12	Chapter Twelve	279
13	Chapter Thirteen	303
	Epilogue	327

Chapter One

Joseph McCoy's philosophy was simple; every woman needs multiple orgasms in order to be happy. Without a doubt, he had done his part in spreading happiness to as many beautiful, deserving women as possible. The latest candidate for his benevolent attention was leaning forward, displaying her silicon enhanced chest for his viewing enjoyment. "Tell me, Mr. McCoy, what do you consider to be your greatest accomplishment?" She asked a follow-up question before he could get his mind in gear to answer. "Was it when you won the Doak Walker Award for being the best running back in college football?"

Tearing his eyes from her impressive cleavage, Joseph flashed the reporter one of his trademark dimpled grins. "No ma'am." Like all the McCoy brothers, you could rake southern charm off him with a stick. "I consider what I achieved *off* the gridiron to be more important." He was referring to family issues, but she couldn't get her mind out of the bedroom.

With a sly little wink and a cheeky little smile, the interviewer from **Texas Extreme** flirted for all she was worth. "I've heard rumors of your - uh - prowess in many different areas, Mr. McCoy."

As he felt his dick rise to the occasion, Joseph checked the clock on the wall. Hell! He didn't have time to diddle with this little darlin'. If he was going to make it to Marble Falls in time for the pre-race show, he needed to be on the road in the next fifteen minutes. "In this case, the rumors happen to be true." He watched her eyes turn dark with passion. She was turned on, bless her heart. Damn his charm! Knowing it was up to him to get her mind back on the interview, he took charge. "My greatest achievement is my family, Ms. Warner. I'm proud of the fact that Aron, Jacob and I have been able to band together and create a good home for our younger brothers. We've made sure they received a good education and we've built Tebow Ranch into a successful enterprise. After the loss of our parents, we never considered any other option; we worked hard, stuck together and made family a priority."

Pushing her platinum blonde hair over her shoulder, the reporter couldn't resist. "When you played for Texas, they called you 'The Stallion'. Would you care to elaborate on how you acquired that particular nickname?"

Stretching his long muscular legs out in front of him, Joseph crossed one custom cowboy boot over the other. "Well darlin'," he graced her with a slow, seductive wink, "I'm not certain how I got HUNG with that handle, but I assure you that I've tried to live up to the image." He couldn't help but chuckle when her gaze slid down his body and got slowed down by the speed bump of his erection. Teasingly, he put his thumbs in his belt, one on either side of his signature Superman belt buckle – and caught her eyes as she looked back up, letting her know that he knew she was ogling his manly credentials.

She swallowed hard, but managed to find her words, "We know you've set a free-fall speed record when you made that jump last month sponsored by Red Bull." He nodded, but she continued. "You've also broken diving records for the longest cave passage when you proved those underwater springs near Tallahassee, Florida were linked."

Joseph laughed, "That's one experience I don't care to repeat. We swam seven miles in six hours, then it took fourteen hours to decompress before we could surface."

Carrie visibly shuddered at the thought. "You seem to live for the thrill, Mr. McCoy. I understand you also hold the record for free-climbing *El Capitan* in California."

Getting antsy, Joseph sought a way to give the reporter what she needed for her article. He needed to be on his way. Maybe if he got her phone number, they could hook up after he finished the cross-country race. "Yea, I conquered 'The Nose' in ten hours; it was grueling." Getting to his feet, he joined her on the settee. Automatically, she scooted closer to him. At the flush on her cheeks, he knew her heart was racing. Steeling himself against her charms, he asked, "Is there something you wanted to ask me about the GNCC Off-road race today?"

She licked her lips, and he wanted to help her moisten the plump rosebud. Joseph could tell her panties were damp; a whiff of her arousal was in the air. With a shaking little voice, she managed to squeak out her question. "This new course you'll be racing on today is supposed to be very dangerous. Do you ever get afraid?"

Her question was so unexpected he was stunned. Joseph McCoy afraid? With an arrogant snort, Joseph put that matter to rest. "Honey, I've taken more chances than you can count. Didn't you know?" At her puzzled look, Jacob spread his arms and proclaimed. "Put this in your article, so everybody will understand - Daredevil Joseph McCoy is invincible!"

On the Road

"God's gift to women," Joseph laughed. Usually that term was thrown out as an insult, but when Carrie had breathed it in his ear, it sure had sounded like a compliment. Maybe, he was God's gift to women. Who knows? Everybody had to have a purpose in life. Pleasing beautiful women was certainly a high calling. And one day soon, he would please Carrie Warner. Today, he just hadn't had time to do a seduction justice. He hadn't gone away from the interview empty handed, however. Joseph had traded a kiss for her phone number. She had clung to him, letting him know she would come to him anytime, anywhere - all he had to do was call. He stored the number in his phone, alongside a dozen other hopeful females, all vying to capture the attention of the modern-day desperado.

Since Marble Falls was only a few hours from Kerrville, Joseph had decided to drive. Only his crew had accompanied him in a caravan of trailers and dual cab pickups. He had spoken to Jacob right after the interview and assured him that he didn't mind making the trip alone. Joseph hadn't made too many trips without at least one of his brothers traveling with him.

Rolling down the window, he let the Texas breeze keep him wide-awake and alert. Smiling, he admitted that the winds of change were blowing at Tebow Ranch. Aron had fallen for sweet Libby Fontaine, who had come to them as their temporary cook for the summer. Their older brother had vowed to never love again, after being hung out to dry by his ex-wife Sabrina. But Libby had changed his mind, and Joseph couldn't be happier. Jacob, the second oldest, had bought a piece of Texas scrub property and discovered it was sitting on a huge pocket of natural gas and blue rock. So, his time was split between family business and his own interests. Isaac, just two years younger than Joseph, was home less and less these days. He spent his time riding with a motorcycle gang or playing pool at the local bar. Something was going on with his younger brother, Noah and a local blonde bombshell named Harper, but Joseph hadn't figured that out yet. And Nathan - well Nathan was their joy. At thirteen, he was all boy and feeling his oats.

Turning on the radio, he let the sweet sounds of Travis Tritt lull his spirit. Joseph thought he was one lucky bastard. So far, he had met every challenge - jumped every hurdle - climbed every mountain. People say he led a charmed life, and that he must have one helluva guardian angel watching over him. Joseph didn't know about that - he did know that life was meant to be lived, and he intended to live every day like there was no tomorrow.

If only he could shake off the funny feeling that haunted him in the middle of the night. There was something missing in his life and he couldn't quite put his finger on it. It couldn't be women - he had plenty of pussy any time he wanted it. It couldn't be excitement; he had all of the adrenaline rushes he could handle. So why did he feel like something was missing? In the dark of night - when all was still and quiet - why did he feel lost and alone?

Texas Motocross - Marble Falls Raceway - Joseph's race

He had to be first. Joseph would accept nothing less. The track was new; a first cut through a fearsome rocky terrain that should have sent chills down his spine. Curves that bent out over fifteen foot drop-offs were taken at breakneck speed. Leaning into the curve, Joseph threw his body sideways to counterbalance the weight of the bike. Terry Rhodes was hot on his heels. Giving his bike a little extra gas, he sent it into a jump over a dry creek bed. If he could win today, the Yamaha sponsorship would be a sure thing. Afterwards, he would call that hot little reporter and ease the ache in his dick.

Flying through the air, his mind was racing as fast as his bike. After this race he was going to slow down a bit. He had been away from the ranch too much in the past year. There was plenty of excitement to be found around the Hill Country, and he should be able to keep himself entertained on the extreme sports circuits and off. It was time he did his part in the day-to-day operations at Tebow. Besides, Aron and Jacob were worried about Isaac. Maybe he could spend more time with his brother, and find out exactly where his head was at these days.

Coming down out of the jump, everything went into horrible slow motion. As he got closer to the ground, he could see the rock. It was too big to miss. There was no way he was going to avoid a crash. It wouldn't be his first one; he knew how to dump the bike to cause the least amount of damage to it and to his body. It would have worked, - if Terry hadn't been right on top of him. As Joseph's bike came down, hit the rock and spun crazily to the left - Terry's bike followed the same trajectory and as his friend was flung to the right; his bike came sailing through the air right over Joseph's prone body.

The world spun crazily as Joseph landed hard. He felt his ankle twist and white-hot pain radiated up his leg. Then a roaring noise filled his head and a blow from above knocked the breath from his body. Shit! A bike had come crashing down on him! He tried to turn over and . . . something was wrong! His mind kept telling his body to move, but nothing was happening. O, God! O, God! O, God! Joseph began praying. What had he done? All he could do was lay there and wait until someone came to help.

Joseph's Guardian Angel
New Orleans, Louisiana - Cady's mysterious dream
　　Sometimes things aren't necessarily the way we think they are.
　　Sometimes they're not even close.
　　For example, there have always been tales of angels and guardian angels - beautiful winged beings who hover near us and guide our steps, protecting us from danger.
　　And they're right.
　　In a way.
　　Sort of.

　　But angels aren't always invisible. And they don't necessarily have wings. Sometimes they are disguised as people we know, or at least people we think we know. They exist in this world to guard and protect, but they are bound by gravity and time and all the other weighty worries of this flawed existence. And they have feelings - - and hopes - - and dreams - - and hearts that can be easily broken.
　　"Why?" she screamed. "Just tell me why?" Acadia paced across the marble floor, her slippers making no noise on the cool, smooth surface. "I could have saved him. That's my job. I could have prevented this from happening."
　　"Sit down." The voice brooked no argument.
　　"What kind of watcher am I, if I'm not permitted to intervene when my human needs help?" Her spirit was in

agony. Joseph had been badly hurt and they had not allowed her to do a **damn** thing." She could have cried – but tears were not permitted.

"I heard that, Acadia. Cursing is not permitted, even in your thoughts. You know that."

"Sorry." She wasn't.

"Lying isn't permitted, either."

Huffing in consternation, Cady started to get up. She needed to check on Joseph.

"Acadia, you must sit still and listen." At the stern reprimand, Acadia slid into her seat and narrowed her attention to the gentleman sitting in front of her.

"Sorry. I am a bit preoccupied." She smoothed out the folds of the soft shift she wore and tried to calm down. "Joseph is scared and sad and I don't know what to do for him."

A breath of pure frustration erupted from the terse lips of Master Gabe. "It has never been your responsibility to affect the happiness of your subjects, just their safety."

"If that is true, why wasn't I permitted to stop that horrible crash from happening? I was there, hovering right over him. It would have been easy to push that flying motorcycle just an inch to keep it from landing square on his back. I could have stopped this!" Cady knew she was dancing right on the edge of insubordination. And the consequences of that charge could be dire – eternally dire – and warm.

"It was meant to be Acadia. There is a purpose for everything – even tragedy."

"What possible purpose could hurting my Joseph have?" She hung her head in despair, not knowing what the future would hold for her charge – or for her.

"Everything has a purpose. The events of human lives are woven together in an imperceptible tapestry. And neither humanity nor the angels are permitted to see the big picture or know the reason that bad things happen to good people.

Our knowledge is limited to protect us."

"I understand that. I just don't happen to agree with it." Master Gabe looked at her sharply.

"Irregardless, circumstances have changed for you. You are leaving."

"Leaving?" Acadia was stunned. "Where in the heavens would I go?"

"You are going to earth." At those impossible words, Acadia almost swooned. "Joseph, your charge, requires more interaction than you are able to give him here. He's about to face the ultimate challenge – even greater than what he has already gone through. Because of the importance of his life mission, we can't take any chances that he will veer from his destiny. You cannot fail, Acadia. Failure is not an option."

"I would never fail Joseph. I love him."

And she did love him. Acadia loved everything about Joseph McCoy. His looks. His personality. His intelligence. His stubbornness. His daring. And most of all: his soul. Acadia loved Joseph almost more than she loved God. And that fact could get her in serious trouble. Angels are supposed to love God above all else. Acadia tried, but Joseph owned her heart.

"Things are going to be difficult for you on earth, Acadia," Master Gabe cautioned. At her puzzled look, he leaned back in his chair and tried to explain. "You are loved here in heaven. In fact, you are one of the favorites, despite your tendency toward stubbornness. Your beauty and goodness is unchallenged in heaven. It won't be like that on earth."

"I can live with that. As long as I am with Joseph, I can endure anything," she assured him.

"You may think so, but it's still going to take some getting used to. Beauty is not defined on earth as it is defined here. What makes you beloved here - will not be valued down there."

Acadia did not understand. "What difference does it make if I am beautiful or not? I only want to help Joseph. He won't care about how I look. Will he?" Her innocent question caused Master Gabe to take a deep breath and consider carefully before answering. Acadia was strong in many ways, but her little spirit was fragile. She didn't realize how easily she could be broken.

"That remains to be seen." Lying was forbidden, but the truth was sometimes as devastating as a lie. "There is one more thing you should know." Reaching into his desk for a file folder, he took out a form. "We are going to send you back to the beginning. You can't just drop into the time/space continuum fully grown. We've processed the paperwork; you are going to have to be born and grow up and make your way in the world just like any other human being."

"How will I find Joseph?" Acadia was afraid. This sounded entirely too complicated. She knew Joseph needed her – now more than ever. But how could she be more effective as a human than an angel. It didn't make sense.

"Don't worry about those details. Leave that to me. Joseph will find you when he needs you the most." He filled out his part of the form and handed it to her with instructions on where to go to arrange for her transfer.

"When will I return here?" There was so much she did not know. Acadia's head was spinning.

"You will return here when your job has been completed. We'll be in touch." With that he hurried her off. Master Gabe shook his head. It would take a miracle for this mission to go off without a hitch.

Cady jerked awake. Good Grief! Throwing off the cover, she fanned herself. It was unlike her to suffer from nightmares. Lying there she tried to remember the dream. It had definitely made her uncomfortable. Try as she might, she couldn't remember the details. All she could remember was a name. Joseph. Joseph. Who the hell was Joseph?

Rolling over, she soothed her hand over the empty space that loomed so large beside her. Cady Renaud slept alone. What she wouldn't give for someone to snuggle up to. At times, she would hug herself tight, imagining what it would be like to be held in a lover's close embrace. Like a teenager, she grabbed her pillow and practiced kissing. She ought to be good at it by now; this pillow had seen a lot of action over the years. As she laid one on her pale pink Egyptian cotton pillowslip, she got tickled at herself and giggled out loud. She was truly pitiful; twenty-eight years old and never been kissed. Flopping backwards, she growled her frustration. Why couldn't she have been born beautiful - or at least passably cute?

Unable to sleep, Cady made her way to the bathroom in the dark. Knowing what she would see, she dreaded turning on the light. Click. Wish. Wish. Wish. Opening her eyes, she was met with the same tiresome reflection that she always saw. Bland. Boring. Washed out. Nondescript brown hair, brown eyes, light olive skin - as unexciting as a gift adorned with plain brown wrapping - no frills, no thrills - a face that was as appealing as a stale piece of white bread. Disgusted, Cady flipped off the light and did her business in the dark. Back in the bed, she let out a long breath - hating how loud it was in the tomb silent room. Sometimes she wanted to scream. She was so lonely. How could someone with so much love to give exist in such miserable isolation? As always, she clung to what her grandmother had told her.

Nana Fontenot was an old hoodoo woman who lived deep in the bayou country of Terrebonne Parish. She was a Creole; which meant that she was a mix of French, Spanish, American Indian and Black. By the one-drop rule of the Old South, Nana Fontenot was black and she clung to that like a battle cry. Cady's mother had been raised white - and Cady - was just Cady. She lived her life using the gifts God gave her and trying to find whatever happiness she could.

Nana Fontenot had taught her many things. Cady could read someone's future in the bottom of a teacup, or she could read the lines on your palm. With the right herbs and a crystal or two, Cady could make a mojo bag that would help your chances at the casino or give you safe travels on the road. More importantly, Nana Fontenot had taught her how to mix oils, herbs and other mysterious ingredients to help in the healing of the sick. This was Cady's special gift. Her grandmother and her aunt had worked with her and she now surpassed even what they could do together. Her aunt Anglique had held her hands and told her than she was a traiture, a healer, and an empath. As an empath, she could lay hands on the sick or injured and draw out the other person's illness or pain and absorb it into herself. Cady had to be careful with this gift, because it was dangerous and extremely draining on her health, as well as her emotional well-being.

Cady had cured many people of different injuries and diseases with a combination of traditional and magical healing. But, in her work as an empath, her aunt and grandmother had cautioned her to take into herself only what she could throw off. "Every empath is different," her aunt had said. "So, we can't be sure. But until we know – do not take burns, broken bones or crippling diseases. If you do, you may find they are with you forever. Heal these people with your magick, but don't open your body to accept their afflictions. You must protect yourself." So Cady had healed the sick and comforted those in pain, and over the years she found the only thing she could not cure was her own heartsickness. At the end of every day, no matter how many other people she helped - Cady was alone.

The one memory she held onto with her whole heart was the night that Nana Fontenot had looked into her cauldron for Cady. She would only do it once for each child and grandchild - she always said that there are some things you are better off not knowing. The old woman had no desire to know when she would lose a loved one to death - she had no heart to see a future she could not change.

That night had been one Cady would never forget. Her grandmother had pulled the cauldron close and had pushed both of their hands down into the dark water. Cady would swear on a stack of Bibles that the water had gone from stone cold to almost boiling in a few seconds. Afterward, Cady had lain her head on Nana's knee and as the old woman soothed down her hair and spoke softly, "Sweet girl, one day you will be as beautiful on the outside as you are within. There is a man destined to fall in love with you, never doubt it. At first, he will be attracted to your sweet and gentle personality. Soon, he will begin to see you in a different light - and when he does, you will grow more beautiful everyday. His love will make you beautiful - not only in his eyes, but in other's eyes as well." Her grandmother was rarely wrong. So, Cady clung to that prophecy, praying she was right.

Her room was so familiar to Cady that she didn't even need to turn on a light. She left the bathroom and walked around her bed and looked out the window. Since it was cool enough, she had slept without the A/C; which was saying something for New Orleans. She went to her knees by the window and looked through the screen. It was a dark night; the moon was barely a sliver in the sky. Constance Street was quiet, only the sound of a tugboat broke the silence. The mighty Mississippi was only a few blocks away, and Cady strained to hear other river sounds. She was tempted to put on her clothes and stroll down to the riverbank. There was one place where she could maneuver between the warehouses and docks on the city-side, and actually reach the water's edge. It was tempting, but dawn was only a few hours away, and she needed to rest. There were a million little chores waiting on her attention.

When Cady was on a job, personal errands and house repairs took a back seat to her patients needs. It was her policy to move in with the client for several months. It took time and effort to get the patient into a rehabilitated state where they were comfortable taking care of themselves. The one-on-one attention in the patient's home meant all the difference in the world to them, but it also meant she spent very little time at her own home during the course of a year.

After high school, Cady had gravitated to a career that would compliment her natural abilities. She had received her degree in physical therapy and had also become a licensed medical masseuse. Combined with her magical acumen, Cady had been known to work miracles. Several clients who had suffered severe paralysis from accidents and war injuries had benefited from her expertise. She had to be careful with her gift, not everyone welcomed the idea of alternative medicine - and boy, was what she did 'alternative'. Sometimes, she could use her empath gift without drawing a lot of attention to the more mystical aspects of it, but in order to do that, she had to earn the complete faith and trust of her patient. Only a few people actually knew and understood what she could do. And that was probably for the best.

Joseph lay in the hospital bed and wished he were dead. There was no way he could live like this. The doctors tried to tell him the paralysis might be temporary due to swelling around his spinal cord. But in all honesty, they were only spouting off guesses. Hell, he couldn't even piss by himself. Every time a nurse came in and wanted to mess with the catheter that was stuck up his dick, he just wanted to throw a fuckin' bedpan at 'em.

Rolling his head from side to side, he tortured himself with a mental list of things he might never be able to do again.

Ride a horse.

Climb a mountain.

Take a shit in anything besides a damn bag.
Walk.
Feel a warm, soft woman beneath him.
Get an erection.
Hell! Damn! Fuck! Joseph heard familiar footsteps coming down the hall - three sets of them. The steel-toed boots and the long determined strides of the McCoy brothers were unmistakable. In anguish, Joseph realized that he might never walk beside them again.

As the hospital room door creaked open, he reset the muscles of his face into a devil-may-care expression. He couldn't let them know he was scared shitless. They didn't deserve to have to put up with a brother in his condition. He would have to see what he could do about that.

"I can't believe the lengths you'll go too to get outta work," Aron stood at the end of the hospital bed. Joseph could see how tightly his fists were clinched. There wasn't a doubt in his mind that Aron had dug his fingernails into his palms to keep from losing it. His big brother was looking at him, lying in a hospital bed, possibly paralyzed for the rest of his life and he was trying to be strong, not only for him – but for the rest of the family.

"Whatever it takes, man. You know I hate grunt work." Joseph was determined to put on a brave front. They didn't have to know he was losing his mind.

Jacob and Isaac flanked either side of the bed. Joseph looked at them both and tried to smile. "You didn't all have to come. I'll be out of here before you know it."

"You're our brother. Where else would we be?" Jacob wasn't one to put on a front; he led with his heart. "Noah would have come, but he stayed behind with Libby and Nathan."

"What do the doctors say?" Isaac pulled a chair up next to the bed. Decked out in his signature black leather, he was a sharp contrast to his cowboy brothers.

"I can't walk." Joseph was still trying to make a joke out

of the situation.

"Do they think it's temporary?" Aron asked with hope in his voice and in his eyes.

Joseph closed his eyes, turning serious. "They can't be sure, but it doesn't look good." After all the chances he had taken – all of the dangerous things he had done and survived – why had this happened now? He had thought he was invincible. Where in the hell had his guardian angel been when he needed her? She, sure as hell, had let him down. Of course – he didn't really believe he had ever had one – not really. That was just stupid childhood imaginings. When he had been small, he had an imaginary friend – a beautiful girl who would come to him at night when he was afraid. After his parents were killed, this friend had helped him make it through many nights of sorrow and loneliness. The image of the girl who picked him up and dusted him off haunted him. She must have been his way of dealing with the tragedy of his parent's death. As he got older, the memory had faded – he couldn't even remember her face now. Aron's voice broke his reverie.

"I want to move you to Austin. I've already made some phone calls and found you a real good doctor. Besides, I want you closer to home." Aron cleared his throat, looking around at the men that meant more to him than anything - except Libby. "We'll start renovating the house, make it . . . . ."

"Handicap friendly?" Joseph couldn't help but let a note of bitterness filter into his voice.

"Joseph, we're going to stand by you, support you, and do whatever it takes to make sure you have the best possible care until you are healed." Jacob's words were almost prayerful. Joseph knew his brother was a great believer in miracles, having worked closely with cancer research – he had shared with them how he had seen people recover when medical science had all but given up on them. Jacob always preached to them that having a positive attitude was ninety percent of the battle.

"What if I'm not healed? What if I have to live like this for the rest of my life?" All pretenses were gone and Joseph's fear was as evident as the nose on his face. "What are we going to do?"

"We're McCoys." The way Isaac said those simple words – it was obvious, as far as he was concerned, they said all that needed to be said. They were McCoy's. "Together we can beat the shit out of anything."

Back at Tebow

The phone rang a little after six; Noah grabbed it, anxious to hear news. He spoke quietly for a few minutes; then handed the phone to Libby. She took it and Noah got up, giving her some privacy. "Hey, baby." Aron's voice sounded tired.

"I love you, Aron." It was the most comforting thing she could think to say. "How's Joseph?"

"I love you, too – more than you'll ever know. I wish you were here; I keep reaching for your hand. Jacob's slapped me twice; he thinks I'm getting fresh with him." Libby laughed at the mental picture. Aron's voice grew serious. "The tests are coming back, and the doctors say that Joseph has a spinal cord injury. They still can't tell us the full extent, but they know there is damage around the T10-L2 level."

"What does that mean?"

"I may be saying it all wrong, but right now Joseph seems to be fine above the waist, but he has very limited sensation below. That's not to say he won't regain some or all of it, but, right now? I can tell he's scared to death." Aron's voice revealed to Libby that he was worried and weary.

"What's next?" she asked.

"We're bringing him back to Austin in the morning. I want Dr. Cassidy to see him; he's the absolute best. Oh, yeah – and I've called a contractor to come out and put in some ramps and do some work on the back wing to make a place for Joseph to have all the room that he'll need – for –

whatever."

    Libby understood. Joseph's ordeal was going to be a long drawn out battle, at best.

    "Tell him I love him." Libby whispered.

    "I'll do it; you get some rest Libby-pearl. I'll kiss you awake when I get there."

    "So, you're coming back tonight?"

    "Yes, Jacob is going to stay and come back with Joseph when they transport him. Isaac and I are coming home and then we'll all meet him at Brackenridge, tomorrow. They have a woman there who is doing wonders with patients like Joseph."

    "Be safe," Libby said softly. "I'll leave the front porch light on."

    "I will be, and doll – keep the bed warm, I need you so badly. I just know if I could get my arms around you, everything will be all right."

    "Hurry home, I'll be waiting."

    The word spread. At first, reporters came to talk to him, all of them eager to get the latest word on his condition. Finally, Aron had cleared the place, calling them all a bunch of buzzards as they left. Joseph didn't want anybody around. Lying there unable to move from the waist down, he felt his life was over. Desperately, he tried to reach out to those that he was used to staying in touch with. Some of them responded, but it wasn't the same. Friends of his would say a few words and find any quick reason to hang up. Others, like the reporter from Extreme - wouldn't even pick up the phone. After three tries, leaving messages, Joseph finally got the idea. Carrie Warner did not want to talk to him – not even for a story. She wasn't interested in half a man. Joseph threw the phone across the room; he no longer had a need for it.

    He endured every test imaginable. Joseph had been poked, prodded and x-rayed. And still, there was no consensus on an outcome. The most they could tell him was that spinal cord injuries like this were uncertain; sensation and mobility might return in time – and it might not. They did encourage him to hire a physical therapist ASAP who could teach him how to cope and start exercising his muscles so they wouldn't start deteriorating. He had the sneaky suspicion they weren't telling him everything – and that pissed him off, royally.

Damn, he needed a drink of water. They said he needed to sleep, but he dreaded closing his eyes – every time he dozed off, he dreamed he was completely paralyzed, unable to blink or even swallow. So, they had given him some shit and it made him feel woozy. His mouth felt like it was full of cotton.

Joseph McCoy was big, with superior upper body strength. And before he thought – his mind told his body to get out of bed. His upper body moved, powerfully – but his lower half didn't cooperate. He lunged off the bed, and flopped on the floor like a dead carp. "Shit! Damn!" Joseph had never felt more helpless or humiliated. Right now, it was a good thing he didn't have a gun - he just might use it.

Cady awoke with a start. Something was wrong. Opening her eyes, she tried to make some sense of what she was seeing. What in the world? She wasn't in her room – hell, she wasn't even in her house. Where was she? Sitting up, she tried to make out her surroundings in the deep shadow. A groan to her left almost made her jump out of her skin.

Sitting up, she realized the bed she was in was higher than her own – it was a hospital bed.
Another groan. Good lord in heaven. It was a man! Stepping down, she saw his large body lying on the cold tile floor. He had fallen, and he appeared to be hurt. Kneeling she started to touch him, and it was like she was reaching through a fog. It was a strange sensation, like she could feel the billions of air particles her hand had to push through in order to touch his skin. He wore no shirt and touching him

seemed so momentous – so life-changing. As her hand hovered over his shoulder, he turned his head and Cady felt lightning bolts of recognition flash through her whole body. She knew this man – this beautiful man! His flesh was warm and smooth and his muscles were so well-defined as to be masculinity personified.

At her touch, his upper body jerked toward her. Her hand pulled back as if she expected to be burned by his heat. Still, she knew he needed her. "Can I help you? What happened?"

God! Was he dreaming? There was an angel hovering over him – or she looked like an angel – her face was exquisitely beautiful. His dream-time visitor had perfect features, rosebud lips and eyes that seemed to be the color of warm honey. Her hair hung in thick luscious waves to her waist and seemed to be the color of the night itself. God, he hated for her to see him like this – laying here – helpless – he had tried to pull himself off the floor but he was in pain, weak and these drugs didn't help. "You can't help me," Joseph grated at her, embarrassed for her to see him like this. Shit! What he would have done with an angel like this just a few days ago. "I'm beyond help."

Acadia knew what to do – and she knew what she wanted to do. Cady wanted to give this man comfort, love and strength. Leaning forward she placed her lips, gently, into the middle of his forehead and held them there, blessing him with all the grace and love in her heart. "No, no one is beyond help." Standing, Acadia offered him her hand. "We can do this together if you will trust me."

"Who are you? Are you a nurse?" He struggled to turn and look at her, and Cady knelt beside him, wanting to be closer, aching to show him compassion. "You don't look like any of the hospital employees that I've seen. Hell, you don't look like any woman I've ever known. You look so pure, beautiful – ethereal." He wiped a hand over his eyes, as if to clear his vision. "Shouldn't you call an aide to help?"

"You are strong," she encouraged. "You can do this. I will assist you. You can do anything, Joseph." Joseph. Yes, this was Joseph. She had never been more positive of anything in her life. With her steadying hand, he was able to turn and pull his useless bottom half up from the floor. She stepped closer – shielding, supporting until he could pull himself into the bed. He turned; fell back – exhausted, embarrassed, but she would have none of it.

Straightening his covers, she tucked him in. Anticipating what he had wanted, she handed him the water and held it as he drank. Then she enveloped him, cradling his head to her.

"Everything will be well, Joseph. I will see to it." With all the confidence in the world, Acadia placed a hand on his face and gave him what she hoped was the sexiest, most sensual kiss of his life.

Acadia knew true happiness for the first time. For she had not only kissed Joseph, but he returned her kiss – and oh, it was glorious!

Peace. Homecoming. Hope. Emotions welled up in Joseph that he thought had been lost on the racetrack at Marble Falls. Her kiss was so precious; her taste was the sweetest nectar. For a few seconds, they shared something that Joseph did not even know existed. It was nothing like the meaningless, faceless lust he had exchanged with countless women whose names he could not remember. He felt something – he could swear he did – below his waist – a twitch – hell, was he dreaming!?!?

Acadia raised her head – knowing it was time to go. She didn't want to. But, she had no choice – she could feel the pull. Grasping air, she fought for control – but – one moment she was there and the next – she was gone.

Joseph opened his eyes. He was alone. She was gone. Hell! It had been a dream.

Cady awoke with a start. Feeling around her, she made

sure she was in her own bed. It had been so real! What was it about this man? Joseph. His name was Joseph. And their lives and souls were intertwined in a way she did not understand. Aching from longing, Cady curled into a fetal position and wished she were with him. He needed her - but not nearly as much as she needed him. The only problem was – she had no idea how to find him.

Cady's Aunt Angelique had summoned her presence to her home on St. Charles Street. Having been unmarried for her entire adult life, Angelique shocked the family when she wed a medical doctor from the Island of Martinique. Angelique had spent the last twenty-five years, before she married Phillipe, as companion to Nanette Beaureguarde. The two women had been inseparable. Angelique hadn't just worked for the family; she was family. She also shared Nanette's magical way of life. The two ladies practiced witchcraft, or their version of it. In New Orleans, traditional witchcraft is a combination of the Celtic craft, voodoo, hoodoo, with a little Appalachian Granny Magic thrown in for good measure. If you asked them what their religion was, they would tell you Catholic. Their everyday life, however, was filled with mojo bags, spells, charms and a constant awareness of the supernatural.

Cady didn't know why she had been called, but a trip to see Aunt Angelique was never wasted. Parking on St. Charles was impossible, so she had walked the few blocks that separated their streets and rode the streetcar to the elegant Greek Revival home. She had not had an opportunity to visit with them since their marriage. Stepping off the clanging streetcar, she made her way into the lush yard. It was full of banana trees and magnolias with all manners of hostas, ginger lilies and other tropical plants. Before she could climb the steps to the wide verandah, Angelique opened the door and smiled at her niece.

"Were you watching for me?" Cady asked.

"No, Patrice told me you had arrived." This gave Cady a distinct chill for Patrice was Nanette's mother and she had been dead for some thirty years. However, goings-on of the ghostly variety were quite commonplace in their family. Angelique had a gift. Cady knew all gifts had their reasons, but this ability was a great burden for her aunt to bear. Angelique could see and speak to the spirits of the dead - and the dead were everywhere. She once said that New Orleans was awash in the dead. And that even after several years, the Katrina dead were very active, they lingered because they were angry for what had happened to them and what had happened to their city. Cady was grateful she could not see beyond the veil.

"Oh, that's nice. Tell her hello for me." Cady's eyes shifted around nervously. The problem was – she didn't doubt Angelique for a minute. Hugging her aunt, she let her eyes rove around the impressive entrance way and the grand staircase that swept up to the second floor. "Your home is lovely, Auntie."

"Thank you, dear." Angelique led her into the parlor. "I'll give you the grand tour later, but first I have something to discuss with you." They sat in front of a coffee table laden with a tea service. She had forgotten Angelique's penchant for tea.

"Is there something wrong?" Cady had some psychic ability, not as much as others in her family, but no one read Angelique unless she permitted it. Her aunt could throw up a ward around her thoughts no sensitive could penetrate.

"No, not exactly," Angelique took Cady's hands. "I've learned something – about you." Her aunt was such a beautiful woman. Cady would have given her eyeteeth to have inherited some of her genetic material.

"What is that?" Angelique was making her nervous.

"You are about to face a tremendous test. Soon, you will receive word that you are needed to help a man who has been severely injured."

At first, she was confused. "I'm sure I can help, Aunt Angelique, that's what I do." But the look on her aunt's face told her this was no ordinary client – this was special. Every nerve cell in Cady's body began to vibrate. Was this it? Was this what she had been waiting for? "What do you know?"

"When you are contacted by this gentleman named Joseph, I want you to refuse the job."

Cady stared at her, realizing how momentous this was. There was that name again. Joseph. Frozen, she listened; anxious to hear every word her aunt would say. "Why?" All she could think about was the strange interlude she experienced the night before – and that kiss. She had daydreamed of kissing someone, but this was the first time she had been kissed in her dreams. What a shame that was as close to a real kiss, as she had ever been fortunate enough to enjoy.

Cady sat and watched her aunt carefully. She could sense her forthright concern and determination. Despite that, there was one irrevocable truth as far as Cady was concerned. If Joseph needed her - and she got the opportunity - she would help him, no questions asked. "So, you know about Joseph? Tell me what you know." Neither one of them disputed that he was a real person – a person that was important in her life.

"I won't tell you all I know, not yet – it's not time. But hear my words, if you choose to walk the path that will take you to this man, you will experience the greatest joy of your life and the greatest sorrow. I see darkness ahead for you. I don't know what that entails, but I am afraid for your life."

Cady knew Aunt Angelique did not intend for her advice to be taken lightly. "Thank you, Aunt. I will certainly weigh your words."

"That's all I can ask." Her aunt studied her face silently. "You're going to do it, anyway – no matter what I say. Aren't you?"

Cady sat silent for a moment. Their relationship had always been based on trust and truth, and she didn't intend to change that now. "Yes, I don't feel like I have a choice. I think it's my destiny. I have been having dreams and visions – it is as if I already know him. He's important to me, Aunt."

Angelique covered Cady's hand with her own. "If you do this – take care, not only with your life – but with your heart. You have a great gift, but this will be the greatest challenge you have ever faced."

"Can you tell what type of challenge? What will Joseph need from me?" She had worked with people recovering from diseases, burns, accidents – she needed to know how to prepare. If this was going to be as life changing as Angelique felt it was, Cady wanted to be ready.

"I can't be certain, but something is weighing heavy on my mind that might be related. Not too long ago, I witnessed Nanette and her granddaughters rescue a man from the brink of oblivion. They, literally, gave Jade Landale his life back. I saw Nanette use a method I'm sure you could utilize. When the time comes, they will be glad to come and help you."

"What was wrong with Jade Landale?" Cady held her breath.

"He was paralyzed from the neck down."

God, Cady thought. Poor Joseph. She had dealt with some paralysis victims, but none that had no feeling whatsoever. Even the war vet who had been paralyzed had some sensation below the waist. This was going to be difficult. She would need help, and she would accept it gladly.

After tea, and a tour of the house - they both stood, and faced one another. Angelique came near, pushed Cady's braid off of her shoulder, and ran one finger down the bridge of her nose. "Ah, my Cady," she spoke softly. "You are very special. One day I'll tell you how truly special you are."

Cady left her aunt's more unsettled than she had ever been. Her existence was always so full of other people, not much of Cady was really there. She existed to serve, not to partake of life's excitement. After returning to her little home and working herself into exhaustion, Cady contemplated her choice. It hadn't really been a hard decision to make – at all. She would welcome this Joseph into her life. Angelique's warning of sorrow was unnerving; but the promise of joy was too wonderful to contemplate. Cady had never experienced joy with a man. If there was any chance of knowing a man's love, even for a little while - Cady was willing to step into hell for the opportunity.

Libby and Aron entered the hospital room expecting to find an invalid; instead they found an agitated, unhappy McCoy – which is a fearsome thing. "I want to go home, Aron," Joseph demanded.

Even as he bellowed at his brother, he held his arms open to Libby. She sat a requested pan of brownies down on the rolling table and hurried to step into Joseph's hug. "How are you?" she whispered for his ears only.

"Holding up," he whispered back.

"I'm getting you out of here as fast as I can," Aron assured him. "I've got two crews that will be there today and they are making all the modifications necessary so we can get you set up for anything you may need."

"Sounds good to me, I'll go crazy if I have to stay in this place too much longer."

"Can I get you anything?" Aron asked.

"How about fetching me some coffee to go with these scrumptious smelling brownies?" Joseph wanted to get Aron out of the room. He needed to talk to Libby. Aron left for the coffee, willing to do anything that would perhaps bring a smile to his brother's face. Once the door shut behind him, Joseph changed. "Libby, you've got to do something for me."

"I don't like the tone of your voice, you're scaring me."

She sat by him on the edge of his bed. "But having said that, you know I'd do anything to help."

"I want the truth. I need you to find out from Aron exactly what my expectations are. The doctors are just feeding me a line of bull. I know I'll never walk again, there's no way. I can't feel my feet, hell I can't even feel my balls unless I reach down between my legs to see if they're still there." Joseph knew he sounded desperate. And he could tell by Libby's face she was very near to screaming in frustration. "I don't know if I can face life as half a man, Libby."

Libby knew exactly how he felt. She had experienced dismay and desolation herself. There was one huge concern, however. Even though it shouldn't be so, with a man it was different. Libby recognized the symptoms. She had seen it more than once. A man's identity was so tied up in his strength, how tall he stands, and in his virility. She heard panic in his voice; raw panic that can eat away at your sanity and leave you wondering at the value of facing another day. Joseph was questioning his legitimacy as a human being. This scared the crap out of her. She had to get through to him.

"Joseph Anthony McCoy, you listen to me – and you listen to me good." Libby got right up in his face, desperate to get through to him. "Life is worth living – in whatever state you're offered it. I'm going to level with you. Aron doesn't know this yet, and I shouldn't be telling you before I tell him – but this is an emergency – so, here goes. I have spent the last eight years of my life living on borrowed time." At Joseph's puzzled expression, she sat down beside him and took his hands in hers. "At present, I am in remission. My disease of choice is leukemia. The type that I have is fairly aggressive and remission doesn't usually last over two years. Yet, during this unexpected and perhaps brief reprieve – I have fallen head over heels in love with your brother. He wants a future with me; a future that I have no assurance even exists."

Joseph was flabbergasted. "Libby, you have cancer?" Pulling her to him, he held her close.   "No, you've got to be all right! We can't do without you."

"Exactly, my point – and we can't do without you!" she spoke in an adamant, no-nonsense tone. "Joseph, I have hope. It may be stupid, but I don't have a choice. In one week, I go and sit down in front of a doctor and he will tell me whether my blood count is still improving or whether it is taking a nose-dive. Just yesterday, I had waves of nausea knock me to my knees. Yet, I can't give up. I want to live too badly to throw up my hands and quit. I love your brother, and I want to live for him. And you – you don't know yet what the final verdict is. You have to get a grip and find a way to hold on. Joseph, you have got to have hope, also. Your family loves you. I love you. And, there's a woman out there – somewhere, that was meant just for you. She's not here yet, but she's coming. Love is worth holding on for."

Libby could tell she had hit a sore spot. He looked at her sadly. "I don't have anything to offer a woman, Libby. My injury has stolen my manhood." His mind kept going back to the woman he had met in his dreams. God, what he wouldn't give to have a woman like that in his life and be man enough to satisfy her.

"Don't say that, Joseph." She clasped his hands. "Let's make a pact. I'll pray for your miracle, if you'll pray for mine. Deal?" She waited, expectantly.

He hesitated for a few long moments. Finally, he answered. "Deal." Solemnly, they shook on it. This is the way that Aron found them.

"I just leave the room, and come back and you two are all lovey-dovey. Should I be jealous?" he asked with a smile.

"Yes, you should." Joseph kissed Libby on the forehead soundly. "If the day ever comes when you don't want her – I'll be standing, hopefully, standing by."

27

"I want you standing, Joseph - walking, running, jumping – whatever." Aron assured him. "But you can't have my Liberty Bell."

"Your what?" Joseph wasn't privy to Libby's real name.

"Liberty Bell Fontaine," Libby dryly explained. "Aron just found out my real name – and he's highly amused."

Joseph was ready to go home. He had one of the cute little nurses' aides get all of his gear together. Isaac and Noah would be after him and in a matter of hours he would be back on Tebow land.

If he had to live the life of a cripple – at least he could live it at home. The doctors and nurses were optimistic, but an optimistic outlook was hard for him to maintain. Was he going to have to live like this forever? Was there anyone in the world that could help him?

The soundless cry rose from his heart and reverberated out into the universe – and lo and behold – as the old fairy tales read – someone was listening. A connection was made. Help was on the way. Sometimes there are wonders in this world that will literally blow your mind.

Chapter Two

Joseph never anticipated that fitting into his own home would be a problem – but it was. He was torn between feeling like a burden and feeling like an outsider. And it wasn't his brothers' fault; they, and Libby, did everything humanly possible to make him comfortable and a part of everything that was going on.

In the last few days, so much had happened. He had returned to Tebow and his world now consisted of what might as well be a rehab center. Aron always true to his word had a rehab wing built on to the main ranch house that any physical therapist would envy. He knew his family had every intention of providing him with anything and everything he would need – but Joseph couldn't help comparing it to some medieval torture chamber filled with unknown and horrifying devices meant to inflict pain and humiliation. There were lifts and exercise contraptions and bathroom helps. Joseph wanted no part of any of it. He had enough sense to know he was being unreasonable, but it just felt like if he gave in and submitted to these devices he would have no hope of ever being the Joseph McCoy he once was – that he wanted to be again.

Looking around his prison, Joseph let his mind wander to what had slipped from his life forever. None of his friends were calling – except Beau – and the day Beau turned his back on him was the day he would hang up his hoe for good. None of the women who had once been at his beck and call would even answer his emails, much less their cell phones. He supposed they just didn't know what to say to him. On some level he could understand – but he didn't think he would have done any of them this way. Maybe his current situation was a testimony to how shallow his life had become. Before the accident, he had spent his time running from one point on the globe to another, always trying to conquer – to win – to beat a record, to prove he was the very best – at everything. Now – he had all the time in the world and not a friend – except his family – that would even give him the time of day.

 Snarling, he realized he hadn't 'evacuated his bowels'. What a crock of shit! He couldn't even tell when he needed to take a dump! Leaning over the side of the bed, he checked his catheter bag. Hell! It needed emptying and he couldn't stand for Libby to do it – not that she minded – Libby loved him, and he loved Libby – but it was goddamn humiliating for his brother's fiancé to empty his piss bag. Groaning, Joseph wondered how in the world he was going to survive such a miserable existence.

Trying to calm himself, he stared out the window. From his vantage point, all he could see was sky and the top of the barn. A hawk flew over the barn and he knew it was after a mouse or a ground squirrel. Maybe if he could just look out the window, he would feel better. Unwilling to try and use the steel monster that hung over his bed to lift himself, he reached for the wheelchair – determined to hoist himself out of bed and into the chair without calling for Libby or anyone else to help him. Reaching – grasping – straining, Joseph leaned over to grab his wheelchair – and he almost had it – but not quiet. Damn! Overbalanced, he found himself falling – for the second time. It was a slow motion trip to the floor. Hell! He couldn't live like this – no way.

Libby came rushing in when she heard the crash. "Joseph! My God! Are you all right? I didn't hear you call me. I'm so sorry." She knelt by him and Joseph was so mortified he couldn't even answer. "I'll go get help." She ran from the room screaming for Jacob as she went and Joseph managed to roll over and partially right himself before she came rushing back.

"I'm so sorry, Joseph." Libby was crying. "I shouldn't have left you. Please forgive me."

Shit! Could he be less of a man? "Don't cry Libby. It wasn't your fault. You just went to check on lunch. I could have waited. I shouldn't have tried to do it by myself."

"Holy Hell! How did this happen, bro?" Jacob fell to his knees next to him. Joseph looked up into his brother's face and saw that it was blanched white with fear. "Easy," Jacob strained to lift and maneuver Joseph's bulk into the wheelchair.

"Thank you," Joseph murmured, avoiding his brother's eyes.

"Libby, honey – go check your food and give us a couple of minutes. Okay?" Jacob winked at Libby, letting her know he just wanted to spend a few minutes with his brother. He waited until he could hear Libby moving around the kitchen. "So, what happened?"

"Hell, Jacob! I used to jump out of airplanes; I have to find my excitement where I can these days." Joseph's poor attempt at humor didn't elicit a laugh from Jacob. Using his strong shoulder and arm muscles, Joseph steered his chair over to the double picture window. He pulled back the curtain and looked out over Tebow land. "Do you know what I was doing when I fell?" At Jacob's soft negative answer, Joseph continued. "I wanted to come to the window to see outside. Isn't that a hoot? I thought I could do it myself." Jacob laid his hand on Joseph's arm, lending wordless support. "I just wanted to look out the fuckin' window!"

"I'm so sorry, Joseph. Is there anything I can do for you?" Jacob sounded sincere. And Joseph knew his older brother would move mountains for him if he could.

"Yes." Their eyes met. "I want you to run across the south meadow for me. I want you to climb that big spreading oak down by the creek; go all the way to that limb that stretches out over the blue hole, where we've always swam. And I want you to have sex with a woman for me. Stand on your strong legs and bounce her on your cock till she screams your name. And when you're through, hold her in your arms all night long. You should be thanking God that you're a real man, not half a man like me."

Jacob was stunned at the emotion that was pouring from his brother. He knew Joseph was feeling a tremendous loss; but he had no idea the depths of his despair. Jacob did his best to comfort him. "You will make love to a woman again, Joseph. Don't you dare give up! We're going to find some way and somebody to help you. You will walk again, run again, swim again – all of it. I promise." How in the hell he was going to keep that promise, he didn't know – but he would. He would, if it was the last thing he ever did.

Maybe, he could take Joseph's mind off of his problems. "This morning, Nathan went out to look for Noah's phone. He spotted something in the stock tank, and came barreling back in the house swearing that there was a mermaid out there taking a swim. Nothing would do, but for me to go check it out." Jacob grinned.

Joseph feigned interest, embarrassed by his own outburst. "I guess he was imagining things – or did you find a beautiful woman from the sea?"

"Yes, as a matter of fact, I did." At that, Joseph jerked his head up and looked at his brother, trying to see if he was kidding.

"You found a girl in the stock tank?" Aron and Libby had a stock tank story, but they wouldn't share it. Aron said it was too precious and personal to talk about, even with his brothers. Joseph wanted a chance to make memories like that with a woman. He was afraid those dreams would have to be placed on the shelf with his parachute and his running shoes.

"No, I found her in our barn. Stunningly naked." Jacob drawled the information with the most satisfied smirk Joseph could ever remember seeing on his brother's face.

Joseph snorted. "Lucky bastard!"

"She may not be a mermaid like Nathan first thought," Jacob smiled, fire in his eyes. "But, he was close. She's a goddess."

Joseph looked back out the window. "If she's in the barn – stunningly naked – what in hell are you doing in here?"

Good question.

Cady was tired of waiting for Joseph to call. If she didn't hear from him soon, she would have to accept another client – after all, she had bills to pay. Checking her bank statement, she decided she could afford to wait two more weeks. She could feel his need for her growing every day. Just today, she had felt his distress – but it had been during the day - not part of a dream. And she knew no way to reach him except in her dreams. Over and over, Cady had relived the strange happening of a few days ago. Had it been real – or just a figment of her imagination? If she ever saw him and he looked like the man in her dreams – she guessed she would know. Sending up a silent prayer, she prayed for Joseph. "Hurry love, I can't wait to meet you."

The family was gathering in from every direction; the big log home was brimming with joy, laughter and the smell of good food. It was Saturday, and for everyone to be present for the morning meal was a special event. Libby had made such a difference in their lives, the difference only a woman can bring into a household full of men. Oh, they had always been a family, and they had always loved one another. But since their parents died that fateful day ten years ago, nothing had been the same. A heavy rainstorm had flooded the vast, Hill Country river system; the normally lazy waterways had quickly become frantic, white-water devils. A flash flood had torn through their county and washed out some of the bridges. To the McCoy family, that freak weather event had brought on the greatest of tragedies. Their mom and dad had been on one of those bridges when it collapsed and they were swept away into a treacherous whirlpool of death.

At twenty-one, Aron stepped up and took the weight of the world on his shoulders. He accepted the responsibility of raising his brothers long before he should have known such duty and obligation. In his desire to make a home for his siblings, he had married a woman who had almost torn their family apart. After the fiasco with Sabrina, Aron had sworn off women – that is until sweet Libby walked through their door and into his heart.

The table was set with Libby's offerings for the first meal of the day: French Toast and Biscuits with Sausage Gravy. "Good Lord, Libby, this looks fantastic." Jacob pulled out his chair and sat down, jerking a biscuit out of Aron's hand. Aron, who was busy kissing Libby, while simultaneously trying to fill his plate without watching what he was doing.

"What the hell?" Aron pulled his lips from Libby's neck and glared at his brother. "Can't you get your own damn biscuit?"

Jacob tore off a hunk with his teeth. "Looks like you got your hands full, brother. Since the rest of us aren't as blessed, we have to take what we can get."

Aron's eyes softened. "Man does not live by bread alone." He sipped from Libby's lips and counted his blessings. "Sit over here darling, so I can concentrate on my food."

With a satisfied smile, she slipped from his lap and perched on the adjacent chair.

The front door slammed. "Isaac's home!" Nathan announced. They all recognized Isaac's signature entrance; his biker boots made a heavier echo on the hard wood floors than cowboy boots and the chains on his black leather pants and jacket jangled as he walked.

"Boy, when you tear that front door off the hinges, I'm gonna make you take up residence in the barn!" Aron tried to look at his brother sternly, but failed. "Did you find me a band to replace those goat ropers who cancelled on us?"

Isaac turned his chair around backwards and sat down noisily. "Yeah, I've got you a band. If you'll come to the bar tonight, you can hear them." Isaac started to go ahead and tell them his big news, but he figured it would be more to fun to show them. He was tired of bearing the family reputation as the bad boy – the badass – the family troublemaker. It was high time he proved he could succeed in whatever he set out to do.

The whirr of a wheelchair motor got their attention. Joseph had more than one chair and he usually preferred the manual one, but this time he was in his Cadillac version. "Nathan, you've got a phone call." He handed the portable house phone to his little brother, who broke out in a big smile. A call on a Saturday morning could only mean good things. Stepping into the den, Nathan's whoop of delight was easily heard.

"Wonder what that's all about?" Libby mused. She liked to keep up with what everybody was doing – especially Nathan. Libby was a little mother hen.

Joseph handed his plate to Jacob to fill, "Be sure to get enough of that gravy on my biscuits, I don't like 'em dry." He added, "That was Bo Barkley's mom, he's having, and I quote – an impromptu swimming and ice cream party this afternoon." Joseph paused for effect. "Coed."

As Nathan came back in with a silly grin on his face, the older brothers decided to have a little fun. "So, big man, what little girl are you hoping to see in a bikini this afternoon?" Isaac couldn't resist.

Immediately, Nathan's face reddened. "Nobody."

Joseph picked up where Nathan left off. "How about that little Morrison girl? She's gonna be a knock-out one day."

"She's just a kid," Nathan mumbled. "Not like that girl I saw this morning in the stock tank." At his words, Jacob's heart leapt with the memory.

"What's that?" Aron asked. He had his own fond memories of the stock tank. That was the first place he had seen his Libby in the altogether. Glancing at her, Aron wasn't surprised to see a pink glow wash over her perfect skin. "That old stock tank seems to see more action than the Playboy mansion." He watched Libby remember the night she had pleasured herself, not knowing that Aron was watching from his second floor studio in the barn. When Libby had cried out his name in climax, Aron had lost his heart and nearly lost his mind.

"I saw a really pretty girl swimming there this morning, I guess she was visiting one of our neighbors and just wanted to cool off." Nathan had backed off of his mermaid story; it sounded a little childish, he guessed.

Joseph pounced on the story with relish. "Nathan thought she was a mermaid and Jacob can vouch she was the catch of the day. He caught her in the barn in her birthday suit." He was getting into this – after all, the longer he could keep his mind off of his own problems – the better off he would be.

Nathan's eyes got big as saucers. He might be young, but he was growing up fast. "No joshing?!"

Libby started clucking her reservations, "Don't you think we should talk about something else at the dinner table?"

"No, I definitely want to hear this," Aron put his fork down so he could pay close attention. "I want all the dirty details, Jacob." At Libby's poke in the ribs, Aron rephrased his demand. "I want the clean version of all the dirty details, Jacob."

It was obvious Jacob didn't really want to share. He hemmed and hawed, and gradually spilled the details. "Yeah, I walked in on the pretty girl as she was getting dressed. We didn't get a chance to talk, because when Libby screamed, I . . . . ." Seeing Joseph's face fall, Jacob paused.

Aron looked at Jacob, Libby and Joseph. "What's going on?"

Joseph let out a sigh. "I did something stupid. Libby came in here to check on lunch and I tried to get in my chair by myself. I fell. It was nothing."

Aron realized Joseph wanted to down play the whole thing. Well, too bad. Some things just had to be dealt with. "I'm glad you didn't hurt yourself. I guess you realize we've got to get you some help. I've put out feelers all over, and it won't be long 'til I have a couple of physical therapists out here for you to talk to." Aron knew Joseph didn't want to hear it, but it was absolutely necessary. "It's gonna have to be a live-in person. We want you to have the best of care – we want you to walk again."

"That would take a miracle," Joseph slammed his glass of ice tea down. If it hadn't been nearly empty, he would have sloshed it all over Libby's snow-white tablecloth.

"We're in the miracle business, aren't we baby?" Aron ran a gentle thumb over Libby's cheek. It had only been days ago they had thought Libby's leukemia had returned. She had been nauseous and dizzy – the typical symptoms of her body coming out of remission. But, it hadn't been her cancer reemerging – it had been the first signs she was pregnant.

"Yes, we definitely believe in miracles." Libby covered Aron's hand with her own, but it was Joseph she looked at intently. "We're going to find you the very best help there is. I've been praying about it, and it's going to happen. That's all there is to it."

Aron chuckled at his baby's adamant statement. "I guess you all heard that." Remembering where this conversation started, he returned to a lighter topic. "So, what happened to the naked woman?"

Jacob filled his plate, making sure he left enough for Noah. "I don't know. When I went back to the barn she was gone."

"Bummer," Isaac sighed. "Misplacing a good looking, naked woman is never a good thing."

The front door opened and shut again, this time with a bit less exuberance. "Noah's home!" Nathan was the town crier; he announced all comings and goings with enthusiasm.

"Hey." Noah started passing out mail as soon as he came to the table. "Sorry, I'm late, Libs. This certified letter came for you," he handed it to Jacob. "Nelda let me sign for it." Jacob stuck it in his back pocket to look at later, "It's probably a copy of the deed to the last piece of property I bought."

"I bet she did; Nelda has the hots for you." Isaac loved to pick at Noah. As far as he was concerned, Noah was a tight-ass who needed to loosen up.

"You're just jealous because Nelda is a classy lady." Noah got right back in his face. "The women you date have all been rode hard and put up wet."

Isaac arched one eyebrow at his brother. It was best if he didn't comment on his own love life, so he pounced on Noah's. "Nelda may be a lady, but she's not the lady you want, is she? We all know what you've been doing, Noah. You're using all these other women to try and make yourself forget one blonde honey who won't give you the time of day."

Instead of answering, Noah threw a hunk of biscuit at Isaac; Aron caught it and went right on eating.

"Hey, did I get any mail?" Nathan asked, eyeing the magazine Noah held in his hand. "It's time for me to get my gaming magazine," Nathan looked forward to seeing the tips and reviews on the latest video games for Wii and PlayStation 3.

"This isn't yours, big guy. This is Joseph's." Noah tossed a magazine wrapped in brown paper. Joseph caught it with a funny look on his face. Suddenly, it dawned on Noah what it was – Joseph's beloved Playboy. He almost snatched it back, knowing his brother couldn't put it to the same use he always had before.

Seeing Noah's remorse, Joseph laughed it off. "Hey, I can always read the articles, can't I?" Silence. Nobody knew what to say.

"I'm going to have to learn to use these damn pulleys and shit," Joseph grumbled as he eased himself back in the bed. He was tired of waiting for one of his brothers to help him up and down. It wasn't that he hated the idea of a physical therapist; he knew it was inevitable. What he dreaded was the idea of someone seeing how truly helpless he was, especially a woman. The only characteristic he was going to insist upon for a physical therapist was that she be homely. He couldn't stand it if a beautiful woman were privy to his shame. Besides the only beautiful woman he wanted to see what the one from his dream. God! He couldn't get that angel off his mind!

Tearing the paper cover off the current issue of Playboy, he went right to his favorite page – the centerfold. Lord. Have. Mercy. He let his eyes appreciate the picture-perfect physical attributes of Lisa Reinhart. She wasn't as beautiful as his nocturnal visitor – but she was stacked; with a rack that made his eyes water. Out of habit, he let his hand wander down to his dick. When he touched it and realized he felt nothing – it hit him. He might never get an erection again. Desperately, he rubbed his penis, hoping against hope to feel something – anything. He stared at the luscious breasts and the tempting mound of the Hollywood starlet. Before the accident, a sight like this would have had him hard and beating it in a matter of seconds. But, now – his dick was deader than a doornail. Giving it a second or two more, he feverishly rubbed his flaccid flesh between his thumb and forefinger. How many girls had he brought to orgasm? How many times had he made a woman scream with pleasure? Not enough. Not damn near enough. In disgust, he threw the Playboy against the wall and watched it slide to the ground as limp and useless as his cock.

Cady's Dreamtime

"Acadia!" Master Gabe caught up to her just before she stepped onto the escalator. "I need to give you a bit more advice."

Respectfully, she stepped aside, allowing the ones behind her to continue on their way. She was in a hurry. Joseph needed her. Plus, she was so excited at the prospect of seeing him that she resented anything that would delay her departure. "I read every word of the memo you sent me," she assured her superior. "But since I won't have any memory of my existence here, how will any of this information be of help to me?"

Clearing his throat, Gabe tapped his foot, counting to ten so he wouldn't lose his temper. Acadia's comment made it clear that she had not read the memo as carefully as she would have him believe. Stretching the truth was frowned upon here, as she should well know – but losing one's temper was equally forbidden. Acadia was about to depart, so she had to be allowed some leniency, he supposed. "My dear, I shall communicate with you in dreams. That is standard operating procedure for cases such as this." He didn't bother to reveal that 'cases like this' were not the norm.

"Oh – okay," she supposed that would be fine. "I know all about dreams," she smiled sweetly. "I visit Joseph when he sleeps." She had never experienced a dream, herself, of course. Sleep was not required in heaven. But Joseph dreamed – of races and winning – sometimes, he dreamed of his parents and his childhood. Often, he dreamed of women and the pleasure he received from touching them. Acadia did not enjoy those dreams of Joseph's, nor did she enjoy the reality of his associations with female humans. It wasn't seemly or angelic, but Acadia was jealous. She really wasn't sure what it meant, but she did know what she wanted. Acadia wanted Joseph.

"Yes, I will visit you, periodically, but more often when it gets nearer to the time of the fulfillment of your quest." He watched her glance at the exit sign. Acadia was eager to begin her adventure. But he had to make her understand how difficult this might prove to be. "I know you love Joseph, Acadia. But, don't fall in love with him," he warned.

What did he mean? "Fall in love?" Acadia tried to grasp his meaning. "I already love Joseph. He belongs to me."

A horn blew and a bell rang out – heralding the last call for those who were scheduled to depart the hallowed halls. The conductor motioned for her to follow him. "Hey, cutie! If you're going with me – it's time."

"I've gotta go, sir." She still didn't understand what Master Gabe was trying to tell her, but she would figure it out. Acadia felt certain all things would work together for the best in her attempt to protect and help Joseph. After all, it was meant to be – or she would never have been given the assignment in the first place. Heaven did not make mistakes.

"Heaven does not make mistakes," Cady whispered. She rolled over in the bed and hugged her pillow close. "Heaven does not make mistakes."

Chaos. Pure chaos and Joseph felt utterly helpless. Just moments before Libby had screamed and he had nearly broken his neck trying to get the damn wheelchair through the kitchen to get to her. He had pulled her down into his lap, attempting to give her comfort. "What's wrong, sugar?"

"It's Nathan," she sobbed. "Aron just got a call and he's hurt! There's been an accident! Aron and Jacob have gone . . .. " She hiccupped, trying to get her breath. Joseph rubbed her back, trying to calm her enough so he could understand.

"What kind of accident?" Hell! If he were anything other than a damn cripple, he would be out the door with Aron and Jacob instead of sitting, helpless, in this damn chair!

"He was riding his bike over the Guadalupe Bridge and a truck sideswiped him and knocked him into the water. They say he almost drowned!" she broke her words with a wail and Joseph felt the coldest dread of his life creep up his damaged spine.

"Nathan will be all right," Joseph assured her. He had to be. God couldn't be so cruel as to take their baby brother from them – not after everything else He had snatched from their grasp. Frankly, Joseph was beginning to wonder about the benevolence of His maker. First, his parents had been taken and then there was his accident – and now Nathan. What the hell was going on? "He'll be fine, honey. Don't cry."

"I've got to call Isaac and Noah," she sniffled, as she rose from his lap. "They need to know what's going on." As Libby went to call his brothers, Joseph rolled to the front door and out on the porch. If only he could get around. What he needed was a pickup that he could get in and out of in his wheelchair. He knew they made them.

"Joseph!" He heard Libby calling him.

"Out here!"

Libby barreled out of the house and flung her arms around his neck. "Aron just called! He's going to be all right, Joseph! He's going to be all right!"

Joseph let out a breath he hadn't realized he had been holding. "Thank God," he sighed.

"And that's not all! Jacob found his mermaid. He's bringing her here – any minute!"

Joseph smiled. Could things get any crazier at Tebow? They could.

"I can do it, myself." Joseph spoke each word in a clipped, terse voice. It wasn't that he didn't appreciate his family's concern – but enough was enough.

"I'll be right out here if you change your mind," Noah spoke through the closed door, obviously intending to go nowhere until Joseph finished in the bathroom. Aron had spared no expense. The bathroom was large and everything was easily accessible – but he had no intention of using all of the grip bars, handrails, or fold out seats. There was even a transfer ledge on the big tub – and swear to God – he could roll his entire chair into the huge shower. But in Joseph's mind, accepting all of this would be the same as admitting defeat. So he sat in front of the sink and wet a wash rag, and began the arduous task of washing his big body with a piece of terry cloth about the size of a postage stamp.

Turning on the tap, he let the temperature get almost to the boiling point before he put the stopper in and squirted some liquid soap in the hot water. Gingerly, because it was too hot, he dipped the rag in and squeezed it out. *Don't look,* he told himself. *If you don't look in the mirror and see the chair, it won't be real.* Rubbing his face and neck, he realized he needed a shave. How was he supposed to shave himself without looking at his reflection? *Fuck!* With a challenging, arrogant stare he finally looked himself in the eye. Why didn't he look different? How could he be the same? His hair looked the same – a little long and tousled, but the shaggy brown locks were familiar. The eyes, nose, and chin - all of his features were unchanged – so why didn't he recognize himself? He knew why. Because Joseph Anthony McCoy had died in that accident – what remained behind was just an empty shell.

"Hey are you all right in there, I don't hear anything. Do you want me to get Libby to help you?" What Noah meant as a joke, Joseph heard as ridicule.

"Fuck, no!" He shouted before he could stop himself. Immediately, he felt ashamed. Noah didn't deserve his ill temper and Libby certainly had been nothing but supportive. Thinking of Libby, he smiled. "I can handle it," he snarled in a much less combative tone. He should be more excited that Aron and Libby were going to bring a new life into the world. Instead, all he could think about was that

43

he would never father a child. God, how selfish could he get?

Noah actually chuckled on the other side of the door. "Just because you're off your feet for awhile doesn't mean you have to be so damn cranky. You make me think of that bull we used to have – you remember Hannibal?"

Washing behind his ears and the back of his neck, Joseph actually laughed out loud. "Yea, I remember him. He was a big, grey Brahmin bull. His dick was so long when it was hard, he stepped on it." As soon as he said the words, he sobered. Would he ever get hard again? Would he ever know what it was like to slide into a woman's hot, wet pussy again? Shit!

"I have that same problem." Noah was so matter-of-fact that he had Joseph laughing again. "When I piss, I have to stand back so I don't flush my dick down the toilet."

"Yea, right." Joseph guffawed. "I've seen your wee willie. I used to change your diapers, you idiot."

"I've grown since then." Noah assured him. "Most men walk up and stick their cock in a woman. I stick it in and then walk closer." He was talking so loud Joseph was sure he could be heard in the kitchen. This could be fun.

They needed some laughs around this place. Nathan had almost been killed a few days before. If it hadn't been for Jessie Montgomery, their little brother would have drowned. Now Jacob was involved with Jessie, and what was going on between them was a mystery to him. Jessie was several months pregnant – with Jacob's baby – yet they had never laid eyes on one another until just a few days ago. There was something odd going on - mistakes at sperm banks and surrogate parents gone crazy - but Joseph had enough problems of his own without trying to figure out Jacob's. "So your dick is big, huh? How big is it? And talk loud, I can barely hear you." He snickered at what was about to happen.

Noah fell for the bait – hook, line and sinker. "My dick is so big; I can run three legged races by myself."

He was plenty loud, but in order to attract an audience – he needed to be louder. Joseph re-wet his washcloth and began working on his chest. If any of the family was within earshot, they would be hearing from them soon. "Louder, I'm having trouble hearing you through the thick door." Noah was way too serious most of the time and to coerce him into making a fool out of himself was just too good to pass up.

"Well, I'm having trouble hearing you through my thick dick!" Joseph could hear Noah nearly choke on his own bad joke. "Can you hear me now?" Noah was practically yelling.

"Yeah, that's good." *Idiot.*

"My dick is so big that it beeps when I pull out." Just as soon as Noah said the word 'out' Joseph heard his bedroom door slam.

"What in God's name is your problem, boy?" Aron was mad! Joseph couldn't see him, but there was no mistaking that meat-grinder monotone. "Did you know that the Baptist preacher is in the kitchen? He's come to ask after Joseph. And what do we hear in here? How fuckin' big your limp little dick is?"

"Sorry, Aron." Noah didn't sound contrite. He sounded like he was about to bust a gut.

By this time, Jacob, followed closely by Isaac, had joined Aron. Joseph had the bathroom door open because this was just too good to miss.

"Aron," chided Jacob. "The Baptist preacher just heard you say fuck – really loud. And Jessie, my little mermaid, is out there. I've just found her, and I don't want you to run her off with your vulgarity before I get a chance to make a good impression."

"The preacher just left and told Jessie and Libby it was a good thing Nathan was still in school and had missed all of the vulgarity." Isaac was enjoying this. "And Noah. . ." Isaac grasped his crotch and strutted closer. "My dick is so big; it looks blurry unless you stand WAAYY back."

"Will you dumbasses get outta here so I can wash *my* limp dick?" It felt sorta good to joke about his problem. Maybe, he might make it without going crazy, after all.

Libby crossed her arms and looked at the brothers, pointedly. "Who's going to Shorty's to hear the band with me, tonight? Y'all do realize the hayride and dance is this weekend? We have a ton of work to do to get ready." The end of summer Harvest Dance at Tebow was a community tradition. And Libby was determined this would be the best one – ever. It would be her first time to play hostess and she wanted everything to be perfect. As a family they had a world of things to be thankful for and she wanted their friends and neighbors to share in their happiness.

Joseph replied first. "I want to go. Kane is supposed to meet me there for a beer." He had known Kane, and his brother Zane, for years. They had met on the extreme sports circuit, competing in rock climbing, snow boarding, motorcycle racing – you name it – they had tried it. When the previous sheriff retired, the McCoys thought of Kane and urged him to apply for the job. And even though Zane was legally blind, he let nothing or no one stand in his way. Besides being a tremendous athlete, he was one of the best lawyers in the state.

"Good," Libby was pleased Joseph was getting out of the house. "Isaac will be there, of course." She hadn't meant a thing by it, but a shadow crossed Isaac's face. "And Pookie has promised to teach me how to line dance."

Jessie laughed out loud. Jacob put his arm around her. "You'll have to get used to all of this nonsense around here." He kissed her on the cheek.

'Pookie' shot Libby a look that was at the same time sheepish and full of more love than Joseph had ever been privileged to see. Aron McCoy would do anything for his beloved, even be 'Pookie'. In retaliation, Aron scooped Libby out of her chair and started blowing raspberries on her neck. "Don't you remember your pet name for me is Krull the Warrior King?"

Giggling, Libby spilled the beans. "That's not *your* pet name, sweetums. That's what I call your . . ." Realizing what she nearly confessed, Libby cuddled close to him and hid her face in his neck. Aron wouldn't let it go.

"Yes, that's right. She calls my . . ." Seeing Nathan looking at him curiously, Aron immediately switched gears. Clearing his throat he rephrased his sentence. "That's right. Libby calls my **horse** Krull the Warrior King." Guffaws went around the table. Even Nathan didn't look convinced.

"How about you, Noah? Are you going with us?" Libby asked shyly, still cradled in Aron's arms.

"I'd like to go. I hear Tequila Sunrise is a great band." And Harley Summers was back in town. Not that she'd come to the bar if she had any inkling he'd be there. Harley avoided him like the plague. "But, if I need to stay with Nathan, I will."

"We'll stay with him," Jacob volunteered quickly.

"Are you sure, Jessie?" Libby asked. "Don't you want Jacob to take you dancing?"

Put on the spot, Jessie was flustered. "Oh, no. You've got it all wrong. Jacob and I aren't dating. We aren't a couple. I'm only here, because . . ." her voice trailed off.

"She's here because I want her here." Jacob settled the matter.

The music that greeted them at the door of the bar was good. Libby was pleased. "I think they'll be just fine. Don't you Aron?"

Aron hadn't told Libby what was going on. Not yet. When the news about Nathan had hit her, he couldn't worry about Nathan for worrying about her. Libby was strong of heart, but her little body had been through a world of hurt

47

in her lifetime, and he didn't want her to worry about a damn thing. He wanted to wait and see what the night would bring. Tomorrow, if Jessie was still at the ranch, he would tell Libby that she wasn't the only one having a baby. He couldn't believe Jacob might have the first child. Lord, you never knew what one day could bring!

"They sound great, Libby-love. And we're going to dance up a storm. Let's get you settled in a good place and I'll go over to the bar and get us some drinks. I see a couple of people I need to speak to and then you and I are going to do some serious cuddling on the dance floor. Okay?"

Libby threw her arms around Aron's neck and squeezed. "I love you so much. Nathan's safe and Joseph's outlook is better. I can't wait to hold you close. It will only be a foretaste of what I want to do with you when I get you home. I can't wait to feel you pushing deep inside of me. Right now, my panties are soaking wet. " At her risqué teasing, Aron almost went to his knees.

"Hell, yeah! I'll hurry back. We may just skip the dancing and go home and . . ." Aron was so obviously turned on that Joseph pulled him away before he said an unmistakable sexual expletive in public.

"Come on, Aron, before you get us all thrown out for lewd behavior." Joseph winked at Libby as he led his lust-struck brother to the bar.

"Don't rush. There's Denise Lyons. She has promised to loan me some decorations for the dance. I need to talk to her for a few minutes, anyway." Libby blew a kiss at Aron and watched him adjust his package to a more comfortable position. Lord, she loved that man!

"I need to put some ice down my breeches," Aron groaned.

"That could be arranged." Joseph mumbled dryly as they made their way through the crowd. "Did you see they were taking the sign down out front?" The two handsome cowboys didn't notice, but dozens of pairs of eyes followed their progress. The McCoy men always drew attention from the women and envy from the men – a wheelchair hadn't changed Joseph's sexiness one bit – even if he didn't realize it yet.

"Yeah, I did. I wonder what that means." Aron drawled.

Joseph mulled it over; it was strange. Shorty's was an institution in Kerr County. "I hope they're not going out of business. Where would Isaac live?" He snorted, knowing he was just being a horse's ass.

Aron ignored the jibe at Isaac. "Why don't we ask Kane? Maybe he's heard something."

Aron sat down at Kane's table, flipping the chair around backward – Isaac style. Next, he slung another chair backwards, making room for Joseph's wheelchair. "What's going on with the bar?" He took his beer from Doris and handed the other one to Joseph. "Thanks," he saluted the sheriff with the amber bottle.

"What do you mean?" Kane knew exactly what Aron was talking about, but he enjoyed playing the game. Isaac was the new owner of the bar. And he knew they didn't know, which was going to make the evening highly entertaining. Kane leaned back in his chair and surveyed the two, big McCoy men. In Kerr County, there were no men more respected than these two.

"It looks like Shorty is pulling up stakes. Did he win the lottery or is he retiring to some damn beach in Mexico? Or do you know, you ornery old cuss?" Joseph had known Kane so long he didn't feel the need for any pleasantries.

"I know more than you do, pretty boy." Kane noticed they were about to be joined by another of the McCoy clan. He decided to stir the pot a little. "I suggest you ask the owner of this fine establishment. I think he may be able to help you."

As he followed Kane's gaze, he saw his own brother walking toward them. Where was Shorty? "I don't understand."

"Well, I'll be damned!" Aron was watching Isaac carefully as first one employee and then another stopped him to ask questions. "I don't believe it."

Joseph was missing something. "What?"

When Isaac pulled out a chair, he motioned for Doris to bring another round. "Welcome to **Hardbodies**, gentleman. Now, we have two things to celebrate: Nathan's alive and well, and I'm not the total screw-up you thought I was."

It took a few seconds, but finally Joseph got it, "You bought the bar." He said it with a tone of incredulity.

"I bought the bar," Isaac echoed. "Now, I won't be so apt to tear it up or drink up all my profits."

"I'm proud of you," Aron's voice was deep. He was dead serious. "This is what you've been doing for the last month isn't it?" The whole family had thought he was just avoiding Joseph and shirking his responsibilities.

"I wish you all the success in the world, man." Joseph raised his bottle and winked at his brother. "This suits you, brother. You're going to do great – a life of wine, women and song. What could be better?"

"Dancing with my baby. I'll see you two goons at home. Nice to see you Kane." With that, Aron left, and in a few moments he had a smiling Libby in his arms and they were dancing to Tequila Sunrise's version of **Breathe**.

Isaac sat with them for a few more minutes, excusing himself when a cowboy got a little rowdy on the dance floor. "Catch you guys, later. And I'll tell Doris – all your drinks are on the house." They thanked him and watched him walk away with a new confidence. Joseph thought it looked good on him.

"So, how have you been Joseph?" Kane missed hanging out with the daredevil McCoy brother. They had been in the same rock-climbing club and had even been white water rafting together a couple of times.

"Not worth a shit." Joseph didn't feel the need to hide from Kane; they had shared too much during the last few years.

"What's your prognosis?" Kane had a reason for asking.

"Depends on who you ask," Joseph wasn't holding out much hope. "Right now, I'm useless from the waist down. Kane, I wouldn't say this around my family – but, I don't know if I can face a future like this."

Kane leaned closer to Joseph. He wouldn't say something like this to just anybody, but Joseph was desperate. "I'm from New Orleans, man. I've seen things that can't be explained by science or common sense."

"What do you mean?" Joseph was a skeptic. He only believed in what he could see with his eyes and touch with his hands.

"I had a buddy that was injured over in Iraq. He was basically in the same shape you're in – not quite as bad, maybe. But the doctors told him he'd never walk; have to use a colon bag for the rest of his life, plus he had no hope of ever getting another woody again as long as he lived."

"Sounds familiar," Joseph sighed. "Even though my family has this idea a miracle is possible, I don't hold out much hope."

"I've seen a miracle, Joseph. I can give you the name of a woman who can give you back your manhood."

Joseph searched Kane's face for any sign of a joke. Kane was a friend, and he didn't think he was cruel enough to make light of something so important. "What do you mean?"

"There's this woman back in New Orleans. Her name is Acadia Renaud. She's a licensed physical therapist; but the lady is much more than that. She's got a hoodoo background. I've heard her called a traiteur, and I've heard her referred to as an empath."

Joseph couldn't believe his ears. Here was this man of the law – a reasonable man – a man with an education, and he was spouting off the most ridiculous drivel he had ever heard come out of a grown man's mouth. "What the hell is a traituer or an empath?" He didn't know why he was humoring Kane Saucier. Perhaps, he was just a nice guy. Or desperate.

Sensing Joseph's disbelief, Kane almost got up and walked away. But, he believed in what he was about to tell McCoy; plus, he had a genuine desire to help the fool. "A traiteur is a Cajun healer, a faith healer basically. Since Cady is part Creole and part Cajun she combines laying of hands with herbs and whatever hoodoo people do. I'm not claiming to understand it, but I did see the result of her talent with my own eyes."

"What about that other word you used?" Joseph couldn't help himself. He was intrigued.

"An empath is a healer who can absorb another person's pain or disease into their own body. It's supposed to be very painful for the empath, but the end result is that the patient is healed and the empath's body deals with the disorder in a shorter amount of time with less damage to their own body. So, it's a talent that they have to be careful with and use sparingly or they devastate their own health."

"So, what are you telling me in plain English?" Joseph dared to hope for a miracle.

"I'm telling you that Cady Renaud might be able to help you."

"What do you mean she could give me back my manhood?" Joseph was pushing Kane for details.

"All I know is that Jack Reardon was paralyzed and unable to get it up. After Cady worked on him for a couple of months, he could walk with crutches and he was making love with his wife again."

"How did she do that?" Joseph's imagination was running wild, but hope was also coursing through his veins like a drug.

"Lord, I don't know. It was a lot of hands on therapy such as massage, and rubdowns with homemade salves. Lord, if I said anymore – I'd just be making it up. What difference does it make? If it works, it works." He could tell Joseph that Jack said Cady slept by his bed and involved his wife in some pretty kinky treatments, but he didn't really know enough to say.

"What does she look like, this miracle worker?"

"What difference does that make?" Kane was a little insulted for Cady. It seemed to him that Joseph would be more concerned about results than what his therapist looked like.

"I don't want a beautiful woman to see me this way. If I'm going to let somebody watch my urine flow through a tube into a bag, I want her to be so ugly that I don't care one way or the other." Joseph knew that sounded cold, but pity from a sexy woman would just about do him in.

Kane considered Joseph for a minute. Poor bastard. He let Cady Renaud's image run through his mind and then answered as honestly as he could. "I guess she would fit your bill. She's no raving beauty, but I don't suppose you'd have to put a bag over her head." Kane felt uncomfortable talking about Acadia Renaud in such a disrespectful manner. She was from a powerful, powerful family. And by powerful he meant people who could call lightning bolts from the sky.

"Can you get me in touch with her?" Joseph didn't know if he was crazy or not. But, if there was a possibility he could be healed, he had to pursue it.

"Zane has her number. He handles some of her legal affairs." He picked up his cell and dialed his brother. In a few moments, Kane handed Joseph a card with a number on the back that might be the miracle he had been looking for.

Chapter Three

Cady had just about given up on hearing from Joseph. Unable to wait any longer, she had taken a temporary job, filling in for a therapist in Baton Rouge. Just in case, sherenewed her contract with her answering service, packed her bags and headed north. The patient was an older woman, a Cajun by the name of Renee Adams. When Cady walked into Mrs. Adams' bedroom she knew instantly the old woman was a kindred spirit. Power recognizes power. Rheumatoid arthritis had twisted the old woman's hands and feet until she lived in constant agony. "Come in, Miss Renaud. I've been expecting you."

Cady knew that wasn't possible, not by traditional means, anyway. The service requested a substitute, but the patient had not been informed who that replacement would be. "You have?" The room drew her in and when she began to look around, she realized why. There was an altar in the corner with a pentacle in plain sight. There was also a bowl of water and a bowl of salt, a large white pillar candle and an amethyst crystal as big as her fist. She looked back at her patient and smiled. "You are a practitioner of the magical arts."

"Yes, I am." The old woman raised one gnarled hand and beckoned her forward. "And so are you. I felt the warmth of your light before you even arrived. " She patted the mattress beside her and Cady sat as she bid. "You can heal me, can't you?"

A sense of humbleness hit Cady. This woman was full of faith and hope – in her. "I believe I can, yes."

Eyes the color of a winter sky gazed at her with all the knowledge of the universe in their depths. "Your aura is pure white. Did you know that?"

"No," Cady shook her head. "I can see the emanation of other people's spirits, but never have I seen my own." She didn't know why hers would be white; Cady knew she was far from perfect. She took the old woman's hands in her own. "Let's get started. Shall we?"

"Yes, please." Her old face crinkled in a smile. "I called you forth, you know. I saw you in my scrying mirror."

As Cady held the arthritic hands, she massaged the fingers and felt heat begin to emanate from her palms. The magick of her ability never ceased to amaze her. "You intrigue me," she smiled at the old woman. "Tell me what you saw." She knew all about her family's gifts and Nanette's family, the Romee witches – but every magical person approaches the craft differently.

Ms. Adams began to talk as Cady performed her unique type of therapy and what she said was absolutely unbelievable. "When I look into the darkness of the mirror, I see a person as they really are. Many times I see that person's past – sometimes even their past lives." As Renee spoke, Cady took out some herb salve and applied it to the swollen joints.

"Okay – so tell me about my past, pretty lady." As Cady worked on her client's body, she repeated scriptures from the Psalms. *O LORD my God, I cried unto thee, and thou hast healed me. Many are the afflictions of the righteous: but the LORD delivereth him out of them all. He keepeth all his bones: not one of them is broken.* The words were so familiar to her that they came easily to her memory.

"I see a young woman who is waiting for something," Renee began. "You have always felt like you were unworthy of love and tried to be invisible. People's unthinking and careless words have wounded you. They don't see the real you, do they?"

Cady's hands stilled. None of what Renee said required much magical ability – after all, her physical appearance was self-evident. But no one had ever been so frank with her, certainly not someone she just met. "What you see is all there is of me, Ms. Adams. My lack of attractiveness is as plain as the nose on my face."

"Ah, Ms. Renaud, there is more to you than your looks." A lilting laugh and a big smile lifted years from her countenance. "You are an extraordinarily gifted woman with a kind heart who asks for nothing more than to be treated with respect. If the average person could see you through my eyes they would know exactly how beautiful you are."

Cady's cheeks were flushed pink with discomfort. "Let's concentrate on your hands. What are you feeling?" Better to get the attention off of her and back where it belonged.

Ms. Adams wasn't very cooperative. "You know what I'm feeling; you can sense the healing energy leaving your hands." In Cady's palm, she could feel Renee stretching her fingers – farther than she had been able to do before they started the procedure. "Don't you want to ask about your past existence, or do you already know?"

Her question was just too tempting to pass up. "I have had past lives? Was I Cleopatra or Jezebel?" She rarely heard of anyone claiming to be just a regular person in a past life.

Renee Adams sobered – completely. "Your pre-existence is unlike any I have ever come across before." She seemed to pause for effect. "You are eternal, my dear. You are a watcher."

Her revelation was so unlike anything Cady had ever expected to hear that she laughed out loud. "A watcher? What do you mean?" Ms. Adam's hands were responding to her ministrations. Good. Relieving another person's pain was the most satisfying things she had ever done.

For a moment, Renee didn't answer. It was as if she were debating the wisdom of telling what she knew. "Watchers were created to guard and protect those who have been placed within their charge."

Cady was floored. "Are you saying that I am a guardian angel, Ms. Adams?" That was the most ridiculous thing she had ever heard. Wasn't it?

Joseph tried calling Cady Renaud three times. He was beginning to get nervous, wondering if she was avoiding his calls. Punching in the number one last time – he prayed she would answer. Click. Finally. "This is Acadia Renaud's answering service? May I help you?"

Better than nothing. Joseph left his information and hoped for the best. At dinner that night, he broke the news. "I think I've found me a physical therapist. I'm just waiting for her to get back with me and schedule a meeting."

All noise and movement stopped. "No shit!" Aron wanted to stand up and shout. It was a huge step forward that Joseph had even consented to get a therapist. And that he would find one himself!?! This meant he was serious about beginning intense therapy.

"Tell us, Joseph." Libby urged. "We want to know everything."

All eyes were on Joseph as he pushed his chair a ways back from the table. He put down his fork and looked from face to face. "Actually, Kane gave me her name. She's from New Orleans. A buddy of his that was injured in Iraq was paralyzed like me and with her help he's almost made a complete recovery."

There were looks exchanged. Jacob felt a niggle of trepidation. Even though they all hoped for a miracle, he wanted Joseph to keep sight of the fact that it was going to be a long hard road to travel. "What's her name and credentials?" Jacob asked.

Joseph was excited, they could all tell. He had hope for the first time in a long time. So the best thing they could do was be happy with him, until they had reason not to.

"Her name is Acadia Renaud. She goes by Cady. I think she's Creole, but what that means, I'm not sure. She uses traditional methods mixed with some uh – unorthodox treatments." Joseph could see a few skeptical glances, but he went on. "I'm not sure how I feel about all the extra stuff, but I'm willing to give it a try. If she can bring one guy back from the brink, maybe she can bring two."

Noah said what everyone else was thinking. "By unorthodox treatments, do you mean some sort of New Age mumbo jumbo?" Jessie caught herself wanting to smile. Noah was just a breath of fresh air on every hand. He wouldn't look at her, but Jessie wasn't upset about it. She respected Noah for his concern for his family.

Joseph was ready for this question. Hell! He had asked himself the same thing. Still, the intriguing possibility that Cady could help him could not be ignored. "I wouldn't call it New Age, or New anything. In fact, I understand her methods are pretty old. Her family is into hoodoo, voodoo, witchcraft or some New Orleans type of bullshit."

Aron snorted at his brother's answer. Joseph's attitude made this question easier to ask. "Well, if you think its bullshit, Joseph, why are you willing to let her within a mile of you?"

Joseph pinned him with a stare. "Kane told me that not only did his buddy walk again – she gave him back his manhood."

Instantly, every man at the table understood why he was willing to take the risk. None of them could imagine living a life unable to make love to a woman. Aron grabbed Libby's hand under the table and Jacob did the same with Jessie, caressing it with his thumb, promising her with a touch that their night was going to be very active indeed.

"Well, Joseph, you've got my support. Whatever you decide to do is fine with me." With that, Aron gave his blessing. Then, he went on to give another one. "Jessie, that was one fine meal. And to think – now we have two good cooks in the family." At Aron's surprising statement, seven pairs of eyes turned to stare at him.

Libby chimed in, backing him up. "We're glad to have you with us, Jessie. It's as simple as that." Aron kissed his little peacemaker.

Later, alone in his room – he got his answer. A buzzing noise alerted Joseph that his cell phone was ringing. For several days, he had made the foolish mistake of keeping it on vibrate. He had forgot he couldn't feel the stupid vibration. Today, however, he had changed it to the least annoying ring he could find. Pulling it from his pocket, he answered. "Joseph McCoy."

"Mr. McCoy? Hello. This is Cady Renaud. I believe you've been trying to get in touch with me?"

Her voice was soft, but had a deep sultry tone – a breathy quality that sent chills down his spine. And that was quite an accomplishment considering he had damage between his S3 and T12 vertebrae. "Yes, Miss Renaud. A friend gave your name to me. He's our sheriff, Kane Saucier."

"Yes, I know the Sauciers. How may I be of service?"

If Kane hadn't already told Joseph that Ms Renaud was unattractive, Joseph would have been completely fooled by her voice. She sounded damn sexy. Visions of low-hanging Spanish moss, slow-moving bayou waters and sweet blooming magnolias filled his mind. In fact, her voice sounded familiar – almost like the voice of the woman in his dreams. "I'm paralyzed, Ms. Renaud. I flipped a dirt bike and I only have function above my waist. I can't walk, I wear a catheter and I am no longer a functioning male. Do you get the picture?" His voice had grown harsher than he intended.

"My methods are somewhat unorthodox," she advised, making sure he understood. "And it is not an immediate cure. Although it varies, my treatments usually last at least a month."

A month. Jacob thought he could put up with anything for a month, even an ugly woman's hands on him. Anything, if he could just reclaim some of the precious things he had lost. "I do not question your methods, Ms. Renaud. I respect your results."

"Very well. I will come to you in two days. Will that fit in with your schedule?"

She sounded self-confident. He had to ask. "Do you think you can help me? I understand you worked a miracle with Kane's soldier friend who was injured in Iraq?" Joseph knew his reference would give her an insight into his torment.

Her voice dropped and Joseph could have sworn the temperature in the room went up about ten degrees. "Call me Cady, Mr. McCoy. There will be no room in our association for formalities. If I am to help you, we will definitely have to become better acquainted."

Now wait a minute. He didn't need some wallflower getting any ideas about him. He might be paralyzed, but he wasn't desperate. When he didn't answer; Cady Renaud laughed. "Don't worry, Mr. McCoy. I don't take advantage of helpless males, no matter how attractive they might be." She made Joseph nervous. Was reading minds part of her bag of tricks?

"I'm not worried, Cady. I'm not the type of man who can be taken advantage of. If you'll give me your email address I will send you directions to the ranch and we can exchange details of what you charge for your services and anything else you might require." Joseph had gone all business. He didn't want to give the woman any ideas. It wasn't a lie that he needed what she could provide. But that was all he wanted from her. Joseph had never been comfortable around unattractive women. And now, he wasn't comfortable around attractive ones. Lord, he was in a mess – in more ways than one. At least now he had hope. There was a light at the end of the tunnel, and it was drawing him to it like a moth to a flame.

Cady hung up the phone and curled into a ball. Joseph. "Joseph." She said the name out loud. She had no idea why she felt like she had been run over by a steam engine at the mere sound of his voice. It was obvious he had been told of her lack of beauty. She did not know Kane Saucier well, but Zane was her friend. And it hadn't been Zane who shared that sad truth – for he had never seen her face, or her body - Zane was blind. But Kane had been kind to her at several neighborhood gatherings. Once, he had even danced with her. Cady could remember things like that, she could count the number of times she had been held in a man's arms on one hand – with several fingers left over. Despite the hurt feelings, she couldn't muster up any resentment toward Kane for something as simple as telling the truth.

Joseph was afraid she was going to get a crush on him. She read that thought of his as clearly as she could read the bright numbers on her digital clock. As she looked into her heart, she knew it was a great possibility – especially if he was as devastatingly attractive as the Joseph she met in her dream. But right now, Cady Renaud planned on keeping her feelings - however tender they may be – to herself. If there was joy to be experienced, it would have to be private joy. Rejection from Joseph would hurt more than any other ever had – so she vowed she wouldn't give him a chance to reject her. Despite her intention to push him from her mind, when she dropped off to sleep, it was to dream of Joseph McCoy.

Joseph tossed and turned, his body felt like it was going through a heat. Ripping off the covers, he let the cool air from the ceiling fan blow away the tatters of his dreams. Something wasn't right. His eyes tried to adjust to the darkness. There was a movement across the room. "Who's there?"

The rays of the full moon gave very little light, for clouds passed darkly over its pearly surface. The room was eerily quiet and Joseph felt like he was looking through a dark glass – into a realm of lights and shadows. Straining to make out who was walking so slowly toward him, he was shocked to see it was the angel from the hospital – the goddess from his dreams. Again he asked - "Who are you?" Not that it mattered; she was someone that he wanted to know, desperately.

"Joseph. My Joseph," her voice was warm and sultry and caused his heart to race with desire. As if on cue, the clouds passed from over the moon and the room lightened, becoming bathed in a heavenly glow that illuminated everything around him – including the vision advancing toward him. It was her! Joseph licked his lips. She wore a thin white gown that emphasized every exquisite curve of her body. He could see large, round nipples that pushed at the gauzy fabric like they were trying to get his attention – they were damn successful.

Unable to resist, he held out his hand. "I want you, angel." His beautiful visitor walked up to the bed and placed her small hand in his. He raised it to his lips and kissed the tender center of her palm. With her free hand, she released a single toggle at her breast and the filmy material floated to the floor. Joseph's mouth went dry and he felt his cock become engorged with passion. Gracing him with the sweetest smile, she pulled the sheet back; then sent his blood pressure into orbit as she ran her hand down his chest to tangle in the short curls above his manhood.

Joseph was panting with desire. Fascinated by her perfect body, her flowing hair and her incredible loving eyes, he held out his arms and she climbed into the bed with him, fitting herself to his body as if she were created just for him. He pulled her over on top of him, her hair creating a sensual curtain that enclosed them in magic. "I live for your kiss," she whispered to him as she offered him the gift of her lips.

Sucking at her tongue, Joseph reveled in the joining of their mouths. Nothing had ever been more perfect than this! Enclosing her firmly in his embrace, he ran his hands up and down her body – learning the curves, the dips, and the valleys – memorizing the silken smoothness of her perfect skin. "Sit up, beautiful," Joseph urged. "I want to see all of you." His wish seemed to be her command, because she straddled his body and sat up, revealing to Joseph's hungry eyes two round full globes topped with dark colored nipples that were clearly aroused and eager for his attention. She wiggled her pussy against his abdomen and cupped her breasts in her own palms – leaning over to rub one nipple over his lips – Eve tempting Adam. Joseph took a bite of the apple – opening his mouth and latching on to the tempting tit like it was the food of the gods.

"Oh, yes!" she keened as he sucked to his heart's content. As he fed at her breast, his siren caressed his chest and shoulders, running her hands over his face, revving up his sexual appetite like the engine of a powerful car before a race. "I want more!" she announced as she took hold of the headboard and moved herself up his body. Joseph was entranced as he realized she was about to sit on his face – demanding something from him he was more than willing to give.

Paradise! Joseph made himself at home in her pussy, licking and sucking and nibbling at the cherry of her clit. She tasted like honeysuckle – sweet and wild. Her aroused moans and groans were making him more excited than he could ever remember being, and he repaid her enthusiasm by reaching up and taking both nipples in his fingers and working them until she began to ride his face with the same erotic rhythm. Much to Joseph's delight, his angel's juices began to flow – coating his face with her passion and ensuring that his cock was as hard as a steel beam. God, he couldn't wait to fuck her!

"Now!" he growled. "I've got to have you now!" He pushed on her waist, angling her down. Joseph was so near to cumming he wondered if he would manage to actually get inside of her treasure house before he exploded.

Looking up into her beautiful face, he was gratified to see she was as hungry for him as he was for her. Her eyes were glazed over with passion, her cheeks were flushed – and her breaths were coming in little pants specifically designed to turn him inside out with longing.

Steadying his angel with hands on her hips, he lifted her high enough to accept his rampaging organ. She was as eager as he and reached between them, taking hold of his cock and guiding him into the hot depths of her body.

"Joseph," she moaned. "It feels good – so good to have you inside me," Immediately, she began moving – sensuously, gracefully, and passionately – like she couldn't get enough of him

"That's it, baby – take me – make me yours - please." Joseph groaned as she rode him with abandon – her head thrown back, blatantly relishing his hard cock throbbing deep inside of her. His encouraging plea caused her to meet his gaze and she smiled, causing Joseph to erupt – he had never come so magnificently – jetting hotly into her body. And as his hips jerked, she cried out his name, "Joseph!" and shattered. Her body began to shake and her pussy fisted down on him in rapid, repeating milking motions – the most intimate caress known to man.

God in heaven! Joseph pushed his hips upward, striving to put himself as deep in her as he could – Lord, he wished he could stay inside of her forever. No orgasm in his past even came close to the rapture of this one. Enchanted, he watched her come down from her high – her palms covering those gorgeous breasts, rubbing her own nipples – her pussy still working his cock in tiny aftershocks. And when she focused on him – giving him her attention – laying down on his chest and resting her head on his shoulder – Joseph felt the most intense happiness of his life. Folding his arms around her, he squeezed. She kissed his neck, he kissed her temple – and sleep stole their thoughts and brought them contentment.

Daylight broke and Joseph reached for her. His hands closed on empty air. God, he could still smell her! Sitting up, he started to swing his legs off of the bed – and he remembered. He was paralyzed... and impotent.

"Fuck!" It had been a dream. Again. That incredible woman, that incredible release had been a figment of his deteriorating reason. "Damn! Shit!" He almost cried from the crushing weight of disappointment that crashed down on his heart and soul. He wanted her – so bad. But, she wasn't real. She was just a dream. And Joseph wanted to die.

She was going to have to change the sheets. Cady looked at the huge wet spot staining her pale pink bottom sheet. Her encounter with Joseph might have all been in her mind, but her orgasm and ejaculation were real enough to force her to strip her bed and do a load of laundry. Good Gracious! Cady could never remember having that type of climax in her sleep. For a moment, she allowed herself to sink down on the bed and relive the ecstasy she had experienced in his arms. Could sex actually feel that good? Feeling her face flame, she covered her cheeks with her palms. Whew! Forcing herself up, she resumed her task. Jerking off the bottom sheet, she threw it over in a pile and started to take off the mattress liner as well. The sudden ringing of her cell phone halted her movements and she instantly knew her grandmother was on the line. "Nana!" she greeted her warmly.

"Acadia, my love," the ancient voice was forceful with will, if not with strength. "How are you?"

Cady sank down on the edge of the bed, again - the events of the night before still primary in her mind. Attempting to put them aside so she could have a legitimate conversation with her relative, she forgot the incredible insight of the woman on the other end of the line. Before

Cady could answer her question, Nana answered it for her. "You are going to him, aren't you?"

Even though she knew it was useless, she stalled for time. "Going to whom, Grandmother?" Anytime she switched to the more formal address for her Nana, Cady betrayed her guilt at whatever her grandmother was interrogating her about.

"Your destiny, child; you are about to embark on the greatest adventure of your life." Nana's voice had dropped an octave and took on that tone of prophecy that Cady recognized from countless times before. "You've been dreaming of him, haven't you?"

Surprise cascaded over Cady. Nothing her grandmother could do should come as a surprise, but invariably this mysterious woman could catch her off guard. There was no use to hedge – she was caught. "Yes." She didn't have to tell everything she knew, though.

"That is normal, Cady, we have all done it. Women of power can bring their dreams to life," she stage-whispered to make her point. "I can promise you this – whatever you experienced last night - - - so did he." Having delivered the message she intended, a soft click met Cady's ears and then a dial tone. Her grandmother was gone.

Cady was stunned. Joseph had dreamed the same dream? About her? Would he remember their encounter? Her hand automatically flew to her hair – to her face – would he recognize her? Did he know it was Cady Renaud who was making love to him? Flashes of her aggressive behavior caused her to flush with a combination of excitement and embarrassment. How was she going to face him now?

"Damn rocks," Joseph growled as he tried to maneuver his manual wheelchair down the pathway toward the barn. He might not be able to ride, but at least he could visit his horse. This old barn had seen a lot of action over the years –

in fact, he had lost his virginity up in the hayloft with Tiffany Robinson. Stopping to take a breather, Joseph was struck by how odd his surroundings were. It was home. Tebow looked the same, but it was like he was seeing it from a different perspective. There wasn't a breeze, not a leaf was stirring. In fact, the ranch was the quietest he had ever noticed. An eerie feeling crept down the back of Joseph's neck. He couldn't wheel around fast – but he turned as fast as he could. Looking out toward the hay meadow and the stock pond, he halfway expected to see somebody watching him – but he could detect nothing amiss, nothing out of the ordinary. Still, there was – something – wrong. Studying the horizon, taking in the livestock, Joseph surveyed his domain. Shit! He knew what was wrong – it was him. Blowing out a frustrated breath, Joseph turned and made his way to the big double doors.

Before he could reach for the handle, the fast pat of running tennis shoes alerted Joseph that Nathan had spotted him and decided to join him. "Hey, Joseph! Wait up! I've missed you!" Who could resist a request like that?

"Come on up here and help me get in this door. I'm glad you came along." He looked up at Nathan. When had he gotten so tall! He was going to be grown before they knew it!

"Sure thing. I brought some apples for Palladin and Sultan and some sugar for Molly – she loves sugar cubes." He threw open the doors and allowed Joseph to roll past him into the cool shade of the barn. "Guess what? Haley Morrison made me some cookies!"

"Cookies? What kinda cookies?" The horses heard them come in and Joseph inhaled the sweet smell of hay and the pungent scent of livestock. The aroma of animals and their natural odors had never offended him – it all just smelled like money to him.

"Oatmeal raisin; I would rather have had chocolate chip, but they're all right, I guess." Nathan followed Joseph deeper into the barn. "She said she made them for me because she was glad I was alive – that I didn't get killed in the accident."

"We're all glad you survived, bud. What would we do without you?" They stopped in front of old Molly's stall. The horse was the favorite of the family; she'd been the first mount the boys had ridden in their younger days. He could still remember putting Nathan on her back for the first time. Molly was gentle and loving – a perfect way to introduce the love of horses into a boy's life. Nathan held his hand out flat and let the gentle mare take the sugar cubes. Her big brown eyes were getting cloudy with age, but the affection she had for the two males in front of her was obvious. "And Haley made you cookies because she likes you and she is glad you're still around."

"Did any girls make you cookies?" Nathan's innocent question hit Joseph like a two-by-four. His life was so different. There was no interaction with women. As far as friends, he had only heard from Beau who called him every day and was planning on coming to see him as soon as he was back in the country. The golden palomino snorted, trying to gain their attention.

"Libby and Jessie made me cookies and cake and pie." Joseph patted his belly. "Give me an apple and let me appease Palladin. He's getting jealous." Nathan handed the piece of fruit over to his brother and gave Molly one last scratch between her ears.

"Jessie and Libby don't count. They're family. They have to be good to us." Nathan's reasoning was sound.

"That's true." Even though no wedding had taken place between Libby and Aron, Libby was family. And Jacob was in love with Jessie, Joseph could tell. He wasn't jealous of his brothers, but he wondered if a wife and a family was an impossible dream for him now. Before the accident, there had been no special woman – he thought he had all the time in the world to meet a girl, fall in love and bring some more

McCoy's into the world. Now that dream had gone up in smoke, just like all of his other dreams. That is - unless Cady Renaud could work a miracle.

"We had better pay some attention to Sultan, he's gonna break down his stall door." Nathan distracted Joseph from his pity-party and led them deeper into the cool confines of the wing where they kept their personal mounts. "Joseph, are you going to get any better?" Out of the mouths of babes.

"I don't know, Nathan. I hope so." Honesty was hard, sometimes. "There is a woman coming to help me. They say she has had a lot of success dealing with people in my condition."

"I love you." Strong, young arms wound around Joseph's neck and his eyes began to fill with tears.

"I love you, too, Bud." A commotion at the door broke the heavy moment.

Aron stuck his head in and let his eyes adjust to the lower light. "We got trouble, Joseph. I'm going to be gone for a while. Sam radioed me and he found some dead calves and three of the fences have been cut. I don't know what the hell is going on, but I'm gonna find out. Will you keep an eye on Libby for me?"

"Is that all they told you? No word as to who might be responsible?" Joseph felt so helpless. His place was at Aron's side, hunting down the culprit that dared to invade Tebow ranch.

"We're stumped." Aron confessed. "I've called the authorities, but I'm not waiting around for someone else to protect my family."

Joseph and Nathan started toward their older brother. "Don't worry about Libby. Nathan and I will take care of things here." As they made their way out in the yard, Joseph looked out over the outlying pastures and fields. Earlier, he had felt an uneasy foreboding. Hell, maybe he was getting psychic. He just hoped his future was worth looking into.

"Why didn't you call me?" Jacob asked Aron. "We could have headed back earlier." He had been stunned to find out someone was coming onto McCoy land, killing cattle and vandalizing property.

"Hell!" Aron was at his wit's end. "I don't know what you could have done. I've got every man we have on full alert. We're taking shifts riding the perimeter – but its damn hard trying to police a hundred thousand acres. It would take a damn army!"

"How many cattle have we lost?" They sat on the front verandah. Aron was tired, sweaty and disgusted. Libby brought them each a glass of iced tea, but it was going to take more than a cold beverage to cool Aron's temper.

"At last count – nine, five of those were registered. That's tens of thousands of dollars lost for God knows what reason." The cattle had been mutilated, butchered and skinned. None of the McCoy's had a clue as to what the possible motivation could be.

"Put me on a shift," Jacob urged, ready to do what he could.

"All right. You can have first light," Aron drained his tea glass and set it on the banister. "The pitiful thing is that we don't have a clue who is doing this, or why. I had to call Roscoe and get him to assign another PI to help us with this mess."

"Good" Jacob racked his brain trying to think of anybody that would hate them enough to do this. They sat in silence for a few moments, till Jacob shared part of his good news with Aron. "Jessie and I have come to an understanding."

From the satisfied smile on Jacob's face, Aron had to know. "Must have been some understanding," Aron leaned forward on his knees, his hands clasped in front of him.

Despite the problems that had arisen, he had a look of complete peace on his face.

"She agreed to marry me, Aron. Jessie loves me."

For a long minute, Aron didn't say anything. He understood completely how a little woman could worm her way into your heart and life before you turned around. The only reason he wasn't married to Libby right now was because she was determined to get married on The Sweetest Day, which the calendar said was October the sixteenth. When Libby had fallen ill a few weeks back, Aron had been horrified to learn she lived with leukemia for nearly a decade. All the time she had been on the ranch, she had been in remission. In Libby's mind, she had been living on borrowed time, determined to experience all that life could offer during the remaining months she had left to live. During that time, she and Aron had fallen in love – so when he had found her collapsed on the floor, it had nearly scared him to death. On the way to the hospital, he had told her that she was going to be fine. And not only was she going to be fine, they were going to be married two months from that date. Jacob had been driving, and he had told Libby the date was October the 16th, The Sweetest Day. Now, she felt there was magic in the day and refused to be married at any other time.

"Do you love her?" Aron thought he knew the answer to that question, but it was his job to ask.

"More than you can possibly imagine," Jacob spoke with a reverent tone, as if the idea of loving and marrying Jessie was sacred.

Aron started to complain that they hadn't known each other long enough, but he had no room to talk. He and Libby only had a few weeks together, when he found himself completely besotted with her. "You have my support," Aron trusted Jacob's judgment. He almost brought up a prenup, but he had no intention of asking or allowing Libby to sign one, so bringing it up would have been hypocritical. He'd let

Zane play the bad guy, that's why they paid him the big bucks.

"I haven't seen Joseph, where is he?" Jacob felt like he had been gone a week instead of just over a day.

"He's with Isaac; they're in Austin checking about the possibility of ordering Joseph a custom pick-up truck he can use with his wheelchair."

"Excellent," Jacob was thrilled that Joseph seemed to be getting a handle on his rehabilitation and his search for recovery. "Did he get in touch with that woman Kane recommended? She was from New Orleans, wasn't she?"

"Her name is Acadia Renaud and she'll arrive tomorrow." Both men felt conflicted over Ms. Renaud's arrival. There was so much going on it was hard for them to give their full attention to any one thing.

"How do you feel about that?" Jacob asked his big brother.

"Let's see; how do I feel about a female who practices magic moving into our house?" Aron had the good grace to laugh at himself. "Women have enough of an advantage over us poor males without throwing witchcraft in the mix." Crossing one long leg over the other at the ankle, Aron tilted his hat down over his eyes like he was going to nap. "Bottom line, if she can help Joseph, I don't care if she dances naked in the front yard swinging a dead cat over her head."

"As long as that dead cat ain't Timmy, we'll be all right." Jacob asserted as he picked Timmy up and scratched him behind the ears.

"Tell me about this land you bought from old man Keszey." Aron was proud of his brother. Jacob was turning out to have a good head for business. Noah wasn't the only one in the family with the Midas touch.

Jacob set Timmy down who scampered off after a butterfly. "It was pure dumb luck," Jacob began. "I had no idea Henry wanted to sell or that he would consider selling to me."

"You've been good to him. In the past couple of months, you helped him get his tractor out of the ditch, you delivered his calf that was breach and you took the time to stop and drink coffee with him when he was lonely. Gestures of kindness mean a lot to old people."

"I like Henry," Jacob stood up and walked to the porch railing and sat down, facing Aron. "The surprising thing was that he sold me his mineral rights. That's unheard of in this day and age."

"Especially since the mineral rights appear to be worth a fortune to you," Aron drained his tea glass, the ice clinking loudly.

"Look, I offered to settle with him after the tests came back positive for natural gas and blue rock." Both of the discoveries would yield millions and Jacob felt guilty about the small price he paid for the acreage. "But he said he sold it for what it was worth to him and he wasn't interested in being rich."

"Knowing you, you'll turn that money into something good." Aron had no doubt about the big heart of Jacob. He was active with cancer research, youth programs, the volunteer fire department – you name the charity and Jacob was in the middle of it.

"I know what I wish," Jacob let out a long breath. "I'd give every cent I have to give Joseph his life back – every red cent."

Robert Keszey took his wirecutters out of his back pocket and snipped the barbwire. He pulled the strands to one side and made a wide avenue of escape for the big red Beefmasters that lined the McCoy coffers with greenbacks.

Jacob McCoy tricked his uncle. The old man was senile and had allowed McCoy to talk him into almost giving away the whole Moore Plantation Section of his – Robert's –

inheritance. Robert was livid. He felt cheated and cast aside. After all the time he wasted on that old goat of an uncle. He couldn't believe he had been passed over – slighted – robbed of what was rightfully his.

The promise of new territory where the grass is always greener drew two of the cows to nose around and walk through the gap. Robert stood there and watched as the large beasts walked out to the roadside to graze where they would put themselves, property and innocent lives in jeopardy. And the McCoy's would be blamed – and he was just getting started.

"Let's go somewhere else," Joseph muttered self-consciously. The two women were looking at him like he was some kind of lab-rat. Hadn't they ever seen a man in a wheelchair before? Tracy Damon and Rosalee Bale were their names; he had dated them both and slept with Tracy. Now, all he could see was curiosity in their eyes. They weren't giving him the same attention they were showing his brother. Him, they looked at with pity – Isaac they looked at with lust. And Joseph didn't know if he could stand it. How would he ever get used to being seen as a cripple instead of a virile man?

"Now, where else would we go?" Isaac reasoned with him. "You want a King Ranch don't you? And this is the Ford place that we've done business with forever." He was oblivious to the two women. "What's wrong with you?" He didn't cut Joseph much slack. It was Isaac's opinion that if you didn't treat Joseph any different than they always had – he wouldn't be any different.

"Not a shittin' thang," Joseph spit out as the two blondes looked at Isaac like he was a stick of licorice candy they'd like to suck. "I just hate to run into women I used to date – especially since they look at me now like I'm something they found stuck to the bottom of their shoe. They can't keep their eyes off of you – you dickhead."

"They're looking at me because I'm hot," Isaac snorted. "A man can't help when he's attractive to the opposite sex. You ought to know that, you've had your share of women since you were out of knee-pants" Truthfully, he wasn't interested in either one of them. There was only one little gal that owned his heart and it wasn't the two bleached blondes that were advertising their multiple charms in low cut blouses and too short skirts.

"Its just all that leather," Joseph started to see the humor in the situation. "You look like a Dooney and Burke purse."

"I look like sex on a stick." He did look good. Isaac did own a mirror, but his ego wasn't nearly as big as he played like it was. "And speaking of leather, wait till you see the interior of that pickup I want you to order. That is the fanciest damn super-cab I've ever seen." Raymond Dawson came waddling toward them with a pair of keys.

"McCoys!" Dawson was always glad to see good, faithful customers. "Boy, have I got a truck for you. It's as black as sin and powerful enough to make even a Texas boy smile; and we can add all the bells and whistles you'll ever need Joseph. A mobility conversion setup can be custom installed that will give you all the freedom in the world." It sounded good; Joseph knew he needed a truck that he wouldn't have to transfer out of his wheelchair in order to drive. "Check it out, and tell me what you think. It's parked out back. I'll be in my office when you make up your mind."

Joseph's mind was spinning. He couldn't drive at all without hand controls for the brake and the gas. Those were a necessity. This would at least get him back on the road. But buying it seemed to say that he didn't expect Cady's treatment to help. Shit!

"You'll have to take us for a ride sometimes, Isaac." Tracy sidled up to Isaac like a cat up to a bowl of cream. Isaac could have strangled her with her own string of pearls.

"This isn't gonna be my truck – it will be Joseph's. You'll have to talk to him if you want to take a spin."

Evidently, Rosalee had a bigger heart than Tracy – because, she had the good grace to at least look guilty and try to cover up their rudeness. "That would be nice, Joseph. How are you doing? We've missed seeing you on the racing circuit."

"I'm making it just fine, Rosalee. How have you been?" He ignored the half-hearted come-on and started rolling over to the office manager's desk to tell him to cancel the truck. He needed more time before he made a commitment this big. He could hear the girls giggling as they flirted with Isaac. They sounded so silly. What had he ever seen in bimbos like those two? All he could about was his undercover angel – his midnight dream girl. Now, that was a woman.

Acadia Renaud drove under the Tebow Ranch sign. As soon as she did, she felt it. Evil. Flashes of red obscured her vision. Something was very wrong at this place. A sense of foreboding enveloped her. Parking, she sat for a few moments; waiting to see if she could glean more information from the black cloud of ominous emotion that had crashed into her spirit. Crossing her arms over her breasts, as if to shield herself from attack, Cady waited for the uncomfortable feeling to pass. As if the source of the darkness was moving farther away, she felt the danger recede.

Biting her lower lip, Cady shored up her strength and courage. This was not going to be easy. Every magical instinct she possessed told her the man who summoned her, asking for her help, was in great pain – but she had been told he possessed the ability to cause her great pain as well. Pulling down the rear view mirror, Cady looked at her reflection. She was not a beautiful woman. She was passably attractive, if the viewer was half-blind and intoxicated. With all the immense power her family possessed, it seemed plausible that they should have been able to come up with some potion or trick that could bestow beauty upon one of their own. With all her heart, she held onto what her grandmother had said. Her beauty was one of spirit and soul – and the man who would truly love her would be able to see past her limitations to the beauty within. And when he saw her for what she truly was – then his love would make her beautiful. Fine. She just wished he would hurry up. Mostly, she wished that man were Joseph.

A rap on the window almost caused her to bite her tongue. Some psychic she was, she hadn't even seen the young man approach the car with either of her visions – physical or psychic. Cady took the key out of the ignition and grabbed her purse, giving the handsome boy a nod of greeting. He opened her door, "Hey, I'm Nathan. What's your name?"

Cady took the hand that was offered to her. "I'm Acadia Renaud, but you can call me Cady." She smiled at him. He was engaging and had the purest gold aura she had ever seen, a sign of a pure spirit – one that was under divine protection. This young man was destined to do great good in the world. That thought made her remember what Renee Adams had said about her own spiritual reality – a watcher – that ridiculous notion still made her laugh. "I'm here to meet Joseph McCoy."

"Oh, yeah!" Nathan nodded; remembering that Libby said Joseph's physical therapist would be arriving today. "You've come to help Joseph." He walked with her up the verandah steps. Cady stopped at the door, an overwhelming feeling of destiny swamping her senses. She didn't know what the future would hold for her here at Tebow Ranch, but whatever was ahead was going to be a wild, wild ride.

Lord, he was nervous! You'd think he was meeting the Queen of England instead of a woman that had been hired to crack the whip and see if his muscles would respond to whatever form of torture she could come up with. When he heard Nathan come through the front talking to someone, he had a sinking feeling Acadia Renaud had arrived. And he was right.

"Joseph! Cady's here!"

Great. He had hoped she wouldn't come until after the party tonight. Hopefully, she wouldn't expect for him to entertain her. He'd have to pawn her off on one of his brothers for the evening. "I'm coming!" Damn! Might as well face the music. He was in his manual chair today, so he took the wheels in his hands and pushed himself to the living room. As he maneuvered toward the door, he reminded himself that she was his choice – she was here because he wanted her here. He needed Cady Renaud.

Cady saw him before he saw her. The movements of the strong muscles in his arms and shoulders almost took her breath away. Now this was a man! Her man! The man of her dreams – literally. Remembrances of what they had done together caused Cady to grow warm, a blush stealing up her cheeks. What a crying shame that he was confined to that chair instead of striding in on those long, powerful looking legs. She knew it would be up to her to make sure those legs stayed powerful and didn't shrivel up into useless appendages. And she intended to heal him – if it was in her power and the fates were kind.

"Hey, my face is up here." Joseph spoke before he thought. He hadn't meant for his tone to be so rebuking. It was just that he didn't like for anyone to stare at his legs. Before his accident, he had enjoyed women eating him up with their eyes. Now he knew they weren't lusting after his physique, they pitied his condition.

Cady jumped at his harsh words. The flush turned into a flash of red shame that washed up her features. She had been caught looking, appreciating his beautiful body. How unprofessional! "I apologize. Please forgive my lack of manners." She stepped forward to offer her hand. If they were to have a good working relationship, she needed to get a handle on this powerful attraction she felt for him. After all, Cady knew what she looked like. Mud fence was a term she was too familiar with.

Joseph had to call Kane and thank him. He didn't know how effective this woman would be at her job, but she sure did fulfill one of his requirements. Cady Renaud was not a pretty woman. Her dark hair was pulled back into a neat bun, with just a few stray tendrils that did little to soften her plain features. She wore wire frame glasses that made her brown eyes look as big as an owl's. And her body was covered from shoulder to toe in a shapeless denim jumper. There wasn't a curve in sight! In spite of himself, his face broke into a grin. He didn't care how many times this woman emptied his pee bag. If he had special ordered a homely woman feature by feature, he couldn't have done a better job.

Slowly, she stepped back. That was when Joseph realized she had extended her hand in greeting and he had failed to accept the friendly gesture. Shit! He hadn't intended to be so rude. Damn! "Sorry." This time he rolled forward a couple of inches and held out his hand. Graciously, she took it and pressed her fingers to his in greeting. "Hell!" he exclaimed as an electrical shock sizzled through his system. "You shocked me!" He was startled. That hadn't happened to him in years, and never had it been that strong. Many was the time he and Isaac had scrubbed their feet on the carpet, lying in wait for one of their brothers to come by so they could shock the shit out of them. Rubbing his arm, he wondered at the tiny smile she gave him. Did she enjoy his discomfort? Lord, that didn't bode well for his physical therapy. That's all he needed – a woman who would get off on causing him pain.

"Forgive me again, Mr. McCoy. I didn't realize I had such an electrifying personality." This time she smiled, a real smile, and Joseph was amazed at the difference it made in her face. Not that it made her pretty, but at least it made her more pleasant to look at.

Voices from the kitchen made Joseph sigh in relief. Saved by the women! Libby and Jessie came skipping through the living room on their way inside with big bouquets of flowers from Libby's garden. Now, this was how women were supposed to look! He couldn't help comparing Cady's drabness to the vivacious pair that had just entered the room like a breath of fresh air. "Libby, Jessie; stop for a minute and meet Cady Renaud. Cady these two beautiful women belong to my brothers Aron and Jacob. This is Libby Fontaine and Jessie Montgomery." Libby, always the perfect hostess, put down her flowers and hugged their newest houseguest.

"How wonderful to meet you, Cady!" She put her arm around her and began to lead her to the back.

Joseph saw a problem in the making. "Libby, honey – don't you think you should show Ms. Renaud to her room? She might like to get freshened up before the hayride."

Libby looked at him like an innocent lamb, "Why, that's what I'm doing, sweetie. We've put Cady in the room next to yours. That way, she can be right there in case you need anything during the night." Lord! Libby's voice sounded like warm syrup flowing over hot flapjacks. She was up to something!

At least Cady had the good grace to blush, Joseph noticed. She must realize there was no way she could ever be his type. Why, Joseph McCoy had dated some of the most beautiful women in the great state of Texas. "I don't think . . . "

One look from Libby quelled Joseph's unruly tongue. If Cady picked up his reluctance to have her sleeping near him, she didn't let on. Instead, she countered his argument. "It would be better if I were close by, Joseph. Some of the treatments we will be trying require that I'm near you while you sleep."

As Cady and Libby disappeared into the new wing, Jessie pulled out a chair and sat close to him. "She seems nice, huh?"

"I suppose," Joseph grunted.

"If she can help you, does it matter how she looks?" Jessie was smarter than the average bear.

Jacob snorted. "You don't understand, Jessie. Cady Renaud looks exactly like I want her to. When I started looking for a therapist, there was one qualification that I insisted upon." Jessie tried to get him to hush. She kept cutting her eyes toward the door, but Joseph was on a tear. "In addition to her having the right certification, I insisted that she be homely. If I'm going to let a woman see me at my worst, I don't want it to be a good-looking woman. And Cady Renaud suits me just fine. She's coyote ugly." As soon as the words left his mouth, Joseph was sorry he said them. The shock on Jessie's face was painful. She hadn't thought him capable of being so insensitive. But, when she cut her eyes over his head, he knew he was in deep shit.

Hell! When he swung his chair around slowly, he knew exactly what he'd find. Cady and Libby stood there. Dead still. Libby looked like she wanted to take a broom to him, but Cady looked. . . Joseph was dumbfounded and baffled. Cady's expression was cloaked. There was no hint of surprise or shock. None at all. The only difference between the woman that just left, and the woman that returned was a certain light in her eyes. The light that had spoken of hope and anticipation had been extinguished. Now, her eyes just looked – blank. "If you'll excuse me, Joseph, I think I'll unpack. Since, it's getting late; why don't we delay our first session until first thing in the morning?" Backing up, she nodded at Jessie and Libby, and then she walked off.

Chapter Four

"Joseph McCoy!" Libby got right in his face. "I didn't know you could be so mean! What's got into you?"
Joseph didn't like for Libby to fuss at him. He loved Libby. And, frankly – he didn't know what had gotten into him, either. Cady Renaud had come to Tebow in good faith. She was here to do a job – and – in spite of wishing it were otherwise, Joseph needed her and her unusual powers more than he needed to eat. "I don't know, Libby. I guess I'm scared. What this woman could do for me might mean the difference between living and just existing for the rest of my life."
"Then why did you go out of your way to hurt her?" Libby wasn't letting up, he'd never seen her so mad. Lord, Aron was going to kill him for upsetting Libby.
"I've been where Cady is right now, Joseph, and it hurts." Jessie spoke softly. "I haven't told Jacob, yet. But I can't read, Joseph." Her voice got soft and pained. "And look at me! I'm about thirty pounds heavier than I should be for my height. Plus, I clean people's houses for a living." She didn't know why she was telling him all of this. Jessie felt sorry for Cady Renaud and she wanted Joseph to know how much people's comments could hurt. "All of my life, people have been snide to me. Jacob is the first man that has ever seen me as a beautiful woman."
"You are a beautiful woman, Jessie," Joseph insisted. "Both of you are." Closing his eyes, he knew what he had to do. He left to go and apologize to Cady.
Joseph knocked and knocked. Finally, he just opened the door of her room and rolled in. "Cady!" There was no one there. The room was empty. Her things were on the bed where she had left them. She hadn't unpacked. But she was gone. Crap! He hadn't seen her go by, and he had been outside in the hall the whole time. To leave the area, she

would have had to go by him; there was no other way out. Huh! Joseph was bamboozled. How had she just disappeared? Out of nowhere, Joseph felt a chill down his back. He remembered that Ms. Renaud practiced a form of witchcraft. Suddenly, he couldn't get out of the room fast enough. He'd catch up with Cady later.

Just outside, Cady slid down the wall of the house until she could sit on the ground. She had barely got through the window and out of sight before he entered the room; the curtains were still flapping in the breeze. God, she hoped he didn't notice. There was no way she could look him in the eye at that moment, facing down a grizzly bear would be far more preferable. Desperate to just get away, she had gone out the closest exit she could find – the window. Often she had done this as a child, coming and going by her bedroom window. It just seemed more private, somehow.

Above the sound of the crickets and the occasional mooing of a cow, she could hear the rolling of the wheels of his chair on the carpet. Holding herself completely still, she didn't dare breathe lest he come to the window to look out and see her cowering down here like a crazy person. Finally, she heard him leave and she let out a deep breath. This was crazy; she had to get a handle on her emotions.

Clutching her stomach, Cady bent over almost double. She felt like she had been kicked in the gut. Tears made ragged tracks down her cheeks. Joseph's comments had cut her like a knife. She hadn't really harbored any hope he would be attracted her – but she had expected him to, at least, be friendly or have the courtesy to pretend he could tolerate her presence. No, that wasn't true; she should at least be honest with herself. All of the fairy-tale like words of her grandmother had given her false hope. What had she expected? In her heart, she had dreamed he would take one look and recognize her, or at least be drawn to her on some level. She had come at his behest – for his benefit –

and he had lashed out as if being in the same room with her offended him.

Rocking back and forth, she debated what to do. Could she deal with this? Could she put aside her crushed hopes and take care of business? Cady acknowledged that even in her suffering, she felt childish. Here she sat, an adult with a job to do. And what was she agonizing over? Her feelings had been hurt. Well, so what. He was still a patient and she was still a professional. Straightening her back and wiping her eyes – Cady made a decision. She couldn't force Joseph to treat her with kindness or respect, but she could control how she reacted to him. Strangely, she still felt some kind of final responsibility for the man. She wanted, no she needed to protect and help him despite his rejection of her as a woman. Chewing on her lip, she decided what she would do: she would toughen up, get in his face and do everything in her power to get him back on his feet. And along the way - if they became friends – so much the better, friendship was better than nothing.

"Miss Libby, I think your party is a success, sweetheart." Aron twirled Libby around the dance floor.

"I think you're right, Mr. McCoy." She laid her head on his shoulder and sighed in contentment.

"How do you feel? And don't even think about lying to me, girl." Aron rubbed his cheek on her hair, wondering how he would ever survive without her. She was so precious to him. Just knowing her leukemia could return at any time was a burden that weighed heavily on his soul. He vowed to enjoy every moment they had together and he prayed every day her cancer stayed as far away from her as the east was from the west.

She brought her arms up to wrap around his neck. "I feel good, Aron. I'm just tired." He could hear the weariness in her voice.

"We're not staying out here too much longer. We'll let Isaac and Noah play host and you and I will go snooze, how's that?" Aron had more irons in the fire than he needed. Roscoe, the PI, had called three times wanting to give a report on Jessie and the surrogate parents, but Aron kept putting him off. He had said it was important, but – God Almighty – what wasn't? He couldn't worry about that till they dealt with whatever nut was trespassing on the ranch. But the one thing he refused to ignore was Libby. She had to come first.

"Sounds heavenly."

Tequila Sunrise played songs that the crowd loved. The dance floor was crowded and Aron worked his way to the side, scoping out the crowd as he went. "Who's that woman over there?" he asked Libby, "the one who's wearing that loose mumu looking outfit?"

"That's Joseph's therapist. She arrived this afternoon."

Aron could tell by her voice that something was wrong. "Spill it, munchkin. What's got your little mind a spinning?" As they swayed to the music, Aron scanned the room, the trouble they were having with vandalism and animal deaths never far from his mind.

"Joseph had the strangest reaction to Cady, Aron. He was downright rude; I've never seen him that way, before. I had taken Cady to the room she'll be staying in, and when we returned we walked in on a conversation he was having with Jessie. Cady overheard him say some unkind things about her appearance."

"How did she react? Do you think she'll stay?" Aron wasn't sure how he felt about Ms. Renaud. After Joseph said he was going to contact her, Aron had made a few phone calls. He wasn't one to leave anything to chance when it came to his family. What he had learned, however, had eased his mind. She was very well respected in the medical community and had a high rate of success with her patients. On top of that, there had been some reports of complete recoveries; one doctor actually used the words 'miraculous recoveries'. For that reason, Aron hoped that whatever burr Joseph had up his ass wouldn't jeopardize giving this woman a chance to see what she could do for him.

"I've never seen anyone be so gracious. It was almost like she expected to be treated that way." Libby didn't like it. She hated to see anyone bullied because of their appearance, race, or any disability. That was one reason she had started gathering articles, books and other information to find anyway she could to help Jessie. From further conversations they had, she knew that Jessie's form of dyslexia was not the same as Nathan's, and would require a different approach in treatment. "Do you think you ought to go ask her to dance?"

Aron was about to steer Libby in that direction when he saw Joseph pull his chair up next to her. "Looks like another McCoy is on the job."

Seeing what Aron saw, Libby frowned. "He'd better be nice to her or I'm gonna short-sheet his bed."

Aron laughed. He had no doubt his little spitfire would do that and more.

"I can't believe he didn't buy his truck." Aron mused as he held Libby close.

"It didn't surprise me," she nestled her head against his chest, loving the feel of his hand rubbing up and down her back.

"Why is that?"

"Because, buying a truck outfitted for the handicapped would mean admitting defeat," Libby said simply. "You never knew, but Joseph almost gave up when he was in the hospital. He didn't think he could face life as a paraplegic. You'll have to forgive me, but I told Joseph about my cancer before I told you." Aron's grip on her tightened. "It was the only thing I could think of to get him to stop dwelling on his own problems. Now that Cady is in the picture, he has some hope to cling to."

Aron watched his brother talk to the woman he was counting on to salvage his life. "She damn sure better not be feeding him a line of bull – that's all I've got to say."

"Can I get you something to drink?" Joseph had debated coming over to talk to Cady, but he knew his mother would roll over in her grave if he continued to act like an ass. He hadn't meant anything by what he'd said; it certainly wasn't personal. In fact, he was glad that Ms. Renaud looked the way she did. It would make working with her that much easier. But she was a woman, and he knew that no woman wanted to hear that someone thought she was ugly. He had been unforgivably rude and he knew it. Now, if she'd just give him a chance to make up for it.

"I've had something, thank you." She gave him a slight smile that didn't quite make it to her eyes. "You have a marvelous home. I'm certain I'm going to enjoy my stay here very much."

Joseph let out a sigh. She was going to give him a free pass, and he didn't deserve it. "Cady, I'm sorry about what you heard me say. I'm not usually so stupid." He tried not to look at her and judge – but could she have picked a more unbecoming outfit? He tried to decide if she were overweight. Hell, it was hard to tell. Her clothes didn't touch her anywhere and she was wearing one of those dresses that women usually wear when they want to cover up a multitude of sins. Her hands were small and delicate and the feet that were peeking out from her floor-length skirt were narrow and sorta pretty. But a woman had to have more than cute hands and feet – what was in-between was pretty damn important. Hell! He was doing it again! What the fuck difference did it make how she looked? Wasn't she exactly what he had hoped for? "It's none of my business how you look or how you dress. I respect your ability and I need you. From this moment on, I promise to treat you with the respect you deserve. Okay?"

Cady looked at him. She had spent all afternoon learning everything she could about this man. Joseph McCoy was one of a kind. He was talented, generous, and smart as a whip. Women loved him, yet he didn't make enemies when he wined them, dined them and sent them on their way. And he was easily the most handsome man she had ever met. Cady wasn't kidding herself. Touching him and being with him hour after hour was not going to be easy. To top it all off – she knew what making love to him felt like – and it was heavenly. But that would never be – not in real life. The fantasy was all she would ever have. She just prayed she was able to build up her immunity to his good looks and forget all of her grandmother's bedtime stories. The worst thing that could happen would be if she were foolish enough to develop a lasting crush on him. Right now, it was just wishful thinking.

What she needed to maintain between them was emotional distance. But, that would be impossible. The very nature of an empath was to connect with another person to such an extent that you could draw their pain out of their bodies and take it upon yourself. It was already becoming clear to her. Her aunt was right about one thing- Joseph McCoy was going to bring her untold pain, both physical and mental. With that realization, she accepted his olive branch and offered one of her own. "Let us not think of it anymore. It is forgotten."

"I'd ask you to dance, if I could," Joseph looked around, hoping to see Kane or one of his other friends who he could coerce into spending time with her.

She must have realized what he was up to, because she stood and straightened her back, giving him a somewhat regal nod. "My journey from New Orleans was a long one. I feel it would be wise if I retire for the evening. Please, enjoy yourself. Tomorrow, we begin a regime that will have you railing curses on my head. So I recommend that you, also, get a good night's rest." As she walked away from him, Joseph was relieved the apology was over with. It hadn't been as bad as he envisioned – but that was because Cady had been generous. He only hoped what she did to him in physical therapy would be as painless. Somehow, he doubted that would be the case.

Their first session was delayed by a horrific event – one that went a long way toward explaining the odd sense of foreboding that had met Cady at the ranch gate. Jacob's Jessie was kidnapped and the whole family went into battle formation. Even Joseph rode the roads with Aron, seeing if they could find any clue as to what could have happened to their brother's fiancé.

Cady stayed out of the way, and did what she could – which was quite a bit. While the family and the authorities searched for Jessie, she lit candles and laid out a map of the local area. Being alone in the house, she visited Jessie's bedroom and took a bit of hair from her brush to use as a spiritual connection. Braiding it into a heart shape, she held it tight in one hand while she let the pendulum swing over the map. After a few moments, it settled and stopped very near to the ranch. Jotting down the locale, she placed a discrete call to Kane Saucier.

"Kane? It's Cady Renaud. I know you're busy investigating the kidnapping of Miss Montgomery. But, I think I can help."

After a few brief words, Kane hung up the phone and didn't even hesitate to act on the information he had been given. If Cady Renaud said Jessie was just off Blanco Road, near Tebow Property – then he would bet his life on it. A camera at a red light had given them their first clue that Jessie's kidnapper hadn't left the area and now they had Cady's tip. The only thing she asked was that her involvement was kept secret. He could do that for her, no problem. No one would believe it anyway, and he wouldn't know how to start explaining the mystery. Placing an emergency call to Tebow Ranch, he informed Noah the sheriff's department and all the back up he could muster were on their way to the Perry Place to rescue Jessie Montgomery. He knew the McCoy's wouldn't be far behind.

Celebration was a mild word. Cady had never seen so much happiness in one place. All of these people loved one another dearly. Libby and Jessie were fortunate beyond measure and the McCoy brothers were open and honest in their affection for everyone in their charmed circle. Cady lingered on the perimeter, offered her well wishes, never letting on that she had anything to do with the miraculous rescue. Anonymity was always far the best, as far as she was concerned.

Finally, the second morning after Jessie's safe return, she approached Joseph about his therapy. Going to his door, she tapped on it lightly. "Come in," she doubted he expected it to be her, or he wouldn't have sounded so welcoming. Joseph avoided her, for the most part, since he had apologized at the dance for his rude behavior. Well, that was about to change.

She opened the door and stepped into his rehab suite. It was beautifully furnished and had been spared no amenity that would benefit a person in his condition. "Joseph, would today be good for us to begin our program?" He sat up in his hospital bed, reading a magazine. She walked a bit closer and saw he was reading a sports magazine, **Texas Extreme**, and the man on the cover was none other than Joseph McCoy. When he saw her looking at it, he flipped it over quickly. He was so handsome, it made her heart hurt just to look at him. If any man had ever been blessed with a perfect face, it was Joseph. Dark lashes framed eyes so blue they looked like the Caribbean on a sunny day. A mouth so chiseled and kissable, it made her lips tingle remembering what it was like to kiss him in her dreams. Smiling to herself, she knew it would be more fun to French kiss him than her queen size feather pillow.

Joseph let his eyes rake over her. Was he ready for this? "Sure, I'm ready when you are." Didn't the woman own anything to wear besides a toe-sack? Her hair was braided today, which he much preferred to the tight little bun, but she was still about as sexy as his high school English teacher. Cady Renaud didn't try very hard to be attractive - maybe she didn't know how. Shaking his head, he tried to get his mind on his own problems. "Give me your best shot, Ms. Renaud. I'm ready to see what you can do."

Cady tried to still her mind. She could not read his thoughts, but she got impressions from him. And right now, she knew he disapproved of her for some reason. It made her uneasy. There was no way she was going to be able to focus if she couldn't learn to tune this sensation out. Self-consciously, she soothed her hair and wished she had thought to put on some lip-gloss. Helping Joseph McCoy was important to her – very important – best to keep her mind on that. "All right, let's start with the basics. Have you conquered this lift to transfer yourself from the bed to the wheelchair and back?"

Joseph gave her a hard look. "One of my brothers or Libby has helped me so far; I can't seem to make sense of this contraption." He hated to perform for her like some kind of trained seal. What he wanted was for her to start her healing magick, make him well and get the hell out of his life. Raising his eyes to meet hers, he was surprised to find her looking at him with obvious displeasure. "What?" He hadn't said any of that out loud had he?

"I know you hate having to rely on a machine to help you do something you used to do by yourself – with ease – but that's your reality right now. Your reaction is normal and every man who has ever faced these unfortunate circumstances has felt the exact same way. You are a very handsome man, Mr. McCoy and I am sure you have lived a life that most would envy, but you need to quit feeling sorry for yourself and take some responsibility for your well-being."

Well, shit! The little brown wren had a backbone. The lecture she had so eloquently given him put an attractive rosy glow in her cheeks. Damn! "Well, show me how to use the friggin thing." He gave her a tentative smile and she rewarded him with a dazzling one. Dazzling? His paralysis was affecting his vision.

She stepped closer to him and pulled the rolling base underneath the bed. "You appear to have ample upper body strength." That was an understatement; his shoulders, arms and chest muscles were body-builder beautiful. Honestly, she couldn't wait to get her hands on him. He was going to be a joy to touch. "You won't need the sling, you just have to learn to stabilize the bar and use it to swing over into your chair." She positioned the lift and showed him how to tighten the knob to keep it from slipping. "The only thing you have to make sure is to leave your wheelchair close enough so you can reach it without falling out of bed." When she heard him snort, it didn't take a mind reader to know his thoughts. "You've already fallen out of bed, haven't you?" She didn't tell him she knew about his spill at the hospital first hand, he wouldn't have believed her anyway. Apparently there had been other incidents. For the first time, she heard Joseph chuckle. What a beautiful sound.

"Fell flat on my ass. Twice." He watched what she did, carefully. "I think I can do this. Watch me." For some reason, Joseph wanted to please her. She seemed so interested and concerned, like she really cared. Now, that was pitiful, wasn't it? Now, he was reduced to pleasing a woman by doing cheap acrobatic tricks. This was hard for a man who prided himself in making women dream, cream and scream on a regular basis.

Cady felt her insides go warm, sympathy tugged at her emotions. "Go for it. I know you can do it," she encouraged him. When he grabbed the bar and began hoisting himself over, she almost fainted at the beauty of his body. What a magnificent man he was! She was fascinated by his arms, they were so strong and all she could think about was how they felt wrapped around her. Oh, well – that wasn't going to happen again, not unless he started to fall and she caught him. Maybe, she could trip him. Lord, she had it bad. She held her breath and hovered like a mother watching her baby take his first step. Unable to resist, she stabilized the chair and was relieved when his gorgeous tight ass landed firmly in the seat. "Wonderful!" she praised him.

He flashed a triumphant grin, and her knees went weak. What was it about this man? It was as if he belonged to her. Every little thing about him was perfect. Right then, she vowed that she would move heaven and earth to restore him to full and perfect health – even if it killed her. "I did it!" he exclaimed.

"Yes, you did. Good job!" She wanted to hug him, so she clasped her hands behind her back to keep from grabbing him. "Now, tell me about your bowel movements and your catheterizations? Are you managing them satisfactorily?" This was a routine question for her job, but she had to admit that thinking of those necessary functions for this man was – different.

He blushed. He actually blushed. "Everything's coming out fine." He acted like this was one topic that was off limits as far as he was concerned.

"Don't be that way," she placed a hand on his arm. "That's why I'm here. We have to make sure you have this mastered. If you don't, you can get sick – fast." Seeing his discomfort, she tried to make light of it at her expense, maybe that would put him at ease. "Remember, that's why you wanted a homely therapist." She spread her hands in concession to the point. "Well, here I am - coyote ugly –

whatever that means. So, don't think of me as a female, think of me as asexual – just a person."

Joseph watched her being far nicer to him than he deserved. Her eyes were the warmest golden brown, exactly the color of an amber jewel. Why did they look so familiar? And her cheekbones were high, and her lips were full and looked so soft and suckable. "Don't talk about yourself that way." He wouldn't go so far as to tell her he had been wrong, but he was beginning to think she was kinda cute. And she reminded him of someone – who?

"What is coyote ugly, by the way? Just for future reference." Cady put her hands on her waist, and Joseph couldn't help but notice how small it was. He would give a good hunk of change to see what kind of figure she was concealing so completely.

Her question registered and he felt lower than a snake's belly. "You don't want to know."

"Sure, I do. You might as well tell me, I can always look it up on the Internet. Is it some 'dog' reference? I've heard that before."

That she would admit someone had called her a 'dog' brought a funny feeling to Joseph's chest. That was a shame. But hadn't he done the same – or worse? She folded her arms under her breasts and he could see that she did have a pair – a rather large pair. Nice. Looking down, thoroughly embarrassed by his own behavior, he explained the derogatory term. "It's something I never should have said. It's cruel." He stopped, hoping they could drop it. She waited, so he gritted his teeth and went on with his explanation. "It alludes to a man being so drunk in a bar that he takes any woman home with him. The next morning when he wakes up and looks at her, he realizes she is – very unattractive. She's lying too close, on his arm, and he can't get away from her without waking her up. The stupid comparison comes from a coyote's willingness to chew off his own leg in order to get out of a trap."

95

"Oh." Cady suspected what it meant, but still – hearing the words in reference to herself coming out of his mouth hurt more than she could say. A wave of sorrow almost knocked her down. In self-preservation, she took a step away from him. "I see." One more step backwards. "That is a serious insult." She could feel tears welling up behind her eyes and she called upon every magical atom in her body to quell them. It would humiliate her even more if Joseph saw her cry over something he said.

"Cady, I'm sorry," Joseph reached for her, but she took another step back. "I've been feeling so sorry for myself; I've lost all good sense and manners. Forgive me, please." He really meant it. Seeing the hurt on her face was far worse than he could have ever imagined. Miraculously, he watched her shake it off. It was one of the most generous things he had ever seen.

"It's all right. There's no use for me to worry about something I can't change," she wrung her hands, as if trying to steady her nerve. "Now, answer my question. Are you being able to perform your bathroom functions?" She put it in the kindest terminology she knew.

Blowing out a breath, he answered. "Hell, yes. I got that shit covered." He smiled at his own joke. "And you could make some changes. I'm not a beauty consultant, but I am a connoisseur of women and I can see some things you could change easily enough." Why did it matter so much to him? Was it just his guilty conscience?"

This line of conversation was making Cady decidedly uncomfortable. Still, she was curious what he thought. "I tell you what; I'll let you analyze my shortcomings, if you'll let me help you in the shower. Or have you figured that out as well?" She straightened the mat on the floor. After his shower, she wanted to get him started on some stretches. "One day when you were out with one of your brothers, I went over every piece of equipment. It was apparent that you haven't made use of the shower, yet. And since you smell like a sexy, clean male, I have to assume you are taking sink baths."

Was she flirting with him? After everything he'd said to her? The hint of sexual tension in the air was pleasurable. "I don't think that's a fair exchange," grumbled Joseph. He loved to share a shower with a woman, but this wasn't the same thing. "How will this work exactly?"

Out of the blue, Cady laughed. It was a beautiful sound. "Don't worry. I'll try and control myself. There's another lift and a seat in the shower for you to sit on. I think that will work much better than a wash rag, don't you?"

"I wasn't worried." Joseph led the way to the bathroom, nervous as a teenager on his first date. Would she like his body? Or would she just see him as the half-man that he was? At least he wouldn't have to worry about his dick getting hard and giving her the wrong idea.

"You will feel so much better after you shower. I'm sure your brothers would have been happy to help you." On the way, she stopped at his closet. "Do you want to change into something more comfortable than those jeans?"

He paused, "Grab that Longhorn lounge pant set, I guess. It's on the second shelf." When she had gathered his things that included a clean pair of underwear and socks, she came back to where he sat, waiting. "This isn't necessary, I can manage by myself. And it wasn't like I was going to ask one of my brothers to wash my pecker for me." He faunched and fussed as he rolled his way to the facilities. Cady just smiled and followed along behind him.

The bathroom was large and fully wheelchair accessible. "Let's go through the process and see how you do. Soon, you won't need my help at all." Taking charge, she did things for him that he would have to do for himself, eventually. Adjusting the water temperature, she angled the sprayers. "Somebody went to a lot of trouble and expense to make everything as nice for you as possible. You have everything here you could want or need," she commented.

"Not hardly," he stated flatly. "I could use a pair of legs and a cock that worked." Boy, that was plainspoken.

"Excuse my French."

"C'est pas grave mon ami."

Her response in French, made him burst out laughing. "Touche! Now, tell me what you said, smarty pants." He was having a good time. He hadn't expected that.

"I said, 'no problem, my friend.' I'm from New Orleans, Joseph. My family is part French." She didn't tell him all the other parts, no use dragging race into the conversation.

Turning to him, she spoke gently. "Okay, let's get started. Raise your arms." He did so, automatically, and she tugged his T-shirt up and then had to bite her tongue to keep from moaning at how utterly beautiful and ripped he was. None of her other patients had been in the same universe as he was when it came to sex appeal. Forcing herself to remain stoic, she sought to alleviate some of his fears. "You have my sympathies, I know you want to be a whole man – walk where you want to go and be able to enjoy your sexuality. If you will place your faith and confidence in me, I may be able to give you back those things." Brown eyes met blue eyes and she shivered at the hope she saw reflected back at her. "I can't make any guarantees, but I have done it before." She knelt in front of him and removed his shoes and socks and went on to unbuckle his belt. She couldn't help but notice her hands were trembling. He was getting to her. Would this give him some sense of sexual satisfaction? Knowing that he could still make a woman shake with desire?

"Tell me what we'll be doing. How will it work? Where does the magic come in to play?"

Sitting back on her heels, Cady looked him full in the face. How honest could she be? She was always afraid that one day her unorthodox efforts would fail and a disgruntled patient would expose her methods to the world, bringing a wagonload of trouble down on her head. "Is that what Kane told you? That I practice magick?"

"He said you could work miracles and your hands have a magical healing touch."

Cady could feel hope rolling off of him in waves. "Joseph McCoy, I promise you this. If it is in my power, I will give you back your legs and your manhood. But, you do realize I am going to have to touch you. Right?" She tried to make light of the situation, in order to put him at ease.

She gave him a saucy little wink and, swear to God, Joseph's heart turned over. What was going on? "What did you just do?" He asked before he thought. How had she made herself look so different – she had looked like . . . . . . no, it wasn't possible.

"What do you mean?" She rose and swung the bathroom size lift over so he could stand up.

Not knowing what to say, he changed topics. "What will we do first?" He couldn't tell her that he was momentarily attracted to her. It wouldn't be wise to get her hopes up. Holding on to the bar, he supported his weight since his wooden legs refused to do so. Kneeling in front of him again, she tugged on his blue jeans and pulled them down until she could help him step out of them.

Cady tried, in vain, to keep her mind on her words. But, as she tugged down his underwear, she could feel the dampness begin between her legs. God in heaven! This wasn't the first cock she had ever seen, but it might as well be. What she was looking at it, flaccid though it might be, was light years different from the others. Jesus! What he must look like aroused! She couldn't help but staring.

Again, a dry chuckle of remorse broke through her thoughts. "No use staring at it, Cady. It's totally out of commission. That is unless you can do that hoodoo you do so well, I hear." How odd it was to have this woman at his feet. She was in the exact position that countless had been in when they gifted him with a blowjob. What he wouldn't give if she would reach out and place her lips over his cock – and that he could feel her do it. Lord, he couldn't live like this. How could he exist knowing he would never know the thrill of a woman's touch or the rush of an orgasm, again? He'd rather be dead.

Removing his underwear, she stood to aid him to the bench seat within the shower. "I apologize. As you probably realize, I am not very experienced." What an understatement. "And you are very beautiful."

Her simple, honest words had a profound effect on him. "I wasn't fussing." When he was seated, she handed him everything he would need and then closed the curtain.

"I'll sit here, just in case you need help." She was quiet for a few minutes. He wondered what she was doing, but then she began to speak again. "As soon as we get you out of the shower, we'll wrap a towel around you and get you back in the bed. I'll give your muscles a work out, and start your massage therapy. Then, if it's all right with you, I'll begin an application of healing herbs and some other traiture techniques. Can you hear me over the water running?"

"Yea, I can hear you?" He answered as he soaped up. "Kane told me that a traiture is a Cajun faith healer. He also said that you practice hoodoo. How does that work together, exactly?" Joseph had to admit; the warm spray of the water felt better than any shower he had ever had.

"I come from an unusual family, Joseph. Each one has a special gift; mine is healing. My aunt can communicate with the dead and our extended family – the Romee' witches – well, they can do everything from making it rain to bringing a serial killer to his knees with a voodoo poppet filled with sharp needles." Joseph let out a groan at the thought. Cady continued. "I have been trained as a traiture by several older friends who have practiced for years. But it's a dying art. The method combines prayers, the laying on of hands and the use of specific herbs that modern medicine is only now beginning to understand. This knowledge only enhances the natural magical ability I inherited – but together – they have given me a special gift. I have been able to cure people of many diseases and injuries and for that I'm grateful."

"Well, I'm game for whatever you want to do to me." Hell, he was counting on a miracle – there was no two ways about it. And Cady was absolutely fascinating. He couldn't resist asking her a few questions. He supposed if she took offense to any of them she would say so. "So, you've never been married?"

"Married?" Had he not heard her? She had said she had little experience. I guess he didn't realize how little. "No, I've never been married."

"Not even close?"

"Close? Hardly, let me explain." She giggled a bit – sounding a little nervous. "Not only have I never been married. I've never been on a single date, Joseph." She spoke slowly, but loud enough that he could hear. When he turned off the water, she hushed. But, he didn't open the curtain; he just sat there, quietly. So, she continued her sad confessional. Why was she telling him this? Perhaps, if he could trust her with his future, she could trust him with her past. "I sleep alone. I've never been kissed. I've never even held hands with anyone – not in a romantic way." She grew quiet. "Since there's a curtain between us – I might as well tell you the rest. How does it feel for a woman to pour her heart out to you?" She didn't wait for an answer. "The truth is, I lie in bed at night and dream what it would be like to be wanted." A small hiccup of emotion erupted from her throat. "I've worn out more pillow slips than you can imagine, practicing my kissing technique. By now, I'm sure I am a wonderful kisser. Oh, well – such is life."

With a whoosh, the curtain opened. When she looked up at him, she was surprised to see heat in his eyes. For her?

Surely, not. "We're going to have to see what we can do about that. A woman shouldn't have to go through life wondering what it would be like to be kissed."

Chapter Five

Cady thought she would swoon. Was he volunteering? Was she about to know the wonder of a man's lips on hers? Sparks of absolute delight danced along her body. What she wouldn't give to know the joy of Joseph McCoy's kiss – for real. "What do you mean?" She needed for him to clarify. This was too wonderful for words.

He looked so pleased with himself, sitting there, dripping water, and looking sexier than any man had a right to look. "We're gonna talk Libby and Jessie into giving you a makeover and then we're going to find you a man. How does that sound?"

Cady felt her heart hit the floor. How stupid could she be? He wasn't volunteering for the job. Joseph McCoy was talking about playing matchmaker. Despair didn't rob her of a sense of humor; she let out a small cry – of laughter. Or at least, she hoped that's what he interpreted it as. "I'm picturing you with short stubby wings and a bow and arrow, Cupid." Offering him her hand, she helped him turn around and gently placed a towel in his lap, tucking it around his hips. Realizing that was probably too intimate a move, she retreated a step and handed him another for drying.

He took the towel and began to wipe off, trying to rid himself of moisture with one hand. "This is harder than I thought. Could you help me with my back parts?" Joseph sat still, like he was anticipating her touch. Was he looking forward to it; or steeling himself against it? Cady blew out a breath and did her best. With gentle, but quick strokes – she removed the water from his body with impersonal movements – careful not to let her skin come in contact with his. He realized he had offended her by his suggestion. "I'm sorry, Cady. I didn't mean to hurt your feelings, again."

Hanging up the wet towel, she gathered his clothes. "Let's get you in the wheel chair and to the massage table.

I'll need you on your stomach to begin with." Her movements were helpful, but impersonal. "And, as for the make-over, I don't think so – but thank you for thinking of it." She did her best, but she knew her voice betrayed her pain. "I've always been told you can't make a silk purse out of a sow's ear. I've resigned myself to a solitary existence, I don't want to get my hopes up and be hurt anymore than I already have. Okay?"

Settling into the chair with her help, he allowed Cady to help him get back in the bed. She carefully arranged the towel so that it stayed secure while he was transferring himself and untied it once he had his modesty concealed on the table. Lord, what a gorgeous butt! It was nicely rounded, muscular and extremely bitable. But, she made no comment; her feelings were still too sore.

Joseph, apparently, wasn't in a giving up mood. As Cady gathered her oils and herbs and more towels, he resumed his campaign. "Okay, so we won't involve Libby and Jessie – for now. Will you just do something for me, just to see how it works out?"

What was he up to now? And why did he seem to care so much? Was this some kind of a game he was playing? Perhaps, he thought if he worried about her problems enough, he wouldn't be spending so much time worrying about his own. So be it. He could do what he wanted – that didn't mean she had to play along. So, she ignored him - for the moment. Cady warmed the oil in her hands. "I'm going to give all of your muscles a work out. Your back muscles, arm muscles – everything has been under a strain trying to deal with the extra burden they've been called upon to bear. I will warn you that it is normal for you to begin to experience pain. And don't be dismayed, that's a really good sign. It means your nerve endings are beginning to awaken. There are things we can do for the pain when it begins, so let's hope it does." Steeling herself against the pleasure, she began to massage his back and shoulders.

'Oh, God,' she groaned inwardly as she let herself enjoy his body beneath her fingertips. Touching him was a heady delight, indeed. Fighting the urge to add her lips to the mix, she decided talking about her own problems was far less dangerous. "What would you have me do, to help my appearance, I mean?" she stuttered at the prospect.

"Just a minute," Joseph moaned. "This feels so goddamn good! You are incredible, baby." The endearment he had used so often just slipped out. Hell, he didn't care. She had magic hands. He had no idea his muscles were so tight and sore. Shit! If he could get hard, he would be shooting his wad from just a simple caress from this fabulous woman. "God Almighty!" He just lay there and reveled in her touch. After a few moments, he was able to talk – barely. "There are several things we could do. But, let's start with something simple. Would you let your hair down for me? Would you let me see it unbound?"

His request surprised her. "You'll only be disappointed. My hair is long and healthy, but totally ordinary."

Working just below his waist, very near the injury, she began to focus on a healing touch. It pleased Cady when her touch brought groans of delight to his lips. "Yeah, that's it. I hadn't realized how much I needed this." She worked her way back up his back. "So, will you do it?

She was so absorbed in her pleasurable task that his question took her by surprise. Shoot. Why not? "Sure, if that's what you want. When we get through and I get the oil off of my hands, I'll take it down for you. I don't know why you'd want to see me like that; it's not going to help my looks."

"Let me be the judge of that." God, he felt good. For the first time since the accident, he was truly relaxed. He felt her move lower on his back. She finally reached a point where he could not feel as much, then nothing. This deadness drove an arrow into his soul.

Cady knew when the change came in his mood. She could feel it. He could no longer feel her hands and it bothered him. Trying to alleviate some of his anxiety, she explained. "It is just as important for me to work these muscles – more important, even. I think you'll find that you begin to have a minute amount of sensation after a few sessions. And if you do, we'll know there's hope. Okay?" He nodded and allowed her to work on his body. When she asked for him to roll over, she moved the lift closer and aided him in the task.

Great, she thought. Now, he would be able to see her drooling over him. Cady began at his neck and tried not to look at his face. Moving on to his deltoids, she tried to view him as an anatomical doll – not a flesh and blood man she would love to eat with a spoon. Rubbing his chest was an unrivaled erotic treat and when his nipples hardened beneath her fingertips, she gasped with awe. Never had the giving of a massage affected her like this. God, the authorities ought to strip her of her license. Her breasts began to swell, nipples hardening with excitement. She could almost cry from the need to be touched. Cady could feel her clitoris – it was throbbing and a trickle of moisture was running down her thigh. Could he smell it? God, she hoped not. She'd just as soon not expire from humiliation today.

But, he knew. He was too experienced of a man not to recognize when a woman was sexually stimulated. "I'm not the only one turned on I see." Embarrassed, she followed his gaze and saw that her nipples were so big they showed clearly through the rough material of her jumper. Obviously, she was totally aroused. Humiliated, she jerked away from him, needing to put distance between them – for her sake. This had never happened to her, before. But, she had never had the privilege of touching Joseph McCoy before, either. "I can't help it," she didn't even bother denying it. "I'll get used to touching you," she assured him.

"It's a simple involuntary response." She would have covered her breasts with her hands, but they were covered with oil – so she just stood there in front of him – head hung and nipples poking out like she was standing in freezing water. "Let's try to finish, shall we?" She bit the inside of her cheek hard – then she bit her tongue and soon there were tears of frustration and pain sliding down her cheeks.

"Hey, hey – what are you crying for?" Joseph was totally amazed and dismayed. Had he made her cry? Ashamed, he realized that all he had done since she arrived was give her a hard time and heap humiliation upon her head. Of course, he had made her cry. She should turn her back on him and walk out. No one deserved to be treated the way he had treated her.

"I bit my tongue," she whispered.

Joseph had an overwhelming urge to kiss her tears away. In fact, it was all he could to keep from taking his arms and drawing her down and cuddling her close. "I'm sorry, Cady." How many times had he apologized already? Her hands were never still. They soothed his abdomen, then skipped his man-parts and traveled down to the sensationless area of his thighs and legs.

"Don't be," she spoke softly. "Let's make a deal." If she didn't feel this overwhelming responsibility for him, she might try to preserve her sanity and back out of the job before she lost her heart and soul. But the wheels of destiny had begun their long, slow grind, and she knew she had to either roll with them or get thrown under the cart and crushed. She did feel responsible for Joseph. Never before had she doubted her aunt and grandmother's predictions, but this time they totally misread the future. The strange dreams - were just that – dreams – her dream – not his.

"What kind of deal?" He looked at her curiously.

"Let's try to be friends. I'll do my very best to help you, and in exchange, you can make suggestions and see if you can change me from an ugly duckling into a swan. I don't think you'll be successful, but I'm willing to give it a try." Why was she doing this to herself? It would only end in heartache, but for some unexplainable reason, she was compelled to see it through.

"Sounds good to me," he looked entirely too self-satisfied for Cady's peace of mind. "I can always use a friend. And as far as your make-over – this is going to be fun, I promise."

Cady wished she felt as confident. After the massage, she lit a couple of candles and helped him turn over once more. "I'm about to lay hands on you now, and apply some healing herbs. This is part of my traiture training. You should feel heat coming from my hands. And if we're successful, in a few days there should be pain." Arranging him, Cady let her mind slip into a place where she could access the healing powers of the universe. Adding pressure to her touch, she envisioned a warm blue light enveloped them both, she prayed for sensation to flow back into his body, for his nerves to heal and knit, for his spinal cord to begin to do what it should – for God to give this man back the future he deserved. She concentrated. She envisioned. She worked with absolute faith and focused intent. Cady demanded results and would not accept anything less. That's how the universe works; we can make and shape our reality, if we have faith enough to create it.

As she worked on Joseph – it hit her. A great revelation. That was what was missing from her life. She had never approached her own shortcomings with any degree of faith that she could change them. Stunned, Cady realized she had never used her own magick on herself. Huh!?! It was time for a change. Excited, she couldn't wait to get time to herself to think this thing through. But, Joseph came first – always. "Okay, I'll let you rest now. How do you feel?"

Joseph seemed to be almost asleep. He opened his eyes and narrowed them as if analyzing his body's sensations. "I feel really good, like a big pile of goo."

"Great! How about below the waist?" She held her breath, hoping he would have a glimmer of feeling. She had poured her heart and soul into the treatment.

Joseph pushed up on his arms, the muscles of his back rippling in the process. Cady had to refrain from licking her lips. God, this ordeal was going to kill her. "That's strange," Joseph began with a disbelieving tone in his voice. "I feel heat. I don't think it's my imagination – I haven't felt anything there in so long, it's hard to be sure."

Cady was relieved. "Good. That's exactly what you're supposed to feel. I'd say our first foray into bringing back the super stud of Texas is right on track." Her voice was happy and she couldn't hide it. "Don't you want to get up now? Lying on that table isn't good for you." He let her help him. "You're really getting the hang of the Hoyer lift. Soon, you'll be pouncing out off this thing."

"God, I hope so. You make it sound plausible. I have to admit you've got my hopes up." Once he was in the chair, he turned and looked at Cady, intently. "You're flushed from the exertion and your eyes are shining bright. Go take your hair down for me, Cady."

Joseph's words curled around Cady's heart like a wisp of smoke on a cool autumn evening – welcome and mysterious. "All right. You'll be disappointed, though." She shook her head; that was not the attitude she should have. She needed to learn how to be positive – after all, disbelief was always a killer of dreams. Okay – let's see what she could do. Going to the bathroom, she took off her glasses and reached in the back for her braid. Slowly, she freed her hair from its binding, letting the long thick curls bounce free and untethered. She had a lot of hair. Too much hair. It hung in abundant, lush waves to the top of her butt. Before going to face the music, Cady tried a little of her own medicine. She placed a hand on each of her cheeks and lifted her plea to the universe. "Make me beautiful, just for a few minutes, in his sight, make me beautiful." Opening her own eyes, she gazed in the mirror. Well, at least she wouldn't make small children go running to their mothers screaming, but she was nothing to write home about. Oh, well. Some spells took more time than others.

"Cady . . ." he called, "I'm getting grey out here."

Giggling, she came out of the bathroom. Joseph could be likeable when he wanted to be. He was much closer than she anticipated and she almost fell in his lap. Her hair swung over her shoulder and she laughed at her clumsiness. "See, I told you."

Joseph held his breath. Wow. Was this for real? Had he ever really looked at her before? "Cady, baby - aren't you sweet." And she was. She had absolutely beautiful hair and without her glasses, her face could never be called plain. "Come here." He held out his hand to her, and she walked to him slowly, placing her hand in his. Joseph was stunned by the electric attraction he felt for her. God, if only he was still a man – he would give her an experience she would never forget. Tugging on her arm, he began to pull her closer. He had an overwhelming urge to kiss her. Absolutely overwhelming.

"Joseph!" A knock on the door brought the whole surreal episode to a grinding halt. It was Jessie. "Cady! Hey guys, lunch is ready. Are you hungry? I've made a big pot of chicken soup." Joseph knew Jessie meant well. But – her timing left a lot to be desired.

"Thanks, doll," he called. "We'll be right out." Damn!

The abrupt interruption seemed to awaken Cady. "Boy, that was close," she murmured. "I almost attacked you," she attempted to tease.

Joseph didn't say anything, for he had been as close to kissing her as he ever had any woman. And frankly, he was as confused as hell. It was as if some magical spell had been on him. Suspiciously, he wondered about that. If the woman could heal – what else could she do? But, as she backed away – he had to admit – she wasn't nearly as homely as he first thought. Cady Renaud was growing on him.

Isaac slammed the phone down so hard he broke it. Hell! Doris sashayed by him with a tray full of empty beer mugs and winked. "No luck, boss?" She was his only confidant when it came to Avery. His head waitress was like a second mother to him.

"Her mother still says she has no idea where Avery is or when she'll return. Do you think they're just feeding me a line?"

Never one to mince words, Doris let him have it. "You know Avery's parents are worried about her. She is their only child and never gave them an ounce of trouble until she met you – bad boy McCoy." At Isaac's frown, Doris laughed. "Most parents would overlook your rowdy ways because you come from a Texas dynasty and you're loaded. But the preacher and his wife are different. They don't know you like I do." She reached over and pinched his cheek. "You hide that heart of gold underneath a thick layer of black leather."

"Do not." He sounded like a petulant little boy. "You still didn't answer my question. Do you think Avery is actually missing?" He couldn't help but be worried. If she were missing, it was all his fault. He had been the one to push her away. Doris refilled her tray and put one hand on her hip giving him her version of the evil eye. Damn, she was scary.

"If I were you, sweet-boy, I would take a little road trip. You are never going to be satisfied until you find out for sure. I can't picture the good pastor out-right lying to you, but - hey, he may be taking the over-protective daddy bit to the extreme." As Doris acknowledged a customer's call with the wave of her hand, she left Isaac with one last bit of wisdom. "You aren't ever gonna be happy till you know for sure how she is, you care more about that little girl than you led her to believe – a hell of a lot more."

"Let's play a game."
Cady was about to kneel at his feet to help him do some stretching exercises. His out-of-the-blue suggestion caused her to lose her balance and sit down on the floor – hard. "Dang!"
"Sorry about that, Cady-did. Did my suggestion take you by surprise?" He didn't look sorry.
"No, I'm just naturally clumsy." She'd rather he think her a klutz than lovesick. Settling in front of him, she placed one hand on his knee and the other under his ankle and began lifting the leg until it was parallel with the floor. She held it there for about fifteen seconds and then lowered it, knowing that repetitions of this exercise would go along way to alleviating the painful spasms he was having at night. "What kind of game?"
"Well, to start with, we could just ask each other simple questions. I'd like to learn more about you and this could make it fun. How about it?" Besides, he needed to do something to take his mind off of her cute button nose. She kept pushing her glasses up when they slid down and he had just noticed how kissable it was. Whew! He must be going through sex withdrawals.
"All right. You go first," anything to take her mind off his sexy calves and strong thighs.
Joseph considered his options. It would be better to start slow and buildup to the wilder stuff. This could be fun. "Okay, let's start simple. What's your favorite color and why?"
Her favorite color – really? She felt like she was taking part in a junior camp icebreaker. "That's easy. My favorite color is purple." As she talked, Cady was transported back in time. "When I was five, I asked for a doll for Christmas – a

special doll. I had my heart set on a baby doll with the same skin tone that I had. And I got it, I don't know where grandmother found it – but it looked just like me and had the prettiest purple dress."

"You have beautiful skin." Joseph had noticed. It was the color of his favorite coffee ice cream.

Cady looked at him suspiciously. "You do know I'm not white, don't you?"

Joseph widened his eyes and tried to look shocked. "No!" It was only a second before he cracked up laughing. "I can see you're not white, baby. You look sorta caramel colored to me."

Without thinking, she playfully pinched him pretty hard. "Ow! Dang-it!"

Cady almost levitated off the floor. "Did you feel that, Joseph?"

It was a second before Joseph registered what had just happened. And then he pulled Cady off the floor and into his arms. "Yes, I did!" It hadn't hurt near as bad as he had played like it did – but he had definitely felt the pinch.

She threw her arms around his neck and hugged him tight. "It's working, Joseph. It's working." He held her close and thanked God for sending Cady into his life.

Gradually, she disengaged herself and slid from his lap back to the floor. Joseph was so elated he found it hard to be still. "Your turn, caramel girl. What do you want to know about me?"

Opportunity doesn't knock very often. As she manipulated Joseph's legs, she mulled over what she could ask. Okay. "If you get back full use of your legs, are you going to continue down the same path you were on or live your life differently?"

Shit! Joseph looked at Cady, pointedly. "This was supposed to be fun." At her shy little smile, he softened. "Let's see. The day I got hurt, I had an interview with **Texas Extreme**. And the reporter asked me what my greatest accomplishment was, I told her that having a hand in raising my brothers after our parents died had to be the best thing I had ever done. I left for the race that day, fully intending to come back to Tebow and reconnect with my family, and cut down on a lot of the hullabaloo of competition."

"And now?" This could be important. Joseph needed to know why he wanted to get better.

"Now, hell – if I get to the point where I can leave this chair behind and be on two strong legs, I feel like I'll have to prove myself all over again."

"Is proving yourself to be the unbeatable Stallion that important to you?" She wasn't judging, just trying to understand.

"Hell, I don't know." Joseph hadn't given a return to competing much thought. All he had done was focus on the possibility of regaining the full use of his body. "I want sex, I know that." He graced her with a devilish grin.

"How about a family?"

"Go for the throat, why don't you, Renaud?" Joseph went serious. "I want a family. Seriously, that's been on my mind quite a bit. Aron and Jacob are both about to become fathers and the idea that the accident robbed me of the chance to have children drives me fuckin' crazy." He ended on a bitter note.

Cady pinched him again.

"Hey!" he laughed.

"Yea, that's right." She petted the spot where she had teased him, rubbing in circles. "Don't you dare doubt what we're doing. Faith is so important in this process." She moved to the other leg. "Can you feel this?" She pinched again.

Joseph frowned. "No. I'm not sure. Do it again." She did. He shook his head. I don't think so – or else it's only very, very faint. I'm afraid my mind is tricking me."

"That's okay." She encouraged him. "It's common that you wouldn't necessarily regain sensation in both legs, simultaneously." She resumed the exercises. "You will have children, Joseph. Beautiful children."

His chest was tight with hope and fear. Needing to lighten the mood, he drawled. "Wanna play truth or dare? Or are you chicken?"

"Chicken? Me?" Cady made a little face at him. She had left her hair down – for him, he suspected. "I'll have you know that I can walk through a cemetery at midnight. And I've swam in a bayou infested with alligators."

"Ooooo," Joseph mocked her. "You are brave. All right – truth or dare. *Strip truth or dare*." He paused for effect. "Now, you can either tell me the truth or accept a dare. Are you ready?" Today, she had on a long loose tunic and a pair of pants. And he knew exactly the piece of clothing he was going to ask her to remove.

Strip truth or dare? Was he kidding? What had she gotten herself into? "You mean I have to take off some of my clothes?" Jesus! "Yes, I'm ready," she sighed. She was massaging his legs now, and she was turned on. What a predicament.

"If you could kiss any man in the world – movie star, rock star, athlete – who would it be?"

Cady jerked her head up and looked at him. Was this a trick? He was looking at her with such smugness. He knew, damn him. *He knew*. Cady wanted to kiss Joseph more than she wanted to see tomorrow. She felt her heart go up into her throat. It would have been easy to just lie. But her damn moral code wouldn't let her. "Dare." Now, she was in for it.

Joseph rubbed his hands together. "Chicken." He bit his lower lip and chuckled. "Who did you want to kiss? Anyone I know? Isaac, maybe? He's popular with the ladies." He kept up his teasing, winking at her, making her blush. "Let's see. What can I get you to take off . . . . . hmmm?" He had to make this good. She probably wouldn't play with him, again. His voice dropped, almost an octave. "Take off those pants, baby. I want to see your legs."

Cady breathed a sigh of relief. She had thought he would ask her to remove her top. The pants weren't so bad – thank goodness the tunic came to just above her knee. It wouldn't be any worse than a mini-dress. Standing up, she realized she would have to lift up the tunic to pull the pants down. Gracious! She had no experience stripping in front of a man. Without asking, she took off to the bathroom. "I'll be right back."

"You'd better." Joseph warned.

In the bathroom, Cady glanced in the mirror. He didn't realize what a big step this was for her. Most girls showed their body all the time, but she had always covered up just as much skin as she could. The less exposed she was – the less vulnerable she felt. Raising the tunic, she pulled down the cocoa brown pants. Again today, she was almost invisible – everything about her was brown – hair, eyes, skin, clothing. Blending into the background had always been her style. Stepping out of them, she glanced in the mirror. Not too bad. Now, she looked like a million other women in a short dress – except, not so pretty. Sticking her tongue out at herself she went to face the music.

Joseph waited. Why was he doing this? Teasing Cady shouldn't be so much fun. But the truth was – he enjoyed her company. And he was curious about her body. He was a red-blooded male. He heard the door open and a few moments later; Cady came in and started walking toward him. Holy Shit! He stared at her delicate little feet and moved up. Slim ankles, shapely calves – God in Heaven! Long, perfect legs – gorgeous skin – he had never seen a more perfect little figure on a woman before. Granted, he couldn't see her top – but what he could see was Grade A Number One. Suddenly, he found himself without words. She was a woman and he was – he was – hell, he felt . . . pressured. God, he had to get out of here.

Cady stood there and waited. Hesitantly. Tentatively. She approached him. Did he like what he saw? Would he find her a little bit pretty?

Gruffer than he intended, Joseph spoke as he wheeled around to leave the room. "Put on some clothes, Cady."

Cady stood there for a moment after he had slammed the door, leaving her all alone. Then, she cried. Sinking to the floor, she drew herself up into the smallest knot she could make with her body. Hugging herself tightly around the knees, Cady vowed that she would never put herself into a situation like that again. The next time he wanted to play a game – she would cheat.

"If you don't feel good, Libby, why don't you go lay down." Joseph urged his soon to be sister in law. "There's no law around here that says I can't fix my own sandwich." He opened the fridge door and started taking out cold-cuts. "Where's Jessie? I thought she was doing most of the chores, now."

"She's been doing more than her share, but Jessie's a lot more pregnant than I am." Libby slumped down in a dining table chair and rested her head on her arm. "Please don't tell Aron you saw me like this."

"I'm not a blabbermouth, doll-face, but if you think something's wrong – you need to tell him. He loves you more than them damn cows he's chasing out there." There was no doubt of that. Joseph pulled up to the table and spread out his goodies. He was worried. Libby was pale and her breathing was shallow. "Do you want to go to the doctor? Noah's upstairs trying to find some more hay up in Oklahoma to buy. With this drought, we're just not growing enough to take care of our needs. But – he'll break away. You're much more important."

"No, I don't need to go to the doctor. What I need is somebody to help around here. We've got the extra crew Aron's brought in help catch the vandal. Plus, the branding and vaccinations start in two weeks. I just don't think I can do it without help." She looked so guilty that Joseph couldn't help but laugh.

"Love-bug, all you've got to do is bat them big ole' eyes at that man of yours and tell him what you just told me – and he'll have somebody here to help you before you can say Kinky Friedman." Libby laughed. She liked Kinky Friedman. He was a Texas legend.

"You think so?"

"I know so." Joseph bit into the thick sandwich.

"Your appetite sure has improved," Libby noticed. "That's good. And you seem happier."

Joseph knew she was fishing, and he couldn't deny her curiosity. He and Libby were close. "Sugar, I am cautiously optimistic."

"What's going on?" Now that he had started the conversation, Libby, obviously, wanted him to finish it.

"Don't tell anyone, yet. But I think the treatments are working. Cady pinched me last night and I felt it."

"Really?" Libby sprung up and hugged Joseph, almost knocking the sandwich out of his hand. "I am so happy and proud of you!" She kissed him loudly on the cheek and then straightened up. "Wait a minute. Why did Cady feel the need to pinch you? Were you misbehaving?"

Joseph snorted. "Me? Of course, I was. Aren't you glad I feel like being bad?"

"Yes, I am." Libby poured him a glass of milk while she was up. "Where is Cady, by the way?"

"I don't know, I haven't seen her since last night. I thought you might know where she is." As he said the words, he realized this was the first time Cady had left without telling him where she was going or when she would be back.

"No," Libby said slowly. "Is something wrong?"

Joseph sighed. Shit! He had been so happy about the sensation he had felt in his leg that he had forgotten how he had left her. She had walked out with such an expectant little look on her face – having bared half of her body for his viewing pleasure. And instead of telling her how delectable she was – he turned around and left her, telling her to put her clothes back on. All he had thought about was protecting himself, not how she would feel. Damn! Joseph had some fence mending to do.

"Are you a witch?" Nathan asked.

Cady made room for Nathan up in the hayloft. She had been hiding up here for the last two hours, dreading when she would have to face Joseph again. "Not exactly. Does it bother you that I'm different?" She would never want to scare this child.

"Nope. I think it's neat." His black hair shone in the rays of the sun beaming through the window. "You can see right into Joseph's room from here," he observed.

Busted. Cady had sat up here and watched Joseph move around his room. It was past time for his therapy session and she had to get off her bottom and head in to do her job. "Yea, I've been keeping an eye on him – just in case." That sounded weak – even to her ears. Nathan seemed satisfied, however. "I visited with your horses downstairs, and took a walk down by the pond and looked at some of the cattle. You have a wonderful home, Nathan. I didn't have any brothers or sisters, you are lucky to have such a big family."

Nathan flopped backwards in the hay and stared at the ceiling. "Things sure have changed around here. It used to be just us boys, and Sabrina – but I'm glad she's gone. She was mean. Now, we've got girls coming out of our ears."

Cady was amused. "Is that bad?" Since, she was one of the girls, his answer interested her.

"Nah," he sighed. "The food is much better. Bess, who used to take care of us, she fried everything and her biscuits were hard."

Just like a man, thinking only of his stomach. "Well, I'll only be here until Joseph no longer needs me. So, that will be one less girl to worry about. And there are babies on the way, how do you feel about that?"

Nathan rose up on one arm and began sifting through the hay. "I like the idea of babies, but I hope they're both boys." He looked up at Cady and grinned. "Can you pull a rabbit out of a hat?"

She picked up a handful of hay and threw it at him. "No, but I can turn inquisitive little boys into mice."

"Can you really?" His eyes got big. "Tommy Ross that lives down the road is a bully. I sure would like to see him with a pink nose and beady little eyes."

"We'd better not," she sighed. "His mom would probably not like that very much."

"I like you, Cady. You're fun. I wouldn't mind if you married Joseph and stayed with us. Libby and Aron are getting married and so are Jessie and Jacob. We could have a triple ceremony." He was sincere. Bless his heart.

"No," Cady had to be careful here. "Joseph and I are just friends. He has lots of girlfriends, but I'm not one of them. My job is to help Joseph get better."

"Are you going to use magic?" Curiosity seemed to run in the McCoy family.

"Magick is a big part of my life, Nathan. But it's good magic. My family only uses it to help people or to protect those we love. Mostly, my magick is in my heart and in my hands. There are those that say I have a healing touch – a magick touch. I'm going to do my very best to heal your brother." Cady ruffled his hair and Nathan grimaced.

"Shucks, I wanted you to fly on a broom and stir stuff in a big black pot."

"Sorry to disappoint you, Sport." A movement out of the window across the way caught her attention. "I need to get back over to Joseph. It's time for his therapy."

"Okay, I've got to turn on the windmill and check the soaker hoses in Libby's garden." Before Cady, could get down, he stopped her with a hand on her arm. "Cady, I think you're pretty."

His innocent, boyish compliment took Cady's breath away. "Thank you, Nathan. I appreciate it."

"I knew there was something different about you, the first time I saw you," he confided in a low voice. "Ever since I almost died, when I nearly drowned and Jessie saved me – I can see things now and know things that I couldn't before."

She remembered their first meeting, also - the incredible gold aura that had surrounded Nathan, signifying he was special and powerful in his own way. From what Nathan was telling her, his near-death experience had given him a connection to the realm of the invisible. This happened sometimes. It would be a heavy burden for a young person to bear. "I'll be glad to listen if you need to talk. Why do you think I'm different?" Cady knew this would be important – out of the mouths of babes.

"I can't explain it – but when I saw you, you had wings."

"Are you ready?" Cady breezed in with a smile on her face. She was determined that Joseph would never know he had hurt her yesterday. On top of that, Nathan's revelation that he had seen her with wings coupled with Renee Adam's comment that she was a watcher had her in stitches. If they only knew how far off base they were. All she could think about was that children's story about the angel who was clumsy, always late and sang terribly off key. The rest of heaven hadn't really known what to do with her. Cady imagined that if she were an angel, which she wasn't, that would be the kind of angel she would be. No angel ever had the risqué thoughts that she had about Joseph McCoy – a fallen angel, maybe.

Today, she wore another denim jumper. It wasn't quite as loose and the bodice was embroidered with fall leaves.

Actually, it was one of Cady's favorite garments. But she fully intended to keep it on and to refrain from engaging Joseph in any game playing. Today, would be all business.

"Sure, I'm ready."

Joseph was in his favorite athletic shorts and muscle shirt and he looked good enough to eat. Lucky she was on a diet. "I want to take you through the exercises and then we'll test those sensations you were having yesterday. Finally, we'll finish up with a massage and healing session." She spoke breezily, trying to project a carefree attitude.

Maneuvering over to the exercise mat, Joseph weighed his words. "About yesterday . . ." That was as far as he got.

"We made a lot of progress yesterday. Hopefully, we'll make more today." Cady never gave him another chance to apologize. She worked his butt off, and every time it even seemed like he was going to say something personal, she countered it with a comment that steered the conversation to safer ground.

"Lay here and let me do the leg extensions and we'll see if you have any more sensation than you had yesterday." So far, so good. Cady knew Joseph was trying to apologize for yesterday, but she didn't really want to hear it. It would be better if they just forgot about it. He let her help him lay down on the mat. As she worked his muscles, she talked. Filling the silence with conversation seemed easier than giving him an opening to remind her how pathetic she was. "If it would be all right with you, I have arranged to spend some time at the Children's home here – at least once a week. I do this in New Orleans and other places when I'm near – there is always work I can do helping with therapy and leading the children in developing good exercise habits."

Joseph was surprised. "Sure, that sounds great. I'd like to go with you, sometimes." He hadn't thought about Cady's private life. Surely, she had one. She might not date, but she had to do something with her time. "Tell me more about yourself, what other things are you interested in?"

At last, he wanted to talk about something besides her lack of looks. "Oh, I have lots of interests. I'm involved in the Louisiana Trust for Historic Preservation. I know that sounds boring, but we try to save buildings, cemeteries, and sites such as Indian Burial mounds and even rare swing bridges."

As Cady talked, it was evident to Joseph how much she cared about her home and preserving the past as a gift to the future. "Could you use a sponsor?" The McCoy Foundation was always on the lookout for worthy causes.

"Yes, of course." Joseph's offer surprised Cady. "How generous of you, I'll see that you get the paperwork." While he was thinking – Cady took advantage of his distraction to test out his right leg for sensation. Yesterday he hadn't been certain if he was feeling anything or not. Sometimes patients 'felt' things because they expected to – this would be a surprise. Taking a sharp instrument from her pocket, she quickly jabbed it into his calve. She waited a moment. Nothing. So, she did it again.

"Cady, sweetheart. What are you doing?" She looked up and caught Joseph grinning at her. "I can feel it, Cady. I felt it both times."

"Perfect. Now, we can advance to the next step."

The next step was just more work for Joseph. He hadn't realized what physical therapy actually entailed. His respect for Cady grew by leaps and bounds. She worked tirelessly and with very little positive feedback from him – because most of what she did was pushing him beyond the bounds of what he thought he could do. Hell, it hurt! And Cady didn't care. She only pushed him more until she fell over on the mat from exhaustion. "That's enough."

"Hallelujah, I thought you were going to kill me." Joseph was out of breath, but exhilarated. He could tell they were making progress. Maybe, his future wasn't going to be such a bad place to be, after all.

Three days later:

God! Joseph was in agony. Everything below his waist was on fire. His back ached and he imagined his muscles were being sawed in two with a rusty knife! He would scream if they wouldn't come and take his man-card away. Curling in on himself in the bed, he tried to keep his head. It had been three days since Cady had started her advanced treatments – and by God, they seemed to be working – but the pain! The pain was ungodly!

One thing that he had insisted upon, and finally got accomplished was to be rid of that stupid hospital bed. He had his own bed brought in – thank goodness, and the lift was stationary at the head. He also had a safe place to store the wheelchair within easy reach. But what was the use of that if he died from excruciating agony?

"Cady!" Finally, he gave in to the temptation. He knew she was tired; she had been working herself to death with him. But, he couldn't stand it. He had never, ever hurt this bad. "Cady!" he cried.

It seemed like an eternity, but finally she came rushing into the room. Turning on the bedside lamp, she gasped. "Oh, you poor doll. The pain pill didn't do you any good at all did it?" She knelt by him. "Joseph, listen to me," He turned toward her face.

God, she was pretty. When did she get so pretty? She wore a white eyelet gown that was cut low enough so he could see a vast amount of intriguing cleavage. "It hurts, Cady."

"I'm going to take your pain. But, you have to have faith – in me." Her voice was insistent. "Can you do that?"

"I trust you," he groaned as another wave of knife-hot pain cut through him.

Chapter Six

Cady didn't just touch him with her hands; she placed her whole upper torso over his lower back area, covering him completely. She didn't put her weight on him. She enclosed him within the heat of her embrace, laying her head on his hip. She crooned to him as she rubbed his legs. Cady commanded the pain to come out. She invited it into her own body. She forced wave after wave of psychic energy into his back and spine – ridding him of the pain and ripping sensation. She ordered the fire to leave his nerves and for peace to reign supreme. After about ten minutes, she felt the first lava-like flows of fire wash down her own spine. "Tell me when you start to feel better," she gasped. There was no way she was going to let him know where the pain was going. If it killed her she would take it upon herself and let him have a good night's rest. If only she was able to walk, she prayed that she would be.

Joseph held on to his thoughts, forcing himself to breathe through the pain. Finally, it seemed to be easing up. Gradually, he became aware of the woman who cradled him to her breast. She was so still – was she even breathing? "Cady? It seems to be better."

"Good," she whispered. He felt the bed sway as she tried to rise, and then she stopped – seemingly unable to move. Sinking slowly to the floor, he watched her curl up on her side on the carpet. She had assumed a fetal position, yet she never said a word.

"What's wrong?" She was scaring him. Where she was lying- there was no way he could get his chair near enough to get in it. "Cady! Talk to me. What's wrong!?" he demanded. Then, he remembered her explanation – Kane's explanation of what an empath could do. His pain was gone because Cady had taken it from him. She had taken his pain into her own body. Just the idea of her little body being wracked with that terrible agony broke his heart. Why would she do something like that? He knew the reason – because she could. He laid one hand on her shoulder, and saw her flinch – he knew exactly how she felt. "Are you paralyzed?" God, what if she was? He would never forgive himself.

"No," she gasped. "Just let me be still here, I'll be better in a few hours."

No way. No way in hell. "Come up here, let me hold you." He couldn't stand it. If he didn't get her in his arms in the next few seconds, he was going to go mad. "Please. Please. Do this for me." He watched her little body struggle. Never opening her eyes, she raised up enough that he could grasp her around the waist and with his strong arms and upper body strength he easily drew her to him. "Now, now," he crooned to her. "Hold on to me, I'll keep you safe." He kissed her forehead, pushing back the damp strands of hair that clung so sweetly. "I'll keep you safe."

Cady seemed to take him at his word. She cuddled up against him like it was the most natural thing in the world. He wanted his arms to be a haven for her – a place of rest – a harbor of safety. Fitting herself to him, he thought they must be like two puzzle pieces that had been apart for eternity and had been reunited at long last. "That's my baby. That's my baby." He hugged her up – tight – trying to give whatever comfort he could, knowing it wouldn't be enough. "Go to sleep, sweetheart. I'll hold you – I'll hold you all night long. And he did.

Wonder of wonders. Her lips were so soft, and they tasted like cotton candy. God, had anything ever been so sweet? Only in his dreams, he reminded himself. He rubbed his hand down her back pulling her even closer enjoying the feel of her unbound breasts pushing into his chest. God, she was sexy. A tiny little moan growled from her throat and he wanted to shout in exultation. A faint stirring of sensual excitement seemed to nestle in the base of his spine. Joseph was sexually excited! He didn't have an erection – but by God – he never thought he'd feel this much ever again.

Cady woke up slowly. Surely, she was dreaming. Things like this – wonderful things – didn't happen to her. But, by glory – she was lying in Joseph McCoy's arms and he was kissing her. On the lips! "Wait! Stop!" she pushed against him. "Start over," she begged.

Joseph drew back a fraction. "What's wrong, baby? Can't I kiss you some more?"

"Yes, please," she begged. "But start over. This is my first kiss, and I don't want to miss any of it." This was so good – so near to her dream – she couldn't bear to miss a second of it. Cady thought she would expire from the pleasure. She was being kissed! A man was kissing her! And not just any man, but beautiful, wonderful, sexy Joseph McCoy. Her beloved. Her Joseph. She didn't really understand that, but it didn't change the truth of the matter. Joseph was hers, in some mysterious, miraculous way. With reverence, she placed her hand on the side of his face and felt the warmth of his skin. He pushed his tongue deep in her mouth, groaning - greedily, hungrily.

Oh, damn. He shouldn't be doing this. He started to draw back, but he looked at her face and it was so, sweetly expectant. If he stopped now, it would break her heart. Shit! He was going to hurt her, either way he went. What the hell! He might as well please them both. Oh, so slowly, he let his lips touch hers, so lightly – the gentlest of caresses. Rubbing softly, his tongue licked out, learning her taste. He coaxed her lips open, showing her how to welcome him into the hot velvet of her mouth. He caught a low moan as it escaped her throat. Had anything ever been so sweet? He fisted one hand in her hair – holding her still – angling his mouth so he could eat at her lips with renewed vigor; he had a voracious appetite for little Cady. The other hand slid down her body, cupping and molding her breast; rejoicing in the perfection of it – the fullness, the softness; the wonderful way it responded to his touch. He pinched her nipple and she writhed against him, aching for more. Pleasantly surprised at his hunger, he took the top of her gown in both hands, "I'll buy you another, baby," and ripped it wide open. Joseph stared at her breasts – they were utterly beautiful - perfect, round, plump, berry-tipped and swollen – just for him. "Lovely, you are absolutely lovely." Enclosing them in his palms, he rubbed them luxuriously, causing her to arch her back, letting him know how grateful she was for the attention he was giving her. "Do you like that, precious?" He could tell she did. Giving her what she needed, he massaged them – kneaded them – rolling the nipples between his fingers, causing her to cry out at the unexpected pleasure.

"Oh, I love it, Joseph. Thank you," she managed to put a couple of coherent words together. Oh, how she wanted to beg for his lips on her breast, but she wouldn't. What he was giving her was so much more than she ever expected – she wouldn't dare jinx it by asking for more. As he fondled her breasts, she fell her sex grow wet – God, would he touch her there? Did she want him to touch her there? Cady felt her sex answer with tingles and jerks – she was so hungry for him that she could die. She marveled at the sheer erotic decadence of being loved on by Joseph – the man of her dreams. And that's what he was – she had been dreaming about him her entire life.

Joseph wanted. . . . . . Joseph wanted . . . . Licking her neck, he kissed a trail down the smoothest, softest skin imaginable - - - Joseph wanted . . . . . . .Hell! In his mind, his cock was hot, hard and ready, but in reality it was just hanging between his legs – useless. He couldn't stand it. "Get up." He pushed her away. "Get up and get out."

"What?" It took a moment for Cady to realize that Joseph was through with her. He pushed her – not hard – but hard enough for her to realize he wanted her gone – now. Trying to get her body to follow her mind's directive – she hesitated. He pushed again and she became overbalanced and tumbled off the bed backwards. With a small cry, she hit the floor. Her torn gown gaped open and she rushed to pull it back together, totally mortified. "I'm sorry. I'll go."

He had a hand over his eyes, as if hiding from the world. With a sinking heart, she realized he had probably not realized who he was kissing. He must have been dreaming and awakened to find himself making out with the homely girl. Eeegads! Scrambling up, she proceeded to put as much distance between them as she could. "I'm sorry, Joseph."

When she shut the door, Joseph let out a blue streak of choice words. "Hell-fire! Damn!" He ought to be horsewhipped. He had pushed her out of his bed! No matter how embarrassed he had been at his impotence - that was the stupidest thing he had ever done. What must she think of him? What if she left? He had already made progress, and he had more faith in her than he could say. It was obvious – he had to make this right. Using the Hoyer, he raised himself up, and after four tries, he finally managed to reach the wheelchair that had been dislodged from its proper spot when Cady had scrambled to get out of his presence.

"Cady!" he called to her as he transferred himself. "Cady! Come back, I'm so sorry!" He didn't even take time for his bathroom duties – getting to her was more important.

Cady let the water run over her body as hot as she could stand it, trying to wash the shame from her very soul. How humiliating! What he must think of her? She should have known that Joseph McCoy would never willingly kiss her. And she had been laying on him – wantonly – his arm around her – just like the coyote ugly definition. Fresh waves of embarrassment took her breath away. Flipping off the water, she stepped out and grabbed a towel to dry off with. Having been so upset, she had thrown her ruined gown on the bed and neglected to get anything else to put on. Leaving the bathroom, she walked into the bedroom and met the surprise of her life.

Joseph hadn't hesitated, he had to apologize. Without thinking, he had entered her room – he wasn't sure what he had been expecting – but it sure wasn't what walked out of the bath, her skin still glistening like diamonds from the shower. Joseph stared. He couldn't help it. God Almighty! He couldn't believe it! He knew this body – he had made love to this body in his dreams! Impossible! He was going crazy! Still, he was going to burn every damn dress she had. Those baggy dresses had been hiding a killer body. "Damn, baby." He stopped his wheelchair and feasted his eyes on luscious breasts that he had only glimpsed in the dim light of the bedroom, a tiny waist and the curviest, sweetest pair of hips he had ever seen. Joseph didn't get to look closer, because she froze in her tracks and held the towel up longwise like a curtain, hiding paradise from his eyes. "Now, this is more like it. We've got to get you some new clothes – some that will play up all of these assets you've been hiding."

"Why didn't you knock? Are you determined to humiliate me to death?" Cady carefully walked sideways keeping the towel draped between them, trying to keep as much of her body out of his line of sight as possible. Going for the lesser of two evils, she whirled around and faced away from him, endeavoring to get her robe on.

Joseph smiled; the view of her perfect little ass was almost as good as those two handfuls of delight in the front that made his mouth water. "I was wrong." Joseph stated flatly.

Cady huffed in consternation as she got one hand hung in the sleeve. She wasn't listening to him. She probably didn't want to hear anything he had to say. "God, please kill me," she mumbled. "Are you still here?" she called over her shoulder.

"Yes," Joseph couldn't have left if he had tried. He was mesmerized. Just as he'd noticed yesterday, her legs were long and delectably shaped and as she fought her robe, her little derriere bounced pleasingly up and down. "I'm still here. I need to talk to you." At least that's what he hoped he said.

Managing to pull on her white cotton robe, Cady belted it and turned to face Joseph. "Why do you hate me so much? What did I ever do to you? I came to help you and you have gone out of your way to insult me, and took away the meager amount of self confidence that I had." Tears rolled down her cheeks and she splashed them away with her fingers. "I want to help you, I really do. For some odd reason – it's very important to me." Joseph didn't saying anything; he let her have her say. "All I ask is that you treat me with just a little respect – you don't have to treat me like a woman – just treat me like a human being."

He couldn't stand it another minute. Using one strong arm to propel himself forward, he caught her by the hand and pulled her down in his lap. "I didn't mean it, precious. I didn't mean to hurt you." Before she could say another word, he covered her mouth with his and kissed her like nobody's business.

Cady didn't know what to do. She wanted to respond so bad she ached, but this might be a trick of some kind. It had to be. There was no way Joseph wanted to kiss her – not her – not Cady Renaud. This time it was her pushing; she placed her palms on his rock hard chest and pushed. He didn't move, but she managed to pull away herself. "No," she managed to gasp. "You're just playing with me, Joseph. It's just some kind of cruel game for you. The coyote ugly thing – that's what happened this morning. Wasn't it?"

What had he done? Her little face was tear-streaked and she was pleading with him not to kiss her because she thought that he was getting some sick kick out of teasing her. "God, no – baby." Overriding her stiff little muscles, he coaxed her closer to him and began kissing her tears away. "I reacted badly – but it wasn't anything to do with you. You were wonderful – waking up with you in my arms was heaven. And kissing your lips, seeing your beautiful breasts – I wanted to ravish you," his voice dropped and so did his head, "but, I couldn't." Joseph pulled her tight against him, and he placed his head in the curve of her neck, kissing the soft skin there. "It hit me that even though I wanted to make love to you so much, I might never be able to."

He clutched her so close she almost couldn't breathe. Unable to deny him, she cupped the back of his head, letting her fingers sink into his soft, dark hair. He was trembling against her and she slipped an arm around his shoulders and cradled him to her. "I know it's hard," she would concentrate on his feelings and not think about his claim that he was attracted to her. That was just too unbelievable to comprehend. "You've made progress. The pain and the localized sensations in your legs, they are both very good signs. Today, we'll start a new treatment and I'll double my efforts to awaken the nerves that will allow you to have an erection." She felt him stiffen. "I want this for you. Are you willing for me to use my gift as well as the traditional techniques I have been using?" Raising his head, she was touched to see tears in his eyes, also.

"Whatever you can do for me," he tugged at her bottom lip with his thumb, amazed at the petulant softness. How had he ever thought her plain? Had the accident affected his eyesight? "I will do anything you tell me and believe anything you say," he whispered. "Can I kiss you now?"

Cady lay in his arms, so close to him – so aware of his masculine perfection. "No, thank you." It killed her to say that, but she had to try and preserve her sanity. "I appreciate the offer, but I think I'd rather stick to our original agreement. You can advise me on how to become a little more attractive and maybe, if I do what you say, I'll be able to find a nice man who can look beyond my homeliness, to the person I am inside. I have a lot of love to give someone who will take the time to see the real me," Cady had kept her hands flat on his chest, desperately trying to preserve a distance between them.

"Sweetheart," Joseph sighed. "I've been wrong about a lot of things in my life – but none more than when I ever thought you plain. You are not homely – you are fuckin' gorgeous. A moment ago, when you walked out of that bath – all those pearly drops of water on your satin skin – you took my breath away." Joseph let her pull out of his arms. As she moved away, he felt oddly bereft. What had he done? God, he was confused. In his mind, Cady was becoming intertwined with the woman of his erotic dreams. At times, he thought they even looked alike – even though there was really no similarity – except in their bodies – and in their eyes. Was he losing his mind?

She stood before him, her little arms crossed under her breasts – her eyes shining with unshed tears. God, she didn't know how adorable she was.

Cady closed her eyes – put a shield over her heart and willed herself not to listen. He didn't mean what he was saying – he couldn't. She had to be strong. Change the subject – that was what she would do. "Would you mind if I brought in some help? Would that offend you? I told you about my family and the Romee witches. They have as much or more experience in a healing of this magnitude as I do. Together, we could make this happen – and happen quickly." She didn't say that the faster she could get him or her feet – the faster than she could go home. Being with Joseph was wonderful – but it was also the most painful experience of her life. Her grandmother and aunt had been right. If she was going to preserve her heart and what was left of her pride – she had to get out of Texas and back to Louisiana.

He shook his head, looked her straight in the eye and smiled. "It's simple, Cady. I trust you. Bring in whoever you want – do whatever you want – I put myself totally in your hands."

"Good. I'll call them this morning. Warn your family that they are being invaded," she couldn't help but smile a bit through her pain. The two she wanted to see together was grande dame Nanette Beaureguarde and Joseph's brother Aron – now **that** would be a pair.

The McCoy brothers all stood in a row on the porch, Joseph was in his chair, of course. They were watching three vehicles park in the circular drive in front of the Tebow Ranch house. "They're driving Jaguars and a Lexus," Aron mused as he watched the people Cady invited exit their cars.

"What did you expect them to arrive on – brooms?" Isaac laughed then roared when Aron had the good grace to look sheepish.

Libby opened the door and saw the brothers in a line like the Cartwright's on Bonanza. They were just looking, not making a move to greet their guests or anything. "Move, you big baboons," she fussed. Libby could turn into a little tornado when she was riled. "Where are your manners?" Unwilling to let their guests have a completely bad impression of the McCoy clan, she took off out in the yard to greet their visitors.

Joseph felt decidedly uneasy. Cady worked with him diligently, but he could tell that something had changed. She was there – but she wasn't. It was as if she had built up a protective barrier between them.

And now – eleven people – all, incredibly normal looking, were greeting Libby and several of the other brothers who ventured out to help them in. They didn't have much luggage so, apparently, this wasn't going to be a long drawn out ordeal. Hell! He was nervous. He heard the screen door open and Cady emerged. She was still dressed in an outfit that hid every incredible attribute she had, but to Joseph she was radiant. How had that happened? "They're here!" she exclaimed with a smile. To Joseph's surprise, she stopped and hugged him, the feel of her arms around his neck and the sweet scent of her body made chill-bumps rise on his skin. "Soon you will be chasing dreams and chasing women, love; just like you used to." Then, she kissed him on the temple, rendering Joseph absolutely speechless. In a few minutes, between Libby and Cady, they had everyone in and seated in the living room with appropriate refreshments in their hands.

Joseph looked around at the crowd in the living room. Cady's guests were not at all what he had expected. Smiling to himself, he knew he had pictured black clad women with too much eye makeup and long, long fingernails. Cady's aunt Angelique was dressed a bit oddly and her husband spoke with a distinct island accent, but other than that - these folks could be anyone's neighbor or best friend. And they were witches?

"Not all of us are witches, Joseph." The voice from across the room answering his mental question almost caused him to fall out of his wheel chair. He looked into a pair of serene eyes set in a lovely face. She appeared to be in her late thirties and was decidedly pregnant. A handsome man held her hand and looked at her with obvious devotion. "Surely, you recognize Jade Landale," she pointed at a tall blonde man who held a small baby like it was made of spun glass.

Jade Landale. The name did ring a bell. "Well, I do," Aron got to his feet and shook hands with the dignified visitor. "Congressman, it's a pleasure to meet you."

"Aron McCoy, your name is familiar to me, also. Tebow Ranch is an example of what makes Texas great. It's an honor to meet you."

Cady took that opportunity to rise and make introductions all around. Joseph was surprised to find that there was an Austin firefighter, a police detective and a doctor in the group. Joseph couldn't help but feel a sense of pride as he watched Cady bring the two groups together. She said something personal and special about every individual, making the guests feel at home and his family at ease with those who had arrived on their doorstep. Finally, she addressed him. Stepping over to his chair, she placed a small hand on his shoulder. "These people are special to me and I trust them above all others. Together, we can help you."

"That's right, honey." The old matriarch of the family stood up and walked across the living room and stood in front of the McCoy brothers. "I know we must seem strange to you," she began, looking at each one of them individually. Finally, she settled on Aron - realizing he was the undeniable leader of the family. "My family has power. I don't pretend to understand everything there is to know about it - but I will tell you this - it is a real power that we choose to use for good. We can trace the roots of our gifts back to the 1600's. In our magical heritage we have Celtic beliefs, African beliefs, even Egyptian and Native American. Our powers are an amalgam of our past - not tied to a religion or to a nation - but tied to the great truth that exists in the universe - there is a higher intelligence that wishes only good for its creation and that good is there for the taking if we will only ask."

Aron made the mistake of coughing and Nannette Beaureguarde pinned him with a stare. "I can feel the concern and the skepticism emanating from you, Mr. McCoy. But, I can also feel the hope that is pouring from your brother's heart. You say you are familiar with the Congressman," she pointed a finger at her grandson-in-law. "Do you recall his near fatal accident, the reports that he was condemned to live the life of a paraplegic?"

At her words, the McCoy men looked at one another - understanding dawning. Noah spoke up first, "I remember that. It was all over the news."

Jacob put his arm around Jessie, stealing a hug. "They wrote you off, didn't they?" He addressed his comment to Jade. "Weren't they planning on taking you off of life support?"

Jade kissed his little dark haired daughter and handed her over to his wife. "You remember correctly, Jacob. I was completely paralyzed from the neck down. I couldn't even breathe or swallow on my own." A shadow fell over his face as he remembered. "My only escape was in my dreams and there I met the most beautiful woman in the world. It's a long story - but my dream was more than just a night fantasy - it was real and it led me to this group of women who gave me back my life and - more than that - gave me my family, my reason for living."

Joseph felt his hands shake as he listened to the other man talk about meeting a woman in his dreams. That sounded a lot like what he was experiencing. What could this mean? He listened to the Congressman tell about how he had been pulled back from the brink of despair. If this incredible miracle could happen for Jade Landale - why couldn't it happen for Joseph McCoy?

Aron eyeballed the older, rotund woman who seemed to exude confidence and a bigger than life presence. "I don't want to see my brother hurt, Ms. Beaureguarde. What you're proposing to do seems a little too good to be true."

Nanette was graceful for a large woman, and she was in Aron's face before he knew she had moved. He met Isaac's face over her shoulder, his eyes wide with surprise. Isaac barely held back a snort of amusement. "The magick we are offering your brother would be considered a miracle by most, but that doesn't mean it is beyond the realm of possibility. Cady has made great progress, we are merely going to seal the deal – give her therapy and healing a boost of magical power and get this boy back on his feet and into the game." Aron backed up a step, held up his hands in defense and took backwater.

"Hey, if you can do that, I'm all for it. I didn't mean to imply . . ." he began and took comfort from the fact that Libby had slipped an arm around his waist and was coming to his rescue.

"We trust Cady, Ms. Beaureguarde. And we trust Sheriff Saucier. He has vouched for you all, and that is good enough for us."

"Then let us begin." Turning to Angelique, she nodded in secret communication. Angelique knew what to do. As Nannette left the room with her granddaughters to begin setting up for the ritual, Cady's aunt approached the McCoy clan.

"We will need three things from you."

"Anything, you name it. We want Joseph to get better, no matter what it takes." Aron was subdued and thoughtful, holding on to Libby's hand for all he was worth.

"Good," Angelique turned to Nathan and placed a hand on his head. "Could you get me a bucket of fresh water from a source on your land? It needs to be from a free flowing creek or a spring. Can you help me?"

Nathan jumped at the chance. There was nothing more important to him than helping his brother. "I'm on it – I'll be back in two shakes of a sheep's tale."

As he started off at break neck speed, Isaac called after him. "Be sure and get a bucket, bud!" When he looked back around, Angelique was in his space, standing close enough to startle him. "May I help you?"

This unlikely reaction for his biker brother caused Noah to chuckle. "Boo!" he quipped.

Pulling himself up to his full height, Isaac awaited the mysterious woman's words. "I need something from the rest of you," she looked at them one by one. "We need an object of sympathy, something that has become frozen in time – unable to move or give life."

"Lady, I'll move mountains for my brother, but you've got to be clearer than that. I don't know what the hell you're talking about." Isaac wasn't in the best of moods to begin with. He had traveled to Avery's parents and found they were telling the truth. They didn't know where Avery was – and he was frantic with worry. He intended to do something – just as soon as he figured out the best course to take. Roscoe was still chasing vandals and had contacted Vance to come talk to Isaac. Together, maybe they would come up with some ideas about where to start looking for the woman who haunted his every thought.

Angelique's eyes softened. "She will return." Those simple words caused a flash of hope to spark through Isaac, and he narrowed his eyes trying to be sure this wasn't some kind of trick.

"Who will return?" He wasn't going to make this easy for the woman. If she was going to toss quips around like that, she had better be able to back them up.

Angelique looked into the macho man's soul. What she saw was a tender heart, a need to be loved and a desire for one woman that burned white-hot in its intensity. "You know of whom I speak. Your desire to protect her led you to push her away. She will return."

Isaac swallowed and glanced around at his brothers who were watching him intently. "What kind of object of sympathy do you want?" Lord, this was creepy and way too close to home for comfort.

Angelique stepped back and let her eyes clear of the prophetical clouds that marred her vision. "The best that you could offer would be a fossil that was harvested from this ground, or a piece of petrified wood that was gathered here."

"I'm on it, let's go." Jacob always the giver, started toward the stairs. "Does anybody remember that box where Mom used to store all of the weird stuff we would give her?" Isaac was right behind him.

"I remember the box. She used it to store every marble, wild flower, crayon drawing – you name it – anything we brought to her." Isaac was racking his brain trying to remember the last time he saw that wooden box of keepsakes.

"Remember that time you brought her a lizard?" Jacob was taking the steps two at a time.

"Yea, it was the day of a first frost. I thought she would squeal and turn him loose; instead she got him a box and made me hunt flies for him all winter. What did she name him?" Memories of their mother were precious and the smiles on their faces were nostalgic as they recalled her kind and loving touch.

"Lewis Lizzard. She named him that after southern humorist she liked so well, Lewis Grizzard." They laughed at the memory.

Light footsteps behind them announced Libby. She hurried toward them, "It's in the hall closet, I saw it while I was cleaning yesterday." She stepped ahead of them and was almost about to climb up on a stool.

"Munchkin! Hey, no climbing!" Isaac gently set her aside and reached for the box himself. "Aron would skin our heads if we let anything happen to you. Remember that time Jacob let you fall off of Molly?"

"That's wasn't Jacob's fault, it was that big old chicken snake," Libby defended Jacob who would rather cut off his own arm rather than let harm befall any of the women in his life.

"Let me see that," Jacob took the box from Isaac and opened it. Letting out a sigh of relief, he took out a piece of petrified wood. "Here's what I was looking for. Do you remember this, Isaac?"

"I sure do." Isaac picked up the piece of agate that was shaped like a heart. "Nathan found it in the yard. He was still in diapers and he came toddling in and gave it to mom with a big sloppy kiss. She cried." Both of them fell silent, because that had been the day before the accident where she and their dad had been lost to them forever.

"Libby! Are you up there?" Aron came bounding up the stairs two at a time. "You're not climbing on anything are you?"

Jacob laughed and pushed little Libby toward his brother who was stalking down the hall like a bull moose in mating season. "Now's who's psychic." Hiding his grin, he answered his brother. "No, Aron. Libby is safe and sound." He tossed the fossil in the air and started down the stairs, wondering where the day would take them.

"Are you ready?" Cady knelt down by Joseph. "This is going to work, you know."

"Damn straight, I'm ready." Joseph began wheeling toward the back. "Are you coming?"

Cady smiled. "Right behind you."

"Where do you want me?" Joseph was determined to take an active role. He was fascinated; watching Nanette's granddaughters light candles and arrange crystals. They seemed perfectly at home with the whole situation, laughing and talking and catching up on family gossip. Cady's eyes watched him observing the other women.

"They are beautiful, aren't they?"

For a moment, Joseph didn't know what she meant. "Yea, sure they are. But you could be just as pretty if you fixed yourself up a bit," He intended for his words to encourage, but saw from her expression that they did just the opposite. Before he could repair the damage he had inflicted; he watched her face fall.

"You need to be in the bed," she spoke slowly. "And we'll have to get you undressed."

"Are you gonna strip me naked? I knew it," Joseph tried to tease. "I've always heard about these lascivious rituals you people have." He had to laugh – it was better than crying. God! He wanted this to work and it all seemed so incredibly unbelievable. What could these people do? They all looked so normal. It was impossible that they possessed supernatural powers that could restore him to the man he used to be – wasn't it?

Cady managed a weak smile. "Let's get on with this shall we?" She provided what help was needed to get him in the bed and undressed. Frankly, he was getting quite proficient at it. Even though they weren't alone, she couldn't help but grow aroused at the sight of his body. Her mind tried to fight the possessive feeling that always bombarded her heart when it came to Joseph. He belonged to her in some mysterious spiritual way, but she would never belong to him.

"Are we all set?" Angelique asked. "Your brothers have brought us the water and the talisman." She held back a smile as she watched Cady protectively cover Joseph with the sheet. "You probably should get a hand towel to preserve his modesty."

"A hand towel?" Joseph chided. "You had better make that a beach towel. My modesty is pretty good sized." As Cady left to fetch something to cover him with, Angelique stepped closer.

"Cady is like a fragile wildflower; a quiet beauty that can be easily crushed." She said no more but gave him a long hard stare that spoke volumes. Joseph felt like he had been warned.

"Cady has nothing to fear from me, ma'am. She's not my type." Angelique's eyes narrowed, telling him she knew he was lying. They both knew. Joseph felt guilty, and he when looked up and saw Cady had heard yet another put-down from his lips, he could have ripped his own tongue out by the roots.

Cady stepped out from behind her aunt. She wasn't his type. Okay, she knew that. Refusing to meet Joseph's eyes, she addressed her aunt. "Please let me deal with this in my own way, Aunt."

"Very well, it is time to proceed." Angelique turned to join Nanette as she added the herbs to the spring water.

Cady pulled back the sheet and draped the cloth over Joseph's manhood. Her face was flaming, but not from his nakedness. She was ashamed her aunt had scolded Joseph and put him into the position of having to deny her, yet again. "Remember, everything that happens is for your good." With those terse words, she walked off.

Damn! Joseph watched her go. Now was not the time to get into it with her – but he would, and soon.

Cady was nervous. This was so important. She deferred to Nanette, everyone did. She watched as Nanette walked up to Joseph. "Sweetie, we are going to heal you. What I need you to do is to have faith. What I am about to do to you is an ancient ritual. I am going to bathe you with water that has been empowered by herbs. I am going to rub your body from head to toe with a lodestone. This stone will draw out the malady and transfer it to this water." She picked up the piece of petrified wood that Jacob and Isaac had provided. "This piece of the past has been frozen in time, it will aid our efforts." She placed the heart shaped talisman at the base of his throat. "And we're going to have to turn you over after we wash your front side, so don't be alarmed. Soon, all will be well."

The others stood around and watched her work. First, she lit the candles and bowed her head in prayer. Next, she dipped a lodestone in the water and began at the crown of his head, stroking all the way down his body, from top to toe. Then she dipped the lodestone in the water and started again. She went on for twenty five times, stroking completely every inch of his body. "Roll him over." Very carefully they did as she asked, replacing the fossil at the base of his neck, right where his brain stem was located. Cady knew this was difficult for Joseph; she could see the muscles of his shoulders tense with nerves. Nanette repeated the procedure on his back.

As she did she chanted.

"I banish this paralysis
I banish the pain
I command feeling to flow through this body
I demand that the nerves be reknit
And power flow through these limbs once again."

When the fifty strokes had been completed, she instructed Elizabeth to take the basin outside. "Be very careful not to splash any water on you. That water contains the source of this boy's problem. Take it to the first crossroads you can find. Empty it and then walk away and don't look back. When we leave, we must not drive through that crossroad. So be careful and choose appropriately." To the rest of them she ordered, "Now come with me and let us all lay hands on his body." They did as they were told. "Cady, this is your calling. You are a traiteur, my dear. That is your greatest gift. You have healing in your hands. Over the years I have seen you place your hands on those that were sick. Even though you didn't realize you were doing it, your love and concern – the intent of your heart healed them. You can do it again. Come on baby, the lodestone has done its work. This is the time, place your hands on this boy and will his legs to move."

    Mesmerized, Cady listened to the older woman's voice. Her hands were hot as she placed them on the small of Joseph's back. "Joseph, are you feeling okay?" So far, no one had addressed him, and she didn't want him to feel disconnected and ignored.
    Joseph cleared his throat. "I'm okay." He had kept his eyes shut for most of the time. It was all just too strange. As the woman had stroked his body with the cold lodestone, he had steeled himself not to react, not to shiver. When her hand had passed from above his waist to below his waist, he had concentrated on trying to feel it and toward the end, he could have sworn he could – although, it could have been

his imagination.

"You may feel some heat now, and if you do that will be wonderful." Cady willed the nerves to mend and feeling to flow back into the extremities of his body. She willed his legs to move and his manhood to awaken. Cady Renaud willed Joseph McCoy back to life.

"Now pray." Nanette directed, and Cady stepped back. The others took her place, all laying their hands at varying places on Joseph's body. Nanette, Angelique, Elizabeth, Aimee, Arabella, Evangeline and Zak; all powerful, all committed to healing her charge. She felt empowered. She felt connected. Kneeling at the side of Joseph's bed, she lifted her hands palm upward and began to call upon the God, the Goddess and the archangels. Grace flooded her soul. Cady felt like a conduit of power as she called upon the quarters – the North, South, East, West – she acknowledged the elements - Earth, Fire, Air and Water – and asked their assistance. Raising her eyes to the heavens, Cady begged the universe to grant her request and send down power to restore Joseph's body to the perfection he once enjoyed.

Joseph opened his eyes and what he saw took his breath away. Cady was on the floor – but she didn't look like Cady – and yet she did. The rays of the evening sun were shining on her, cloaking her in magnificence. What was different? Her hair was the same, yet alive and vibrant – not ordinary by any stretch of the imagination. And her face, he blinked his eyes and looked a second time. She was absolutely gorgeous! She looked like - - exactly like - - My God! - - Cady was the image of his nighttime visitor! How could that be? But, for some reason, it made perfect sense. If anyone in the world cared enough to come and be his angel of mercy, it was Cady.

Pulses of power seemed to throb through her body, Cady could feel the energy in the room and she visualized Joseph getting feeling in his legs, the nerves sending messages to his brain so he could move, walk, run and make love like he did before the accident. "Harm to none, my will be done, so mote it be." Cady sent her plea out into the heavens, begging the powers that create and sustain all life to grant her request.

Joseph was entranced. Absolutely baffled. What they had done, he could not explain. At first, he felt nothing. Then it started. He began to feel heat. At first he thought it was wishful thinking, but then the tingling started. Sensations began to shoot down his thighs and down his legs. Hope began to bud in his heart and mind. How could water and a rock heal him? There was more to it, he knew. Right now, he didn't care. With everything he had, he attempted to move a toe. As he concentrated, he was not aware that he had begun to talk. Everyone in the room turned to look at him as he hoarsely said, "Cady? Cady, love. Something's happening. I can feel my feet, they're tingling!"

Cady trembled with joy as tears streamed down her cheeks. Rising to her feet, she walked to his side, took his hand in hers and went to her knees. "You can feel your legs?" She kissed the hand she was holding. One by one the others filed out of the room, leaving them alone.

He powered himself up and Cady helped him roll over. Concentrating with all of his might, Joseph tried to ascertain just what he was feeling – God, how could he be sure? So much had happened; it was hard to separate reality from wishful thinking. "I don't know, I can't be sure," he ran his hands down his legs. Could he feel his hands? Damn!

Cady walked to the end of the bed, she was watching him carefully, the strain showing clearly on his face – sweat beaded out on his ripped chest – his skin glowing golden, the hair on his chest matted from the perspiration and the ritual bath. He was drop-dead gorgeous that was what he was. "Can you move your toe for me?" She trembled as she laid the palm of her hand on the bottom of his foot so she could be sure and feel any movement he made. "Try, Joseph, try," she encouraged. The look on his face tugged at her heart – she saw hope, pride, vulnerability and fear. And as he focused she prayed harder than she ever had in her life. 'Please, Goddess, please,' she begged.

"Come on," he whispered. "God, please." Ten thousand pounds of pressure seemed to be pressing down on his back. His muscles were so tightly tensed he thought they would break. Finally, it seemed as it something loosened and one big toe moved barely a half-inch.

"Joseph!" Cady exclaimed. "You did it!" She propelled herself forward and threw her arms around his neck and he absorbed her weight easily, enfolding her in his arms and holding her close.

"Yea, I moved one toe," he didn't know if that was a lot to celebrate. If there really was magick involved, shouldn't he have been totally healed, instantly?

Cady pulled back, hearing the disappointment in his voice. "Yes, you moved one toe," she reiterated. "And that's huge. What it means is that you are going to get better. It won't be instant, but healing has begun."

With his heart in his eyes, he looked at her – his face pale with the ordeal he had been through. "Are you sure? I thought their magick would do more than this."

Encouraging him, she tried to explain. "Magick works in its own time. You will get better, everyday; I will do healing rituals along with your regular treatments. We will even get more locale specific, if you know what I mean." She didn't show any emotion – but she could tell by the heat in his eyes he understood she would be massaging his penis, hoping to get it to show some signs of life. Needing to change the subject, quickly, she added. "And we're going to need a walking course installed in here. Because you, sweet Joseph, are going to be up and on your feet before you know it."

"I look forward to it. All of it." And he did, more than she would ever know.

Chapter Seven

"Aron, I need help." It was hard for Libby to admit it, but nausea and an increasing sense of fatigue was just about to get the best of her. "I'm not complaining, but with branding and vaccinating coming up and knowing how many extra mouths we're going to have to feed - I'm afraid that Jessie and I just can't do everything that needs to be done. And Jessie is already doing more than her share"

At Libby's sweet request, Aron's guts twisted. "Do you think you need to go to the doctor?" He was terrified that Libby's cancer would return. Every time she looked the least bit uncomfortable, Aron imagined the worst. "And now we've got a houseful of company for you to take care of, to boot," he blew out a breath. "We'll have a cook-out tonight; that will take a lot of the pressure off of you and Jessie. We men can throw some steaks on the grill and do baked potatoes and corn on the cob. How does that sound?"

Just that simple of an answer seemed to give his beloved such sweet relief. She melted into him and hugged him tight. "Thank you, Aron." He could feel the little swell of her abdomen between them and his heart did a cartwheel, just from her nearness.

"Hell!" Why hadn't he thought of Kane's phone call before this? "I think I have the answer, baby." He explained how Kane Saucier, had called to inquire about any leads for a job for a friend of his, Lilibet Ladner. She had lost the lease on her house and was having to give up her food service job. She would have to leave town if she couldn't find other employment. Smiling, Aron realized there was probably more going on between the sheriff and the little lady than he let on. He planned on teasing him, unmercifully. "I might know where we can get you some help."

Joseph made his way through the crowd; a McCoy party was always well attended – no matter how little notice was given. More than once he had to veer his wheelchair to one side to miss a careless sidestep or an overly exuberant dancer. "Why don't you ever use that high-powered fancy wheel chair?" Isaac drawled leaning up against a pavilion support post. He was sipping a beer, avoiding two or three women who had their eagle eyes glued to his leather clad form.

"I'm not a weakling, asshole."

Instead of getting angry, Isaac laughed. "Never said you were weak, knot-head." Isaac dug in a cooler and tossed Joseph a beer. "I thought you would be walking around by now. I heard the hoodoo razzamatazz worked. What's the deal?"

"Hell, if I know." Joseph popped the top. "I can move my big toe. How's that for progress. Where's Cady?" He had plenty to say to her and there was no time like the present.

"Sounds like a big deal to me. If your brain can communicate with your toe, it can talk to your dick, dumbass." He knew there was no use pushing it; Joseph would realize the significance of what had happened, eventually. At his brother's pointed stare, he gestured across the room with his free hand. "She's with Zane, over there. They seem to be having a good time."

Cady was with Zane. Jealousy flashed over him like a grease fire. He stopped his chair and just sat – watching them. They did look like they were having a good time. Zane Saucier was a handsome devil – and he didn't let his blindness slow him down any. Cady was playing with Rex, Zane's seeing-eye dog. Joseph raked his eyes over her. She looked happy – she was laughing at the antics of the lab who was enjoying the attention. The dog looked up at the bachelor lawyer like he hung the moon. With one hand, Joseph wheeled his chair around and headed to the bar – one beer was not going to be enough.

"I can't explain it, Zane. I just know it isn't over. Would you talk to Kane for me?" Cady had been so concerned about Joseph that she had ignored a nagging sense of darkness that kept pulling at her thoughts. "Just yesterday I bumped into Jacob and I could feel it – something is wrong. He is the trigger – I really need to do a reading." Cady grasped Zane's hand and squeezed it, as if holding on to him would connect her to the answer. "The man that was after Jessie was part of the problem – but not all. Evil is still near – I don't know who or why – but there is more trouble coming."

Zane didn't doubt it. He had heard about the wire-cutting incidents and Kane said that he thought some of them had happened after he had arrested Jessie's kidnapper. "I'll talk to him first thing in the morning, Cady. Now, how about a ride home?"

Cady pulled back into the parking lot. She had taken Zane and Rex back to his apartment. He arrived with his brother, but the sheriff had left early with Lilibet, leaving the lawyer to find his own way home. Exiting the vehicle, she scanned the pavilion area, her eyes searching for Joseph. She really needed to talk to him, evaluate how he was feeling. Who was she kidding? She just wanted to be with him.

"Back so soon?"

Turning to face him, Cady could barely make him out in the shadows. "I gave Zane a ride home. He has an early deposition."

"Now that's the man you ought to set your sights on," Joseph drawled.

His tone was odd. "How many beers have you had?"

"Not enough." He rolled up right in front of her, a belligerent expression on his face. "Yea, Saucier is perfect for you."

"Why do you say, that? Because he's a lawyer or because he's from Louisiana, like me?"

"No, Zane Saucier is perfect for a woman who looks like you Cady - - he's blind."

Cady stumbled back to the house. The blatant insult Joseph had just thrown at her knocked the breath from her body. There was no way she could go on like this. Picking up her skirt, she sank down on the steps. Tears were running down her face – this was the second time she had let his cruel words make her cry, and it was going to be the last. He must truly hate her – why else would he intentionally hurt her over and over again.

"Cady? What's wrong?" Libby sat down beside her, concerned.

"I need to ask you a question," Cady screwed her courage up to ask the beautiful woman for help. At Libby's kind smile of encouragement, she nervously smoothed her skirt. "Would you and Jessie give me a make-over? Maybe, you could help me buy some different clothes, show me how to wear make-up like the two of you do?"

Libby brightened. "It will be our pleasure." She ran a hand over Cady's long brown hair. "I know exactly what I want to do with you. We'll go shopping tomorrow and pick you up some outfits that will make the men around here drool."

Cady didn't admit that it was just one man she wanted to make drool, but she was sure everyone suspected she had a huge crush on Joseph. "Drool isn't necessary, I'll settle for them not running the other way when they look at me." At that pitiful comment, the tears began to flow. Libby put her arms around her and hugged tight. Cady laid her head against Libby's cheek and when she did, she felt the heat. Libby had a temperature. "Libby, are you sick?"

"Yes, but don't tell Aron." Her voice shook and Cady pushed her back to arm's length to look at her.

"Aron is the first person you should tell." At Libby's stricken look, Cady helped her up and they retreated into the house. "Let's get you upstairs and I'll lay hands on you, but tonight you tell Aron and tomorrow you go to the doctor." Cady didn't want anything to be wrong with Libby, but she was grateful for anything to take her mind off of Joseph.

They went to Cady's room so they wouldn't be disturbed and also so she would be in her own bed when the exhaustion and debilitation hit. If it was just an infection – that would be bad enough. But if it was a return of the cancer that Libby was battling, when Cady took it upon herself – it was going to make her sick – really sick.

Joseph felt sick to his stomach. He was the most stupid son-of-a-bitch in the world. Jealousy caused him to lash out at Cady in the worst way. And now, Cady had disappeared. Using the ramp that Noah and Jacob had built for him, he made his way into the house. Heading back toward her room, he heard voices. Easing to the outside of the door, he shamelessly eavesdropped. "Do you feel better, Libby?" he heard Cady ask.

"I do," Libby whispered. "I feel stronger and my temperature is gone."

"I am so glad," Cady's voice was so low, it seemed weak. "You go lie down and rest, and tell Aron what we did. He loves you – there's nothing he wouldn't do for you."

Hearing Libby's footsteps, Joseph hurriedly backed down the hall so he wouldn't be seen. But as soon as she was down the hall and out of sight, Joseph was back at Cady's door. Turning the knob, he pushed it open – it made little to no noise, but he wasn't trying to be silent.

"Cady?" The room was dark and smelled like her – the scent of jasmine and vanilla permeated his mind and set his pulse to racing. As his eyes adjusted to the darkness, he could see she was in the bed, on her side hugging a pillow to her chest. "Are you okay? Was Libby sick?"

A muffled groan came from the pillow, "I pray that she will be well. Aron will get her a check-up tomorrow."

Joseph rolled closer to the bed. "You took her sickness, didn't you? Come here, let me hold you."

"No!" Cady launched herself backwards in the bed, and Joseph jerked forward, thinking she was going to fall over backwards. "Please go, Joseph. I can't deal with you right now." A note of panic was in her voice that Joseph had never heard before.

"Hell!" He was torn – she needed him, despite what she said – but something weird was going on. "I moved my leg, Cady." He couldn't hold back his wonder. When he had thought she needed him, he had actually picked up his leg and sat it on the floor – as if preparing to get out of the chair – pure reflex.

Even though she was incredibly weak, Cady went to him. "That's wonderful, Joseph!" She left the bed and knelt by his chair, running her hands over his jean clad leg. "You picked your foot up, and your calf muscle is flexed." Sitting back on her heels, she gave him the sweetest smile. "I am so proud of you!"

Her face was damp with perspiration; tendrils of her hair were clinging to her temple. Joseph couldn't have stopped himself from touching her if his life depended on it. "You did it, Cady. You are my miracle." Her skin was so soft – she was so sweet, so beautiful – so forgiving.

"No, not me, Joseph; I am no miracle – I am merely a conduit for the power that is available to anyone who has the faith of a mustard seed." She held onto the bed and pushed up, obviously shaky and fragile. "Let me rest, and I promise – tomorrow I will do my best to show you what a miracle truly is." Without looking at him, she lay back down; her back turned toward him. He was dismissed. For a moment, he considered getting into the bed with her – but her stiff little back sent a clear message. He had gone too far - - and he didn't know if he could make up lost ground or not. The truth was - seeing her with Saucier had nearly killed him, but she wasn't ready to hear that and probably wouldn't believe him if he tried.

Leaving her – knowing that she needed him – was the hardest thing he had ever done.

The Next Day

He was fifty-five fuckin' years old and what did he have to show for it? Nothing! Robert Keszey threw his leg over the four-wheeler and started it up. Life wasn't fair – it just wasn't fair. When he was in high school, for a brief period of time, it had seemed that everything would work out for him. He had been a rodeo star and he had the prettiest girl in Texas on his arm. Marian Swann had belonged to him. "Shit!" He was almost out of gas. What else could go wrong? Climbing off, he started back over to his uncle's run-down barn. Looking around, he surveyed his inheritance – all twelve acres of it. It was a crock of piss, that's what it was. Swann property had adjoined his Uncle's and if he could have hung on to Marian, Tebow would have been his – if damn Deke McCoy hadn't moved to Kerrville. Deke had waltzed in and took over. He became the football star, the basketball star – hell he had even been a damn fine bull rider. And Deke had stolen Marian right from under his nose.

After that, everything had gone downhill. Deke had gotten richer and Tebow had gotten bigger. And he had given Marian six boys – boys that should have been his – not McCoy's. Marian and Deke were gone now, but Robert's hatred lived on. Damn that Jacob McCoy! This last insult was the final straw. He had told that stupid idiot of an uncle that there was oil or gas on that scrub land. But did he listen? Hell, no! And now it was in McCoy's hands. The McCoy's had stolen everything he had and it was about to stop. Grabbing the gas can, he started back toward the four-wheeler. The war had just begun. He was going to wreak havoc on the whole McCoy clan. What he was about to do would make the original Hatfield-McCoy feud look like a Sunday picnic.

"Do you really think this outfit looks good on me?" Cady wasn't so sure – there was more of her showing than she thought was wise.

"Cady, you look absolutely stunning – you have the sweetest figure," Jessie was walking around her, checking out the short yellow skirt and white lace top. "And I love your hair. That stylist knew just what to do – look at all of those soft waves. Sexy is not the word."

"And look at her eyes – they are so big and sensual – Cady, I'm jealous!" Libby leaned against the dressing room wall and studied their creation. "You are beautiful. Truly, you are."

"I don't believe a word you're saying, but thanks." Staring at the mirror, Cady could see some improvement, but not the sexpot image they were describing. "What did the doctor say?" She wouldn't have wished harm on Libby for the world, but she was glad of an opportunity to take the focus off of her questionable looks.

A broad smile covered Libby's pretty face. "I'm still in remission, it was just an infection – although who knows what he would have found if you hadn't helped me last night."

Cady just smiled, she didn't know for certain – but the degree of discomfort she had endured after the ritual had felt like more than a mere infection. "That's wonderful – what a relief."

Jessie gathered up the outfits they had selected. "I can't wait until Joseph sees you in these. His eyes are going to bug out of his head. Do you want all of them?"

She was anxious for Joseph to see her too, but not for the same reason. It was her intention to get Joseph McCoy on his feet and get the hell out of Dodge before her heart was so irreparably broken it could never be mend. "Sure, I'll take them. Obviously, I need a new wardrobe." Gathering everything up, she followed the chattering duo out into the crowded department store. Today hadn't been nearly as painful as she imagined, tonight would be a different story.

The calves were playing with each other. Joseph watched them gambole about, bouncing and running at each other in mock war games. Would he ever be able to have that much freedom? The sun glinted off the lake in the distance and then he saw it reflect off of another surface. Someone was on McCoy land! Joseph watched a four-wheeler cut across the pasture. He moved closer to the window. Damn! He couldn't see who it was. The son-of-a-bitch wore a cap, he couldn't even tell what color hair he had. But he wasn't a McCoy that was for sure. This was a small man – all of his brothers were bigger than this man – except Nathan.

God, what he wouldn't give to just get up out of this chair and run out of the house. Wheeling around, Joseph started for the door. Shit! If only he could get around! That healing ritual might have been a good start, but he wasn't cured – not yet, anyway. Damn! The man would be long gone before he could maneuver out into the yard and find someone to go after him. Hell! What had he been doing so close to the house? He had no idea, but he intended to find out.

Making his way outside, Joseph looked all around. The hair on the back of his neck stood up. There was that funny feeling again. Hell, their troubles were supposed to be over. The villain had been captured – or at least they thought he had. But if that were the case, who was the dude who was trespassing this afternoon? All of their hands rode horses or drove three-wheelers. There wasn't a four-wheeler on the property – Aron didn't like them. He said that it was much easier to flip a vehicle with four wheels that one with three. Since Joseph's accident, Aron had insisted that safety be their highest consideration. What the fuck? The barn door was standing open and something small and gray was lying right in the door. Timmy! It was Jacob's cat and he looked dead. Joseph tried to reach down for him, but he couldn't reach down far enough. God, he needed help. "Hey! Can anyone hear me? Hey!" Shit! Fishing his cell phone out of his pocket, Joseph punched in Jacob's number.

"What's wrong?" Jacob asked, quickly.

Knowing what he was thinking, Joseph assured him. "I'm fine. But somebody's been up here at the barn, and I think they've done something to Timmy." Looking around, he saw an open can of tuna fish. Only part of it had been eaten. "It looks like he's been poisoned."

"Is he still alive?" They all kidded Jacob about his cat, but Joseph wouldn't have anything happen to him for the world. Looking at the cat hard, he saw that his sides were still moving – barely.

"He's still breathing. Hurry."

"I'll be right there. I'm only about five hundred yards away, fixing a fence." Jacob assured him.

Joseph moved around Timmy carefully and entered the barn. A funny smell hit his nostrils. What was that odor? Damn, the whole fuckin barn must be on fire! Frustrated, Joseph made his way down to where the horses were shut up in their stalls. They could smell the smoke, too and they were nervous. Unlocking their stall doors, Joseph began to release them. They took off toward the front entrance at a gallup. He hoped, to hell, they didn't step on Timmy. That would be the last straw.

"Where the hell are you?" He could hear Jacob's voice. "My God!" He could hear Jacob calling 9-1-1, and after that, he called Aron.

Joseph made his way deeper into the barn and found a smoldering hay bale. "I found it! Bring the water hose, Jacob! I think we can put it out."

"I've got it, Joseph." Nathan came running in with the hose. "Jacob took off to take Timmy to the vet." He turned the water on the smoldering straw and put out the fire. "Boy, that was close. If you hadn't come out here, this would have caught and burned the whole place down."

"Yea, it was luck. I just happened to be looking out the window and seen someone leaving on a four-wheeler. It looked suspicious, so I came to check it out."

"It looks like our troubles aren't over." Nathan spoke solemnly. "Somebody doesn't like us very much."

"Can you believe somebody set the barn on fire?" Noah looked out over the yard, as if he thought they might have missed a clue or something.

"If Joseph hadn't seen the intruder and gotten a funny feeling, we would have lost Sultan, Paladin, Molly and all the rest." Patting his brother on the back, Jacob thanked him. "You saved the day. And the vet says Timmy is gonna pull through. He has to stay at the animal hospital overnight on an IV, but I think he will make it."

"That's good." Joseph was listening, but his mind was on other things. He had to make things right with Cady – again. All he could think of was how she had looked when he told her that Zane Saucier was perfect for her, because he was blind. Truthfully, he'd rather face half a dozen intruders and barn fires rather than one small woman with big, sad eyes.

"Who could have done this? Do you think it's just a mean kid making mischief?" Noah sat with his feet on the railing, drinking a longneck beer.

"I don't have a clue." Jacob shook his head. "When Kane caught Kevin, I thought that would be the end of this mess. I've racked my brain, but I just don't have an answer."

"I'm headed to Argentina next weekend," Noah announced flatly, trying to move the topic to something more pleasant.

"Bull semen?" Jacob asked dryly.

"Yea, there's a bull down there I want a piece of."

"I'm glad no one else can hear you but us, numb-nuts." Isaac drawled as he walked up behind his brothers. Joseph snorted his amusement as Noah realized what he'd said and how it had sounded.

"Hell, you know what I mean." He shot Isaac the finger. "That bull's genes will add a lot of good blood to our herd."

"How are your legs?" Noah couldn't stand it; he asked Joseph the question everybody was dying to know the answer to, but all were afraid to ask.

Pushing his black Stetson back on his head, he turned his torso sideways in the chair to face them. "Fuckin' fantastic, I can move a little – watch." He moved one booted foot a bare inch or two – the strain evident on his face – but it did move.

"Hot damn!" Jacob breathed like a prayer. "She did it."

"I prayed for you to get better, but I never dreamed their magic would really work." Noah had left his chair and sat on the banister in front of Joseph. "Is everything – uh – waking up?"

"If you mean my cock – no, not yet." Looking off into the distance, Joseph didn't know what to say and what not to say. Finally, he confessed. "Cady said it would, eventually."

Isaac laughed; a low rumble in his chest. "Sounds like Cady has the magic touch, maybe you ought to let her – you know – touch."

Joseph started to throw back a scathing remark, but the rumble of a truck engine drew everyone's attention. A cloud of dust heralded the arrival of Aron's big, double cab dually.

"He's got a full house don't he?" Noah commented dryly, noting he had a truck full of women. "Where's he been?"

Jacob spoke up, "He took Libby to the doctor and the other girls went along as moral support."

"Is Libby all right?" Isaac frowned, this was the first he'd heard about it.

"She's all right. Just an infection," Jacob knew because Jessie had called him as soon as the word had come down.

"I bet Aron is relieved." Joseph was too. There had been enough sickness and despair in this family to last a lifetime. It was time for good things to happen to them all.

"Good God! Who is that woman with them? Damn! She's hot!" Isaac stood with his mouth open.

Noah whistled, "Fresh meat, baby."

Joseph narrowed his eyes – "Lord Have Mercy!" That was Cady. His Cady.

"Hey, Joseph – isn't that . . .?" Noah was looking at his brother, amused at Joseph's thundercloud expression. Three of the ranch hands had miraculously appeared to help Cady with her bags.

God, she looked like a dream. Her skirt was barely long enough to cover paradise and those tanned, firm legs were a mile long. And her face – holy fuckin shit – without the glasses her eyes were huge and he wanted to pull her close and drown in them. Libby said something and she laughed – and Lord help him, but he thought his heart would stop. Lance Rogers was walking far too close and when they got within earshot he could hear, "I sure would like to take you to dinner tomorrow night." Instantly Cady's eyes collided with Joseph's and he held his breath, waiting to see what she would say.

She was being asked out on a date! Cady held her breath waiting for the thrill to come - - but it didn't. And the answer was simple – it was the wrong man popping the question. "Thank you, Lance. How kind of you, but Joseph and I have some intense therapy to get through - but I appreciate being asked more than I can say." With a kind smile, she shook his hand solemnly. "Joseph, are you ready?" Without a backward glance, she headed in to finish this deal or die trying.

"If you don't make a move on her, I will," Isaac warned. He didn't mean it – for some ungodly reason he was still hung up on sweet, innocent Avery – but Joseph needed a kick in the balls to aim him in the right direction.

"If you want to live to see your next birthday – you'll keep your big mitts off my woman."

Isaac snorted his approval, "Your woman, huh? Well, you'd best get busy – or the real McCoy will have to show you how it's done." Joseph shot him the bird, before following Cady into the house.

"You look incredible," Joseph didn't beat around the bush. He was half undressed and more than ready for whatever she had in store for him – the only thing missing was a hard dick.

"Thank you," Cady tried to ignore the thrill his words gave her. He didn't mean them – but at least she knew she looked her best. "Today, we're going to put you through the paces, so don't take off any more clothes – not yet, anyway. After that, I'll massage you with some healing herbs."

"Paying me back with torture, huh?" Joseph was afraid of that. He deserved anything she could dish out. And dish it out she did. She wasn't kidding, she put him through the ringer – working his muscles – stretching – exercising. By the time they were through, they were both covered in a fine sheen of sweat. The heartening thing, however, was the fact that he could stand – not very long – but, stand he did, holding on to the rails. "That's marvelous!" she praised him. Cady felt like she had been awarded a gold medal. Joseph was going to be all right.

Joseph couldn't believe it; he was standing up – actually standing up. Not walking – but at least he was able to put some weight on his legs – and shit, they hurt like hell!

"You're hurting, aren't you?"

"You don't have to smile about it."

"But, it's wonderful – come on. Let's get you on the bed and let me massage those muscles." She hadn't told him yet – but if he would let her – there was one muscle she intended to give a thorough working over. Damn! Her voice shook – it actually shook. This was going to be one of the hardest things she had ever done. With God's help, she would be able to do it without making an utter fool out of herself. But the thought of touching that part of him was absolutely intoxicating.

He let her help him to the bed. She smelled heavenly – the heat of their workout activated the body wash she used. And he couldn't keep his eyes off of her tits. The top she wore accentuated their lushness and he had no trouble remembering how the hard, succulent nipples had tasted in his mouth. "How do you want me?"

Cady almost laughed out loud. How did she want him? Anyway she could get him. "On your tummy first, please." She picked up her heavy skein of hair and let the cool air rush over her neck. 'God give me strength,' she prayed. She stood by the bed and watched him settle in, the muscles of his back rippling, causing her breath to catch in her throat. "Joseph," how did one say this with a straight face? "Today, if you'll allow me, I'm going to try and make you hard."

Instantly, he jerked under her hands. All he was able to do was groan.

Cady closed her eyes tightly and made herself speak, slowly. "I know how you feel about me and let me assure you that this is necessary. I wouldn't do it, if I didn't feel like it had to be done. Okay?" Joseph started to turn over, but she placed a hand in the middle of his back. "Let me loosen up your muscles, first. You are very tense." She called on every ounce of professionalism she had. She could do this. And it wouldn't mean a thing – except to her.

Joseph closed his eyes in prayer. "You don't know a damn thing, Cady." But, he wasn't going to elaborate. There was no use declaring his interest in her if all he could offer her was a limp dick and a promise. But if her magick worked – then he planned on making some magic of his own.

She chose to ignore his sarcastic remark. Somehow, his scathing words made it all easier. Taking some oil in her hands, she warmed it and began soothing it over the wide shoulders, the bulging biceps – the smooth tanned back that looked capable of bearing the weight of her world. "You have made remarkable progress. I'm so proud of you." Knowing their time together was drawing to an end, she grew a bit reckless. "I've dreamed about you, you know. Even before we met – I felt a connection to you – a mysterious bond that seemed to transcend time and space."

Despite his anticipation of what was about to happen, Cady's hands were making him feel relaxed and, almost normal. He could feel tingles in his legs and a slight twitching in his balls – but that might be his imagination. What was she saying? Dreams? That woke him up. "You've dreamed about me?" The fact that she so closely resembled his midnight goddess made her admission doubly outstanding.

"Yes, I have. Let's turn you over." When he was on his back, she began at his feet – rubbing them, working the toes and the ankles. She could feel him looking at her, and when she gave into temptation and glanced at his face, his eyes were hooded and intense – he almost looked aroused. Yeah – like she would recognize the look. Her hands moved up his legs – molding the muscles and kneading the flesh. As she worked, she repeated the healing chant in her head – willing strength, sensation and movement back into every nerve cell and fiber of his being.

"I've had some strange dreams, lately." His mind was so turned on – his body had to follow – it just had to. "I want you to touch me," Joseph spoke quietly. "I've dreamed of your hands on my cock," his words were heated and low. "I just hope to God I can feel them." He had refrained from touching himself – he was too afraid he would feel nothing.

Biting her lip, she began to work on his thighs – the sight of that miniscule washrag covering his manhood was tempting her beyond measure. "All right, let's give this a go. It would probably be best if you shut your eyes. I won't be so nervous – and remember – I'm not experienced at this." She lifted the rag.

Then she laughed out loud which caused Joseph to snort, "What's so damn funny?" It was never a good thing for a woman to laugh when she looked at your cock. He knew she wasn't being cruel – it wasn't in Cady to be so.

Twirling the rag on her finger, she explained. "When I was telling you I wasn't experienced, I almost added – 'so don't expect a miracle'. Then I realized that is exactly what we're expecting – a miracle."

Oh My God! She finally had her hands on Joseph's cock. In order to get the best angle, she had straddled his thighs – her skirt riding high. She had instructed Joseph to close his eyes. Not that it would help, magically, but he would be able to concentrate on whatever sensation he was feeling and more importantly, he wouldn't be watching her face. She didn't want him to see the longing that would be reflected there.

Wrapping her right hand around his flaccid shaft, she began massaging it, rubbing her thumb up and down – milking it between her fingers. Even in its unaroused state, it was more than a handful. As she worked his organ, she repeated in her head – over and over – 'I ask for healing. I ask for strength. I ask that this man's body once more react to the desires of his mind and his heart.' With her left hand, she cupped his sac, working the balls between her fingers, she sought to awaken the nerves, the synapses, the cells to respond to the directions of the brain – to come alive – to produce the seed that announces rapture, yet gives life. Cady's breath was coming in hard pants and even though she was fighting to control it, her body was on fire and it was all she could do to keep her body still – she wanted to rock on Joseph's thighs – feel the friction of his skin rubbing against her pussy.

He once read that the brain was the major sex organ, but he never believed it until now. It was all he could to keep from reaching for her – watching her little face as she gave him a hand-job was something he would never forget. And desire? Desire for her was raging through his body – his nipples were stiff, his heart was racing, his temperature rising and his cock wanted to be buried deep inside her. Joseph groaned. Realization slapped him between the eyes. Hell! He could feel. Damn! He could feel her fingers on his cock - - he could feel her rubbing his balls! "Cady!" Joseph rose up suddenly, took Cady by the shoulders, and pulled her forward for a heated kiss.

One moment she was totally absorbed in manipulating Joseph's organ – the next, her mouth was being devoured by the man of her dreams. "Wait. . . ." she managed to say between bites of his lips.

"God, no," he groaned. He sucked at her lips. "No waiting. No more waiting." He was turned on – gloriously aroused – and his cock was filling up, growing – getting hard. Glory Hallelujah! "You are a fuckin' miracle – did you know that? I can feel, baby!" He cupped her head and gazed into those beautiful eyes. "Do you know what that means?" Not waiting for an answer, he swooped down and captured her mouth again. For a few seconds, she just accepted his kiss. His tongue coaxed at her lips, probing – seeking entrance. Finally with a little heart-catching sigh she opened her mouth and let him in.

Bliss. Absolute bliss. Every dream she ever had of being wanted and desired seemed to be within her grasp – but it was a mirage, she understood that. But at this moment - - this miraculous moment - - Joseph wanted her. Obviously, it was because she was the only female around – handy – but that didn't really matter – not at this glorious moment.

"I need you. Please." Joseph begged. He was erect, ready and he needed to fuck. He needed to feel like a man again. God – he had to feel like a man again. "Make love with me, Cady. I've got to have you. Now!" His voice growled with uninhibited need.

"Okay," she whispered. "I'll make love with you, Joseph. Once." Only once, that was all her heart could stand. Joseph was going to be all right, and it was time for her to go home.

"Take off your clothes, beautiful. I want you so much." He was helping her unbutton as he cajoled and persuaded. His hands literally shook with need. It had been months since he had made love and – to be honest – he hadn't held out much hope he ever would again. And now – now he had a hard on between his legs and a beautiful woman in his arms and – by God – life was worth living again. "Lord, you're pretty." Her skin was so warm and smooth – and the color was exquisite. Parting her blouse, he unveiled a pink lacy bra that was almost see-through – her swollen nipples made his mouth water. He couldn't wait to get them in his mouth. "Do you know what the sight of your tits does to me?"

"Could we not talk, please?" Joseph was a master seducer, and he was following a script that he had probably used a million times, and she couldn't bear the thought of just being a much needed dress rehearsal for his next big performance. "I mean, you can tell me what to do. But don't say nice things to me. Okay?"

Joseph was too far gone to argue. "Take off your bra," he growled and she instantly obeyed, while he clasped the top of her panties in both hands and literally just pulled them apart. "I'll replace them." Voraciously, he opened his lips and sucked her nipple and areola deep into his mouth, making deep groans of appreciation as he feasted on her soft flesh. His right hand rubbed her slit, spreading the juice from stem to stern, making her buck on his hand. "God, you're wet. Mount me, Cady. Please."

How could she deny them both what they wanted? "All right, Joseph. But this is therapy for you." She wanted it too, more than she could ever imagine. Lifting her hips she took his wondrously stiff cock in her hand and began to fit herself over it. "Remember, I've never done this before, so don't expect much." Strong hands stopped her downward descent.

"I want you like crazy, but I don't want to hurt you," he spoke through clenched teeth.

She put one of her hands on each of his and pushed. "No, it's all right. You won't hurt me," she met his eyes – he had the most beautiful face – every time she looked at it she was stunned. "I've used tampons and dildos – I'm just a technical virgin – no virginal barrier. I promise." She couldn't help it – as happy as she was – as aroused as she was – this was probably the saddest thing she had ever done. Cady Renaud was making love for the first time and last time with the man she loved – and he didn't love her.

Lord, what had he done to her? She looked like she was about to cry. A moment like this should be precious and special for her, and he was making a helluva mess out of it. "God, I need you – but. . . ." Suddenly, his words – thought – breath – reason – all was stolen from him when Cady began to take him into her body. Fuck! Heaven! Rapture washed over him as he once again felt his cock being enveloped in hot, wet female flesh. His hips automatically pushed upward, seeking to embed himself just as deep in paradise as he could. Cady winced, but pushed back against him. "Sorry, baby – it feels so damn good."

Placing her arms on his shoulders, she held him still, as best as she could. "It might be wise if you let me do the work." He was on the mend, but there was no use risking an injury. Looking at his face, she could easily see how much he was enjoying being inside of her and how necessary this was to his whole recovery and mental attitude. Joseph needed to feel like a man – and she was the only woman within reach. He stilled – and Cady let herself be aware of how her body felt being stretched and filled with her soul mate – because that was what he was. True, something had went awry in the grand scheme of things, she was born lacking what was necessary to please the man who had been created just for her. And that was the biggest tragedy of all. Ripples of pleasure sparkled from her vagina. "Joseph," she whimpered.

"Jesus!" God, he thought he might pass out from the absolute rightness and ecstasy of being inside Cady Renaud. "You are so damn tight!" He wanted to buck up into her. Cady's wet heat provided a snug, haven for his starving cock. And then she stole his fuckin' breath away. . . . . . she began to move. "Damn, baby!" Her body began to gently rock on top of his. When she reached for his hands, he grasped hers and held on tight. She had her eyes closed and her expression was one of beatific wonder. Instinctively, she just knew what to do – the muscles of her vagina began caressing him – undulating around him like a massaging glove.

Cady couldn't think – she could only feel – and it was heaven. She was making love! No, she corrected herself – she was having sex. Waves of bliss flamed up from her vagina – God, it felt wonderful. Rising up on her knees a few inches, she slid up and down his pole – careful not to jar his body.

She was caressing his cock, loving it – massaging it within her velvet channel. Joseph laid back and let his body revel in the sweet reality of being balls deep in a woman again. She was holding his fingers tight, letting her little body rise and fall, rock back and forth – every move specifically designed to drive him fuckin' insane. "That's it baby – ride me – make yourself feel good."

It did feel good – too good. She was going to cum. This hadn't happened to Cady very often, but she had experienced it once or twice. And it couldn't happen now . . . . . if it did she would be lost. Sharing an orgasm with this man would be something that would stay in her mind and heart forever – and that she would never survive. So, she fought her feelings – determined to give him pleasure yet deny herself the ultimate joy. Focusing on pleasing Joseph, Cady bit her lip as hard as she could – trying to distract her body from the building sensual onslaught that was threatening to overtake her whole being.

"That's it doll, you cum first." She was trembling, and making sexy little noises. God, she turned him on! He had enjoyed sex with countless beautiful women – but this one – this little doll was screwing him six ways to Sunday. He had never felt more perfect muscle control as she milked his dick with her throbbing little pussy. He closed his eyes and just enjoyed it - - his excitement building - - his balls swelling - - the passion boiling up inside of him. He wasn't going to be able to hold back much longer. A fever of molten delight began to rise in his loins - - God, he was about to erupt! This wasn't like him. Joseph prided himself in his ability to ensure the women he bedded were satisfied – several times. But – it had been too long. He was too desperate for release; too desperate to prove to himself he was still a man. He couldn't stop it - - he couldn't hold back. With a deep guttural growl of completion – Joseph achieved that mountain top release he thought was no longer in his grasp. Throwing his head back and groaning – loudly – he arched his back and shot his seed up into Cady's welcoming sanctuary. His cock throbbed its joy – relishing the clasp of her tender flesh fitting so tightly around him. Slowly, he became aware that she was saying something . . .

"No, no, no, no," and even though she was moving her body in all the right ways, she was trying to deny herself pleasure. "I don't want to cum. I can't cum. No, no, no."

"Cady?" Joseph let go of her hands and reached for her. Avoiding his touch, she eased up and off of his shaft. It was as if she had awakened from a trance. She was shivering and flushed, obviously sexually excited. Lifting herself off of him, she carefully got up from the bed and, hesitantly, met his gaze. "What's going on? You gave me an incredible release. Why wouldn't you take yours?"

"It's not important," she looked around, frantically, for her clothes. "You were able to perform – perfectly." Pulling on her skirt, and shrugging into her blouse, she looked like she wanted to be anywhere rather than with him. "We don't lack too much rehab – in fact, a few more days and you will be able to get another therapist." She turned to go.

"Do Not Walk Away From Me." Joseph was emphatic. He had just made love with the sexiest woman in the world and he wasn't about to let the moment end like this. "We have things to clear up – I need to make you understand."

"I understand – perfectly." She couldn't bear to hear any more of his quips. "Rest for a few minutes, I'm going to take a shower – then we'll see where we stand." *Please let me get out of here; just let me get out of here.*

To Joseph's amazement, she was walking away – from him. "Not so fast." He didn't know if he could do it, but he was going to damn sure try.

Cady turned, anxious to get out of the room…. She heard him fall.

"Hell!"

"God, no." All thought for herself fled Cady's mind. Turning, she wheeled to find him on the floor – but he had miraculously made it about ten feet before faltering. He was down, but not flat – he was kneeling on the workout mat, his legs obviously supporting his weight. "Are you all right?" She was at his side in seconds, her hands moving over his shoulders and back. "Are you hurting?"

"You better damn well know I'm hurting – my pride most of all."

In a move that made her head swim, Joseph had her flat on her back in seconds. "Joseph!"

"Now, I've got you." He covered her body with his, from head to toe. Still nude, he appreciated the fact that her blouse was undone and her breasts gloriously unbound. She held up her hands as if to fend him off, and he easily captured them and held both arms over her head. Leaning on one elbow, he supported his weight enough so as not to crush her – but he had her – down and out for the count. "Now, what was all of that nonsense before? Why did you hold back when we made love?" He searched her face, noting the uncertainty, self-doubt and sorrow that colored her features.

Was he serious? Did he not know? "I didn't want it to be good for me. I may never get the opportunity to experience something like this ever again, and I didn't want to know what I was missing, it would hurt too much. Remember, just yesterday, you said a blind man was perfect for me – because he wouldn't have to look at me when we had sex. Yet, it was me you had to settle for the first time you were able to make love again. I can just imagine how hard it was for you." Tears were threatening to well up in her eyes. Why did she have to love him so much? At this proximity she could see deep into his eyes – there was the sexiest sunburst around his dark pupil – the scruff of his beard was appealing – God, even his breath was sweet. "Let me go," she begged. "You know I'm not going to struggle, I don't want to injure you."

"I'm not about to let you go - not this time," he whispered as he rubbed his nose on her cheek. "I didn't

settle, right now, you are exactly who I want." Cady tried to ease from his embrace, but he settled more firmly on top of her. "You are so soft." Her breathing was rapid and he could feel every intake of air – her tits were molding themselves to his chest with every movement.
Miraculously, he felt his cock began to rise. "God, you are a miracle worker, baby. I want you, again – so much."

"Remember, only a blind man would want to make love with me. That's not desire you're feeling, Joseph. It's gratitude." She licked her lips, fighting the urge to kiss his cheek.

"The hell it is, I know desire when I feel it," Joseph grumbled. "Cady, do you know why I said those awful things to you?" Unable to stop himself, he began kissing her face, letting his lips trail over the beautiful features, the sexy contours, the silken skin. "I was suffering from a fit of puredee black jealousy, baby. Seeing you laughing and smiling with Zane turned me pea green with envy."

"Jealous?" She said the word as if the concept was foreign to her. "You were jealous – of me?" Disbelief was evident on her face and in her voice.

"God, yes. I knew that Zane could offer you something I couldn't. He might be blind, but he's all man with a cock that works." He wanted to explain everything to her – and he would. But right now, he wanted something else. Her. "But you have given me back my life, Cady. And my parts are all in working order, thanks to you. I need you, babe. And this time, I want you to love me back."

Every part of Cady Renaud went femininely soft at his masculine demand. "Joseph. . ." she wanted to protest, but she couldn't.

"Shhhhh – open up for me, butterfly. Spread your wings, I can't wait to be inside of you, again." Joseph was engorged and pulsing with pure lust. As he felt her body moving to accommodate him, Joseph could have shouted for joy.

"Are you in any pain?" She couldn't help, but ask.

"Quit worrying," he protested as he lifted himself up a scant inch to allow her to open her legs wide enough for him to be cradled in the valley of her thighs. "You're always pestering me to exercise –I'm just doing what I'm told." His wry comment made Cady smile, which was just what he wanted. She was beautiful when she smiled. "You get more beautiful every day. How do you do that?"

An odd feeling of destiny settled on her spirit – her grandmother's prophetic words echoed through her mind. "Magic?" she offered, hesitantly, with a slight laugh.

"I can believe that," Joseph couldn't wait another moment. "I'm going to kiss you, now," he warned her as he slowly lowered his head until their lips were just touching. They had kissed before, but it had been nothing like this. This time was real. He took her lips tenderly, fitting hers in between his, caressing and nibbling. And bless her heart, she responded. She tugged on her hands to get loose and he let go, and her arms went around his neck, her fingers sliding in his hair, as if to hold him in place. Tentatively, her tongue slipped out to gain entrance to his mouth. With a groan, Joseph met her advance and opened his lips to welcome her home. They kissed wildly, devouring one another – their tongues tangling, sliding together in a feast of tactile sensation.

Through their slight movements, his cock found itself nestled between her labia lips. And, lord-in-heaven, his dick was being bathed in her passion. Pulling back for a breath, he took a moment to take in her beauty. She was gorgeous – her lips were wet from his kiss – her eyes were shining with excitement and her nipples were poking at his chest with every breath she took. "I need to be inside you, Cady. Am I welcome?"

"You are welcome," and she repeated her invitation by spreading her legs wider and lifting her hips.

Placing both palms on the floor, he levered himself up and let his shaft prod at her tenderness until he could slip inside the sweetest place he had ever been. "Oh honey, baby," he groaned, biting his lower lip and rolling his head from side to side in absolute ecstasy. "There is nothing in the universe better than this – nothing."

Cady thought she would have to agree. Before, she had been so intent on not cumming that she hadn't let herself enjoy the miracle of being possessed and pleasured by Joseph McCoy. He was pumping his hips, thrusting his manhood into her – deep, sure strokes that made her molten center pulse and throb. In and out, grunting and pressing into her – hard – over and over again. Cady was lifted and pushed with each ramming motion of his body. It was an amazing feeling. She belonged; Cady belonged to Joseph. He had claimed her - the very thought tossed her whole body into a maelstrom of wanting. Lord, she wanted to clasp her legs around his waist and hold tight – but she was afraid that might be more weight than his back could stand. So, she lifted her pelvis, meeting each motion of his body with one of her own. Together, they set a rhythm that sent heat racing toward her core – causing spasms to begin deep within that felt like mini-earthquakes of rapture. "Joseph, my God – I never knew – I never knew." And when they came – they came together.

Chapter Eight

Joseph rolled off of Cady and rested breathlessly on the mat. Laughing out loud with complete and total jubilation, he announced, "You are fuckin' magnificent!" Turning back to her, he placed a hand in her middle, as if to anchor her down. "You've given me my life back. Did you know that?" He kissed the side of her face tenderly.

Placing her hand on his chest, she reveled in the moment. "I'm glad." Her body was still quaking with tiny sensual aftershocks. "That's what I came to do. You are making marvelous progress. It won't be long, now. You won't even need me."

With ease and a dexterity that surprised them both, Joseph threw one leg over both of hers. "You aren't going anywhere. I need you – more than you will ever know."

"You can get another physical therapist, one that will just come in, periodically. I can recommend one for you."

Growling, Joseph bit her ear lobe – making her squeal softly. "That's not what I'm talking about. I need more lovin' from you – what we just shared was incredible and I'm not ready for it to end – not yet."

"It wasn't me that made it fantastic. Don't you think it was because you were hungry for sex – like a starving man's first meal?" Cady wasn't judging; she was being honest.

Joseph took her chin in his hand, to make sure she was looking straight at him. "I don't think I'm that shallow, Cady. I know what I'm feeling."

Cady was silent. She wanted to believe him.

"Will you stay? Will you let me love you for a little while?"

The 'little while' was what she was worried about. But before she could talk herself out of it – Cady's heart answered for her. "Yes. While I am here, until we have you

177

up and walking, it would make me very happy to share your bed."

"Come on, Cady. Joseph will be fine. We want you to go to the spa with us." Jessie pulled on Cady's arm. "If we have to suffer through a Brazilian wax job, so do you." Cady almost died.

Joseph sent her a wicked grin. Since they had made love the night before, Joseph hadn't been able to think about anything else. He couldn't wait to get his hands on her, again. Turning their exercise regimes into erotic wrestling sessions sounded like a good idea to him.

"All right." Cady huffed. Before she was dragged from the room, she went to Joseph's chair and bent down. "I know you want to show off for your family – but do not try and walk by yourself until I get back."

"Yes, dear." With a snort, he pulled her down for a kiss right in front of the other two girls.

"Whoot! Whoot!" Libby couldn't resist. Pumping her little fist in the air, she was happy with what she saw. "Atta boy, Joseph!"

"Look at him," Jessie teased. "He's blushing."

"You two troublemakers get outta here, while I give my woman some sugar."

Cady blushed from the tip of her toes to her hairline. "Joseph!" She couldn't believe that he had called her his woman.

"Come on!" Jessie tugged on her shirt. "We're gonna be late! You two can smooch, later."

Joseph watched them leave. Funny, he just realized that Cady was the prettiest of the three women. When had that happened? Her face was classically beautiful – high cheekbones, wide-set dark eyes and a luscious mouth. And her body was perfectly proportioned – a sweet hourglass figure that set his heart to pounding. Jessie and Libby were stunning – but Cady was drop-dead gorgeous.

Hearing voices from the den, Joseph maneuvered his chair into the room that served as the center of all macho related activity in the McCoy household. The door was ajar and he could hear his brothers' voices as they discussed the latest problems with the wire-cutting vandal who had been plaguing the area ranchers. "I think we need to set up some cameras and see if we can catch any suspicious activity out on the farm-to-market road." Isaac offered as he sipped on a shot of rum and coke. "Do you think it's the same idiot that set the barn on fire?"

"That's my gut feeling. The cameras could work, I guess." Aron mulled over the suggestion. "But, it would be hit-or-miss, that's a five mile stretch – we'd need a dozen cameras to cover that amount of distance."

Jacob, always the voice of reason, stood by the fireplace and watched Nathan play with the new puppy that Isaac had picked up on the side of the road. Isaac had a soft heart for strays – he was always giving away hamburgers to passer-bys who were down on their luck – and had brought home countless animals over the years. "Yea, and we need some type of surveillance here at the ranch, too. In addition to the cameras, maybe we ought to set up a patrol; have some of the guys make rounds every hour on the hour."

"That would work," Noah interjected. "We need to do something. It's just a matter of time before somebody wrecks and kills themselves, and some of our herd to boot. All we need is a lawsuit hanging over our heads."

"I think we ought to invest in electric fencing; that would give him a shock." Joseph stated calmly, waiting for them to notice he had entered the room. He couldn't hold it back – the smile on his face was from ear to ear.

"Why are you such a grinning fool?" Aron asked grumpily. He wasn't in the best of humor – not with the vandalism and Libby's recent health scare. Lord, he would be glad when that baby was born. That thought brought a slight smile to his face.

"I'm back." That was all Joseph said.

"Back from where?" Isaac asked - a perplexed frown on his face.

"Back from the dead, dick head – what do you think?" Noah whopped Isaac on the back of the head. He might be younger, but he had more on the ball upstairs, usually.

"Oh – you mean you can walk." Isaac said it off-handedly – like it was no big deal. And then it hit him - - - **"You mean you can walk?!?"**

Every eye was trained on him as Joseph grasped the arms of the wheelchair and stood – slowly. He wasn't the steadiest thing in cowboy boots and he didn't let go of the arms of the chair – but he did stand on his own two feet. "See?"

All of the McCoys came to him. Aron wiped his eyes. Jacob patted him on the back. Isaac and Noah shook his hand and Nathan hugged him tight around the waist. Joseph cleared his throat, "Nathan, would you go get me a glass of water."

"Sure thing," he took off to the kitchen.

As soon as he was out of the room, Joseph grinned. "That ain't all I can do."

There was silence in the room and then Isaac snickered. "You can get a boner, can't you? Hot Damn! Congratulations!"

"Hell, yeah!" Noah shouted.

"That's fuckin great man," Aron patted Joseph on the back, careful not to overbalance him.

"So, Cady fixed you up, didn't she?" Jacob asked in all innocence.

It was perfectly normal for the McCoy brothers to razz each other about their sexual exploits. Aron and Jacob had become more reticent since becoming involved with Libby and Jessie, and Joseph hadn't really understood their reluctance to discuss intimate details about their current relationships. Now he did. "I owe Cady everything, so don't even go there." Protective – that's what he felt. Protective and possessive.

"If that little girl has you back on your feet, she will always have my eternal gratitude, no matter what her methods are."

"I didn't mean nothing disrespectful," Isaac apologized seeing his brother's discomfiture.

What was he doing? Joseph looked at his brothers. They loved him. They only wanted the best for him. His body worked again – thankfully – and Cady was responsible. And he didn't care who knew it – or who knew what he felt for her. "It's okay. Look, we're involved and it's complicated. It's not forever, but – for right now – she's what I need."

"I hope you work things out, man. God, it's good to see you on your feet again." Jacob slapped Joseph on the back – not hard, but enough so that it seemed like old times in the McCoy man cave.

He had to be careful. Keszy sat and plotted his next move. It had been easier when that other guy had been around making mischief. As long as the doctor had been vandalizing Tebow property and butchering cattle, anything he had done had been laid at the other man's feet. But now that he was in custody – Keszy had to be more careful and more creative. The barn fire hadn't gone off as planned. The cripple brother had spotted him – or so he had heard at the bar. Going to the biker boy's hang out had given him other ideas – it was time he branched out. The McCoy brothers had other interests than just the ranch. There was a lot of places he could cause problems – all he needed was a little patience.

"Come on, you can do it. Just three more reps and we're through for the day," Cady steadied him from the back, taking the opportunity to enjoy the play of his muscles under his skin. "You are doing so well. I am so proud of you." As he held on to the rails, raising and lowering himself, working the muscles in his lower back and upper thighs, Cady sent up a prayer of thanksgiving for the miracle of his recovery. "Perfect." She playfully planted a kiss on his shoulder and whooshed out a surprised grunt when Joseph grabbed her by the arm and pulled her around in front of him.

"God, I want you." Moving her hair to one side, Joseph began kissing her neck. "See what you do to me," he took her hand and pushed it down between their bodies and let her feel his engorged cock. As she palmed it, he pushed it deeper into the cup of her hand.

Cady knew what she wanted to do. "Go sit on the bed. I want to kiss you."

Joseph slid his mouth up her soft throat to intercept her mouth. "I'll kiss you here."

She opened her mouth, gladly accepting his butterfly caress; rubbing her tongue against his while she cupped his jaw. Gradually, she pulled back, "Don't get me wrong – I love to kiss you. But that's not exactly what I had in mind."

"God, yes – if you're talking about what I think you're talking about." Joseph took it slow; walking to the bed in measured steps - when what he wanted to do was vault over the furniture.

"Wait, a second – stand still and hold on to my shoulders." She went to her knees in front of him and began pulling down the burnt orange Longhorn lounge pants. Cady was shocked to find that he didn't have on a stitch of underwear. "My goodness!" she laughed. He was already aroused and ready for her attention. "Look at you!"

"I have to say that of all the awards and races I've won – being here with you, like this, is a helluva lot better."

He sounded agreeable to her trying out her unskilled seduction on him, but she had to be sure. "Are you sure this is okay with you – that I take you in my mouth?"

He sank down on the bed, took her by the shoulders and pulled her close enough that he could bury his face in her neck. "Is it okay with me? Baby, I'm beggin' you to give me that pleasure – that incredible gift." Seeking her tender flesh with his tongue, Joseph kissed a path that led, ultimately, to her lips.

Pulling back, she looked into his face, reassuring herself that this was what he really wanted. What she saw made all the difference – Joseph was looking at her like she was the most beautiful, desirable woman in the world. And at that moment – she was. Moving between his spread legs, Cady allowed herself to enjoy this unique experience. She moved her palms lightly up his legs – and was surprised when that small gesture produced a groan of excitement from him. Encouraged by that response, she smiled and granted herself freedom with a man's body for the first time.

Joseph was enchanted. Cady began kissing his thigh, running her hands up the outside of his legs and when her lips reached his cock – she placed an open mouth kiss right at the base – the root of his cock - then licked a path up his rod that sent tingles down the length of his spine. His whole cock bobbed in appreciation and Cady giggled. "I think he likes me."

"Hell yeah, he likes you." Joseph growled. "Take me in your mouth, honey. Please?" One last glance at his expectant, handsome face gave her the courage she needed to proceed. Grasping his hard shaft, she slid her hand upward, squeezing gently. This garnered her a moan and a tightening of Joseph's leg muscles. He placed his hands on the bed on either side of him and pushed his cock upward toward her face. Emboldened, Cady pumped her hand up and down his shaft and then opened her mouth and took him in. The head of his dick was large – like a big, juicy, purple plum and she sucked on it greedily and if there had been any doubt in her mind that Joseph wanted this – it was dispelled. "God, baby!" he exclaimed. "Oh yeah – that feels so damn good. Fuckin' paradise!"

Thrilled at his praise, Cady doubled her efforts. She held his staff at the base and took as much in her mouth as she could – tightening her lips around his sizable girth. Sucking for a few moments, she let go, moving her tongue up and down his length, lapping and soothing as she went.

Surprised by the taste and texture, she concentrated on the enjoyment she was experiencing by giving him this pleasure. And it was obvious he was getting off on her unschooled technique. "More – God, please, more," he chanted. "Cady – my Cady," he pushed her hair over her shoulder, caressed her face – cupped the back of her head – all encouraging touches that proved he was grateful for the attention she was giving him.

Joseph couldn't get over how good it felt. It wasn't the most professional blowjob he had ever received – but it was, by far, the most precious. Cady was loving him – there was no term that could better describe the way she was treating his cock. "Play with my balls, baby," he encouraged and she instantly complied, rolling them between her fingers and massaging the sensitive globes.

His testicles seemed to tighten in her fingers and Joseph increased the motion of his hips until he was fucking her face, her hair twined around his hand. If someone had asked Cady how she would react to being controlled and used in this manner, she would have said she wouldn't like it – but she would have been wrong. Cady gloried in the act – the fact that she could please Joseph made her feel more feminine and powerful than anything ever had. "Tighter, baby – deeper," he commanded. "God – I'm cumming!" he shouted and he bucked and groaned and jets of hot, liquid cum shot to the back of her throat. Cady fought the gag reflex – she didn't want to disappoint him in any way. Instead, she swallowed – and when he was through, she lovingly licked him clean.

And Joseph – he fell back on the bed – exhausted, but more satisfied than he could ever remember being.

"Beau's here to see you." Noah knocked on the therapy room door and Cady nearly jumped out of her skin.

"I didn't think to lock the door," she whispered.

Joseph chuckled. "It's all right love." He sat up and jerked the bedspread over his nakedness before Noah opened the door and barged in. "Just a sec, bro. I'm not decent!" He knew that Noah would know exactly what was going on because they hadn't been shy around one another since they got out of diapers. Cady wiped her mouth and tried to straighten her hair, which was sexily disheveled. "Come here, baby." He laughed out loud at her blush and pulled her close for a quick kiss. "You are so sweet – you swallowed every drop didn't you? Let's straighten your hair." Joseph finger combed the thick strands.

"Who's Beau?" she asked as she luxuriated in the unaccustomed attention.

"He's my best friend. Apparently he's back from Cuba – I knew he would be here the moment he set foot back in the states. Beau was hunting crocodile. He's planning on adding them to his alligator farm over near Breaux Bridge." Joseph framed Cady's face. "Thank you, love. That was unbelievable – and I will return the favor." Noah beat on the door again. "Come in!" Joseph yelled and Cady quickly rose and put distance between herself and the bed before Noah entered.

Noah had a shit-eating grin on his face. "Whatchadoin?"

"Nothing that's any of your damn business, boy." Joseph chunked a roll of towel paper at his brother. "Tell Beau to come on back. I want him to meet Cady."

Noah disappeared and Cady looked at Joseph, nervously. "Meet me? Why would you want him to meet me?"

"Because he's important to me and so are you," he stated flatly and simply as if no more explanation was necessary.

A loud, boisterous, jolly laugh echoed down the hall. "Beaucoup, Podna!" The door suddenly filled up with a big, handsome man who looked like he had never had a sad thought in his life. "T-Jo, I turn my back and you hurt yourself. I told you not to fooyay with dat motorbike. You need to come catch gators with me."

Joseph stood, carefully, and the two men embraced. "I am damn glad to see you, you ugly Coonass."

Beau stood back and whistled. "I glad to see you standing on your own two feet, for true. What you been doin with yourself? I bet you just gumbo, go-go and do-do."

"Merci, my friend. But, you aren't nearly as glad as I am." Joseph held out his hand to Cady. "Beau LeBlanc, this is my lady – Acadia Renaud. Cady is the reason that I am walking again."

"Ca c'est bon – that is good." Beau took Cady's hand and kissed it. "Cher, did you conja de boy?"

"Aucun, no bad gris-gris." The Cajun dialect was as familiar to her as her own backyard.

"So, all he does is eat, make love and sleep?" She translated, correctly, the slang terms gumbo, go-go and do-do.

"Cady is from New Orleans, Beau." Joseph was about to point out what the two had in common.

"I am familiar with the Renaud family, T-Jo." Beau assured him. "You were most fortunate to make her acquaintance."

Joseph wouldn't argue with that statement. "I was blessed, Beau. The day I met Cady was the most fortunate day of my life." He reached for the single crutch that now took the place of the cumbersome wheelchair. "Let's go get a cup of coffee. I'm ready to see the last of this rehab room – I hope to turn it into a pool hall or something."

Cady followed the two handsome men into the kitchen where Jacob and Aron sat at the table and Libby and Jessie were about to put supper on the table. "Looks like you're in time for more than coffee." Joseph pulled out Cady's chair and Beau went to look in the pots. He didn't hide the fact he felt at home with the McCoys.

"What's in there, Beau?" Jacob asked. "Jessie and Libby won't let us even take a peek."

He turned around and looked at Jacob with a glint in his eye. "It's my favorite. Can't you smell?" Cady noticed he had dropped his thick Cajun accent and now sounded like everybody else. She supposed it was a game they played.

"Must be chicken and dumplings," Aron mused. "It's what I thought – but with both pots together smelling up the place, I couldn't be sure."

"You're right – chicken and dumplings and a big pot of jambalaya." Beau turned a chair around and sat by Joseph. "I've missed you guys – you can't find food and friends like this anywhere else in the world, especially Cuba."

"Tell me about those Cuban crocs." Joseph was so glad to see him; he didn't know what to do. He hadn't realized how much he missed interactions with friends until there was none.

Beau's face changed, his expression became more intense. It wasn't hard to tell that this was a subject near and dear to his heart. "Those beauties are an endangered species. I love studying them because they are so agile; they have been known to leap nine feet in the air. And they are incredibly intelligent. Some have been known to learn and follow commands, to recognize their name and to come when called and retreat when dismissed. But they are tremendously aggressive and highly dangerous – right down my alley. So, I've purchased a breeding pair because their natural habitat is quickly shrinking and if something isn't done – the world will lose this magnificent animal."

Cady and the others were fascinated. "Do you have any photographs? I would love to see?" she asked.

Beau pulled out his phone and began to show some pictures he had taken. "Speaking of photographs, I saw that write up about you in **Texas Extreme**. Have you let them or any of your friends know that it won't be long before you're back in the game?"

Cady took the phone from his hand and Libby and Jessie craned in to see. Her attention, however, was on Joseph. Emotions were flashing across his face like a digitally controlled billboard. "No, I haven't talked to anybody in a while. I don't know, Beau. I'm better – but I don't when I'll be in competing form again." He looked at Cady for her input.

What should she say? He had made miraculous progress, but she could make no guarantees as to timing. "There's no reason you shouldn't completely recover – in time. But your body received a devastating injury and even with the 'unique' help I provided, you will need weeks – if not months – to fully regain strength and complete use of all your muscles." There, maybe she said that right.

"Hey, I'm just grateful I've come this for." Joseph was honest. "And I don't know about announcing the prospect of my own come-back. It doesn't seem right to be blowing my own horn like that."

"Do you mind if I do it? It would please me no end to let the world know they wrote you off too damn quick." Beau smiled at Libby as she sat a steaming bowl of chicken and dumplings before him. While they talked, the rest of the family had gathered and were eagerly listening to the conversation as well as helping themselves to the savory dishes. Beau liberally added hot sauce to his jambalaya and black pepper to his dumplings. Nathan's eyes were getting bigger just watching the extra spice the Cajun was sprinkling on his food. Beau laughed, "It takes a lot of heat for me, Nathan. My taste buds were scorched off a long time ago."

"I like a lot of heat, too, Beau – if you know what I mean." Aron pulled Libby backwards until she settled in his lap. Contentedly, she moved her bowl of dumplings closer and began eating right where he placed her. "I, for one, would appreciate you calling up some of them fancy reporters. They're always looking for a story – and this is a whale of a tale."

Joseph leaned forward, "I'm sure there are those who might be interested in a story like this." Cady could tell he was a bit uncomfortable with the notion. She looked around at his family and they were all watching him, too. She didn't like to think about the press having a field day with him – asking him questions he didn't have the answers to – putting pressure on him to prove himself before he was ready. Not to mention what publicity would do to her. Pressing her hands together, she debated whether to say something. But Joseph's next words stopped her. "Do it, Beau. I want those folks to know that Joseph McCoy isn't through – the Daredevil will be back. And they can take that to the bank."

"I like your friend." Cady confided as she massaged Joseph's leg muscles. "He's very colorful and I can tell he thinks the world and all of you."

"Colorful, is one way to put it – I'd say a better label is nuts. He tangles with twenty foot alligators and thinks nothing of pulling a snake out of a tree as he glides under it in his boat." He held back a laugh as Cady visibly shuddered at the reference to the snake. "That ain't all he does – he is an expert marksman and owns one of the most unique weapons businesses in the world. Beau is a first class sniper and demolitions expert. In the world of firearms and explosives – the man is one big son of a gun." He watched her hands as they kneaded his flesh. They were so strong and capable, yet totally and utterly feminine – like the rest of her. He could feel his cock stirring and the rush of arousal and excitement was fabulous. Never again would he take for granted the privilege of getting hard and making love to a beautiful woman. "Hey, when you get through there – let's play – okay?"

There was such boyish anticipation on his magnificent, manly face that she couldn't have resisted him, even if she wanted to. "I would love to play with you." It was hard to finish up what she was doing, for her pussy began to tingle and swell, readying itself to be filled by the man she had been created to love. "What do you want to do?" Playfully, she rose up on her knees and ran her palms down his bare chest. "I love touching you." Before he knew what was happening, she had leaned in and nipped him on his stomach.

"Hey!" He loved that she felt confident enough to tease him. "You'd better watch it Angel-baby." With one smooth move he whisked her top over her head and she squealed with delight. "Now, that's more like it!" Her face was so precious – so sweet – how, in sam-hell, had he been blind to her beauty? Cady was everything a man could want. If there ever came a time he wanted to settle down, it would be with a woman like . . .

"Day-um!" Her next move stole the very thoughts from his head. She had stood before him, skimmed off her panties, unhooked her bra and turned to wiggle her beautiful ass right in his face. He couldn't keep his hands off of it – he traced the shape of it like he was skimming the rounded sides of a Valentine heart. "You have the most beautiful skin" – and she did. "It looks and tastes like wild honey, and I want to lick you till you scream." He pulled her bottom toward him – bent her over at the waist with one strong hand and proceeded to do just that.

Cady held onto the rails of the walking course – because if she hadn't had them to grasp, she would have been unable to stand upright. "Oh, my God – oh, my God," she pushed backwards seeking more. "Joseph!" He was kissing her! Down there! His talented tongue was making forays deep into her slit – and his fingers were teasing her clit and all she wanted was more – God, she wanted more! So this was what all the fuss was about. Many was the night she had laid in bed and tried to fathom what a man's tongue would feel like between her legs – and now she knew. Ecstasy!

"Lay down. I want to do this right." Joseph urged her back on the bed and high enough up so he could roll over and get his head between her thighs. "Now, where was I?" She spread her legs and pointed and he cracked up. "You like this, don't you?"

"Yes," Cady sighed. "I could easily get addicted. You are very talented." Desperate, she raised her hips. "More, please."

"Hell, yeah!"

God, there should be an Olympic event for this – Joseph would be a gold medalist, for sure. He spread her labia lips with his hands and licked her deeply, making her writhe in pleasure. Placing his hands under her bottom, he picked her up and angled her so his tongue could spear down deep into her vagina.

"Holy Mother of God," she groaned. "I've got a G-spot," she announced as if there had been doubt. Joseph chuckled and the vibration of his laughter against her swollen sex was the sweetest feeling. Who knew sex could be so much fun? He tongue-fucked her until she was tossing her head from side to side, and when he licked his way northward and began sucking on her clit, drawing it completely in his mouth and circling it over and over with his tongue - Cady tore at the sheet with her fingers – ripping it from the sides of the bed and winding it around her hand. There was no being still – she bucked upward and Joseph held her in place.

"God! Yes!" she screamed as every star in the universe exploded behind her eyelids. Nirvana! She didn't lose consciousness, but she did seem to leave the bonds of this world behind. Cady floated in absolute bliss. '*Not even heaven could be this wonderful,*' she thought.

Heaven was not amused.

He could get the big head if he wasn't careful. Cady lay there panting like she had run the Boston Marathon in record time. "I still got it, don't I?" He asked as he kissed his way up her torso until he found a ripe breast to munch on.

"I doubt you ever lost it, love." She gulped in air. As he rested on top of her, worshiping her breast, she felt a large, hard object next to her thigh. Joseph was in need.

Exultation flared up inside of her. She had done it. Joseph was fully functioning and – best of all – he could get it up – for her. "There's something on my leg – something big and hard. Could you move it for me?" Teasing a man was a whole new ball game for her and she found that she enjoyed the game.

Sliding up a few inches, he proceeded to move it – just right. When the head of his cock came into contact with her engorged clit, she almost came off the bed. "How's that?" he asked in all innocence.

"I'm not sure," she chewed on her lower lip. "Could you do it again – just for good measure?""

"You!" mHe pretended to bite her neck and growled like a grizzly bear. "I'll show you a good measure." He rolled them over and sat up. "I want you to sit on it," he guided her to turn her back to him and held his cock with one hand as she impaled herself on it - - slowly. "Fuck!" he groaned.

She almost sprang away, but he held her fast. "Did I hurt you?" she asked.

"Not hardly," he managed to groan. "It just felt so damn good. Honey, I've got to tell you – before I lose my mind here. You are one hot little darlin'. Being inside of you is fuckin' paradise." He took her by the hips and pulled her close – her back to his front. Cady pushed herself a bit farther down, ensuring he was buried root deep inside of her. "Now, cowgirl, let's take you for a ride." Joseph showed her how to move – that it wasn't necessary to bounce up and down. The combined movements of her rocking, his hips flexing and the inner muscles of her vagina caressing his shaft was enough to create delightful friction and heat. "God, you're good," he whispered against her back. "I'm so glad I found you."

Cady's heart contracted. She covered his hands with her own and drew them to her mouth, where she proceeded to kiss each one. Then she laid her face in the palm of one hand, cherishing the moment and vowing never to forget what it felt like to be loved by Joseph McCoy.

"Lay your head back on my shoulder," he coaxed. And when she did, he showed her what a Texas boy could do when he was highly motivated. One hand slipped down to cover her mons, a finger slipping between her folds to massage her hot button. The other did double duty – kneading and massaging her tits and all Cady could do was hold her arms over her head and touch his face. "That's my baby," he urged. "Love me, doll." She didn't have to be told to do that – because as he played her body like a fine instrument, she gave him her heart, completely – unequivocally and for all eternity.

"Hold me tight, precious." She didn't know exactly what he meant, so she held him tight – everywhere. On hand behind his neck, the other tucked under his thigh and her vagina squeezing him with everything she had. "I gotta cum, Cady-did." His simple term of endearment flung her off the edge. She was so turned on – so into him – so grateful to be in his arms that the orgasm just burst upon her like a summer thunderstorm, raining down rivers of refreshing, engulfing pleasure.

"I love you," She whispered under her breath. There was no way he could have heard – but she got the extreme satisfaction of having said the words that defined her existence. Joseph hugged her close, his arms like bands of steel around her body. Taking the cords of her neck in his mouth, he bit the skin gently – his teeth scraping, his tongue sucking the flesh. Cady knew what he was doing. He was marking her – as sure as the world. She would never hear him say those words to her - but in his own way – Joseph had branded her as his own.

As he held her, he shook. Waves of rapture bombarded him and he buried his head in her back and bellowed his release. In an instant, Cady felt hot pulses of cum flood up inside of her and begin to drip down – and it was then that she realized a momentous fact. In all of their excitement over his recovery and rejuvenation – not once had they even considered using protection against pregnancy.

Chapter Nine

Now, she had two things to think about. Cady paced up and down in the rehab room, moving things around, rearranging, making notes over what could be sold outright or donated to a hospital or therapy center. Every step she made, the realization that there was a slight possibility she might be carrying Joseph's baby reverberated through her mind and soul. A baby. A million butterflies fluttered through her stomach, but it wasn't unpleasant – it was pure excitement. She tried to muster up some remorse or regret for the new life that might, even now, be growing inside of her – but she couldn't. Although, she knew the chances of her getting pregnant were less than slim. Cady's cycle had never been consistent. She would go – literally months and do nothing but spot – and even that didn't happen every month. Since she had never been sexually active or ever considered the possibility of having a sex life or getting pregnant - having tests to determine her fertility had never crossed her mind. The only diagnosis she could come up with for her lack of periods was, that over the years, she had taken within her body so many illnesses and diseases in her empath work that there was really no telling what damage had been done to her reproductive capabilities.

While Joseph and Beau were huddled up making notes on some new project they had cooked up between them, Cady just basked in the idea of being a mother. A smile played around her lips. The possibility of Joseph's child growing in her body was miraculous. It was something she had never allowed herself to dream about very much. If it were true - what would Joseph think about it? That was the question. Hugging her middle, she debated with herself; there had been no promises, no hint of a future together – only passionate lovemaking and more ups and downs than a playground seesaw. Nevertheless, it was a sweet dream – no matter how impossible.

And then there was the other thing. If Beau alerted the sports world and the media that Joseph McCoy was on the mend – there would be those who would seek out interviews and information. Because his paralysis had been reported as most likely permanent, questions would certainly arise about his treatment and who was behind it. That type of publicity was exactly what Cady always tried to avoid. There was only one thing to do; before any reporter came, she would have to brief the whole family on the necessity of keeping exactly how Joseph was healed a mystery.

"Hey, Cady! Honey! Come here, I want to hear what you think about this idea that Beau has." The very fact that he wanted to include her in any discussion thrilled her. She put her notes on the desk and hurried to see what he was so excited about. When she entered the den, he was smiling and held out his hand to her and she couldn't resist taking it and greeting him with a quick kiss on the cheek – just like a regular couple, she thought. About to take a seat, she was taken aback when he spun her around and pulled her into his lap. "Guess what?" Before she could manage to formulate a query, he provided the answer. "Beau has an idea I think is fantastic. What do you think about a rodeo for handicapped and disabled kids?"

He looked so excited and so animated – totally unlike the first time she laid eyes on him. It just melted her heart. "I think that sounds wonderful." And it did, but as a professional in the healthcare field, she had questions. "How would that work? Would it be safe?"

"We'd make sure it was. We'd call it Rascal Rodeo and it would be specially set up for children with special needs from paralysis to mental disorders. It would take a bunch of volunteers, not only professional cowboys, but also people like you who could make sure we did things right. We could make an annual weekend event out of it – a family affair."

Beau stood up, too excited to sit still. "This would be a tremendous opportunity for kids. We could get them down on the arena floor. They could see everything first hand – get their feet dirty. It would be a great time for them."

"Yea, we could do a little bit of everything: calf roping, barrel racing, bronc riding – even some cow milking. Wouldn't it be fun to introduce rodeo and the western lifestyle to kids who face all kinds of problems and disabilities?" She was about to give her approval, when he kissed her on the cheek and said something that made all the difference in her world. "I would want you to help us, of course." Help him? In order to do that, she would have to be near him – at least once a year. She placed her hand over her chest in an attempt to keep her heart from leaping out of her chest.

"That sounds perfect," she managed to croak. Oh, this was dangerous. She was beginning to see things that surely weren't there, things too wonderful to hope for. Mon Dieu! Next thing she knew she would be expecting all of her dreams to come true. And that didn't happen to people like her. Something had to go wrong – it was just a matter of time.

"I am not asking you to lie, at all." Cady looked at each member of the McCoy family, in turn. "All I need for you to do is to draw as little attention to me as you can." They all sat around the dining table – only Nathan was otherwise occupied.

"Wow, that's not what we usually hear." Jacob was very experienced dealing with reporters concerning patient recovery. "Usually medical professionals don't shy away from publicity."

"They won't get any information out of me." Isaac stated flatly.

"Me either," Jessie sat down a tray filled with tall glasses of cold lemonade. "If you'll tell us what to say, we'll stick to the script."

"That's a good idea," Noah took a glass and drained it in one mighty chugging gulp.

"Thirsty, much?" It never failed to tickle Aron at how much his brothers could eat and drink in a day's time. Jessie and Libby used to spend half their time in the kitchen. Now that Lilibet coming in each day, it had gotten better for them. She shouldered a lot responsibility. And since she was dating their good friend Sheriff Kane Saucier, Lilibet was practically a member of the family.

"Just tell them he improved due to a treatment of exercise and physical therapy which included herbs and massage." That sounded reasonable and was absolutely true – for the most part.

Joseph sat back and considered what he was going to say to the reporter who called this morning to schedule an interview. It was a reporter for the Dallas Morning News, he asked for an exclusive on Joseph's miraculous recovery. Dealing with only one curious scoop seeker and one set of questions seemed like a good idea to him. Every day he was getting better, but he had enough sense to realize he wasn't even close to competing in anything more strenuous that a game of marbles – not yet, anyway.

"Okay, we've got that settled; now what about those two cows that got killed out on the Ranch Road this morning. That just makes me sick – I hate for anything to suffer and I had to go out and put those two poor old things out of their misery. But we'd be up shit creek without a paddle if it hadn't been poor old Henry Kezsey who ran into them. Thank God, he wasn't hurt and he won't sue, but we have got to get a handle on this mess." With a broad gesture, Aron encompassed the whole group. "Between all of us, surely we can come up with an answer. Kane says that, more than likely, this is personal. Somebody has a grudge against us, and I want all of you to figure out who has got a burr under their saddle against the McCoys."

"What about Harper's dad?" Isaac was only half kidding. Noah had seriously teed off the county judge over an unfortunate misunderstanding with his lovely daughter.

"What about Avery's dad?" Noah shot back and Isaac held up both hands, knowing that there was no love lost between him and the good reverend.

"I've been to see him," Isaac confessed much to the surprise of his family. "He's too preoccupied with the fact his daughter is missing."

"Missing?" Libby was shocked.

"She got upset and hightailed it off without goodbye to anyone," the big biker hung his head. "I'm going to have to look for her because it's my fault."

"Your fault? What do you mean?" Aron leaned forward, always interested in his brothers' problems as if they were his own.

"She was hanging out at the bar," Isaac shook his head, sorrowfully as he remembered. "Avery had a crush on me and I . . .I pushed her away – told her to leave, that she wasn't woman enough to please me." At Jessie and Libby's gasp, Isaac looked up, sorrowfully. "I thought I was doing her a favor – she is pure and good and I'm. . ."

"And you are a good man that any woman would be lucky to have in her life," Jessie spoke up – shocking everybody at her conviction. Jacob put an arm around her, enjoying the fact that she felt enough like a member of the family to take up for his brother.

"Thanks, Jessie," Isaac mumbled.

"Don't worry, man – we'll help you find her." Noah knew how it felt to be estranged from the one who held his heart. Harper believed the worst about him and the misunderstanding hurt her so much, for months she wouldn't even let him explain. And then when she had called – he missed it – and he hadn't been able to reach her since.

"One thing's for sure," Jacob reached for the pitcher and refilled his glass. "You know those two old men didn't have anything to do with this. Think. This is someone with a much bigger axe to grind than a love spat."

Cady almost interjected that some of the major wars of the past were fought over love spats, but she felt it wasn't the time to show off her historical acumen. Instead, she could offer her services. "Perhaps, I could help."

"What could you do?" After Cady had helped both Joseph and Libby, Aron had no qualms about her helping out with anything.

"I would need something from the scene; a piece of the fence near to where he touched might be enough." She wasn't certain that it would work, reading an object wasn't her strong suit – but she could try.

"I'll see what I can rustle up," Isaac offered. "Where's Nathan, by the way?"

"Watering Libby's flowers, I promised her we would try to keep them alive. This drought is taking its toll on everybody and everything. A lot of the ranchers are selling their cattle because they can't afford to buy hay and their water sources are drying up." Libby took Aron's hand and held it in her lap. She knew he was worried about his ranch and his family.

"We have a lot to be thankful for." Joseph's simple statement made them all stop and think. Their lives weren't perfect and there were still mountains for them to climb and battles they would have to fight – but they were McCoy's – they could handle it. All in all, their blessings outweighed the problems. "Libby is healthy, Jessie is safe, we have two babies on the way and our Nathan is still with us – and I can walk, by God."

"Damn right," Aron agreed. "We've got our health and each other – everything else will work out in due time."

Cady looked in the bathroom mirror. She did look different. Picking up her hair, she turned this way and that trying to determine what had caused the transformation. Her hair was styled, but it was the same. The shape of her face was unchanged – same eyes, same nose, same mouth. So why didn't the sight of her reflection fill her with the same despair that it used to? A smile lit up her features causing an even greater change in the woman she barely recognized. Cady was in love and that made all the difference. No matter if it was temporary or unreturned – Cady was experiencing joy in a man's arms and that had given her a self-confidence and self-admiration for herself that she had never known before. Nana was right – love made all the difference. Love had made her beautiful.

"Are you coming out, or am I gonna have to come in and get you?"

"Be right there." Holding up the new gown that Jessie had insisted she buy, she gathered her courage to walk out wearing something so seductive. Would Joseph like it? Or would he think she was being silly? Well, she'd know in a minute. Slipping it over her head, she pulled the next-to-nothing piece of black silk over her head and smoothed it down her body. The lace played peek-a-boo with her nipples, clung to every curve and was tighter than a coat of paint. Pinching her cheeks to make them rosy, she considered saying a little incantation to make herself more appealing to Joseph, but she decided that she would rather have his real emotions than any she might conjure up.

With a combination of nervousness and excitement, she entered the bedroom. Joseph insisted he move back to his own wing. And she didn't blame him. He was a man on the mend and even though they still used some of the equipment and the massage table, there was no need to sleep in a room that constantly reminded him of the dark place he had lived just a few weeks ago. Flickers of candlelight danced over the walls. For a minute, she thought the electricity had gone out – but she had just flipped off the switch in the bathroom, so that wasn't possible. As her eyes became acclimated to the dimness – she saw him. And it hit her. Joseph was setting a romantic scene *for her*. There was even soft music playing. And he lay up in the bed, hands behind his head – biceps bulging and a look on his face that would boil water. Her gaze meandered down his body – God, he was magnificently and wonderfully made. She got stuck on his chest, the whorls of dark hair, washboard abs, the wedge shape that drew her eyes down a happy trail to a part of his anatomy that was fully engaged in the moment. His cock was fully aroused, swollen; bobbing with every breath he took. "Damn, you're lovely. That little piece of nothing you're wearing is sexy as hell. Come here, I need you," he held out a hand that beckoned her to join him.

Cady's whole body reacted to him. Her heart contracted at the thought he would care enough to set a mood – not that she needed it. Just the sight of him had her nipples peaking and her sex tingling. His room was large and filled with massive oak furniture, but it had such a different feel than the rehab room, it seemed that they were in some exclusive vacation spot – just the two of them – away from the world. "I can't believe you did all of this," she crawled up on the bed and took his hand. "Thank you for being so nice to me."

"Did what?" What had he done? And then it dawned on him that she was grateful for the candlelight and mood music. This sweet baby never had anyone court her. Hell, he had a lot of work to do. "Why don't you and I go out to dinner some night? Would you like that?"

"Yes," she said as he drew her up to his chest. She wasn't sure what the invitation consisted of or if they would be alone or with a group, but any chance to spend time with Joseph was welcome. "I would love to go out with you." He guided her down to lie beside him and she molded herself to his side and rested her head on his shoulder. "Oh, this is nice." Cady couldn't resist rubbing her palm over his chest and pressing a kiss to his shoulder. Her caress kept creeping lower with ever sweep she made; it was like his cock was a homing device and her hand was on a special mission.

"I wish you'd hurry up," Joseph chuckled. "My dick is so revved up, he's about to explode." He tilted his hips up, meeting her hand and when she closed her palm around him, he groaned. "God, yes. Rub him, baby. He wants you so bad." She followed his direction, her own arousal growing to the point where she could feel herself growing wet with need.

"Do you want me to kiss him?" she offered, longing only to please him.

Underneath her, Joseph shifted until they were lying side by side. She hadn't let go of his cock – unwilling to break that connection. "I want everything, doll." He placed his forehead against hers and looked deep into her eyes. "But, I'm too turned on. I want to be inside of you. Are you wet enough?" He slipped a hand between her legs and encountered the creamy evidence of her desire for him. "Oh, yeah, you want me. Don't you?"

"Oh, yes," she moaned as he rubbed her all up and down her vulva – spreading the cream that would ease his entry. She placed one of her legs up over his so he could have easier access and pressed her breasts into his chest enjoying the rasp of his chest hair on her nipples. "I can't wait to have you inside of me."

"Get up on your knees, baby. I want to take you while I pet that luscious ass of yours."

Excitement coursed through her veins, but one emotion kept her from doing as he asked. Guilt. She took his chin in her hand and confessed. "Joseph, we didn't use protection the other times. Don't you think we should?" There was no use trying to explain that she might not be able to get pregnant – all of that was way too complicated for the moment. The possibility existed and she didn't want to ever take advantage of him.

"Hell, we should have thought of that before." He rolled over and opened a drawer in the nightstand and removed a condom. In a few seconds, he was sheathed and ready for business...."Now, where were we?"

Surprised at how well he took the news of the risk they had run, she vowed they would discuss it more, later. But – right now – there was something more urgent to attend to. She got on her knees and noticed that this put her in full view of the large mirror that covered both closet doors. Immediately she was self-conscious – mirrors had never been her friends. So, she closed her eyes, which only amplified her sense of touch – and by God, there was a lot of touching going on. Joseph was covering her from behind, running his hands from the swell of her hips, up her sides and under to cup her breasts. He followed this same path over and over again, trailing kisses from the base of her spine to up between her shoulder blades. A thousand points of excitement covered her skin – some would call it goose bumps – her granny always called them freesons. "Open your eyes, Cady. I want you to watch me watch you, as I make you mine."

Sizzle! Tingle! His words stroked her from her ears straight to her clit. She felt the head of his cock probing the tender flesh of her pussy. All she wanted to do was lay her head on the bed and thrust her ass up toward him and beg him to take her hard, deep and fast.

"Open your eyes, Cady-did," Joseph whispered. "Look at me. Look at me loving you."

She obeyed and what she saw took her breath away. He towered over her – big, broad, and devastatingly handsome and all of his focus was on her. His body tensed, he flexed forward and she felt his thick rod push inside of her body. "God, yes," she gasped. But she couldn't take her eyes off of him. His face was awash in ecstasy. He closed his eyes and his hand sank back – the cords of his neck standing out prominently.

"Hmmm – oh, baby," he growled. "You fit me like a glove." Placing one hand on the middle of her back, he began to move. His body pressed forward, then drew back in a perfect rhythm, and the sliding of his cock in and out of her body was creating a fire that a thousand orgasms would never douse. She craved Joseph McCoy like she craved the very air she breathed. "Now, look at you, Cady. See what I see."

She didn't want to – looking at him was much safer. "Now, Cady." Joseph commanded. Slowly, she let her vision encompass both of them – and when she did, she caught her breath and held it. Amazing. The woman in the mirror was beautiful. Her hair was flowing across her shoulders in a midnight waterfall, her body was graceful and the look on her face was enraptured. "Do you see her Cady? Do you see that beautiful woman I'm making love to? Look at your tits, baby." God, he was right. She looked decadent. Her breasts hung down like plump, ripe fruit. And as she watched, he reached under her, picked one up and squeezed it – rubbing the nipple – Cady gasped with pleasure. "Your tits are sensitive, aren't they?"

"Yes," she managed to croak. "I love for you to play with my nipples. Everything you do to me feels good." Giving in to her own needs, she lowered her head to the mattress and rested it on her crossed arms. This angled her ass so Joseph could go as deep as possible. Her words seemed to enflame him and he grasped her hips and started pistoning into her with renewed vigor. Sexy slapping sounds filled the air as he rammed into her over and over.

He couldn't think – he could only feel. His cock was tunneling into the warmest, tightest pussy he had ever been privileged to fuck – but that was just the icing on the cake. What mattered to him was that he was pleasing Cady. It was Cady who was kneeling in front of him granting him full and complete access to her body, bestowing upon him the gift of her trust and passion. The pleasure was almost unbearable – he could feel the semen boiling up in his balls – God, he needed to cum. "Oh, Joseph – I can't hold back – I need to . . . ." Cady began to shake and her vagina started fluttering around his cock like a thousand kisses.

"Come, love," he urged. "Come with me." Pounding into her pussy, Joseph let himself go. Pulsating waves of passion exploded in his groin – it was like a high-speed elevator that had pushed upward and upward and upward finally being released and freefalling down in an extreme rush of blissful heat. "Ah – Yes! Yes!" he pushed in deep – held it – pulled out and pushed back in slow, loving the drag of his male flesh against her wet, yielding softness. He did this several more times, allowing her to come down slow, luxuriate in the aftershocks. Not ready to break their intimate connection, he gently pulled her back up until her could hug her body close to his. "How wonderful you are. You have made my life worth living, again. Did you know that?"

Cady sighed her contentment as she rested against his strong, hard body. "I'm glad." Despite all of the things on her mind, she yawned. "Could we cuddle now?"

"You bet." He pulled out, a little stream of her ejaculate coming out with his cock. "Let me clean you up and we'll hold one another all night." Joseph still wasn't bouncing around, but he was moving easier and smoother every day. Going to the bathroom, he removed the condom, wet a washcloth in warm water and cleaned off his cock. Seeing the cum on his dick, he thought about what Cady had said. So, she wasn't on the pill. He stilled – waiting for the dread and worry to swamp him as it had in the past when he thought there was a chance he had knocked a girl up. Hmmm. Nothing. All he could see in his mind was Cady holding a little baby with dark hair and creamy skin. Shit! If he didn't know better, he would think he was falling in love.

Joseph buried his head in her hair. Waking up with a woman wasn't something he had done very often. Usually, he had made his escape long before dawn broke. Spooning Cady, he let himself appreciate how it felt to be nestled against her softness, especially her round little rump. Gently kissing her shoulder, he ran a hand over her hip until he could cup her mons. Rubbing the soft little mound, he slipped his fingers between her labia lips and began to massage the button of her clit that he knew tasted like wild cherry candy. It didn't take but a couple of circles with the pads of his fingers before she moved in his arms, pressing back against him – her body lifting trying to push her pussy farther onto his hand.

Good. It felt so good. Cady had been awakened by erotic dreams before. When you are used to sleeping alone – dreaming alone – waking up to find a handsome, sexy man has his hand between your legs is quite a pleasant surprise. "Oh, yes, yes – I love what you're doing. Don't stop."

"No way, baby. You are so sweet." Joseph pushed his cock against her backside, he was getting rock-hard listening to her little grunts and feeling his fingers become wet from her juices. "But I gotta get closer, a lot closer – I want inside." He couldn't get enough of her, "Put your leg up on mine." She immediately followed his directions and hummed her happiness when he pushed deep up into her. Sliding his other arm beneath her back, he cupped her breast with one hand as he continued to stroke her clit with the other – all along he was humping her – fucking her from the back. It was incredible!

"Joseph – oh, Joseph," she moaned. "How does it keep getting better?" Cady surrendered to him, touching her hand to his face – loving the feel of his scruff against her palm.

Then it hit him – it did keep getting better. How could that be? He knew – and he was man enough to admit it.

With Cady, he was making love to more than just a willing, beautiful body. He was making love to his friend – to a woman he cared about – to a woman who cared about him. Kissing the side of her face, he breathed in her scent, listening to her sexy moans and the combination of his pleasure and hers threw him over the edge. They lay there in each other's arms until Cady started giggling. "What are you laughing about?" Joseph asked. "Do I amuse you?"

"No, I'm just happy."

"Good, so am I."

They fell back asleep, thoroughly relaxed. About an hour later, Cady opened her eyes. How oddly wonderful it was to be sharing a bed with a man. Her mind went back to the last night she had spent in her home in New Orleans and how she had longed for someone to cuddle up against in the dark of night. With a light touch, she skimmed her palm down the smooth skin of his back. He lay on his stomach, his head facing away from her – but he had his right arm slung over her middle, holding her close. Every time they slept together, there wasn't a time during the night that she was aware of - that he was not touching her, somewhere.

She would give anything to grant Joseph's wish of recapturing his athletic prowess. Although he had made great strides in regaining a wide range of movement, plus the ability to have an erection, she knew there was still much progress that needed to be made.

He needed to be examined by a doctor; Cady realized that. The only reason she hesitated was the incessant questions they would have to answer. If only – and then she realized – she could call Philippe, Aunt Angelique's husband.

Not wanting to disturb Joseph, she kissed him on the shoulder, eased out from under his arm and slipped out of the bed. Her gown and robe lay discarded on the floor, so she gathered them up before retreating to her own suite for a quick shower and change of clothes. As soon as she was through, she looked up Philippe's office number and gave him a call. After speaking to his receptionist, he came on the line.

"Cady, how good to hear from you! How is Joseph?"

"He's improving every day, Uncle." He had requested she address him as such, and she was glad she had remembered to do so. "He can stand and walk with a crutch, but there are limitations, especially with his left leg. I'm still continuing with the exercises and the massages, but I would like to know the exact condition of his spine and the connecting nerves."

"Has he recovered his bladder and bowel functions?"

"Yes, thankfully."

"How is his trunk stability?"

"He favors his right side, so I'm concerned that there may be residual nerve damage."

"Has he regained sexual function?"

Here Cady stumbled, "Yes, uh – uh, yes, he has – completely, I understand."

Her aunt's husband chuckled. "Excellent. I'm sure his frame of mind and outlook on life has improved."

"Indeed." She refused to elaborate. "Would you see him, Philippe? I'm just not comfortable taking him to someone who will ask pointed questions that will be impossible for me to answer."

"Certainly. Why don't the two of you come to New Orleans? I'll work him in and we'll get the answers you need. I'd love to do some range of motion tests, an MRI and x-rays." Cady was relieved. They spoke for a few more moments before she hung up and went to make sure Joseph would agree with her plan.

Since he returned to his original suite, Cady's room was on the other side of the house. As she entered the living room, she noticed Jacob was seated on the couch drinking coffee. "Good morning," her voice sounded cheerful even to her own ears.

"Hey, Cady-girl." Jacob smiled at her. "You sure are chipper this morning."

"Yes, I feel good this morning." She was grateful he saw her coming from her own room. Not that she was ashamed of what she and Joseph were doing, but it was unprofessional on her part.

"I'm glad." He stood up and removed a white paper towel from his back pocket. Unfolding it, he held out a piece of wire to her. "I brought this from the scene of the vandalism on our fences. Do you have time to do see what you could pick up from it?"

This was important. She'd let Joseph sleep in for a few more minutes. "Of course." She took the item from his hand and sat down on the couch. "May I have the towel, also?" He gave her the scrunched up paper. Holding it in the palm of her hand she concentrated. As she ran her thumb and first finger over one of the barbs, she purposefully pricked her finger. Jacob made a protesting noise, but she shook her head indicating to him that all was well. "I've had my tetanus." The shedding of blood and the mingling of it with the iron would provide a powerful bonding of her psychic energy with the inanimate object. After a few moments, flashes of light danced over her mind's eye. Scenes began to appear like a trailer from a movie being shown at high speed. Cady concentrated until she could bring the vision into focus. "I see a man. He's middle-aged. He has red hair that is fading to grey. The truck that he is driving is a green flatbed. I see him pull over near a fence and get out of his truck. He has an instrument in his hand. He goes to the fence and clips the strands of barb-wire and then pulls the gap wide enough so the animals will have no trouble going through it."

Cady opens her eyes and looks at Jacob. "A lot of this is directed at you. The whole family is a target, but something you did has set this in motion."

"What?" He looked surprised and concerned.

"This man is thinking that you cheated him and he is doing this to get revenge. And Jacob – the wire cutting thing won't be all he'll do, so be careful."

Jacob stood up and paced the room. "Hell, I'll have to think about this, but it has to be Henry's nephew. He's the only one who has made noise about being wronged." Grabbing his hat, he headed for the door. "Thanks, Cady. Would you tell Jessie that I'll be back in about a half hour. I'm headed over to Henry's place to see if he knows where that no-count nephew of his is keeping himself these days."

A little blood was still seeping from the cut on her finger, so she retreated to her room to clean it up and get a band-aid. As she went through the kitchen Jessie was coming from the patio with Libby. "Are there any clouds in the sky?" she asked knowing how badly they needed rain. More than once she wished she possessed Evangeline's gift. It wouldn't surprise her to find that Austin was getting a little more rain than other parts of Texas.

"Not a one," sighed Libby.

"It's not even eight o'clock and it's already eighty degrees," Jessie sipped her coffee and rubbed her protruding tummy. "I hope it cools off before this baby comes."

Cady placed a hand over hers, feeling a slight kick. "This is going to be a happy baby."

"You're getting psychic vibrations from feeling her tummy?" Libby was fascinated.

"No," Cady giggled. "I know he's going to be happy because he's got such a wonderful family who are going to spoil him rotten." Libby's disappointed expression was hilarious. "Jessie, Jacob asked me to tell you that he has gone over to Henry's and will be back in about thirty minutes."

"Shoot!" she fussed a little bit. "I would have gone with him, I like Henry."

"How's Joseph?" Libby asked with a knowing smile.

"He's improving every day."

"His lungs are definitely strong, I heard him agreeing with you last night. He was shouting, Yes! God, yes! To the top of his voice."

As Libby teased her, Cady could feel the heat rise on her face. "We'll try to be quieter next time."

"Its okay, Cady," Jessie patted her arm. "Don't let Libby embarrass you. After all, the three of us belong to the same club."

"What club is that?"

"The McCoy Joy Club, of course – our boys are the real deal – and they satisfy us every time."

She found him, still in his bedroom getting dressed. He was shirtless, only in blue jeans and sexier than any man had a right to be. For a couple of seconds, she was able to observe him unnoticed and once again she was struck by his masculine perfection. God, he was gorgeous! How she wished she had the confidence to slip up behind him and put her arms around his waist and kiss him on the back. Hell! She was only going to go around once in life. He was leaning against the massive oak dresser, using the furniture to keep his balance while he slid his tooled leather belt through the loops of his jeans.

Truly, he was making amazing progress – but she knew he would never be satisfied until he could climb mountains and jump out of airplanes again. As he centered his belt, she smiled. On the back was one word – Stallion – God, the imagery that conjured. Once she had seen a stallion mount a mare and she never forgot the super-charged sexuality that had been in the air. The men who were standing near had all been frozen, watching the pure eroticism of that magnificent beast piercing his chosen mate with a cock that was enviable to say the least. Last night, she had known what that felt like – Joseph had mounted her and the memory was hot enough to make her pussy melt, even now.

Giving in to temptation, she tiptoed up to him, slid her arms around his waist and kissed him on the smooth skin of his shoulder. "There you are, Cady-did. I dillydallied here, hoping you'd come over. I was watching you in the mirror." He covered her hands with his own, and leaned back against her, encouraging her to do whatever she wanted. Feeling empowered, she traced a pattern on his back with her tongue, nipping the skin. He groaned in appreciation. She felt him take her hand and move it down until it was filled with a huge, hard erection. With hungry fingers, she molded it – worked it – rubbing it until he was pushing into her palm, asking for more. God, she was turned on. What had possessed her? Of their own volition, her hips were pumping, pressing her mons into the hard muscles of his hips, and desperately seeking any friction for her swollen clit that she could find.

Holy Hell! When Cady started humping his ass while she rubbed his dick, Joseph lost his mind. "Around here, now!" he demanded. Taking her by the arm, he pulled her to the front, blindly seeking her mouth. "You make me crazy." Joseph inhaled her. Cupping the back of her neck, he devoured her lips, feasting at their succulent flesh. She kneaded the muscles of his arms, moving her hands up his biceps. He made a growling sound deep in his throat, warning her that there were consequences for her actions. Joseph sucked on Cady's lips, eating at her mouth, and in turn feeding her kisses that she accepted with whimpers of delight.

Closer. She needed to be closer. If she hadn't been afraid to hurt him – Cady would have wrapped her legs around him and climbed him like a telephone pole. God, the man could kiss! Wet kisses. He pushed his tongue in her mouth and she gladly sucked on it. Then he would pull it back as she grunted her protests and appease her with tender smooches to her lips, chin and jawline. He had her literally weak with arousal. "Joseph, God – I came in here to. . . ."

"Love on me?" With gentle pressure to her shoulders, he coaxed her down on her knees. "Please?"

Lord, he didn't have to ask twice. "Yes. I want to, yes." With shaking hands, she undid the snap on his jeans and pulled down the zipper over the huge bulge of his cock. He'd never gotten around to fastening that superman belt buckle. Every time she saw it, she thought how appropriate it was – he was Superman, to her. Cady's mouth was watering as she worked his pants down over his hips.

"Having trouble, love?" Joseph laughed as she struggled to unwrap his straining erection. "Ummm," she moaned as she wrapped a hand around the shaft and captured the head with her mouth. "Shit!" Hot, wet, velvet – that's what her mouth was. "Good girl," he praised her as she sucked him off. As she deep-throated him, played with his balls – took him to the gates of glory and back – he held her head and thanked God he was a man.

Still on her knees, she tenderly redressed him; kissing him on his skin, on his clothes – showing him how important he was to her.

"Lie down, let me pay you back," he offered as she got to her feet with his gallant assistance.

"No." Was she crazy? Must be. But there were more important things at hand than a mind-blowing orgasm. "I need to talk to you."

"Are you sure?" he teased as he tweaked one of her nipples through her camisole.

"Stop that," she grabbed his hand and kissed it. "I talked to Dr. Francois this morning. You remember my aunt's husband?" At his affirmative nod, she continued. "He said he would work you in for an examination if we drive to New Orleans."

"All right."

"I think this is necessary because I need to know where we're at," she continued to explain and then realized he had already agreed. "All right?"

"Road trip!" he was as excited as a small boy. "When do we leave? Will you show me around? It's been years since I was in the Big Easy."

"Yes, I'll show you around," his excitement was contagious. "How does tomorrow sound?"

"Not as good as today," he began taking shirts and pants out of the dresser drawers. "Hand me my duffle out of the closet. A change of scenery sounds damn good."

Before they could make their escape, Joseph got a phone call from Trey Richardson about the interview. He confirmed the request was prompted by a call from Beau. Joseph's Cajun friend was a celebrity in his right, so when he dropped a name – it wasn't ignored. Trey reiterated that if anyone was going to announce the Stallion's miraculous recovery and the hope he would be able to return to the sports he loved, Dallas Morning News wanted to be the one to do it. Trey and Joseph agreed to meet on the upcoming Thursday, three days away. After nailing the time down, Joseph found Aron in the kitchen, "Big Hoss, Cady and I are leaving for a couple of days."

Aron almost choked on his sandwich, "Say what?"

"I'm going with Cady to New Orleans for three days and three nights of debauchery, overeating, hot sex and a check-up." All of this was said with a straight face as he ate French fries off of his brother's plate.

Aron slapped at Joseph's hand. "Quit eating my taters. What kind of check-up and how much debauchery?"

Joseph stood on one foot while he pulled the chair out and sat down, leaning the crutch on the table. "Cady says she needs to know where we're at in my recovery and what she needs to concentrate on to get me up to par. That uncle doctor of hers is gonna run some tests, take some x-rays and check my oil."

"You're such an idiot." Aron was enjoying their carrying on. "I've missed your stupid sense of humor. Did you know that?"

"Cady says I'm funny." Joseph stole another fry. "And as for the debauchery, Cady says that we'll go down Bourbon Street and to the Voodoo Museum and Jackson Square. Cady says we might even eat at Emeril Lagasse's place."

Aron was smiling like a cat eating a canary. "Cady says all that?"

"What?" Joseph didn't get it.

"Nothing," Aron continued to eat one fry after the other. "I'm just surprised Cady has so much to say, that's all."

"Asshole."

"Are you comfortable?" She looked over at Joseph who was as stretched out as far as he could get in her Jaguar sedan. The car was second-hand, having been one of Nanette's, who was a faithful Jaguar customer. This hand-me-down was a big sedan. Cady called it her Tony Blair car, because she had once seen the former British prime minister driving one exactly like it on a news program.

"Yes, dear."

Joseph was in such a good mood. Cady found it hard to keep her eyes on the road; she'd rather look at him. He had slid down in the seat, those long legs in front of him and that rise in his Levis was prominent even without a hard-on. He was looking out the window as they drove over the Atchafalaya Basin Bridge. "This is beautiful country."

"Thank you, Joseph. That makes me happy. This part of the world is special to me. Not everybody can appreciate its beauty." She pointed out several houseboats that floated just below the interstate bridge. Louisiana was her home and the swamp was in her blood. "My ancestors lived off the land, and built their homes on the banks of the slow moving green waters of the bayou." As she spoke, her voice took on a different cadence. "They fished for shrimp and crawfish, hunted alligator and nutria – moving through the swamps in small pirogues. On Mondays we cooked red beans and rice and on the other days, big pots of gumbo simmered on our stoves."

"Would you make me some gumbo when we go home?" Cady noticed that he included her in the home scenario and her heart lurched with happiness.

"Shrimp and oyster or chicken and sausage?"

"All of the above?" He had set up in the passenger seat, taking it all in. The bridge was over eighteen miles long and there was a lot to see. "Did you always live in New Orleans, Cady? Or did you spend time in the swamp?"

"My grandmother and some of my aunts have lived near here and in South Louisiana. When I was growing up, we'd go to fais do-dos, dance parties where zydeco music would float out over the water. The food was out of this world – crawfish boils, jambalaya, boudin and my favorite dessert – bread pudding."

Joseph turned in his seat enough so he could see Cady. "How about voodoo? Has your family ever been into that?"

She could tell he was fascinated with the subject – so she opened up. "In years past, yes. Not so much anymore. Today, my family considers themselves to be Catholic. That's not to say they don't still practice some of the old ways – they do, but it's all melded together in their minds."

"The spell that all of you used to heal me, was that voodoo?"

"No. Nanette does her own thing; she knows so much – she puts a little wicca with some pow-wow and throws in some granny magic for good measure."

"Pow-wow – like native American medicine men?"

"No," Cady laughed. "Unusually enough, pow-wow is Pennsylvania Dutch folk magic. And it's all based on using the Bible and religious phrases for magical purposes."

Joseph couldn't take his eyes off of her. Today, she wore her hair in some kind of a French twist that showed off her long graceful neck, and she wore her glasses perched on the end of her cute little turned up nose. If she had on any make-up, it was applied in such a way to look natural. He couldn't see a thing wrong with her. She looked beautiful to him. "Do you need your glasses to drive?"

Cady immediately took them off. "Not too much. Do they look that bad?"

The self-consciousness in her voice pricked his heart. "No, no – put them back on if you need them. You look adorable." And she did. "Whatever you've been doing to your hair and make-up has made all the difference. The only thing we've got to work on now is teaching you how to flirt."

Cady tightened her hands on the steering wheel. How could she forget? She was Joseph's project. Every time she got to feeling like they were a couple or their relationship meant something special to him – he had a way of reminding her that their association was an affair – a temporary affair. She was Eliza Doolittle and he was Henry Higgins, yet she feared the ending to their fling would not be the same as My Fair Lady. Cady would never be Joseph's Pygmalion, her flaws could not be solved by changing the way she spoke. "I don't need to know how to flirt," she stated flatly. "I don't intend to try and flirt."

"Yes, you do," he argued. "Women have been coming on to me since I was Nathan's age. And I enjoy it – it's a sport – man's favorite sport. There's nothing that gets me going faster than a pretty woman catching my eye across a room – turning her head and body just so – letting me know she would welcome my attention."

Why she felt it necessary to defend herself, she didn't know. "When I came back from shopping that day, the ranch hands found me attractive."

"You are - and getting more attractive everyday. I know how they felt. When you stepped out of Aron's truck your looks stunned me. I almost didn't recognize you."

Joseph's explanation wasn't making her feel any better. "Gee, thanks."

"Now, you just need to learn how to come on to a guy – how to make him want you more than anything." At her skeptical look, he laughed.

"And you can teach me how to do this?" She wanted to ask him why he had wanted to make love to her, but she was afraid of what he'd say. .

"No, I'm used to being a receiver not a passer. We'll go to a bar – your choice – and just observe. I bet we can find some good examples of women making a play for an unsuspecting target."

All the while he was talking to her; he was rubbing her leg from knee to thigh – back and forth – back and forth. Did he know he was touching her? Cady was enjoying his caress, but not the conversation. "Okay," she finally stated, resigned. She had envisioned them seated at a table at a small café in the French Quarter, holding hands; instead he would be coaching her on the best way to pick-up another man. Deciding she might as well play along, she glanced at him. "You'll have to help me decide what to wear."

"No problem," he squeezed her leg. "It'll be fun to let you model clothes for me." As they made plans, he felt a niggle of doubt.

Checking the traffic sign she saw they were a half hour out of New Orleans. "So, let me get this straight – we're going to go out and watch couples hook up. After I make some notes, I'm going to get up and try it out while you watch?" Her mind was working fast. Maybe she could turn this in her favor. The old adage kept coming to her mind – be careful what you ask for – you just might get it.

"Well, uh – we'll . . . ." He actually hadn't thought it through that far. "Maybe . ."

"That's sounds like fun. I'll do it." He wasn't the only one who could have a plan. With everything in her, she hoped she could make Joseph jealous.

Cady was taking him to her home. When she left, weeks ago, she had no idea that Joseph would be returning with her. They turned down St. Charles Avenue and she enjoyed pointing out the elegant mansions that adorned the tree-lined boulevard, the famous streetcar and the beautiful campuses of Tulane and Loyola Universities.
"This is beautiful. Doesn't Anne Rice live down here somewhere?"

He was taking it all in and he looked so interested that Cady couldn't resist turning down 1st street and showing him Rosegate. "Do you like to read about vampires?"

Joseph smiled so big, his dimples made a welcome appearance. "Actually, I liked The Witching Hour best, but yes – I have read most everything she ever wrote." A mischievous look came over his face. "Cady, if there is such a thing as witches, how about vampires, are they real, too?"

Dropping her voice to a conspiratorial tone, she answered. "Every culture has their tales that people can shift into an animal form. It's not all bats and blood sucking. In South America, there is a belief that man can become jaguars; in Ireland its seals – selkies – in Europe there's the werewolf. Here in New Orleans, the vampire has a new home. There are vampire bars and people who have attempted to become vampires by drinking blood, avoiding sunlight and sleeping in a coffin. But. . . . ."

"What?" He was fascinated.

"Aunt Angelique says that where there's smoke there's fire – and there's too much smoke here - too many stories down through time that all point to the same thing, there are those who can cross the boundaries of humanity and take upon themselves the traits of an animal. They can walk among humans undetected with abilities and powers we have a hard time comprehending." As Joseph leaned closer in – she giggled. "But, I've never seen one."

"Shoot! I thought you were going to tell me you knew a vampire, personally."

"Nope, sorry. Although Nanette's grandmother does visit Aunt Angelique, periodically."

"Wow, she must really be old. Nanette is . . ." Joseph looked at her suspiciously. "Her grandmother would have to be way over a hundred."

"Patrice is dead."

"So, not only are witches real – so are ghosts?"

"Yes, I can't see them. But Angelique can."

"And you believe her?"

"I've seen her solve murders after she spoke with the victims." Cady turned into her driveway. "We're here." She was proud of her cottage and she hoped that Joseph would like it and be happy in her home. It was small, but comfortable.

"Wow, Cady. It looks like something out of a magazine. I love it." His kind words made all the work she had done on her home worthwhile.

"It's a side hall cottage with four bays." The fifteen hundred square foot house was painted varying shades of brown – from light taupe to chocolate. "It was built around 1900 and I completely renovated it last year. And the crepe myrtles are all dark purple, my favorite." Pulling into the garage, she parked and cut off the engine. "Your appointment is not til ten in the morning. So, we'll get settled, rest a few minutes, and then go do some fun stuff."

Joseph was a little slow getting out of the car. He stood for a moment, leaning on his crutch, stretching his legs. They had been on the road for ten hours and had only stopped a couple of times for food and bathroom breaks. He had learned a lot about Cady while they had been cooped up in the car. And he liked everything about her – she was fun and kind and could laugh at herself. "You don't have any ghosts here, do you?" He was kidding, enjoying their conversation.

"Not that I know of," she took their bags out of the car.

"Here, let me help." He took the larger bag from her hand. "I'm not helpless, Cady."

She knew he wasn't, but still she watched as he made his way around the car, looking for signs of strain or discomfort. "We see Uncle Philippe tomorrow at ten."

"Sounds good."

She led him into the breezeway that connected the garage to the rest of the house. All the time she was nervous of him seeing her world, you can tell so much about a person from their home – their selection of furniture and accessories – their collections and decorations. And hers were eclectic to say the least.

Joseph took everything in. The furniture was simple, overstuffed and inviting. As he entered the interior, he could see that Cady collected Irish Belleek, there were lighted curio cabinets full of the fragile china adorned with green shamrocks. On the tables sat large woodcarvings of animals like swans and geese, and there were life-size porcelain statues of white rabbits and cats in front of the fireplace. "You have quite a menagerie."

"I'm gone so much, I can't have pets. These statues make me feel less lonely."

She said it matter-of-factly, the fact that she was lonely. Joseph couldn't imagine living alone, not having his family around him. "You shouldn't be alone, Cady."

"It's not so bad, Joseph." She didn't want him feeling sorry for her. "I spend a lot of time on assignment, and I'm not alone then."

"I realize that, but it's not the same."

"You're right. I'm with my patients for a little while, and then I move on." She stopped at one of the bedrooms, realizing he was a patient and soon she would be moving on from him. Joseph seemed to fill the hall, his shoulders wide and strong. If Cady lived to be a hundred, she would remember this moment – seeing him standing here. She pressed the memory in her mind like a flower in a book that she wanted to preserve forever.

Joseph didn't like the sound of that. "We'll be friends for always, Cady. I don't want to lose contact with you."

She didn't know what to say, so she opened the door. "This is the guest room."

"Are you sleeping in this room?" He didn't move.

"No, my room is over there." She indicated the room across the hall, which was open – the bed clearly visible.

"I'm sleeping with you, Cady-did." Turning, he walked into her space like he owned it. "In fact, I'm about ready for a little nap. Would you care to join me?"

Chapter Ten

She was frozen in the hall as he strode into her room and made himself at home. How many nights had she lain in that bed and longed to be loved? How many times had she dreamed of him – not knowing anymore than his name and that he was important to her? If she made love with Joseph there, it would never be the same. He would haunt her dreams for the rest of her life. She only hesitated for a second – if this was all she would ever have – so be it. Cady was storing up memories to last a lifetime. "I didn't want to presume," she teased; glad he made the first move. She just wasn't that brave.

Joseph started stripping. He hadn't realized how horny he was until he had seen her standing in the rays of sunlight streaming into the hall from the guest room window. Her cotton dress was practically see-through and those incredible legs had been clearly visible – and the shadow of the vee between her thighs had beckoned him like the most tempting delicacy. His cock was hard, engorged and ready to play. "Come here." He sat down on the bed, removing shoes, socks, jeans and underwear. "Undress for me."

Cady tossed her suitcase to one side, she would worry about unpacking later, this was more important. The air in the room felt different – it was as if the very walls and furnishings were shocked. They had only known her – spinster Cady. Now, a man had invaded them and his presence upset their normal, inanimate existence. "You want me." It was a wondrous admission, but seeing him sitting on her virginal bed, his penis distended and swollen was a sight to behold.

"More than you will ever know," he said tenderly.

Her dress was cotton, one that Libby had picked out. It was white with tiny purple flowers – a million tucks over the bodice and tiny lace around the neck and sleeves – a thoroughly feminine dress. She might be fooling herself, but she felt sexy – and daring. Slowly, she unbuttoned the bodice, her fingers trembling slightly. The bra underneath was shear and Cady could feel her nipples peaking, pushing at the fabric. They wanted to be free – hell, who was she kidding – her tits wanted to be sucked. Already, she could feel dampness between her legs. Joseph looked at her, while he fitted himself with a condom; his eyes were dark and focused on the movements of her hands. Could she entice him?

This new underwear she was sporting was so different from the plain white, utilitarian garments she had always worn – it made her feel almost sexy. Almost. Pushing the sundress over her shoulders, she let it fall to the ground, leaving her in the bra and a pair of barely-there panties. Joseph gasped, his cock bobbed and Cady almost went to her knees. "Take off the rest," he growled. She obliged, peeling off the scraps of material – leaving her naked, vulnerable and shaking with desire.

"Step closer, baby. I need you." She came close enough that Joseph could reach her; he pulled her between his thighs, trapping her face between his big hands. Cady expected the kiss to be tender and tentative – instead it was hungry and desperate. Joseph kissed the living daylights out of her, running his hands over her body – molding, soothing, kneading her arms and back. She accepted the thrust of his tongue, excitement sparking through her body like electrical circuits overloaded with power. "Cady – come on, straddle me, baby." He scooted back on the bed and hauled her closer, arranging her body so that her thighs were draped across his. "God, I've dreamed of doing this with you. I want to do everything with you – over and over." He cupped her breasts, pushing them together – licking and sucking at her nipples, rubbing his face over their softness. Cady moaned her enjoyment. The man was driving her crazy, setting her blood on fire. "Put your hands on me, sweetheart, please."

Joseph groaned his pleasure when she tangled her fingers in his hair. Lord, she loved him. Feverishly, Cady kissed his head, the side of his face, loving that he was sucking her nipples with single-minded devotion. Her pussy was pulsing, "Joseph, honey – I need you so much."

"Are you wet for me, Cady?"

"Always," she whispered. "All you have to do is look at me and I'm ready for you."

"Damn, baby. You're gonna make me come before I get inside of you." Her words almost sent him over the edge. "Lift up, just enough." He held her up and guided his cock into her honeyed depths.

"Joseph!" she keened, burying her face in his shoulder.

"Look at me, Cady." With passion-blurred eyes, she tried to hold his gaze, blinking at him. Joseph took control – his mouth on hers, his hands on her body. She wrapped her arms around his neck and rode him, her clit rubbing against the hard muscles of his abdomen. "God Almighty!" he ground out as she impaled herself – pulled up – and slammed back down again. "I need – heaven help me – I want . . ." With one powerful move, he lifted her off of him and flipped her onto the bed, breaking their connection for only a heartbeat. Spreading her legs wide, he thrust back into her hard. With smooth, sure strokes, he began pumping, relentlessly. Joseph couldn't take his eyes off of her. Cady's face was a picture of ecstasy and her whole body was flushed with excitement. And, merciful heaven, her breasts were bouncing with every movement of their bodies. With perfect rhythm, he tunneled in and out of her, ramming root deep.

"I love this, Joseph. I love this so much," she panted, trying to let him know what their lovemaking meant to her. Every stroke had her crying out – every stroke brought her closer to cumming. Needing more, she wrapped her legs around his hips and strained upward, giving her clit maximum exposure to the delicious friction. It didn't take much; the convulsions started and just kept coming.

Joseph couldn't hold off. "It's so fucking good! Better. Every. Damn. Time." Her pussy muscles clamped down on his cock so hard he detonated, his cum shooting out in hot spurts. He ground his dick into her – holding it deep, causing her to shatter again. "That's my baby." Relaxing on top of her, he rested his forearms on either side of her head and kissed her deep, sucking on her lips.

Cady stretched underneath him, enjoying his weight pressing her into the mattress. Just that quick, passion morphed into tenderness. Lust had never been so sweet. Yes, this was much better than kissing the pillow – much better.

"Cady!" He bumped the door with his crutch. "Cady, are you ready? I'm hungry!" That ought to get her in high gear. She didn't like for him to be hungry. That thought made him smile. Cady was good to him. "Do you need me to help you pick out an outfit?"

"Give me a second," her frustrated voice sounded muffled through the door.

"Can I come in?" Surely, she wasn't shy. He had touched and kissed every inch of her beautiful body.

"All right." Yes! He opened the door and went in. Hell yeah! She was dressed, all right, and looked damn sexy in a deep red skirt and top. At the moment she was kneeling on the floor looking for something on the carpet. "Did you lose something, Cady-did?" He was about to lose his mind. Staring at her little heart-shaped ass presented to him like a gift from heaven had thrown his libido into maximum overdrive. It was all he could do to keep his hands off those sweet cheeks.

"I dropped my earring. Can you see it?" She was so sincere, wiggling her little rump around. It was all he could do to keep his hands to himself. He'd much rather be cupping that enticing little tush.

"Honey, I can almost see the Holy Land from here."

"What?" Not understanding, she glanced back at him with a puzzled expression. Seeing his sexy leer, she realized the position she had herself in. Apparently, Cady wasn't used to maneuvering around in short-short garments. Grimacing, she wrinkled her cute little nose and yanked on her skirt. Wiggling that delectable rump, she hid her luscious assets from his prying eyes.

Feeling a tad guilty, he moved closer and helped her search. "There it is." He pointed the tip of his crutch at the shiny metallic object. She retrieved it and quickly put it on. "Those are pretty, you don't usually wear jewelry. I like it."

"There are a lot of things you don't know about me." Getting up, Cady sat on the edge of the bed and looked forlorn. "I'm nervous about going out with you."

"Why?" He sat down beside her on the bed, knowing this was a dangerous place to be – if they intended to go out on the town at all. "I'd say we know each other pretty damn good."

Edging away from him, she crossed her legs beneath her – fighting the skirt – and faced him. "Our relationship is mega complicated. Perhaps it would be better if we just went back to our original client/therapist association."

"Cady, we're sleeping together." He watched as a blush rose from her neck and fanned out across her face. "I know this isn't a forever thing – we're just having a good time, but surely we can go out and have a drink and get something to eat. Besides, tonight we're gonna teach you how to flirt. Remember?"

"I remember." The problem was – deep in her heart – even as she understood it was impossible – Cady wanted their relationship to be a forever thing. She was in love with Joseph McCoy and if she was going to survive, she needed to get it through her head that what they shared was temporary. Going out on dates, even faux ones, wasn't the way to begin distancing herself from him. Joseph was used to being adored – he expected it. That was one of the reasons being ignored by women after his accident had devastated him, so.

Nevertheless, when he brushed her hair out of her face and looked at her with those big ole blue eyes, she knew she couldn't say no. "Okay, let's go." She hopped up – not only to show her agreement, but also to put a bit of distance between them. "I'm ready to become a femme fatale."

They went to Arnaud's French 75 Bar. It wasn't on crazy Bourbon Street, but on more sophisticated Bienville, a couple of blocks away. Cady chose it because it was romantic. She always got a thrill from the old school elegance, particularly the window love seat with its back to Rue Bienville. Okay, okay – she knew she wasn't there for romance – but what the hell. Tonight, she had her own agenda.

"Classy place, Cady. I like it." Joseph looked around at the gleaming wooden bar, the comfortable chairs and the whimsical monkey lamps. "Something smells good."

"This is Arnaud's, Joseph. The bar is attached to one of the best Creole restaurants in the Quarter – two birds with one stone." He held out a chair for her. "Thank you."

"You look beautiful, Cady." And she did. In fact, his cock was already twitching, raring to go another round with her as soon as they got home.

"You look great, too." She complimented him. Actually, he was devastating. Dressed all in black, he looked dangerous. They sat side by side, facing the interior of the bar. As soon as the waiter came, Joseph ordered a beer and she asked for their signature cocktail, a French 75; cognac, fresh squeezed lemon juice, simple syrup, topped with cold champagne and a lemon twist. Not waiting for Joseph to take up the game, she plunged in. "Look over there; see that woman at the bar? How about her? She's beautiful and she has her eye on that man in the suit. Let's watch."

The scene played out in front of them. She was seated at the bar stool and she made eye contact with her intended prey. Lifting her chin, she tossed her long blonde hair over her shoulder, thrusting her ample chest out like a knight throwing down the gauntlet. "I think I can do the hair thing, but I'm not as blessed as she is in the bosom department."

"Yes, you are. That woman doesn't have anything on you." He observed the woman in question; she looked a little cheap, if you asked him.

"Uh-oh," Cady put her hand over Joseph's. "She's ramping up her plan of attack." Ms. Hot-to-Trot turned sideways and crossed her legs, letting her skirt ride high. Now, she had her victim's full attention. He waived the bartender over and bought the lady a drink. She accepted it, gave him a wink and slid off the stool; stretching her legs out so he could see the top of her thigh high stockings. "I think she's going in for the kill."

He wasn't watching the action at the bar; he was enjoying her hand on his. She wasn't aware of what she was doing – she couldn't be. She was rubbing his hand sensuously, caressing the fingers, gliding the pad of her thumb over his palm. He was getting hard – no two ways about it.

The woman in question flowed over to her target. Her hips swayed, her breasts jiggled – she was projecting the idea that she was in heat and ready to be claimed. When she got close enough, she didn't pounce – she let herself be drawn in slowly like his body was a magnet. By the time, she actually put her hand on his shoulder; the poor man was vibrating with anticipation. "That's pretty forward, isn't it?" Cady was mesmerized, observing the woman work her hand up the man's back, until she cupped his neck lightly with two fingers, letting her fingernails scratch in erotic promise.

"Huh? What?" He wasn't watching. Cady had moved a bit closer and her leg was touching his from hip to thigh, and her caressing hand had moved under the table and was massaging his thigh. Fuck!? What was she doing to him? "Cady?"

Pulling away from him abruptly, she took a long sip of her drink. "See those two men who have just come in – the Marines? I'm going after them. I think I can do it. Wish me luck." Truthfully, Cady would rather have gone to the dentist and had all of her teeth pulled. But this was a gamble and she was betting all she had. If she didn't make Joseph jealous with this move – they had no chance.

What was she doing? "Cady?" He hadn't intended for her to jump in with both feet. Hell, she was going whole hog. The two sex hungry Marines were checking women out like they were shopping for a good steak. His Cady changed before his eyes. She paused and seemed to lower her head, as if collecting her thoughts and when she rose up and started walking – she was a different person. Her walk became sensuous, her hips swayed provocatively. She picked up her hair and held her arms over her head, which pushed her tits up – God; she looked like a sex goddess. By the time the two Marines saw her, she was moving toward them with a come hither look on her face that was making Joseph question his whole stupid plan. What had he done?

Cady couldn't look back to see if her plan was working, all she could do was hope Joseph wasn't studying the menu or heading out to visit the john. The boys in uniform had honed in on her and stood ready to reel her in. She gave them a smile, chewed on her lower lip and watched their jaws drop in admiration. Hell, this stuff did work! The looks on their face said it all – she was offering and they were buying. So, what did she do now? Unfortunately, she hadn't thought that far ahead. "Can I buy you guys a drink?" There, that sounded good. Now what?

"Hell, yeah!" one of them said. They pulled out a chair and invited her to sit.

"Not so fast." One moment, she had been about to sit – the next she was hauled backwards into a pair of strong arms and cradled against a broad, hard chest that she would recognize, anywhere – Joseph. "Let's get out of here." He didn't give her time to think twice.

"Hey, asshole. Wait a goddamn minute!" One of the marines made a grab for Joseph.

"You don't want to do that, soldier-boy." Joseph met the man's slightly inebriated look with a steely stare.

"If you think I'm letting some crip take off with this tasty morsel – you're a damn idiot." He took a swing at Joseph, but he missed.

"Joseph, I don't think this is a good idea." Cady couldn't stand to see him fight, his body wasn't healed enough to risk it.

Joseph laid down the crutch and turned to face the pair. He was prepared to do battle with both of them. This mess was his fault – and he would face the consequences. "Stay behind me, Cady."

"Why would you fight over some woman who was coming on to us like gangbusters?" the quieter marine asked. "Hey, don't I know you?" Before the question could be answered again, the first marine struck out and Joseph just flattened him – one strong uppercut to the jaw and the man fell like a big pine in a hurricane. While his buddy was helping him up, Joseph grabbed his crutch, took hold of Cady's hand and started for the door. Joseph was moving with determination. He might be a crip, but he was covering the ground he walked on and there wasn't a man in the bar who didn't realize that the cowboy had claimed his woman.

"Joseph, we need to talk." Joseph propelled her out of the bar and down the street to the first alley. Stepping two feet out of the glare of the street lamps, he pushed her back against the bricks. Penning her to the wall, he covered her mouth and began to kiss her wildly – blistering kisses, voracious kisses. God, yes. This is what she wanted. His hunger. His intensity. Underneath the onslaught, Cady smiled. Joseph was jealous. Mission accomplished.

His kisses slowed down – became tenderer. Cady thought her heart would burst. "That was the stupidest damn thing I've ever done." Joseph admitted. "I couldn't stand seeing you come on to those other men."

"But I thought that's what you wanted." She had to know.

"I'm a damn fool," he cupped her face, kissing her over and over. "I should have known, sharing has never been my strong suit."

"Oh, Joseph, I wasn't going to go through with it," she pacified him, returning him kiss for kiss. "It was just a game."

"Games are supposed to be fun," he sucked on her neck, rubbing his prominent erection against her belly. "And that was misery, no fun at all."

"If we were somewhere more private, I'd take care of you," she strained toward him, her nipples enjoying the chafing they were receiving from the pressure of his body against hers.

"Where's the nearest damn hotel?"

Cady racked her brain; she was too turned on to think straight. "Uh, the Royal Sonesta on Bourbon is just around the block. Let me go get the car and I'll drive us."

Joseph took her by the hand. "Can't wait – my cock is about to burst. And I'm not some damn invalid, Cady. I can walk a city block." They hurried through the crowd; he was almost dragging her. She was actually having a hard time keeping up. Truthfully, Joseph was getting around very well. The only thing that concerned Cady was how he favored his right side, it didn't have all the feeling back in it and it was drawn, slightly, making the crutch a necessity. Philippe would shine some light on that situation tomorrow.

The Royal Sonesta was a grand old hotel. Huge crystal chandeliers and ornate furniture filled the lobby. Joseph stopped at a couch and told her to wait while he went and booked a room. The fact they had no luggage was a bit embarrassing for her – but didn't affect Joseph a whit. This was probably not a new scenario for him – checking into a hotel just for sex. Cady had been to the Royal Sonesta before, but she had never stayed in one of the rooms.

"Come on, doll-face. Let's go." As soon as they were in the elevator, he slid in his key card, punched the button for the penthouse floor and backed her up against the wall. Placing his forehead against hers – he looked her right in the eye. "Now, let me make myself clear." Cady jumped as his hand cupped her sex. The thin dress she had on did nothing to cushion the impact of his questing fingers. He rubbed her slit – surely the dampness would seep through the material – massaging her clit and causing her to stand on tiptoe and spread her legs, begging for more. "Never – never again do I want you to flirt with another man in front of me."

She rubbed her lips against his; a tender, welcoming gesture. "I won't. I promise. Those men didn't do a thing for me – I only want you," she whispered.

The elevator dinged and he kissed her hard – a sultry promise of hot things to come. He held the door while she stepped out and tried to walk, he teased her by cupping her butt, making her jump and giggle. Being with Joseph was a heady, exhilarating experience – one she would never, ever forget. At the door to the suite – he slipped the key card in and they entered. Cady was sure the room was sumptuous and inviting, but she didn't pay the least bit of attention to it – her whole mind and body was focused on Joseph who had his hands all over her. As they walked to the bed, he was undressing himself and her. She helped as best she could, but her mind was numb with passion.

Only the bedside lamps illuminated the room, and they were turned on low, casting the big room in shadow. The bed was huge, bigger than any King size she had ever seen. Joseph left his crutch leaning against the dresser and crawled onto the bed, lying flat and spread-eagle right in the center. His cock was fully aroused and pulsing with life. "Seduce me, Cady. Flirt with me."

Cady wanted to pinch herself to see if she was dreaming. Flirt with him? Could she? He wanted her; that much was obvious. Closing her eyes for a split second, she drew upon her courage. A chance like this might never come again. Her inner Cady said, 'Go for it girl, make him drool!' "Joseph, I want you. I am so hungry for you. My body aches for you." As she spoke, she lifted her arms, lifting her heavy hair and exposing her neck. She licked her lips, slowly, running her tongue over the top lip, sensuously. Taking a step or two nearer the bed, she swayed her hips as she walked - Cady became a seductress.

Joseph almost swallowed his tongue. Lord, she was beautiful. She ran her palms down her body, caressing herself. And when she lifted her own breasts – pulling at the tips – offering them to him like a gift from the gods, he almost levitated off the bed. "Sweet Jesus, baby."

His reaction only spurred her on. Emboldened by his obvious appreciation of her efforts, she went a step further, sliding one hand down to her pussy and parting the folds with her fingers. She rubbed her clit and spread the cream, amazing herself. She was playing with her own pussy in front of a man! Would wonders never cease!? "Do you want me, Joseph? I'm going to make you feel so good. My pussy is going to milk your cock so hard. I'm so tight, baby. I'm starving for you." She drove him crazy with her words – her eyes never leaving his. God, he had unleashed a wildcat.

"Over here. Now." His voice was a low warning growl. As she drew near him, she could see the excitement leaking from his cock. Unable to resist, she took it in her hand and stroked from base to tip – a long, slow, luxurious glide of promise. "Fuck!" he gasped. He took her by the arm and pulled her over on top of him. "I need you so damn much."

She fitted her body to him, he was big and hard and every cell in her body responded to his nearness. Framing his face, she began eating at his mouth, sucking his lips and flirting with his tongue. He bucked his hips up, his cock stabbing her in the backside. Cady slid her body up and down on top of his, giving him a full-frontal massage with her tits. "Does that feel good, baby?" she asked as she kissed the corners of his mouth.

"Fuck, yes," he groaned. "Move up." He took her by the waist and pulled her farther up on top of him until he could reach her nipples with his mouth. "God – you are delicious." He bit at her tits – nuzzling and licking, grunting his enjoyment. Opening his mouth wide, he took her whole areola in his mouth, sucking and pulling. If possible, it seemed he would have swallowed it whole.

Cady was vibrating with need. She hadn't known it was possible to be so turned on. She held herself up by her arms while he feasted on her breasts. "Joseph – love – I need more," she begged.

"Turn around," he directed as he positioned her body like he wanted it. "Let's 69."

Of course she knew what '69' was, but that was like saying she knew what The Kentucky Derby was – it didn't mean she had ever been there. Before she knew what was happening, he had her on her stomach on top of him, her pussy in his face and right in front of her eyes was his mammoth cock, erect and badly in need of attention. "Glory be," she breathed. With a jerk on her hips, Joseph pulled her more firmly back against his face. "Joseph!" she yelped. Oh – my – God! With tongue and lips and teeth, he began to eat her out. How was she supposed to pleasure him when she couldn't even think? God, it felt good. She laid her head on his pelvis and let the unbelievably pleasurable sensations wash over her. There was no way she could ever explain to anybody what this felt like. It was out of this world! But, she couldn't be selfish – pleasing him was paramount. She held her head up and wiggled just a tad so she could worship his bounty. All she could think about was a verse in the Psalms – "Thy rod and thy staff – they comfort me." The thought almost made her giggle – she was going to get struck by lightning quoting Bible verses while she gave a man a blowjob.

    She licked. She sucked. She jacked him off. Taking him deep, she fondled his balls while her head bobbed up and down, deep-throating his dick. Joseph could feel his cum rising and boiling – God, this was incredible. He tongue-fucked her, playing with her clit – loving that she ground down on his face, wanting everything he could give her. She wasn't silent. Lord, she was loving him for all she was worth. Cady hummed her appreciation – moaning when he hit the right spot, grinding her pussy on his face. Joseph licked her cream, honeysuckle heaven – that was what she was, all sweet and tangy. As good as it was, he didn't want to cum this way – he wanted to be inside of her. "Stop, sweetheart. I need to fuck," he said with one last long lick to her crease.

    Cady was in the zone – she heard him speak, but she didn't want to stop – she loved the feel of him in her mouth. When he began pulling her body up, she let go and allowed him to flip her onto her back. His wish was her command. Rising above her, his big chest was a playground for her fingertips. "Your body is a work of art." She traced his pecs with her fingers, molding the hard flesh. "I love to touch you." He leaned over farther, offering himself to her tongue. She took full advantage, teasing one nipple while she enjoyed the rough texture of his chest hair with her fingertips. Cady couldn't get over the thrill of having Joseph's body to play with. It was so amazing to touch and kiss where and how she wanted to. It was like being turned loose in a candy store – she wanted a taste of everything!

    "Spread those legs, Cady. I want in." He was so damn strutted with lust that he thought his cock was gonna burst.

He rose up on his arms while she opened her legs, leaving herself completely open to his possession. Bless her heart — she canted her hips, took his dick in her hand and guided him in. "Oh, hell yeah," he moaned. Lord, his baby was tight — but oh, so soft and wet. Her little cunt sucked him in like quicksand — except this was like sinking into hot whipped cream. "Ahhhhh," he moaned, loving the feel of sinking balls deep into her snug little channel. Once again, he was struck with the oddest feeling. He had fucked more women than he could count — but never had he felt this tremendous sense of homecoming, of finding exactly what he had been looking for. Throwing his head back, he enjoyed the rush he got from sliding in and out of her pussy, the way she clamped down on it, trying to hold him in. "Oh baby — you know how to please me."

His compliment only made her want more. Hooking her feet over the back of his knees, she pushed upward with her hips, as much as his weight would allow. It was so wonderful! The pleasure was exquisite. It felt like he was pushing deep enough to touch her soul. Holding on to his shoulders, she watched his face. She couldn't help it, it was just too much. Tears began to trickle out the corners of her eyes. Lord, she loved him. Being here with him like this was more than she had ever hoped for.

Joseph looked down. She was crying! "God, am I hurting you, baby?" He immediately, stilled.

"No, no," she lifted her hips, squeezed him, urging him to continue. "You're not hurting me. It feels wonderful."

He lowered his head, kissing the tears away. "Well, then why are you crying? What do you have to cry about?" Merciful heavens, he loved to make love with her. She was made just right. Her little body housed him like she had been fashioned exclusively for his pleasure.

"I'm crying because . . . because," she stopped, trying to collect herself. All the time they were talking, she was milking him, loving him — working his cock with her pussy muscles – showing him what she wouldn't allow herself to say. Cady loved Joseph - with all her heart. So, she said enough to let him know what he meant to her without making him uncomfortable. "I'm crying because I'm happy and you make me feel so good and I can't believe I'm here with you like this – it's just a miracle." Her confession seemed to enflame him – he stiffened his arms and began pumping into her with hard, jabbing thrusts – making her whole body shift with every pile-driving motion of his hips. "God, yes!" she screamed as she splintered into a million pieces. She arched up, begging for all he could give her – needing him to fill her up so she'd never be hungry again.

How had he lived and not known the difference between sex and lovemaking? As he felt Cady's body shake and quiver beneath him – felt her vagina tighten around his cock in tiny convulsive caresses, Joseph's orgasm hit him like a freight train. He felt a rush of bliss that took his breath away – his cum boiled up from deep in his balls and he exploded – the pleasure was so intense that he bowed his head, laying it on the pillow next to her. She took advantage of his nearness and kissed him over and over – nipping his shoulder – all the time her pussy quivered, the muscles throbbing with joy as she came.

Joseph pushed his cock as deep as he could and just held it there – letting both of their bodies squeeze every second of rapture they could out of their climax. He shook with emotion – his whole body pulsating with pleasure. With awe, Joseph realized he would never be the same. Cady had changed him. She had shown him what it was like to give of oneself expecting absolutely nothing in return. He had made no promises, and right now – he still couldn't make any. The future was so uncertain. Yet, she demanded nothing. Her only desire seemed to be to make him happy. Cady gave him a second chance, but he had to determine what he wanted from this unexpected opportunity. Did he want to return to extreme sports – or invest himself in Tebow – or pursue some other, yet undetermined, dream?

"Thank you," she whispered, kissing his shoulder. "Thank you, I loved that."

He captured her mouth, kissed her with tenderness and nipped her lip.

"Ow!" she squealed – giggling so hard she jiggled his body. "What was that for?"

He couldn't tell her the truth. "Because you're cute." She was cute, but he teased her to lighten the mood. The truth was - he was very near to telling her that he loved her – and that scared the living shit out of him. Love was not in his plans, right now. And he didn't know if it ever would be.

They had made love without a condom, again. Cady lay in the bed beside Joseph while he slept. She rubbed her tummy, imagining it blossoming with child. It really hadn't occurred to her until Joseph pulled out, his semen running out of her, coating the inside of her thigh. She had gone to the restroom, wet a washcloth and cleansed herself. All the while she wondered if she would ever know the thrill of a child growing in her womb. Maybe, she ought to buy a pregnancy test. That way she would know for sure. And the odd thing was – she didn't know which she was more afraid of: that she would be pregnant with Joseph's child or that she wouldn't be. After she had seen to her own needs, she had taken a warm washcloth out and tenderly bathed his cock. The look he had given her as she ministered to him would stay with her forever. On some level, Joseph loved her. She could see it. She could feel it. They were connected on a cellular level – so deep and so abiding it was scary. Cady couldn't explain it. Maybe she *was* Joseph's guardian angel – that was as good an explanation as any.

Listening to him breathe – she committed the sound to memory. He wasn't snoring, but each inhale and exhale was audible. And every few minutes he would say something.

She couldn't make it out, but he was almost talking in his sleep. She covered her lips, catching a giggle when he laughed a little. Whatever he was dreaming was pleasant. Cady turned on her side and looked at him. The light from the bathroom illuminated his face. God, how she loved him. She leaned closer in. He was saying something. What was it? And when she heard it – Cady gasped. For Joseph was talking to her. "I love you, Cady. I love you." They were the most precious words anyone had ever spoken. Cady filed them away in her heart, so she would have them to replay over and over again.

"Hey, get up, sleepyhead." Joseph tickled her in the ribs. "We're gonna be late for my appointment." She raised up from the pillow. When he opened his eyes, she had been sleeping on her stomach and he had been draped over her – an arm around her waist and one of his legs thrown over the both of hers. Since he had begun sleeping with Cady, he couldn't imagine sleeping alone, again. He laughed out loud. She looked so disgruntled. "Look at you. Did you have a bad night?" Her hair was messed up and she had a pillow crease on her face. God, she was adorable! And naked as a jaybird.
"What time is it?"
"Eight o'clock. We need to go back to your house and shower and change."
"Okay," she flopped back on the pillow. "Wake me up in ten minutes."
"Nah-uh," he straddled her. "You aren't going back to sleep. I'm hungry. You didn't feed me last night."
"Sorry," she said in a muffled amused voice.
"You don't sound sorry." He couldn't believe how much fun he was having.
"We ate – each other." She giggled.
"What did you say?" he goosed her sides.

"Stop!" she squealed. She bucked her little butt up, doing her best to unseat him.

"Whoa, baby." He scooted back down her legs, trapping her, swatting her on her butt.

"Joseph McCoy! If I ever get up from here, I'm gonna whale the tar out of you." She didn't sound mad, she was laughing so hard, she was out of breath.

"Hell, baby." He moved off of her, and began rubbing her ass in caressing motions. "Spread your legs." She tried to turn over. "No, stay where you are. You're just fine." Cady opened her legs about six inches, wondering what he was up to. Joseph straddled her again, laying on top of her this time, supporting himself on his arms. "Now, hike your bottom enough for me to get in." He felt between her legs, making sure she was wet. "Damn, you are ready for me, now, aren't you?"

"I told you I'm always ready for you," she groaned as he pushed two fingers up inside of her and played with the spongy area that drove her crazy. "Fuck me, please!" she wailed.

"Demanding little thing, aren't you?" He loved it. She wanted it – anytime – anywhere – unconditionally. It was damn good for his ego. "You want me – baby, you've got me." He surged into her, causing her to gasp.

"Harder, Joseph!" Cady was so excited. He angled himself until he was lying flat on top of her.

"Am I too heavy?"

"No, God, no. You're just pressing me down into the mattress." She found that she could move her hips down and squeeze him even harder. "I like this."

"Lord, I do too." He sucked on her neck, pumping into her, relentlessly. "Arch your back." When she did, he slid his hands under her and grasped both breasts, kneading them in time to his thrusting hips. "Do you like that?"

She whimpered and moaned. "Oh, Joseph! God, I'm cumming already!"

"I can feel it." He scraped his teeth over her neck, wanting to eat her alive. "Jesus, you're tight, baby. You squeeze me so good. Damn!" he bellowed and filled her pussy with his seed. He didn't stop moving, he just slowed down – sliding in and out – loving the feel of her body beneath him. She laid her head down on the pillow, completely out of breath. "Are you okay?" he kissed her hair, her neck, her back.

"Perfect. I'm just perfect."

He was about to agree with her when a sharp rap sounded on the door. "Hell, who could that be?" Joseph pulled out and rolled off of her. She got up, grabbed her robe and gave him a sweet grin.

"That's room service. I ordered it last night after you went to sleep. See, I take care of you just fine."

"Your progress has been phenomenal." Dr. Philippe Francois looked Joseph in the eye. "Although, there is still some nerve damage on your right side."

"What do we do about that?" Joseph reached over and grabbed Cady's hand. "Can Cady help me with more healing spells?"

Philippe locked eyes with Cady. "I never underestimate the power of a woman, especially a woman as exceptional as Acadia."

Cady looked at the good doctor. "We are still following an aggressive exercise and therapy program with deep-tissue massage and herbal treatments."

"Acadia, my new niece, you can speak freely with me. I am married to Angelique, high priestess of Santeria. I have worked beside Nanette Beaureguarde and watched Evangeline McCallister brew up a storm. I am familiar with your family and friends."

Taking him at his word, she addressed the more mystical elements of her work. "I have continued with the healing spells. Each time I've massaged him, I've used the laying on of hands technique. I repeat the chants and call upon the healing energy, but I'm not going to give up. There are still things I can try."

"You are an empath, are you not?" Philippe asked bluntly.

"Now, wait a minute," Joseph began. "I've seen Cady take my pain and I don't ever want to see her do that again."

Cady looked at Joseph, surprised. "The pain doesn't last long." She hadn't considered taking his nerve damage. She had never tried to do that. Her grandmother's warnings echoed in her mind. "Doctor, have you had experience with other empaths?"

Dr. Philippe leaned back in his chair, pausing before he answered. He was very dark skinned, slight of build with a twinkle in his eye. "Yes, I have. I've seen them do some miraculous things. Once, I saw an empath heal a boy of autism. She exhibited the symptoms for several days, but soon they were both normal. Another time I saw a woman with leprosy healed. The empath developed the lesions and other symptoms, but she cured the leper. For a time, I was afraid the empath would retain the disease, but it gradually dissipated.

"No." Joseph didn't look in the mood to argue. "I'd rather stay the way I am right now, than risk Cady hurting herself."

"It's up to you," Philippe spread his hands. "But without the intervention, I'm not sure you will advance much beyond the ability you have now."

Cady made her mind then. She would heal Joseph, completely. "Would you give me a copy of the x-rays and the other tests so I can determine the proper course of therapy?" The doctor stood and gestured toward the door. "Come into my laboratory."

Joseph grabbed her hand. "The answer is still no."

"I'll be right back." She kissed him quickly on the lips and followed the doctor before Joseph could say anything else.

When they were alone, he gave her the information she needed and turned and looked her full in the face. "Tell me what type of diseases or afflictions you have been able to absorb?"

Cady turned and looked out the window. She could see the Superdome where so many had suffered and died during Hurricane Katrina. "My experience has been limited. I have taken pain, some diseases." She knew she could not be certain of Libby's cancer. So, there was no use addressing that issue. "My grandmother warned me not to attempt to take burns or wounds or broken bones. I can take the discomfort – no matter how intense - but not the affliction. She said she could not promise my body would throw those things off like it can fevers or pain."

Rubbing his hand over his short hair, Philippe blew out a long breath, "Every empath is different. Unfortunately, there are no hard and fast rules governing this mysterious power that you have. Only you can be the judge of your abilities."

For a few seconds, Cady debated telling Dr. Francois her plans. After all, he was married to her aunt. "Does patient confidentiality apply to me?" She grinned at him. He raised his eyebrows in a questioning manner. "I don't see how I can deny him this chance to completely recover all that he was before. He's the type of man who will never be happy with less than perfect." As she said the words, she knew this truth applied too more than his former life. Joseph deserved the best. He deserved perfect, and she knew that term would never apply to Cady Renaud.

"My advice is to proceed with caution. I know that's cliché, but only you can know what your limitations are and how big of a risk you are willing to take."

NOLA was crowded. The great chef Emeril Lagasse owned the trendy restaurant on St. Louis Street. Cady had eaten there several times and wanted to share the experience with Joseph. They had ordered the Hickory-roasted duck with the whiskey caramel sauce and the brown sugar glazed sweet potatoes. "Damn, this is good!" Joseph bragged.

"It is, isn't it? I usually get the crab cake appetizer so I can splurge on the pumpkin bread pudding."

Cady made a sigh that sounded exactly like the one she made when he sucked on her clit. "Damn!" he said again, but for an entirely different reason this time.

"The word is Bam! Sir, not Damn!" Joseph looked up to see none other than Emeril Lagasse himself standing there with a big grin on his face. "Hello, sweetheart." He bent down and hugged Cady. "Who's your friend?"

"Emeril, I had no idea you were here tonight. It's so good to see you. This is a – uh – a patient of mine." She would have loved to claim him as something more, but she wasn't sure how he would feel about that. "Joseph McCoy meet Emeril Lagasse, my favorite chef in the whole world."

Joseph stood and shook the jovial gentleman's hand. He was decked out in traditional snow-white chef attire, which contrasted sharply with Joseph's choice of all black. "Great to meet you, sir. I'm a big fan."

"Nice to meet you, young man." Emeril narrowed his eyes. "You're the guy who does everything, aren't you? You're the extreme sports champion? Sure, Joseph McCoy. I, also, am a big fan."

"At the moment, I'm out of commission." Joseph explained without going into detail.

"I heard about your accident." Emeril placed a hand on Cady's shoulder. "No need to explain your vast improvement. I can guess the answer would be our Cady." He kissed Cady on the cheek. "Your money is no good here, dear. I'll take care of everything." With that he slapped Joseph on the back and was off to greet other guests.

Joseph sat back down. "That was fun. Emeril Lagasse recognized me." He was quite amazed. "How do you know him?"

"For years, he was the chef over at Commander's Palace. He knows my grandmother quite well and I have frequented his restaurants here in New Orleans since I was a child. Emeril is one of New Orleans' gifts to the world."

"As are you, my Cady." Joseph raised his tea glass to her. How different she seemed to him now than she had the first day he had laid eyes on her. Cady was amazing, there was no two ways about it.

"Can I have your autograph?" A young, very beautiful woman stood at Joseph's elbow. "I heard Emeril call your name and I recognized you, too." She held out a pen and a napkin to Joseph. Not once did she look at Cady, instead she rubbed Joseph's back like she was about to give him a massage. Joseph shrugged a tiny bit, enough to let the woman know her attention was not welcome. She did not take the hint.

"Sure. What's your name?"

"Make it out to Shelly, write something sexy." As he wrote – 'All the best, Joseph McCoy' – the woman draped herself over Joseph's shoulder resting one large breast on his arm. "I'm glad you are back on your feet." The aggressive fan pushed another napkin in Joseph's front right shirt pocket.

"Thank you. I appreciate that. Here you go," Joseph said graciously. He handed it to her, backing up a bit. It was an obvious dismissal. The woman looked disappointed, gave Cady a haughty glance and whirled around to leave.

Joseph took the piece of paper out of his pocket and saw that a phone number was written on it as well as the name of a hotel and room number. He wadded the paper up and placed it in the middle of the table to be disposed of by the waiter. "Sorry about that, Cady."

None of what she had seen surprised Cady. She had been uncomfortable, but that was all. "It's okay. I'm sure you deal with that type of thing all the time."

"I do." Joseph was surprised that the woman's admiration and obvious come-on had not given him the thrill he had expected. "But, you were here. It wasn't right." His own attitude surprised him. Never before had he taken offense when an admiring fan or a hopeful groupie interrupted a date. Joseph realized the reason was simple. None of the other women he had spent time with had been as important to him as Cady was. That information stunned him.

They made love that night and it was mind-blowing. Joseph lay in the dark with Cady cuddled up to his side. Her head on was his shoulder and she was draped over him – an arm across his chest and a leg thrown over his, her knee resting right on top of his package. He just hoped she didn't bear down hard and smash his wiener. With one hand he rubbed up and down her arm, loving the feel of her skin. Everything that had been going on was racing through his mind. He had feelings for Cady. Deep feelings. And she was falling for him – he knew that. The question was – what was he going to do about it? The worst thing he could do would be to hurt her. But what the answer was, he didn't know.

Joseph dozed. He was hot. God, he was hot. He threw the covers back. Where was Cady? He was alone in the bed. "Cady? Where are you?" There was no answer. Worried, he started to sit up, but a hand on his shoulder stopped him. "Cady?"

"Joseph. My Joseph."

"You!" His midnight angel was beside him, kneeling on the bed. She was bathed in moonlight, and nothing else. Heaven had never created anything more beautiful than she was. Joseph was in absolute awe. "Who are you?"

"I am yours," was her simple answer. She held out her arms to him. He moved toward her remembering the ecstasy he had known in her embrace.

But what about Cady? "Where's Cady?" he asked.

She didn't answer. Instead, she closed the distance between them. Cradling his head in her arms, she pulled it to her breast. "Don't you want me? I crave you above all others."

He couldn't help himself. He kissed the soft, smooth skin of her breast. She was exquisite. Rapture awaited him in her arms; he knew that. But what about Cady? Her hand drifted down to his straining cock. It jumped in her hand. His mind was warring with his body. Something was wrong. Being with her seemed so right, but his heart was telling him to stop. "I. . . I think you are wonderful. And being with you was out of this world, but I can't."

"You have always been mine," she held him tenderly. "You always will be." She seemed so certain of what she said, yet his protests did not seem to upset her.

"I can't do this to Cady."

She said nothing else, only smiled at him serenely, kissed him on the cheek and . . . . he woke up, jerking so hard, he almost fell off the bed. Joseph whipped his head around, curled up beside him lay Cady, sound asleep.

Chapter Eleven

Very early in the morning, while the city is still quite, sometimes you can hear the streetcar over on St. Charles. This was one of those mornings. When she had awakened, Cady had been alone. And for a few minutes she had wondered if all of it had been a dream – going to Texas, meeting Joseph – healing him, loving him. But the pillow she usually made out with bore the distinctive impression of where he had laid his head. That indention drew her touch. Placing her hand into the depression, Cady rejoiced in the evidence that he was more than a dream. Hazy with sleep, her mind wandered – a dream – it seemed she dreamed last night about Joseph, but she couldn't remember what it had been about. That was strange; usually she had no trouble recalling the details. Curious as to where he was, she left the bed, pulled on a robe and went to find him. The smell of coffee led her to the kitchen. He was sitting at her small round dining table with a cup of coffee in front of him. "Couldn't you sleep?"

He smiled at her, pulling her into his lap. "I had some weird dreams." Nuzzling the side of her neck, he said. "You smell good in the mornings, Cady-did."

Cady snuggled up against him, "You haven't shaved. I like the way your beard feels on my skin. It's all raspy." She cupped his face and kissed the exposed skin of his neck. He was already dressed in a pair of blue jeans, but his blue shirt hung open unbuttoned and Cady gave herself a morning gift of tracing the contour of his muscles. "What do you want to do today?"

Kissing her on the forehead, he pulled her closer and said. "If it's okay with you, I'd like to head back to the ranch. There have been a few things on my mind and I'd like to check into them. You know, I've got to start making plans, finding something to do with my life. I have the ranch, of course – but I need more. You heard Philippe; this may be as good as it gets for me."

"We're not through with your treatment, Joseph." Was he trying to get rid of her? Already?

"I know we're not, love." He reassured her with a soft kiss on the end of her nose. "And I want to continue. I have faith in you. After all, you have brought me this far. You don't know what it means for me to be able to stand up and walk under my own steam." When she tried to look away, he caught her face and made sure she was looking into her eyes. "This crutch is a pain in the ass, but I can live with it, if I have to. What I couldn't live without is my manhood – my virility – and you gave me that back completely. For that gift, I owe you devotion and gratitude for the rest of my life."

Cady stiffened in his arms. She didn't want his devotion and his gratitude. Was that what this was? "It was my job. It was what you hired me to do, remember?" As soon as she said the words, she knew she had to correct them. "But you know I would have done it for nothing. Helping you has meant more to me than you will ever know." She knew at that moment that she wouldn't be taking any payment for her time with Joseph. It wouldn't be right. The money that had been transferred to her bank account would be returned and she would accept no more. "Don't give up on a complete recovery, not yet," she urged him knowing what she intended to do.

"I'm not; it's just smart to have a plan to fall back on." He took one of her hands and began rubbing the fingers, almost absentmindedly. "For so long, I didn't think I had a future and now that I do – I want to make something out of. To tell you the truth, I was planning on taking a look at my life when the accident happened. My options may have changed, but I know there are things I can do to make a difference in other people's lives. Beau said some things to me the other day that have been weighing on my mind.

There is a lot happening in the search for answers in how to live with paraplegia. Stem cell research seems to be on the cusp of a breakthrough and there is even talk of robotic suits that people can wear to give them a mobility they would never have otherwise."

"Your family is very active in cancer research funding; I can see you expanding that to aid in the search for a cure for spinal cord injuries. I think it's a wonderful idea."

"Not everybody can have a Cady in their lives to work miracles for them. So, I thought it would be the least I could do to show my gratitude for the blessings I have been given." He was so sincere and so sweet that Cady couldn't resist hugging him. "We'll go back now and I'll do my very best to take you that extra step toward a complete healing."

"Do you have on anything under this robe?" Joseph was still confused about his feelings and torn over the dream he had the night before, but she was sitting in his lap and his cock was beginning to take notice. He untied the cotton belt to see for himself. It was like unwrapping a Christmas present.

"Not a blessed thing." She didn't know how long she would have him in her life. But as long as this precious interlude lasted, she would be a fool not to take full advantage of it. Her robe was tossed to the side and his blue jeans and underwear found their way to the floor.

"Lay back on the table," his voice was urgent. Lord, first her bed – now her kitchen – no room in her house was going to be absent of precious memories. "Now, put your legs around my waist." Cady loved any position that Joseph wanted to try – but face-to-face was her favorite. Looking at him while he took her, while his passion could be read as easily as a book – she couldn't tear her eyes away. "What do you say, Cady? Do you want me?"

She lifted her hips, spread her legs and showed him the physical evidence of her desire. She was swollen and glistening – her vagina was open like a flower, her nectar flowing and sweet – the honey of love. As he slid into her, she answered him and he knew the words would haunt him forever – for it was the exact words his angel had said to him the night before. "I am yours. I crave you above all others."

Back at the ranch, Joseph found the family in an uproar. There had been more fence cutting incidents, one of Jacob's gas wells had been sabotaged and Jessie was having premature labor pains. "If it ain't one thing, it's another." Aron walked beside his brother on the way to the corral. Kane doesn't have anything new to report and Vance is trying to help Isaac track down that little Avery gal. "But, I am sure thankful to hear that you got a pretty good report. How do you feel?"

Aron had slowed down so Joseph could keep up with him. He tried not to let that bother him, but it did. Special treatment was not something he had a hankering for. "Cady is going to keep working with me and the doctor didn't rule out the possibility that I'd get better. He just said there's a chance this will be as good as it gets."

"What do you think?" Aron believed that Joseph's attitude was the key. He didn't discount Cady's ability or her magic, but if Joseph had given up and was convinced his recovery was at a standstill – Aron was afraid it would be a self-fulfilling prophecy.

"I'm praying for a miracle, of course." They came to the fence where Jacob was riding a new horse.

"That's the ugliest mare I've ever seen." Aron called out to Jacob who was putting the little filly through her paces.

Joseph studied the horse in question. She wasn't that pretty. Her coat was a dull brown and her mane looked like it stayed tangled all the time. Her nose had a blemish on it that Joseph couldn't tell whether it was a wart or a cut. "What's wrong with her face?"

Jacob rode to the fence. "She's been abused. Somebody whipped her in her face. She's got scars on her rump, too."

Then, he eyed his brother, hard. "And she's not ugly. She's mine." As far as Jacob was concerned that settled it.

"Does her belonging to you make her pretty?" He didn't know why he asked the question, but the answer seemed important.

"Beauty is in the eye of the beholder, brother. Haven't you ever heard that?" Jacob patted the mare on her flank and dismounted. "The longer I love her, the prettier she'll get, and you just watch what I tell you." He tied her to the fence and stood upon it, looking down at Aron and Joseph. "So, did you hear that somebody sabotaged my well? The main valve started leaking and if my foreman hadn't been alert, it could have been disastrous."

"How do you know somebody messed with it?" It wasn't that Joseph didn't believe him; he was just curious and more than a little troubled. What else could go wrong with their family?

Jacob didn't appear to be offended. "Because they used the wrong size tool and scarred up the surface tree."

"You know we don't know all that fuel jargon." Aron complained. "Suffice it to say somebody tampered with your shit."

"Do you think it's connected with the other vandalism we've been having?"

As Jacob talked, his new horse nudged him in the back of the leg. "Easy Angel, I'll get you some sugar in a few minutes." Turning his attention back to his brothers he floored Joseph. "Just before the two of you went to New Orleans, I had Cady read a piece of barbwire, to see if she got any type of reading from it. And she told me all of this was personal and it was directed toward me. And the clincher is, she told me that the fence cutting wouldn't be all he would try. I guess she was right."

Joseph was stuck on the fact that the horse's name was Angel. Lately, the word had come to mean something special to him – it was all mixed up with Cady and his night visitor. And the fact that Jacob said the horse was beautiful because he loved it – that sounded way too close to how his feelings for Cady had evolved. Lord, he was losing it. Now, he thought he was getting messages from a horse. "Now, say that again – what you said about Cady."

Aron looked at Joseph like he was retarded, and spoke real slow. "He said that Cady fingered the barb wire and told him the perpetrator was out to get him, personally, and that said perpetrator would find some more ways to get back at him for whatever wrong he feels Jacob has done to him." By the time Aron had drawled out his Lincoln-lawyer version of the truth Joseph was laughing.

"Thank you, for your legal interpretation, Ben Matlock." He hadn't known that Cady had read for Jacob, but he wasn't surprised. Cady helped any way she could.

"If you ask me, I think Cady did it," Aron was joking, but Joseph took offense.

"Don't even joke like that," Joseph defended her with a snarl. "Cady would never hurt anybody and she would do anything she could to help this family."

Aron winked at Jacob. "You remember what Daddy said about old Luen. Him and mama visited that old fortune teller when some of their cows went missing. This was just after they got married. And Luen told him they had been stolen, but one of them would show back up and he identified which cow would return." Aron paused for effect. "And he was right. Daddy always wondered where old Luen had them cows tied up. Usually fortune tellers are the type to take advantage of innocent people."

Joseph couldn't see it, but Aron was setting him up for a fall. And it worked. Joseph wheeled on Aron and got right in his face. "Cady is not a fortune teller and she would rather hurt herself than ever think about hurting one of us. I love Cady and I don't want you to say another damn word against her. Do you hear me?"

"Yea, I hear you," Aron laughed. "Loud and clear. Did you hear him, Jacob?"

"I think the folks over in the next county heard him. So, you love Cady?"

Joseph leaned against the fence and blew out a long breath. "Looks like it – but damn, if I know what I'm gonna do about it."

Cady doubled up on her efforts to help Joseph. She didn't cut him any slack, but pushed him harder than ever. And when it was time for his massage, she did more than give him a rubdown. Cady poured her whole self into the act. She prayed, chanted in her mind, laid her hands on him in abject love and supplication – asking the powers-that-be to heal him completely and mend the nerves in his right side that kept him from being whole. That night, she planned on taking it all the way. While he slept, she intended to take the nerve damage into her own body. What it would do to her, she didn't know – but that wasn't what was important. Joseph was important. The reporter from Dallas Morning News would be at the ranch in the morning and she intended for him to have a scoop he never expected.

Libby and Jessie cornered her in the kitchen. "Tell us about your trip. Did you and Joseph have a good time?" Libby was literally beaming. Her pregnancy had passed the morning sickness stage and she had that ethereal glow that women with child always get. What Cady wouldn't give to be as beautiful as Libby.

"We did, actually." Cady reported as she filled a glass with lemonade. "We did some sightseeing, ate at Emeril's restaurant and I practiced flirting with better results than I anticipated." She didn't intend to tell them all the details, but Jessie would have none of it.

"Flirting? Spill it girl. Who were you flirting with?"

Cady debated on how much to say, but she didn't have any other female friends. "I don't know if you realize it, but I'm in love with Joseph."

Libby and Jessie both broke out in laughter. "Of course, we know. And he's sweet on you, too. We can tell."

"I don't know about that," Cady protested. "The sad truth is Joseph sorta took me on as a project. He told me how to wear my hair and he's the one that suggested a makeover. And on the way down to New Orleans, he decided that I should learn how to flirt." Just the memory of what happened made Cady blush. "So, I watched this other woman make a play for this guy and when two marines walked in – I got up and put on a show."

"You didn't?" Libby was enjoying this.

"I did." Cady leaned in conspiratorially. "I flirted for all I was worth and Joseph came over, grabbed me, hauled me out of there . . ."

"And laid one on you." Jessie's eyes were big as she visualized their sensual encounter.

"I bet he did more than lay one on her, didn't he? Did you two do the mattress mambo?"

Cady grabbed her cheeks, knowing that she was scarlet with embarrassment. "Actually, we couldn't check into a hotel fast enough." All three girls squealed with laughter. After a few moments, Cady sobered. "But, I have a favor to ask you two."

"Sure, anything." Jessie assured her. "We love to match make."

"Well, what I need for you to do; is nothing like that. Tonight, I'm going to take Joseph's paralysis that's affecting his right side." The other two sat down and stared at her.

Jessie lowered her voice. "Is this dangerous? You were pretty sick after you helped Libby."

Libby looked guilty, but Cady hastened to assure her. "It didn't last long. In fact, it never does. I've just never done this particular type of empathic healing before. And I don't want Joseph to know I've done it – not for a while, at least. So, what I need you to do is distract him. Tomorrow, before its time for me to get up - I need one of you to call Joseph out of the room and send him on some type of a mission. That will give me time to see what shape I'm in. I may have to hide the fact I am not walking the best in the world." She hoped, as usual, any symptoms she exhibited would be less than what Joseph had suffered - and they wouldn't last but a few hours. But she couldn't be sure; it would be the morning before the symptoms would be evident. If it were really bad, it might be necessary that she leave Tebow for a while.

Jessie and Libby agreed to the plan and Cady felt sure she had done the right thing.

He caught her in the bathroom. It all started out innocently enough, but quickly progressed to an erotic playtime. Cady was running a tub of water and added bubble bath – a little too much bubble bath. Joseph walked in while she was leaning over the tub trying to mash the bubbles down before they floated over the top, just in time to see her fall over headfirst into the tub. "Gottcha!" he pulled her back to safety, she was sputtered with big poofs of bubbles on her face and in her hair. "What are you trying to do, drown yourself, watersprite?" She was slick, soft and sexy – just the way he liked her.

She wiped her face so she could see him. "Thanks, I was about to take a bath and things got out of hand." She smiled at him, sweetly. "Do you want to take a bath with me? Or do all of these bubbles threaten your sense of masculinity?" Lord, she loved to tease him. She was going to miss him like crazy when it was time to go home.

"Baby, I am so much of a man that I could wear pink underwear and still make you cream and tremble."

She didn't doubt it a bit. "You've got on too many clothes, Aquaman."

While he undressed, she spread out some towels, just in case they got rambunctious. She hoped they got rambunctious. "I've never had sex in a bathtub before." Like he didn't know that – since he had taken her virginity and everything else she had to offer.

"Who said we were going to have sex in the bathtub?" Joseph asked with a smirk on his face. "I'm not going to have sex with you in that water." When he saw her pooch her bottom lip out just a tad, he made a grab for her. "I plan on having my evil way with you," he grabbed her and held her hands behind her back. "I plan on seducing you," he bit her on the neck, making her laugh. "And I plan on making love with you," he turned her in his arms so he could claim her mouth. "Nothing as simple as having sex."

Cady wound her arms around his neck and rubbed her body against his. He groaned at the intimate contact. "You get in first and I'll fit myself between your legs." She didn't hold his hand, but she stayed close just in case he slipped. Hopefully, tomorrow would change all of that. She was counting on it.

"I like the sound of that – you being between my legs." He eased down in the tub and the bubbles were displaced precariously close to the top. "Don't worry about those bubbles baby – it's just soap and water." He held his hand out and she climbed over. Just as she was about to sit, he pulled her right down on top of him. "Now, I've got you." Water went everywhere and he hooted with laughter.

"Yes, you've got me." Did he realize how true that was? "Now, what are you going to do with me?" He spread his legs until her bottom fit right in the vee of his thighs. "Oh!"

He wasted no time getting down to business. She was leaning back on his chest and his arms were around her. Facing away from him, she was totally at his mercy and the only part of him she could reach was his oak-hard legs framing her lower body. His hands began their torment, using the bubbles and the water to aid in his play. They started at her neck, lifting her hair so he could kiss the curve of her neck and tease the shell of her ear. He gently rubbed her shoulders, stroked both muscular hands down her arms, and with feathery light touches brought them back up. Then, his hands began their torture of her breasts. It hadn't taken him very long to find out how to absolutely drive her mad, "Does that answer your question?"

Her breasts and nipples were the hot button area of her body—not that her loins didn't scream out for him—they did—but she adored how he worshipped her breasts. "You have all the answers," she laid her head back on his shoulder and swooned. He circled them, cupped them, and weighed them with his hands. He lifted them, massaged them, rubbing the nipples between his fingers until she whimpered with delight. And just as soon as she thought he was through, he would begin again. This time, he pushed her all the way. Not a finger went any lower than the underside of her breasts and he made her orgasm—trembling, her hips pumping up and down, giving themselves the only stimulation he would allow. She arched her neck and begged for his mouth and he met her lips and kissed them reverently as she shook with the richness of her climax. "More," she pushed her toes hard against the end of the tub. "This is the best time I've ever had in the tub," Cady spoke in breathy little pants. Her pelvis shot up and she gasped, "Oh my Lord, Joseph."

"You didn't really want to take a bath did you, my insatiable angel?" He knew he had more on his mind than a good soak. His hands encircled her breasts once more and then they both moved lower. He put one on either side of her most tender flesh and pulled her tightly back against him. She could feel the rock hard presence of his penis right behind her hips and nestled against her lower back. His cock was so big, and it was getting bigger by the second.

He spread her legs wide against his own, and then both hands occupied themselves between her thighs. One hand went toward the place of her greatest need, the emptiness she had longed for him to fill all day. And he filled her vagina with one finger, and then two. The other hand massaged and manipulated her clitoris. The double onslaught drove her mad. "Please, Joseph. I need you so." The combination of the measured insistent finger thrusts and the constant, circular petting of her clitoris drove her into a frenzy. She writhed in ecstasy, she bucked, she rocked against his hand, she threw both arms over her head and around his neck and she thought she would die from the longest, hottest release imaginable. And not once did she worry about the bubbles and water that were sloshing over the tub like a tsunami.

Best of all, it was only just the beginning. Now, Joseph would give her what she really wanted all along. His hands and fingers had brought her pleasure, but what she wanted most lay between his legs. "I want what you want." Her body was still quivering in his arms. "Fuck me, please?"
"Let's go to the bed. I need more room to move." They didn't hurry getting out, but they didn't waste any time either. She grabbed two fluffy towels and followed him to his bed. They dried off just enough to keep from water logging the sheets. Joseph looked up and noticed the expression on her face. "What?"
"Just looking; admiring the view. You do know how gorgeous you are, don't you?" She catalogued his perfect biceps, massive triceps, and thick forearms. The man was bulked up and ribbed. Cady knew anatomy and she had no trouble identifying delts, quads, glutes and the most perfect set of abs she had ever seen. "You take my breath away, did you know that? All I want to do is kiss and lick every square inch of your body." God, what had loosened her tongue? No matter, it was the truth.

"Hell, baby – you know how to make a man feel like a man." He dropped the towel and there was no hiding the fact he was fully aroused and ready to rumble. "Come on, love, I can't wait." He laid her down and brought himself over her, their gazes locked together.

"Condom, baby, condom." She knew they hadn't been consistent, but this time she remembered.

"No, problem, doll." Grabbing one from the drawer, he leaned back until he could fit the condom over his cock, then spread her legs wide and eased himself into her.

"God, you feel incredible. It always amazes me how, impossibly tight you are." Her muscles were toned and strong, she had incredible muscle control and he loved what she could do to his raging rod. Slowly he pushed down into her moist, hot depths. Her inner muscles hungrily grasped him—inch over inch. When they first began making love, he had known she was more responsive than any woman he had ever been with, but now she had tasted the complete banquet, she was beyond belief in bed. Joseph did not know what he had ever done to deserve such a treasure. She enjoyed him and she had no problem letting him know it. She fed his ego more than anyone ever had.

When he was completely buried within her, he watched her face. Her eyes closed with the sheer pleasure of it, her sweet hips lifted off the bed and she began to rock him and stroke him. "I've been dreaming about this all day," she whispered. So had he. He didn't have to move at all, but he wanted to. He let her enjoy herself just a moment longer, and then he took over. He sat up and pulled her up in his lap, with her head still back on the pillow but her hips across his thighs. Her legs crossed behind his back. He braced himself and began thrusting. Over and over again, deeper and deeper. Cady began to moan and grabbed the bottom sheet on the bed and held on to the Egyptian cotton for dear life.

Still he kept pumping into her, slamming against her thighs in the ancient, pagan, rhythm of life. He climbed the mountain of passion and when he reached the crest, he shouted triumphantly and drove into her one final time as his body shuddered with the force and excitement of his climax. She joined him and rode the overwhelming tidal wave of passion until they lie spent and replete in each other's arms. "Cady, my God, Cady. You have no idea how you make me feel. I can't believe how wild and exciting you are."

"Joseph, it's only for you. If we had not met, I would have never known any of this. I would still be the twenty-eight year old virgin, waiting for life to pass her by."

Joseph did not like to think what might have been. There was no doubt in his mind, if they had never met – he would, definitely, be the biggest loser.

That night, she had more on her mind than slumber. Since they had been sleeping together, Joseph had got in the habit of touching her in his sleep. No matter what position they ended up in, he kept one hand on her body. If she didn't know better, she would swear he was trying to make sure she didn't get away. Tonight, he was lying on his stomach with his head turned away from her – but his right hand was across her stomach. Actually, it was a perfect position for what she had in mind. She slowly turned toward him and cuddled close. Placing her left hand on his lower back, she began to forge that connection that would allow her to absorb the nerve damage that plagued him.

Focusing, she concentrated on developing an image of the nerve endings in her mind – his spine – the specific area she wanted to not only heal, but also free from the damage that had been inflicted to it. She traced the path on his back with her hand – up his spine, between his shoulders, all the way to his neck. Cady loved him so much. With all the energy she possessed, with every bit of the magick she could muster – Cady called forth the paralysis that hampered Joseph and invited it into her own body. An electric heat began to build between them. Joseph shifted in his sleep, the difference in temperature causing him to pull away from her the slightest bit. Edging closer, she renewed her efforts, keeping contact with his body to allow her spirit to meld with his and relieve him of the burden that was dragging him down.

After a few minutes, she felt it. Her body began to tingle and not in a good way. She felt her right leg draw slightly and sharp jabs of pain began to stab her in her right hip and thigh. Wincing, she realized that Joseph had been in much more pain than he had let on. He had been protecting her. Numbness snaked down from her knee to her ankle. She knew that until this malady dissipated, there would be no way she could walk normally. This was true sympathy pain – she now knew what he had been feeling all along. As she touched him, she felt Joseph straighten out his right leg and stretch it – he sighed as if a weight had been lifted from him. Very carefully, Cady eased back. Catching her breath, she tried to turn over – but now her body was different – it had limitations she had not known before. Good. If she was hurting, that meant Joseph was free from pain for the first time in weeks.

Turning over slowly, she sought to find the exact angle to hold her body that would be most comfortable. It wasn't easy – poor Joseph. Now, she needed to surround herself with blue light and try to rejuvenate her body. And if she could do it without Joseph being any the wiser, that would be perfect.

"Joseph. Joseph." Libby was calling his name so loud that Joseph was sure the house must be on fire.

"Coming," he called. "Cady, I'll be back as soon as I find out what's going on." He bent over and kissed her on the forehead. Bounding out of bed, he jerked on his pants, grabbed a shirt and headed for the door. Cady didn't move. She wanted him to think she was still drowsy enough to sleep in. One thing was sure and certain: Joseph was his old self. There was no halting, no hesitancy, no limp – nothing. And it was also obvious it hadn't dawned on him, he was operating on instinct. He had been torn from slumber so quickly that he wasn't thinking clearly or he would realize his nerve damage was gone.

"What's up?" he asked Libby as he opened the door. Cady lay perfectly still while Joseph stepped out into the hall with Libby.

"That reporter from Dallas is here. He thought his appointment was at eight, Jessie is serving him breakfast."

Cady lay in the bed and listened as Libby talked to Joseph. Well, it hadn't been necessary for Jessie and Libby to manufacture a crisis – luck was on her side. She just hoped it stayed with her. "Oh, shit," she muttered as she tried to sit up. Where could she go to lick her wounds and get her act together? Her old room came to mind. Now, the only problem was getting there without drawing undue attention to herself. She wondered how long it would be before Joseph noticed he was healed.

"Man, it's good to see you!" Trey Richardson grabbed his hand and pumped it hard. "You look great. Aron's been telling me that you were doing good – but I can't tell that there's anything wrong with you at all."

Damn! Joseph stopped in his tracks. He mentally inventoried his body – testing sensations, functions, abilities – What the hell!?! Everything worked! He felt like a fuckin' million dollars! The only trace of his problem was a tingling sensation like every nerve on his right side was waking up. It wasn't unpleasant – it was like a million tiny needles were jabbing at him all at once. Frankly, being able to feel was absolute heaven. "There's not. I'm a new man." Shit! Damn, he needed to get back to Cady. He was healed. He was friggin' healed! She had done it – now all he needed to do was exercise – get all the feeling back and get cleared by a doctor to drive again.

It was hard to answer Trey's questions intelligently – when all he wanted to do was get up and out and evaluate his new found freedom. They retreated to the den where Jessie had put a tray of coffee and muffins to stave off their morning hunger. "So, what's next – are you going to make your fans happy and unleash Daredevil McCoy back on the Extreme Sports circuit?"

Joseph thought a minute about how to answer. "I don't know. It's going to take some time – I'll have to train, make sure my body responds like it used to. Plus, I'll have to see where my sponsors are. I don't know if they'll be onboard or not." He couldn't help it – Joseph laughed with glee. "Hell, it's fun to think about, though. You'll never know how wonderful it is to actually have a choice. When I was paralyzed and in that wheelchair, I never thought the day would come when I'd even be discussing a possible comeback."

"So, you aren't saying yes – and you aren't saying no. Is that fair to your fans?" Trey was a heavyset man, with more hair on his face than on his head. But he had a faithful reader base that digested every word he wrote. So, when Trey Richardson spoke – people listened.

"You tell them that the Stallion is going to train, be put through his paces and when he's in racing form – he will make a comeback. How's that for a promise?" Even to his own ears, it sounded like he'd made up his mind. But what about all of those things he'd said to Cady about wanting to spend more time with his family or make a difference in the athletic community? Well, he was young – he could do it all – he'd just have to take things slow and work on his priorities. That sounded good. Yea, he could live with that. What he couldn't do was wipe the grin off of his face. Damn, he was happy!

Trey wasn't through, however. "So, tell me, Joseph. To what do you attribute your recovery? Was all the dire news just a poor diagnoses?"

Joseph remembered what Cady had said about protecting her. So he did. "I had a good doctor, a great physical therapist and the Lord on my side. I guess you could say I am highly blessed." Richardson seemed satisfied with his explanation.

"Will you keep me informed?" Trey handed him his card. "I would love to do a follow-up when you've gotten to the point to know if you'll be competing again. Rock-climbing, skydiving, dirt bike racing, free diving – you've done so much. Do you have any idea where you'll start?"

"It's all going to depend on how my training goes." He wasn't about to commit. There were to many factors to consider. The main one right now was telling his family – celebrating – and giving Cady the hottest kiss a woman had ever received.

The only problem was – he couldn't find Cady. He made him think of that night after he had humiliated her and he had gone to her room only to find her strangely missing. The rest of the family was in the kitchen. When he'd taken off with Trey – it had all happened so fast they hadn't got a good look at him and hadn't noticed his crutch was missing. Pausing at the door, he appreciated the sight. They were all around the table – his family. Aron was at the head, stuffing his face and giving orders. Libby sat to his right – beaming, as she made sure everyone had enough on their plate. Nathan sat by Libby and it seemed like he'd grown at least an inch in the last week. He'd be grown before you knew it.

On the other side of Nathan sat Jessie. Jessie was so pregnant; she looked like she was about to pop. Even though tests had determined that Jacob wasn't the biological father – the sperm bank's records had been criminally mishandled – he was as excited about the impending birth as a man could be. The baby might not be a McCoy by blood, but he was Jessie's baby and that made all the difference. Jacob was giving Isaac, who sat at the far end of the table, a hard time. Isaac was feeding the dog under the table and ignoring Jacob who was trying to give him advice on expanding the bar into a franchise.

Noah was all ears. Money was his forte and if there was going to be any expanding done – he wanted to be in on it. Roscoe – their PI – who was on a retainer sat by Noah. He was updating Jacob on the investigation into the ranch vandalism. It seemed that Henry's nephew had been spotted in Kerrville and Kane had him under surveillance. His and Vance's other ongoing case – missing Avery – had hit a strange dead-end. Isaac was much more worried about Avery than he was about expanding so the conversations at the table were varied and layered and nobody was paying the slightest bit of attention to him. "Hey!" he hollered, getting everybody's attention. "Where's Cady?"

Jessie looked at Libby and he knew they had answers to his questions. But eagle eye Nathan didn't miss a thing. "Where's your crutch? Are you walking without your crutch?" His voice grew loud and he jumped up to come and stand by his big brother, amazement on his face.

"Hell Yeah!" he exclaimed and immediately his family was on their feet, surrounding him.

"Damn!"

"This is wonderful"

"I knew it – I just knew it"

"It's a miracle!"

Joseph tended to agree with the last statement made my Jacob. "It is a miracle." There was much hugging and backslapping, but when the dust settled – he still had the same question. "Where's Cady?"

Again, there was a knowing look passed between the two girls. Jessie finally spoke up. "She went to visit her aunt for a couple of days. There was some type of family emergency." Jessie felt guilty not telling Joseph that Cady was the family emergency in question. While Joseph had been talking with the Dallas Morning News Reporter, Cady had got up – dressed, packed and managed to convince Lance Rogers to drive her to New Orleans. When she left – Cady hadn't known if or when she would return. Not that Jessie was going to be the bearer of bad news. She also wasn't going to tell him that Cady had been using his crutch when she left.

"I'll call her," Joseph was concerned. "Was it her aunt or Nanette?"

"I don't think so," Jessie hedged, hating to mislead her future brother in law. Joseph walked off, phone in hand and the family stood watching him – grateful he was walking upright, steadily and under his own steam.

She hadn't gotten very far. It had been a mistake to ask Lance to drive her, but she didn't have much choice. Her right side was basically useless and she didn't know how long it would be that way. Convincing Lance to drop her off at a Holiday Inn Express and then keep the information to himself had cost her the promise of a dinner and a movie. Lance had asked a lot of questions. Apparently, it was common knowledge on the ranch that she and Joseph were more than client and therapist and now Lance was convinced Joseph had dumped her and he was going to be the knight in shining armor there to pick up the pieces. There was no way Cady would even have tried to explain the situation – she didn't really understand it herself.

She sat the crutch down and fell on the bed in an exhausted heap. One problem was that the crutch was way too long and she had almost never got the bolts loose enough to shorten it – and the second problem was that she was scared. What if she was unable to throw off the paralysis? Could she live like this? Shaking her head, she knew the answer. Of course she could. She had done this for Joseph and that knowledge made this burden easy to bear. Now all she had to do was get better. Instead of physician heal thyself – it was witch heal thyself – same difference.

The ringing of her cell phone caught her off guard and it didn't take much of a psychic to guess who was on the other end. "Hello?"

"Where are you?" Terse, and to the point. His obvious concern warmed her heart. He cared.

Cady paused. How could she lie to him? How could she not? If he knew where she was – he would be there immediately. Okay – hedge – that was the answer.

"I'm fine. How are you? Are you feeling well this morning?" She had seen the way he walked out of the bedroom, but she had to be sure.

There was a tell-tall change in his voice. Cady could hear the joy in every syllable. "Cady, I'm walking without the crutch. When I woke up this morning – the drawing and burning in my right side was gone. There's still a lot of tingling and itching, it's like how you feel when your foot has been asleep for a while and you start trying to wake it up. Trey couldn't believe my progress. What do you think it means?"

"It means you are going to be healed completely." Thank God. Her sacrifice was not in vain. And at the moment, she didn't know if her condition was temporary or permanent. And until she did – she had to stay away from Jacob. "I am so glad. That means I have done my job."

Joseph was stunned. "Are you telling me you've left me?" He had never considered that. "I thought there was some type of family emergency. What the hell is going on, Cady?" Why he felt the way he did – that was another story – but he wasn't ready to give her up. Not yet.

Her mind was going a mile a minute. Okay, this wouldn't be a lie. She would just make certain what she said came true. "I'm meeting up with Aunt Angelique. She's going to help me with a case and – then – then – I'll try to come back by Tebow and check on you. How's that?"

"You've got to come back, baby. We've got to celebrate." He couldn't believe she was gone. "I need you, Cady. Please come back. We're not through; I'm not ready to let you go."

Just her luck, he was saying the words she wanted to hear and the very act that had given him his miracle might very well keep them apart. So, she said all she could say. "I'll do my best, Joseph. I'll come to you as soon as I can."

The phone at Tebow started ringing off the wall. Everybody wanted in on the excitement that the Texas 'Stallion' might be on the road to recovery and back in the thick of things. Aron had to post guards at the gate to keep television crews and nosy folks from just wandering up uninvited. Trey Richardson had been extremely gracious and wrote a nice piece on him that let the public and the sports world know it wouldn't be long before he was competing again. Before the accident, Joseph made up his mind to slow down – but now he had something to prove – to himself and everybody else. He had to know he was as good as he ever was. The only cloud on the horizon was the fact that Cady wasn't here. And he missed her – terribly.

Everything was good, but nothing was just right. While he was busy, he didn't notice it so much – but let the sun go down and the nights became too long and his bed way too empty. Isaac and Noah had started to help him train. He had even gone out to E-Rock and scaled one of the medium-ranked cliffs – just to see if he could, and he passed that self-imposed test with flying colors. But – hell, all he could think about was Cady. The whole world seemed overcast – that old song about there being no sunshine when she was gone was the gospel truth.

He had met with the accountants at his family's trust department and the family had given him the go ahead to start the foundation work for the advancement of paraplegic research. After he laid out his initial plans, their people ran with them and they were sending him a mock-up brochure for his approval within the week.

And that wasn't all – Red Bull had contacted him and wanted to showcase his come-back at the Dust Trail Hot-race in Odessa in three months. They promised him a full-fledged promotion campaign and a matching purse for the charity of his choice – bet he knew which one that would be. All in all, everything was falling into place. The only thing missing was the deep desire he had to share his news with somebody important, and although he told his family – he still longed to whisper his triumphs into the ear of someone who would rejoice just in the simple fact he was happy – someone he could cuddle close with at night and share the ebb and flow of life with. Lord, he missed that woman. Not that he was alone – Joseph had all the female companionship a man could ask for - the only problem was none of them was the one woman he wanted to be with.

He had taken to walking every evening to the creek that ran down behind the house toward the north pasture. As he had sat in his room in the wheelchair and stared out the window – this had been one of the things he had longed for most – just a walk through the trees to hear the babble of the water over the rocks. Something had begun to bother him – and he didn't know why it had taken him so long to realize it. God, he was selfish. The day he had met with Trey Richardson, the day he had regained the full use of his body was the day Cady had walked out of his life. Joseph picked up a rock and skimmed it across the water. Damn! Why hadn't he seen it before? This was no damn coincidence – Cady had healed him, took his injuries and left to struggle with it by herself. He wanted to run - he wanted to yell – he wanted to go to her, but he didn't know where to turn. She wasn't answering his calls and he felt more helpless than he had been when he was half a man and pissing in a bag.

It had been a horrendous three weeks. She doubted at times whether or not she would recover. Aunt Angelique and Philippe had come for her and she had returned to New Orleans, but not to her home – just in case Joseph had decided to come for her. Instead she had retreated to Nanette's home and had endured countless healing rituals. This malady wasn't as easy to dispel as a fever or a case of the shingles. Joseph had called and pressed her for information, but she had stood firm – or as firm as she could stand on one leg and a crutch – and told him she was busy and would come to him when she could.

Gradually, Cady regained the use of her right leg - mostly. It had taken two visits with Nanette and intense self-healing sessions where she had channeled natural energy to free the nerves from the binding prison of peripheral neuropathy. Now, she knew what it had felt like when Joseph's injury had prevented the nerves in his spinal cord from carrying information from his brain to his leg. She knew there was pain, loss of sensation and the inability to control muscles – but living with it was much different than just treating someone with the problem. Now, she understood. If she ever got the chance to work with another accident victim like Joseph, she would have a better idea how to proceed with their therapy.

Now, it was time to go back to Tebow and say goodbye. She had no illusions that she and Joseph would pick up where they left off. For all intents and purposes, she had pushed him away. Cady had been in hiding, but word of Joseph's activities always seemed to find her. The papers were full of it – there were reports on cable news shows and write-ups in everything from Texas Monthly to Newsweek. And the women. His many admirers had returned. Gorgeous, amorous females had flocked to him and he was being photographed at every event and function with beautiful women on his arm. Each time she saw one of catches by the paparazzi, Cady had died a little inside.

There had been no visit from the menstrual fairy during that time, either. Cady still couldn't believe that she was carrying a baby, but she had begun to eat right and had refrained from alcohol – just in case. For some reason she had put off a visit to the doctor or taking a pregnancy test – that was something she would rather do when she was back in Kerrville. If she was going to bring a McCoy into the world, she wanted to be at Tebow when she found out. Fantasizing, she envisioned how Joseph would react if she did turn up pregnant. She still remembered the night he had talked in his sleep and said he loved her. It was probably just a dream that he didn't remember – but she would never forget those words as long as she lived. .

It felt good to work out again. The McCoy men had a good set-up. They were all active and got their exercise in natural ways – hard work, active lifestyles and playtime that pushed them to the limits. But they had a weight room, too – one that was outfitted with the best. Before the accident, Joseph could bench press four hundred pounds. He wasn't quite back to that point, but he didn't like much. He had just finished twenty-five reps when the door opened and shut. Thinking it was Noah, who had just left to make a phone call, he called out. "Hey, will you come spot me?"

"My pleasure."

Joseph almost dropped the whole shebang. "Cady!"

She steadied him and then lost her breath when he flipped her over the uprights. "God, I'm glad to see you!" He was wet with sweat and sexier than sin. Not giving her a chance to move, he pulled her down for a kiss. Cady wanted to cry, she was so happy to be in his arms, again.

"If you feel as good as you look, you are in tip-top shape." she couldn't help but comment, even as she slid down his chest, dipping her tongue between the defined ridges of muscle, loving every hard-honed line. The musky smell, the salty taste of his skin made her head spin.

He sat up, taking her with him. "I'm great, Cady." He hugged her tight. "Where have you been? I missed you, so."

She didn't answer him. Instead, she pushed out of his arms and stood up, but she wasn't steady on her feet and wavered enough that he jumped up to make sure she didn't fall. "Thanks," she murmured, looking decidedly uncomfortable.

"Walk across the floor," Joseph demanded.

"Why?" she countered. "What would that prove?" He knew and he wasn't happy. Well, too bad.

"You healed me, and you left so I wouldn't have to watch you suffer with my affliction." Joseph paced across the room, not knowing whether he wanted to kiss Cady or strangle her. "Now prance, baby. Walk that sexy little ass across the room and show me what you've done to yourself."

She didn't want to, and her body language showed it. Knowing she wasn't going to get out of it – Cady called all her inner strength forward and steeled herself to walk as straight and sure as she ever had. Step. One. Two. Three. Small sway – damn! Four. Five. "Is that enough?"

Joseph just stood there; his guts were clenched up in a knot. "You're limping – because of me." There was anguish in his voice.

"I'm much improved," she tried to explain. How could he make her feel guilty for doing what she had to do? "And I'm sure, in a few days – even this small limp will be gone." Joseph covered the space between them in a second –

swept her up in his arms and stalked out of the room. "Where are we going?"

"To my room – do you have any objections?" As he walked, he nuzzled her neck – breathing in that special Cady smell. "You smell like sugar – did you know that?"

"That's because I'm sweet." Had a homecoming ever felt so good? Cady wrapped her arms around his neck and enjoyed the ride.

"Will you let me taste how sweet you are?" His bedroom door was ajar and Joseph kicked it on open with his foot.

Cady was enthralled at the way Joseph was looking at her. His gaze was roving over her face as if he was trying to record every feature. He had missed her – that was as plain as the nose on his face. And he had a perfect nose – he had a perfect everything. She ran her palm over his chest and shoulder, thanking the heavens above that she had the privilege of touching him again. "That would make me very happy."

Laying her on the bed, he stretched out beside her. "I can't believe you did that for me, even after I told you not to. I ought to spank your darling rump for risking yourself that way."

"I'll take the spanking – if you're offering," she teased.

Growling, he playfully nuzzled her on the neck, taking tiny nips. "It is so good to have you back in my bed again." All he had on was his ever-present pair of Longhorn lounge pants and he pushed those off and kicked them off the end of the bed. "Are you in pain?" he asked her, tenderly arranging her hair – fanning it and spreading it out on the pillow.

"No." Not much – and right now, she wasn't feeling anything but love, lust and longing.

"Would you tell me if you were?" he tapped her on the end of the nose.

"No, probably not," she admitted. "It was worth it, Joseph. Just look at you – you're perfect again. Tell me what you've been doing." Not that she didn't want to make love with him — she did. But she was as hungry to reconnect with him mentally as she was physically.

Tucking an arm around her waist, he pulled her as tight to him as he could get her. "The morning you left, I met with Richardson and he put out the word that I was on the mend. News spread like wildfire and - what can I say — I'm back where I was, at least with the opportunities. I'm still training and getting my muscle tone up to par — and, well — we'll see if I've still got what it takes when the time comes for a competition."

Cady lost herself in his eyes. She was listening to what he had to say, but the thought of kissing him, making love to him was hypnotizing her. "I'm glad — that's what we hoped for all along, isn't it?"

"And I couldn't have done it without you, baby." He lowered his head to hers in the slowest of increments — he was going to kiss her and she was shivering with need. And then he dropped a bomb that blew her skyhigh. "I'm going to love on you till I've sated my appetite and then I'm gonna take you out on a date. I've got an important question to ask you and you might as well start rehearsing how to say yes."

Chapter Twelve

He was going to ask her to marry him! He was going to ask her to marry him! Every fiber of her being lit up like a Roman candle. She literally melted in his arms. Throwing her arms around him she held on for dear life. "I think I can manage a yes," she whispered.

"I hope so," he chuckled. "I don't know what I'd do if you said no." All the time he was unbuttoning her blouse, unhooking her bra – pushing down her skirt – getting her nekkid and primed for his loving. Cady arched her back, offering herself to him. In his arms was where she longed to be and right now – she was happier than she had ever been in her life. Joseph belonged to her. Finally, it was more than just a mystical bond, it was glorious reality and she couldn't believe every dream she ever had was about to come true.

With blatant hunger, Joseph began caressing her body. He ran a palm over her tits, down her stomach and between her legs. She opened for him, anxious to welcome him back where he belonged. "Not much chance of a no, I'm thinking," she managed to keen as he began stroking her damp slit, caressing the pussy lips, massaging her swollen clit. "Oh, I've missed this," she sighed, lifting her hips, begging for more.

Chuckling, he slid down in the bed and opened her wider – making room for his broad shoulders. She was spread out, totally vulnerable. Cady could feel the cream of her excitement beginning to flow. "Look at that," he took a long lick – he whole body followed the motion of his tongue, he had to hold her down to keep her still.

"Thank you," she spoke, almost reverently. Her response almost did him in. What kind of woman was this? She never ceased to amaze him.

"Hmmmm, you taste so good." Pushing his face into her pussy he began to feast. Nothing was safe. Flattening his tongue, he licked her cream from every hidden fold. He nipped and nibbled at the labia lips; thrust his tongue deep into her vagina – spearing her, unmercifully, until she almost wept with excitement. And when he took her clit in his mouth and swirled his tongue around it, she - literally – screamed.

"I need you, Joseph – please, my God, I need you." Cady was beyond aroused, she was on fire and desperate to be taken – hot, hard and fast. He didn't make her wait. Pulling her legs up over his forearms, he angled her hips just right and surged into her.

Oh yeah, just like that – home, sweet home. Joseph pushed it and held it, loving the feel of her tight little cunt working his cock. God, nobody loved him better than Cady. "Squeeze me, baby."

She did – and he watched her face – the tip of her tongue dancing out to lick her upper lip. "Like that?" Cady concentrated on pleasing him, her hips pumping in a backward, forward motion, riding his rod. Damn! He couldn't be still any longer – he let loose and rammed inside of her over and over again. She met every hard thrust with the sweetest little grunt. Primal need took over; Joseph yanked her closer, pounding into her with escalating fervor. And even as he took his pleasure, even as his seed was boiling up from his balls – all he could think about was loving Cady over and over again.

If her leg would have cooperated, Cady would have danced across the room. Instead, she settled for hugging herself till she almost passed out. Libby and Jessie weren't surprised that she was back and the McCoy brothers were as gracious and warm as ever. It felt like she had come home. And after their date tonight, and she accepted his proposal – Tebow would be her home. Cady McCoy. 'Cady McCoy', she dared to say it out loud. Holding up her left hand, she visualized how it would look with his ring on the third finger.

With a tiny bounce and a little squeal, Cady celebrated the fact that Joseph McCoy loved her.

Almost instantly, she sobered. He hadn't said he loved her. Not even after their out-of-this world sex – he never said the words. Shaking her head, she pushed those thoughts out of her mind. They were going out and nothing could possibly go wrong. Besides, she could use this trip to town to buy a pregnancy test. And if she was pregnant with their child – it wouldn't be that big of a deal. Starting a family would have been the next step anyway.

"Aren't you ready, yet?" Joseph walked into his room, admiring the way Cady looked in a dark purple peasant skirt and top. "You look like a sexy, gypsy baby." He was just about to lean in for a kiss when Noah nearly knocked the door down – "Joseph, Joseph – I just looked out the window – and you'll never guess who just pulled up. It's that hot little reporter from Texas Extreme."

"Come here, Lady! I've got your ball!" Nathan waved the red rubber football in the air, trying in vain to catch the rambunctious puppy's attention. She was much more interested in the hummingbirds that were flittering around the feeder. Every few seconds she bounced in the air – clearing the ground by a good two feet, but not coming anywhere close to catching one of the tiny ruby-throated creatures.

"Hello."

Nathan looked around to find a pretty blonde woman making her way across the yard toward him. "Hey. May I help you?"

"I'm looking for Joseph McCoy. I'm a friend of his, Carrie Warner. Would you know where he is?"

He might only be thirteen, but the wiggle in Ms. Warner's walk had Nathan mesmerized. "Uh – uh – he's in the house."

Carrie's voice dropped, "Is he able to have visitors? I've heard he's better, but I know he was in really bad shape." Nathan figured the face she made was supposed to show sympathy, but he thought it made look like she had tasted some cow manure.

"Yea, sure," Nathan wondered what he should do. "Come with me and I'll tell the family you're here." He led her across the yard, the puppy bounding along beside her. Lady didn't understand why the woman wasn't paying attention to her.

"Stop that," she fussed. "Don't jump on me. You'll mess up my white slacks."

Nathan snickered under his breath. "Stop, Lady." He caught the dog up and carried her. "Sorry, mam."

She brushed off the paw prints and huffed. "So, tell me. Is Joseph still bedridden or are the rumors true."

"Bedridden?" Nathan didn't like the sound of that. "Joseph was never in the bed except to sleep. He got up everyday." She made his brother sound like he was helpless or something. "And now that Cady has healed him – he's walking around like me and you.

Carrie swung her head around, her reporter's nose already on the scent. "Who is Cady and how did she heal him?"

Nathan walked up the steps ahead of her and held the door. "Cady is a physical therapist, but she's more than that. Cady is a witch, sort of, and she can heal people. Her whole family came and they did a spell on Joseph. She has a magic touch and now Joseph can walk again."

She was beautiful. Cady's heart sank.

"Joseph!" The woman squealed, threw her arms up in the air and launched herself across the room and onto Joseph, grabbing his face and kissing him. Cady held her breath, afraid that the crazy woman was going to knock him down, but Joseph stood steadfast - - - and - - kissed her back. Well, well. The daredevil had returned in full force. With a seductive little laugh, the woman pulled back and purred. "I can't believe you are standing up and looking so handsome." She returned her lips to his and proceeded to kiss him over and over and Joseph tried to dissuade her – but not very hard, it seemed to Cady. Finally, he managed to take her by the forearms and untangle himself.

"Thank you, darlin'. Don't you know they can't keep a good man down?" His stance and voice changed as he talked to the reporter. It became apparent that Joseph was putting on a show, and Cady didn't like it a little bit. He was exuding charm and a certain arrogance that must be part and parcel of his public persona. The Stallion was back and raring to go.

"I couldn't believe it when I heard, I just had to come and see for myself." She closed the distance between them again and rubbed herself all over him. "And, I am so glad I did."

Jealousy boiled up inside of Cady and she felt the distinct need to do some witchy warfare against the bleached bimbo. Noah kept giving her sympathetic glances and that made her feel even worse. She turned to leave when Joseph seemed to come to himself and notice her, "Hey Carrie, let me introduce you to the one responsible for my recovery." When he grabbed her arm to pull her forward their eyes met. He held her gaze for a moment, and then dropped it. "Carrie Warner, meet Cady Renaud, my physical therapist. Cady this is the reporter who did that cover story of me for that flashy magazine called Texas Extreme."

Carrie sidled over to her, raking her eyes from the top of Cady's head down to her toes and back. With a toss of the head, Cady was evaluated as a rival and dismissed in short order. It took calling forth all the embedded Southern manners that she possessed, but Cady managed to extend her hand in greeting. "Hello, Ms. Warner. It's a pleasure to meet you."

Carrie barely touched her fingers and lifted the corner of her mouth in a poor facsimile of a smile. "So, you're the one we can thank for getting Joseph back on his feet?"

"Not entirely," Cady responded. "I provided appropriate exercise and therapy as prescribed by his physician." Boy - that was an understatement.

"I may have some questions for you, later – after this handsome cowboy takes me out to dinner." Turning from her abruptly, Cady was summarily dismissed.

As if emerging from a trance, Joseph spoke up. "Sorry, Carrie – but I already have plans. Cady and I were just on our way out to dinner."

Pouting and petulant was the only way that Cady could describe Carrie Warner's face. "But what about my interview? And the last time we talked, you told me we'd get together real soon." She cocked her hip to one side and pushed her boobs out and gave Joseph a wink and a promise that no one could have misinterpreted.

Joseph hid a grin, Carrie meant business – she had come to collect on the erotic escapade he had hinted at the last time they were together. The only clincher was how she had completely ignored his calls after the accident, and now that he was up and mobile again – she was back and on the prowl. "I don't think so, Carrie. Thanks for driving all this way, but I think I'll have to pass. I gave an exclusive to Richardson of Dallas and promised him the follow-up. So, if you'll excuse us. Cady?" He held his hand out to her. After a moment's hesitation, she took it.

Right in front of them – Carrie transformed. She went hard, that was the only way to describe it. Ms. Warner was not used to being set aside. "You are going out with her, instead of me?" The way she enunciated the question left little doubt what Carrie thought about the development – disbelief was putting it mildly.

"That's right. If you'll excuse us, we'll be on our way." He pulled Cady around Carrie's stationary body.

"You'll be sorry, Joseph. I'm an investigative reporter and if there is a story here – I will find it, believe me."

"Sorry about that," Joseph apologized as they walked down the ramp. "Do you mind taking your car? Jessie borrowed my truck to run some errands."

She knew that. "Of course. Are you sure you still want to go? We don't have to, you know." All the joy had evaporated out of the evening for her. The reporter's visit had opened her eyes to the way Joseph was accustomed to living. Her come-on to Joseph reminded Cady how many women pursued Joseph and she didn't know if she would ever be able to handle that – at least not graciously.

"Of course I want to go." Despite her uneven gait, Cady managed to keep up with him. She tried to hide her discomfort the best that she could.

"Do you want me to drive?" Joseph offered. He could well relate to how she was feeling.

"No, I'm fine." And she was. The limp was slight and she had most of the feeling back – she could drive. Or she'd die trying. The only thing she couldn't do was dance. There was no way she was going to hobble around the dance floor – and she would so have loved to be held in his arms. "While you drive, I can look at you." He placed a hand on her knee and started pushing her skirt up. "We're gonna have a good time tonight, Cady-did."

She caught his hand before it made much forward progress, "I need to concentrate, lover-boy." She was happy that Joseph had chosen to come with her instead of spending time with Carrie, but she had this niggling suspicion the reporter was going to dig until she found something she thought she could use. And that was going to be nothing but trouble. Pulling out on the ranch road, she headed into Kerrville.

He didn't remove his hand, but he did let it stay just above her knee – and only moved the pad in slow circles. "This okay?"

She covered his hand with her own, rubbing his knuckles, and taking her eyes off the road just long enough to glance at his face. What she saw made her heart pound – he was looking at her with heat – that was the only way to explain it. Clearing her throat, she answered. "Yea, I always love to feel your hands on me." Answering him in such a way showed how much she had changed – the time she had spent with Joseph had been a rollercoaster ride of highs and lows, but it had shown her than a man could find her desirable and she reveled in the feeling. Especially since the man was Joseph whom she adored and who would be proposing to her before the night was over.

"Good, because touching you gives me immense pleasure." He laid his head back on the seat and let out a long breath. "Cady, I'm sorry about what happened back there. She was kissing me before I knew what to think and my kissing her back was reflex. It was so much like old times that I lost my head for a minute." His thumb was never still, tracing patterns on her flesh, maintaining a connection that was precious to her.

"I understand," And she did. Attention from fans and women were so much a part of his former life, that receiving it again must be like getting a sign from heaven his prayers had been answered. "Who could blame you? Ms. Warner is an exceptionally attractive woman and you are a very virile man."

"Don't make excuses for me, sweet. It was wrong. I'm with you. This is our time."

What he was saying sounded good – but something about it bothered her. But there was no time to psychoanalyze it now. As they pulled into town, Cady noticed a drug store that was opened and she remembered the pregnancy test. No better time than the present.

"Would you mind if we stopped here? I need to get a couple of girly things."

"Not at all, I'll just wait in the car." She parked and ran in, leaving him to amuse himself for a few minutes. Opening the door, he let in some fresh air.

"Well, well – fancy meeting you here." A sultry voice caught his attention. Sabrina. Aron's ex approached the car and assumed what she conceived as a sultry pose.

Joseph's hackles immediately went up. "Sabrina. I'd say it was a pleasure to see you, but I'd be lying. I thought you had left town after Libby handed you your ass in that bar fight."

"You don't have to be nasty. I just wanted to speak to you and tell you I'm happy you aren't going to spend your life as a cripple." Funny, even Sabrina's niceties were laced with arsenic.

Joseph noticed how much older she looked. Life wasn't being kind to the viper, but that was her own fault. She had brought most of her troubles on to herself. "Well, I do appreciate your kind words and the sentiment." He just wished she'd go on.

"Who came to town with you?"

Joseph was glad that neither Aron or Libby would have to endure her company. "Actually, I'm here with a date."

"Really," Sabrina looked puzzled. "Is she in the drug store?"

"Yep, not that it's any business of yours." *Just go way*, he thought.

Sabrina cackled an evil little laugh. "Oh, really. I just came from in there, and I was the only woman except for . . . . ." She pinned Joseph with a hard stare. "Surely, you're not with that colored girl are you?"

Hearing Cady referred to with a racial slur infuriated Joseph. "Watch your mouth, Sabrina. Cady is more of a lady than you'll ever hope to be." Hearing a bell jingle, he looked up to see Cady coming toward the car. "Now, get outta here, before I sic Libby on you, again."

Sabrina smirked. "I'm going – and you have a good date," and she paused for a few pregnant moments – "Daddy."

"What in the hell do you mean by that?" Joseph sneered.

Sabrina didn't answer but sauntered off, throwing her head over her shoulder in defiance.

Cady slipped the paper bag containing the pregnancy test into the back seat well away from Joseph's prying eyes and fingers. "Who was that?" she asked as she settled herself behind the steering wheel. "I saw her in the drug store. Are you friends?"

"Not hardly. That's Aron's ex – a nastier human being you would likely never meet." That was all he said, but Cady could tell the woman had upset him. "Did you find your womanly products?" He was ready to change the subject off of the scheming gold digger.

"Yes, I did. Thank you." And she couldn't wait to get back to the ranch and find out if diapers and pacifiers were in her future. Her heart palpated with the notion. Putting the car into gear, she asked. "Where are we going?"

"Cattleman's, it's just up on the next block. You can't miss it." Trying to put Sabrina out of his mind, Joseph decided to tease Cady a mite. "What did you buy in there? Did you get some of that his and her jelly that will make our orgasms seem like nuclear explosions?"

Cady blushed. If he only knew. "No." She couldn't keep the smile off of her lips. "What would we need that for? Our orgasms are already explosive enough – or at least mine are. I don't think we need any help in that area. Do you?"

"Not a bit." He laid the back of his hand on her smooth cheek. "I'd have to say what we share is just about perfect. You make me feel like a fuckin' king. I've enjoyed loving on you more than I can say."

Cady leaned into his touch – needing it. "I don't have anything to compare it to. But if it were any better, it just might kill me." Pulling into a parking place, she kissed Joseph's hand, trying to tell him without words how much he meant to her.

A movement outside the car drew Joseph's attention. "Look, there's Kane and Lilibet." He reached over and honked the horn getting their attention. Cady hoped he wouldn't invite the other couple to join them – she wanted this to be a real date not a double date.

Kane stepped up to Joseph's door and opened it, leaving Lilibet waiting for him on the sidewalk. Cady liked the other woman immensely and would have loved to spend time with her if the circumstances were different. At least, she could get out and be friendly. "Well, look at you!" Kane exclaimed. "Man, this is a sight I wouldn't have missed for anything."

Cady left the car and joined Lilibet by the door. Joseph stood up and shook his friend's hand. "Hey, I owe you – you red-neck Cajun, you. If you hadn't told me about Cady, none of this would have ever happened. I'd still be wheeling around the house and pissing in a bag."

"Keep your voice down," Cady chided him, laughing. She looked at Lillibet. "Are they always so rowdy?"

"I don't know," the other woman was a bit shy. "This is our first time to go out like this. Cady could pick up an array of emotions from her and she saw a bruise hidden under Lillibet's makeup that alarmed her.

"It's only our second." Cady confided. "Are you okay?" She tried to read any emotions coming from the woman, but they were unclear. She did remember warning her of danger at the BBQ, the night that her aunt and the others had been celebrating Joseph's healing.

Lilibet looked uncomfortable. She laid a hand over the bruise. "Kane didn't do this," she spoke quietly. "And yes – I'm fine. We're celebrating tonight." She held up her hand and Cady saw a beautiful diamond ring.

"Congratulations!" She admired the engagement ring, wishing she could tell Lilibet what the night held for her and Joseph. Their men joined them and Cady couldn't help but notice the admiring glances they were receiving from passing women. She had to admit the two were exceptionally handsome – each in their own way.

"Yea, we were both fortunate that Cady Renaud came to town," Kane put his arm around Lillibet. "Not only did she work her magick on you, she told me where to find Jessie after she was kidnapped." At Joseph and Lilibet's surprised looks, Cady wished that Kane hadn't been so freely forthcoming.

"Really?" Joseph drawled. "And why I am I just now hearing about this, Miss Cady-did?" He gave her a loud smack on the cheek. "But I'm not surprised. This woman is something else." They all stepped into the dark, cool restaurant. There was music playing and Cady could see that there was a bar and dancing some distance from the dining area. A thrill shot through her in anticipation of sharing this time with Joseph. It didn't matter to her they wouldn't be able to dance – she'd be in his arms, later – in bed.

"I hate to leave good company," Kane drawled. "But my lady and I have some celebrating to do." At Joseph's enquiring look, Kane kissed Lilibet tenderly. "We're engaged."

"Damn! That's wonderful, man." Joseph clapped his buddy on the back. "I'm proud for both of you. You've got yourself a fine man, Miss Ladner."

"Thank you, Joseph." Lilibet looked so happy. "I realize how extremely fortunate I am to have Kane in my life." The adoring looks they were sharing made Cady feel warm inside. She knew exactly how the other woman felt.

"I'm the lucky one," Kane beamed. "A beautiful woman has agreed to spend her life with me. How much more fortunate could I be?" He gave Joseph a pointed stare and

Cady tried to discern the unspoken message but all she could pick up was regret from Joseph. Was he sorry he had to spend time with her? No, that wasn't it. She tried again, but his emotions were too mixed up to read.

Joseph read Kane loud and clear. His friend was reminding him of what an ass he had been when he had expressed the desire that his physical therapist be homely. Pulling Cady close to him, he looked her in the face. "Your good fortune doesn't top mine, Saucier. We're both dining with beautiful women - but mine has a magick touch."

"What looks good?" Joseph asked as they studied the menu. They were seated side by side at an end booth and Joseph was running his hand up and down her thigh – going just a little higher each time. He had a tiny smile on his face – he knew full well she was getting aroused and wet.

"I think I'll have the petite sirloin," she said, trying to maintain a certain amount of decorum. Yet her body betrayed her, because she spread her legs the tiniest bit, giving him better access. She'd never been so grateful for a long tablecloth before.

"Do you feel like dining on a good piece of meat, baby?" His voice was low and sexy sending ripples of excitement dancing over her skin. She knew exactly what he was talking about – and it wasn't a slab of Texas cow. "Lean back, Cady and enjoy." His talented fingers found their way to her swollen slit and as he dipped in between her damp folds, she jumped with a combination of embarrassment and bliss.

"This is wild and decadent," God, but it felt so good. She pushed her pussy closer to his hand and he rewarded her by delving even deeper, massaging her mons with his cupped palm and rubbing her clit with a soft, circular motion. "Don't stop," she ordered him in a breathless voice. "I'll return the favor – I promise."

"Oh – I know you will." Watching Cady cum was one of the most beautiful sights he had ever seen. "I want those plump lips circling my cock." He caught the eye of the waiter and with a jerk of his head sent him back where he came from. First things first and this appetizer was too delicious to miss.

Laying her head back against the high seat, Cady sat there and tried to be still. "I can't believe we're doing this," she whispered. "Is anyone watching?"

"No, I'll take care of you, baby. Trust me." And he proceeded to do just that. With just three fingers, he took her on a trip past the moon. As she soared and shimmered, her fingers twisted the white material draped over her knees, if Joseph hadn't anchored it with his free hand she would have pulled it from the table like a magician doing the old tablecloth trick.

"I can't believe we just did that," she whispered. "What do I look like?"

"You look amazing," he spoke softly, sincerely. "Cady, I am so grateful that no other man has known you like this – never seen this side of you. Despite my accident, I wouldn't have missed this time with you for the world."

"Thank you, Joseph." Drawing her to him, he held her close while she came down from euphoria, trembling in his arms. It surprised her how possessive he acted. There was still no declaration of undying love, but perhaps this was just Joseph's way. So, she decided to just enjoy it and cherish every moment.

After placing their order, Joseph teased Cady about what they had done. "I didn't know you could be so quiet. You're a screamer, Cady-did." She blushed and stuffed his mouth with a piece of buttered bread to shut him up before somebody heard him.

"Hush! Someone will hear you. There are more people nearby now." He chewed on the bite she had given him and winked at her, wickedly. She ignored him. "Look, Kane and Lillibet are dancing." The sight made Cady smile. She knew about her short leg and how self-conscious Lilibet was about what she considered to be her imperfection.

"I wish we could dance. We'll try, if you'd like. I could hold you close, and we could dance real slow," he offered.

"No, it's all right," she assured him. She laid a hand on his knee. "I'm enjoying myself just being with you.

"Would you go with me to the powder room, Cady?" While their attention had been on each other, Lilibet had walked up with Kane on her heels.

"Sure, I need to freshen up." She gave Joseph a knowing look. Both men watched their women walk away, enjoying the view.

"Who would have thought our lives would bring us to this night, with these women? You are on the mend and I've found someone to share my life with."

"We both experienced miracles, you old reprobate. I never thought a woman would get her hooks into you." Joseph lifted a beer in salute to Kane.

"I took one look at Lilibet and fell like a ton of bricks. How about you and Cady? What's going on with the two of you?"

Joseph didn't say anything for a few seconds. Then, he started talking. "Cady's my friend; I owe her my life."

"Are you interested in her?"

By interest, Joseph knew Kane was talking matrimony. "Kane, I've been to hell and back. By some miracle, I have a second chance. I'm not ready to settle down, not even with someone as wonderful as Cady. I do plan to reach some type of understanding with her – in fact, I plan on trying to seal that deal tonight."

Kane looked over to where the women would emerge from the restroom. Cady came out and immediately was surrounded by young, randy cowboys with more than dancing on their minds. "It's a good thing you don't feel overly possessive. Cady's attracted a crowd. I'd say you have a bit of competition, my man."

Joseph looked over to where Cady was being invited to take a whirl around the dance floor by at least five different cowboys. Damn! .

"I think I'll mosey over that way and head my little filly off at the pass before she gets corralled by those bow-legged cowpokes." Kane took off and Joseph sat there with a distinct scowl on his face.

"No, thank you. I'm here with someone, but I appreciate you asking me to dance." Cady repeated herself several times, gently turning down man after man. What was going on? Had someone put these men up to flirting with her – perhaps, to bolster her ego? Lilibet joined her and was hit on as well. Kane came to their rescue and she couldn't say she was upset to be escorted out of the fray. Following closely to him, she searched through the crowd to see Joseph. He was still seated at their booth – where just moments before he had given her an incredible orgasm. But he wasn't alone – three women had joined him. It appeared they were seeking autographs, among other things. At first she was upset, but as they made their way through the crowd, she saw him gently remove one of their hands from his shoulder and distance himself from them by his body language. He was being a gentleman and her heart swelled. God, how proud she was that he belonged to her. And in a few minutes – it might be official.

By the time they reached Joseph, the women had dissipated and he was watching her with hooded eyes. His intent stare sent shivers down her spine. "I had to beat the men off with a stick!" Kane joked. "We'll talk to you two, later. My honey and I have got some courting to do." Joseph turned sideways so Cady could slip back into her place in the booth. Feeling a bit nervous, she glanced at him, unsure of what to say. Their food arrived at that moment, giving her a little reprieve.

Her plate was filled to overflowing. "Are you sure this is the petite sirloin?" The steak covered half the plate and a football sized baked potato took up the rest of the room.

"Look at mine, I need sideboards." He was telling the truth, his piece of meat dwarfed his plate. They doctored their potatoes; adding butter, sour cream, bacon bits and shredded cheese. Cady's stomach growled and Joseph laughed, kissing her on the cheek. Every time he looked at her, something inside him went all warm and electric. He was possessive as hell of her, and – frankly, this was unknown territory for him. He had specialized in the love-em-and-leave-em philosophy for so long that anything else was too farfetched to consider. But Cady – she was something else, entirely. Right now, he wanted to put his fork down, take her by the shoulders and kiss her till she promised she would never look at another man as long as she lived. But – he couldn't – he was scared to death. The daredevil, invincible McCoy had finally found something he was afraid of – and it wasn't so much *commitment* as it was how she made him feel. Joseph felt vulnerable.

He wanted to confess all of his sins to her – to make a clean slate – a fresh start. Where that would lead, he didn't know. But the first thing he wanted to get off his chest was an explanation of his philandering ways. After that, he wanted to tell her about those erotic dreams he had experienced – the ones that were inexorably tied in to her, in some weird way. What good that would do – he didn't know – but he needed to tell her, just the same. "Cady, I want to talk about women."

She almost dropped her fork. "What?" This wasn't how marriage proposals usually started out. "I mean, okay. I guess." Edging away from him on the bench seat, she turned to face him, pushing her plate aside. She was so excited she was trembling all over. Joseph did the same, although he had done away with most of his food. He propped his forearms on the table and with his sleeves rolled up, the muscles bulged, so well defined, covered with a fine dusting of dark hair. Geez! Just looking at him made her weak.

"Cady, after we lost our parents – it was hard. Aron, Jacob and I had to put aside a lot of things that young men fancy and grow up fast. I gave up less than they did, but I carried my share of the responsibility." Cady listened, quietly. "When Noah turned eighteen, I decided that Aron and Jacob could handle Tebow and Nathan, so I took off to pursue my own dreams. Jacob, the philosophical one, he says we all reacted to losing Mom and Pop in different ways – and I became the daredevil – not satisfied unless I was climbing higher, or driving faster or breaking another record, winning another race. I guess, I treated women the same way – I conquered them, collected them, never getting close to any one woman – just using them as much as they would allow." He laughed, with a hint of remorse in his voice. "And I won't kid you, there were a lot of them and they seldom told me no, about anything."

"What are you trying to say? I know that you've had a lot of women. It's okay – I don't care. The important thing is that we're together, now."

"Hell, yes, that is what's important. I'm saying all of this – rambling – to tell you I'm not perfect. But we have something special. I like you. I like you a lot. Now I'm not proposing marriage or asking for a commitment or anything like that."

Joseph kept talking, but Cady stopped listening for a moment. In fact she wasn't breathing – not really sure her heart was beating. Cady was stunned. Had she heard him right? He wasn't proposing or asking for a commitment. Her heart sank to the floor. He'd never had any intention of asking her to marry him. It had only been a micro-second – she took a deep breath and tried to listen to him talk. She was very careful to not let any emotion show on her face – whatsoever.

"What I'm asking you for is an understanding. And I do have an idea how we can make all of this work." Fumbling for words, Joseph wasn't sure if he was even making sense.

"An understanding? What kind of an understanding?"

"Well – for now – while we're together – while we're sleeping together – I don't want any other man anywhere around you." He said the last eight or nine words succinctly and with an obvious growl in his voice.

Cady didn't know whether to laugh or cry. So, she did neither. She controlled her emotions and laid them aside to take out and analyze later. "The only time I ever had anything to do with another man was at your insistence. Have I given you any reason to doubt me?"

"No, that's not what I meant. I'm trying to tell you. . . . . I want you to know. . . . "

She watched him mentally flounder around, searching for the right words. "I understand, Joseph." She did – he was being a dog in the manger. He didn't want her – not permanently anyway - but he didn't want anyone else to have her, either. "But you said you wanted to ask me a question. What was the question you wanted to ask me?"

"I want to offer you a job. I think it would great if you would consider joining my team. I would love to bring you on as my personal assistant. You could help with my training, give me massages and we'd have a lot of time just to be together. I'm not ready to let you go, baby." He touched Cady's face and it was all she could not to pull back away from him. How could she have been so stupid? "And one more thing – while we're together, I won't mess around with any fans or groupies."

Cady had to bite her lip to keep from laughing – or screaming – or crying. He was being so magnanimous. Joseph McCoy was making a great sacrifice. "That's good of you. I appreciate it." It would have been hilarious, if it hadn't been so sad. "And thank you for the job offer. I'm surprised. This wasn't what I was expecting." That was the understatement of the year. "But, I thank you for thinking of me for the position." She had no idea how she kept talking so reasonably. Her stomach had turned into a hard knot and her chest felt like something was pressing hard enough on it to force all the air from her lungs. This was the pain that her grandmother had spoke of – and God, she had been so right. Cady was hurting so bad, she wished she were dead.

This was going well, Joseph thought. He might as well get everything off of his chest at once. "I do want to tell you about these erotic dreams I've been having. Not that I can help what I dream, but I have had a hard time getting that goddess out of my head."

"What kind of dreams?" He was talking about her and the times that she had come to him in the night – she knew it.

"Dreams I started having after my accident, this woman came to my bed. . ."

Cady couldn't stand it. She couldn't resist. "You fell out of bed and she helped you back into it and you . . . . ."

"Yes," Joseph was astounded. "You are psychic!"

"It's more than that . . . " Cady lowered her voice; aware they were in a public place. She didn't want to make a scene. "It was me. The woman in your dream – it was me. I helped you off the floor and gave you water. I kissed you – I made love to you – before we ever met."

Silence.

Absolute silence.

"You?" Joseph was astounded. "Once or twice, I've wondered..." he began. "When you were on your knees – praying – for a moment you looked like her." He was gazing at her with fascination – astonishment. "But, how can that be – she is so – perfect?" The moment the word left his mouth, he knew he had gone too far. Cady shut down – her face became a mask – completely void of emotion. "I didn't mean . . . you know I think you're... "

"It's okay." Cady held her hand up – silencing him. "I know exactly what you mean."

"No, you don't."

He didn't know it – but he had just added insult to injury. This was more than she could stand – she had to get out of here. Now. But there was one more thing she needed to ask.

"What did I look like?" She wanted to know. "When I was experiencing the same dream, or whatever – I felt like myself. Before I came, after I figured out it was you in my dream, I actually wondered if you would recognize me?" She hiccupped a burst of laughter. "Isn't that funny?"

"It doesn't matter. . ." God, his mind was whirling. "She looked like you in lots of ways, now that I think about it." He could tell she didn't believe him. "How can this be? Is it some kind of witchy thing – a spell – did you control it?" Not that he would trade the experience for anything; he was just trying to understand.

"No, it wasn't anything I did – at least not consciously." Then an absurd thought crossed her mind – hell, it was as good an explanation as any. "I started dreaming about you even before I visited you in those midnight rendezvous," she said the word with a bit of disgust. "Your name was familiar to me and I felt this tremendous burden – this need – to help you. Even after all the insults and putdowns you've come up with – I have always felt this responsibility toward you. Helping you was more important to me than my own happiness. Hell, I think I've been visiting you in my dreams all of my life. I've always taken care of you." Looking off to one side, she shook her head in disbelief. "I guess Renee might be right – it is one explanation – stupid though it may be."

"What are you talking about?" He reached for her hand – tried to touch her, but she pulled back. "What explanation?"

"I was sent to help you, Joseph. It was my destiny." There was something weighty about the words as she said them – as if she was quoting scripture or something. "I was born to be here – now – for you." With a wry smile, she offered up the most fantastic theory of all. "I'm your guardian angel, Joseph. I was sent from heaven just for you." With that, she threw down her napkin and stood up. "I need to get by . . . I need some air; I'll wait for you at the car."

He let her push by him. What had just happened? How had they gone from being so happy one moment – to her running out on him the next? Hell!

The ride home was quiet. Joseph tried to get Cady to talk – but she didn't respond with anything more than monosyllables. Damn! Women! He'd never understand them if he lived to be a thousand years old. When she pulled into the ranch and parked in her spot, he put a strong hand on her arm. "We need to talk, Cady."

"Not now," she said simply. "Let me think about everything you've said. And I'll give you my answer as soon as I have one." Without looking back, she exited the vehicle and walked off as gracefully as she could. Looking neither to the left or the right, Cady made for her old room. Pushed the door shut and threw herself on the bed. Folding herself around a pillow, she swallowed gulps of air – struggling to control the urge to break out into sobs. Sorting through the turmoil of emotions, she mourned what might have been. How could she be so stupid? She was pitiful. Cady tortured herself with the notion she had expected Joseph to go down on one knee and ask for her hand in marriage. What a joke? Joseph only wanted a temporary relationship with a woman who was just a flawed facsimile of the perfect woman he desired. And she, plain Cady Renaud, would never be perfect enough for Joseph McCoy.

She wouldn't let him in to her room. "You know I could break this damn door down," he growled. "Look, just let me in. I don't think I made myself clear." He waited for her to say something. "Come on, Cady. I'm drawing a crowd out here, baby." And it was true – Noah and Isaac were standing at the end of the hall ready to whup his ass because he had made Cady cry. And Isaac wasn't in a good mood, anyway, the little dog he brought home to Nathan was missing. Nathan was walking himself to death and calling for the puppy until he was hoarse and making himself sick. No one was in a good mood – least of all Joseph.

The door opened and he breathed a sigh of relief – if he could touch her, he could make her listen. She was on the phone. "I'll just be a moment," she spoke to him. "That's all I have to say to you, Miss Warner. Goodbye."

"Thanks, for letting me in. That was Carrie? What was she doing; pumping you for information?"

"Yea, something like that." She had her back to him and hell if she hadn't put on one of those shapeless jumpers. Her hair was pulled back in a bun and she had her glasses on, again. And she had never looked so good to him. Joseph closed the gap between them and as he did, he saw her stand a little taller – her back a little stiffer.

"I'm glad you got rid of her. Neither one of us needs any negative publicity. Look, I'm sorry if what I said upset you, Cady-did. I had the best of intentions. What I want most is to keep you with me – I'm crazy about you, love. I can't keep my hands off you." He slid his arms around her waist and pulled her back against him.

His nearness affected her as much as ever, but she fought it with everything in her. Before she knew it, tears started to flow. "I appreciate the offer and I'm not saying no." No would be her answer – there was no way she could continue to see him every day and know their relationship wasn't a forever thing. Joseph would never love her. There had been a time if someone had told her a man would like her and want her – that would have seemed like more than enough. But now she had become greedy – she wanted it all. Cady wanted to be loved with the same deep, abiding intensity she felt for Joseph. But that wasn't likely to happen. "I just need to sleep on it. Okay?"

"As long as you sleep with me – it's okay." Joseph almost forgot to breathe – he was so afraid Cady was going to walk away from him. He wished he could offer her more – give her the world. But he didn't know if he could. There was so many unanswered questions for him – untraveled paths – races that had yet to be run. Joseph just wasn't ready to settle down – not yet. "I know it's not night yet, but we have time for a little afternoon delight." He laid his check next to hers and whispered in her ear. "Let's go to bed."

Could she do it? Could she lie in his arms one last time - knowing she would be enjoying the last touch, the last kiss, the last time she would hold him close? "It will be my pleasure," she rested her head on his chest and vowed to make every second count.

Chapter Thirteen

Joseph was horny as hell. He wanted Cady – now and he knew exactly how. "I've been dreaming about fuckin' you standing up. Back when I didn't think I would ever walk again – I dreamed of holding a beautiful woman in my arms and bouncing her on my cock. How does that sound, baby?" Joseph was tearing at her clothes. His pulled her hair down and ran his fingers through it – grabbing her face and taking her mouth – one hot kiss at a time.

Cady couldn't have pushed him away for love or money. He was the most precious thing in the world to her. So, she didn't resist when he pulled her jumper over her head – or unhooked her bra or pushed her plain white panties to the floor. There was nothing of her he had not seen or touched or kissed. Like a drug addict, her body craved his. Instantly, her nipples swelled and puffed and her sex softened with excitement, knowing full well what would happen next. Every part of her readied itself for Joseph's possession, anxious to accommodate his every need. Turning her, he backed up against the wall, and with one graceful movement, he lifted her off the floor. "Wrap your legs around my waist." This was a feat he wouldn't have been able to do just weeks before, and now he was doing it with the greatest of ease. His big hands cupped her hips and as he directed the action, he burrowed his face in her hair and licked a hot trail down her throat, ending with a sensual scraping of his teeth over her skin. "I could just eat you up, baby. I can't get enough of you."

Joseph held her securely, she felt safe and she felt wanted. Clasping him around the neck, she pressed her tits into his chest, loving the feel of her nipples scrubbing against his hair-roughened skin. "I'm hungry for you, too," she admitted. "You don't have to wait – I'm ready."

Her words seemed to release something within him – some powerful need to master and dominate. "Look at me, Cady. Don't take your eyes off mine. Watch my face as I take you." She obeyed. God, she was going to miss this. Supporting her with a knee, he took one hand and guided the head of his cock to the tender opening of her pussy. "Now just feel," he commanded her and slowly pushed inside. Cady drew in a relieved breath as her body stretched to accept him. This was it – as long as she lived – she would never forget how it felt to be complete. When they were joined together, it was as if two halves, long separated had been reunited. Cady's grandmother had once told her about soul mates; that every person had one. One night while they had been sitting on the dock, feeding the catfish scraps of bread, Grandmother had told her that when two certain souls are made in heaven that an angel will cry out – 'this woman is made for this man'. She didn't know about that – but she did know that after loving Joseph, there would never be anyone else for her. Nobody could ever replace him in her life, or her heart – or her body. He was the missing piece in her life and when they were separated she would never be whole again.

Nothing – nothing was better than this. Joseph buried his cock as deep in her as he could get it – all the way to the hilt. Stepping back, he took her with him. "Hold on baby, I've got you," he promised as he fulfilled a fantasy that had been haunting him. Taking her by the waist he moved her up and down on his swollen rod, glorying in the act that proved he was man, she was woman and what they created together was more magical than any spell ever written.

Cady clung to him, wishing this moment could last forever. If only she could preserve this ecstasy, this sense of belonging forever. He was totally in control – he moved her how and where he wanted her and she gave herself freely and completely. Waves of pleasure crashed over her – cumming for him was a given. Multiple orgasms had gone from being a concept that was foreign to her, to one that she now claimed as a right. Finally, he broke eye contact with her – throwing his head back and grinding out a triumphant shout of release. Laying her head on his shoulder she reveled in the rightness of being with Joseph. So, she endeavored to convey to him how she felt without burdening him with her love. "There is no one like you. No one." She kissed him right over his heart, feeling the strong beat beneath her lips. "Thank you for allowing me to share this precious time with you, Joseph. I'll never forget it as long as I live."

"Me either, baby. Let's take a nap, and we'll go another round." Joseph wrapped himself around her. "I'm glad you're back, Cady. I missed you."

As much as she wanted to stay, Cady knew the time had come to go home.

"Are you listening, Acadia?" Master Gabe spoke more sternly than he should have. His beloved Acadia was hurting, just as he had feared she would.

"Yes, sir." Her voice was small and desolate sounding. "I can hear you."

"Feelings such as you are experiencing are not ours to enjoy." He believed what he said, although he did not understand the reasoning behind it. "I warned you of the danger to your heart if you were to allow your emotions to rule your actions."

"I know." She refused to raise her head and see the pity in her mentor's eyes. "I have decided that it is time for me to go. Joseph is safe and well, I have completed the task that you have given me."

"No, you haven't."

"What do you mean?" Master Gabe's words shocked her so that she almost fell off her seat. If it hadn't been for the stabilizing weight of her wings, Acadia would have toppled to the floor.

"Hey," he steadied her. "No fallen angels, allowed." Gabe smiled – sometimes his own humor amused him. Seeing that Acadia did not appreciate his levity, he sobered and got back on point. "You cannot leave. You must stay at least one more day. The greatest test of your devotion is yet to come."

Horror struck Cady's heart. "Joseph is still in danger?" How could that be? She had drawn him from the depths of despair and walked along beside him until he was strong and on the right path.

"The threads of destiny are still being woven, Acadia. Life's tapestry is hard to discern if you stand too close. It's only when you step away that you can see the truth."

"What does that mean?" Acadian did not understand. "I will do anything for Joseph, anything."

"I know." He spoke as one with great insight. "Joseph was entrusted into your care. You have done well. Soon you will have proved that you are worthy of the title Guardian. We have been given the greatest example of all - **The greatest love you can show is to lay down your life for your friend.**

Cady sat straight up in the bed.

She remembered.

Her body was damp from pure fear. A cold sweat emphasized the chill of the night air. Looking over at Joseph, she trembled from the terror she felt at the thought of losing him. There was no way she would let something happen to him now. Her departure from Tebow would have to be postponed.

"Can you believe this? Who let the cat out of the bag that Cady was anything more than a regular physical therapist?" Aron was livid. The family had enough problems – now this. Aron, Noah, Libby and Jessie sat around the big screen TV and watched as Carrie Warner drug the good name of McCoy through the mud.

And it got worse – the report went from slamming Joseph for putting his illness into the hands of a charlatan to actually accusing him of faking his paralysis to create a media storm in order to cut bigger deals with his sponsors.

"Shit," Noah breathed. "Joseph is going to explode."

They sat and listened to the lies being spouted about their brother and outside the door stood Nathan. Holding Lady, he hung his head, knowing he was the one that had talked to the reporter about Cady and had used the word 'witch'. He didn't understand exactly what was going on, but he knew he couldn't face his brother or the rest of the family with what he had done. Turning, he ran out the door and off into the night.

"Joseph! Damn it all, Joseph! What are you doing in bed in the middle of the day? Or do I have to ask? Get your ass out here. All hell has broken loose."

Aron's irate voice broke into Joseph's dreams. Rubbing his eyes, he tried to wake up enough to answer. "I'll be right there." Cady lay curled on her side, with her back away from him. "I gotta get up and see what's going on." He kissed the back of her head and got up to grab his clothes, but she got up right behind him. For the time being, Cady intended to be Joseph's shadow. Her ominous dream might be only a dream, but she wasn't taking any chances.

When she had redressed she joined the others in the den. They were standing in front of the television. "It didn't take her but a couple of hours to screw you, buddy." Aron wasn't pulling any punches. He was seriously pissed off.

"What's going on?" And when they all turned to look at her, she realized, instantly, they considered her to be part of whatever problem had arisen.

"Take a look at your handiwork, Ms. Renaud." He handed the remote to Libby. "Back it up, baby. I can't get the hang of this dang DVR."

What was Aron talking about? Libby and Jessie wouldn't look at her and Joseph was glued to the TV screen where Carrie Warner was appearing on one of those gossip news shows that focused on exposing celebrity secrets. "How did she get this gig so fast?" Jessie whispered.

"She probably already had it booked. But until she visited me, she didn't know which angle she'd pursue." Joseph spoke flatly as if he were talking about the weather.

"I was shocked." Carrie Warner played up to the camera. "Joseph McCoy is a star and seeing him fall from grace is a big disappointment. Either explanation is unacceptable. If Joseph put his health into the hands of some warped faith healer – well that's bad enough. And if the reports are true that his physical therapist is into witchcraft – well, I don't think the public can accept that in a hero they look up to."

"That's very interesting, Miss Warner." The host of The Big Scoop leaned nearer to the sexy blonde. It was obvious he was hanging on her every word and wishing he was hanging on to something else. Carrie noticed that he was eyeing her assets, so she poked her chest out so far it was a wonder she didn't throw her back out. "You said there was a more believable possibility than a magical miracle cure?" He was enjoying this segment – you could rake the lechery off of him with a stick.

"Yes, there is." Carrie looked right in the camera lens as if she was telling a secret. "I have a source – a woman close to the family. She told me there's a good chance Joseph was never paralyzed at all. This whole thing could very well be a publicity stunt. After his supposed cure, the sponsors came out of the woodwork. Joseph McCoy is bigger than he ever was before. And that's a shame, because from all the evidence I've seen – Joseph is a colossal fraud."

Joseph was frozen. He couldn't believe it. This was the worst possible thing that could happen. Cady couldn't have betrayed him? Could she?

"Joseph, I'm so sorry." She placed her hand on his arm and he backed up, as if her touch burned him.

"What did you say to Carrie?" He wheeled around to face her.

Cady couldn't believe the look on his face. He thought she had something to do with this? "I didn't say anything to her."

"That's not true," Joseph, countered her statement. "I walked into the room where you were talking to her, just a few hours ago."

"She was protecting herself, Joseph." Aron looked at her accusingly. Libby's hand on his arm only served to keep him from saying more.

"No," Cady protested. "I would never do anything to hurt Joseph."

"Where is everybody?" Jacob yelled from the front.

"We're back here." Jessie answered. She looked decidedly uncomfortable with the direction the conversation had taken.

"I need help," Jacob looked tired. "We've been attacked. I'd swear one man couldn't do the damage that's been done. The fences have been cut in multiple places. Half the cattle we own are on the roads. There's been an accident and Lilibet is missing. And the worst part is – I can't find Nathan anywhere."

Isaac surveyed the room, it was almost complete. This was something he had wanted for years, and now it was almost within his grasp. None of his family knew his secret. He had managed to keep this part of his life separate. But when Shorty had approached him about buying the club – it seemed like a perfect plan. He could build his playroom here, away from the prying eyes of his brothers. Now, where was that drill. He must have left it in the storage room out back when he had put up those shelves. He'd go get it – then he could put in the last set of bolts and he'd be through for the day.

Keszey crept into the darkness. This was going to be fun. Making his way to the bar, he smiled. The sound of breaking glass was going to be satisfying. Picking up a big bottle of whiskey, he slammed it against the edge of the cabinet. CRASH!!! Yea, this was going to help his feelings, quite a bit. One by one, he broke bottle after bottle. Then he started on the glasses – it would take that biker boy a long time to clean up this mess.

A door creaking in the back alerted Keszey to the fact that he wasn't alone. Shit! Scurrying down the hall, he looked for a place to hide. One door was ajar and he darted into it. What was this place? It was the entrance to the basement, and when he got to the bottom – he was amazed. Dark cherry wood lined the walls and ankle deep carpet covered the floors. Lord, the thick rug was blood red. There was some kind of a cross on a wheel next to one wall and there were waist high benches fitted with stirrups and restraints. Whips hung from hooks on the wall and there were stocks – actual stocks – where some unlucky bastard would be held against his will. Was this some kind of fuckin' torture chamber? What kind of monster was this McCoy freak?

Keszey kept looking and he noticed a huge cabinet against one wall. It was fitted with doors and drawers with fine brass pulls and when he opened them he found dildos and handcuffs – quirts and nipple clamps. By God! This wasn't a torture chamber; this was some kind of wild sex room.

Isaac didn't know what to do. Sabrina had been back in the bar tonight causing trouble. Only this time it had been Joseph she was after instead of Aron. Doris had noticed it first, and had come to tell him that a reporter was asking questions of everybody that she could get to talk and Sabrina was spouting off one lie after another. She had even said that Joseph had faked his paralysis in order to get bigger, more lucrative contracts from his sponsors. Isaac had never heard such drivel. "What the hell?" The smell of alcohol nearly knocked him down! And there was something all over the floor. Flipping on the light, he was shocked to see that every bottle – every glass – it was all broken. All right – this was too much. Flipping open his cell, he called Kane. "You'd better get over here – I've been burglarized."

Methodically, he looked everywhere – nothing – no one. Had the coward ran off? But, then he saw that the door to basement was shut – and he was pretty sure he hadn't left it that way. Easing it open, he slipped down the stairs – and there he was. Robert Keszey was fumbling through his toy chest. "Find something in there you like?"

Keszey turned quickly. "Damn McCoy!" Reaching behind his back, he pulled a gun.

"Excellent." Isaac laughed. "You just made my day, asshole." With one graceful movement, Isaac tore a whip from the wall and let the long black snake slice through the air coming down with a stinging blow on the bare hands of the man who dared to breach his inner sanctum.

"Hell!" Keszey screamed. "I hate you McCoys. You and your scum of an old man have taken everything I ever loved. It was all supposed to be mine. Mine!"

"Isaac!" Kane had arrived. "Where in sam-hill are you?"

Well, his secret was about to be exposed. Oh, well – it was just Kane. Kane would understand. Maybe. "Down here."

Kane and his new deputy came bursting into the room. At once, they took Keszey into custody, handcuffing him and the deputy led him out, but not before he got an eyeful of his surroundings.

"Well, hell – McCoy. I should have known. All that black leather you wear makes sense now. What are you, some kind of a Marquis de Sade wannabe?"

His friend was determined to have a laugh at his expense. So be it. Isaac was serious about his lifestyle – he knew what it took to satisfy him. That was one reason he had fought his feelings for Avery so hard – there was no way she would ever accept this side of him. She was too good, too pure – and Isaac was just what everybody thought he was – a Badass. "I'm a Dom, Kane – a sexual Dominant." He said it so matter-of-factly that Kane sobered.

"Sounds kinky." Understatement.

"I expect you to keep your mouth shut about this and tell your deputy to do the same. This is my private business and I want it to stay that way."

"If that's the way you want it," Kane wasn't a gossip. "And I'll talk to Waters. He's a loner, I don't think you'll have any trouble out of him." About that time, Kane's radio went off. "Sheriff. What? Damn! But, we just caught him at Hardbodies – how could he have been in two places at once? What did you say?"

Isaac watched Kane turn white as a sheet.

"What's wrong?" Isaac was afraid it was something at Tebow – the way their luck was running, he wouldn't be surprised.

"It's my Lilibet. She left your ranch a few minutes ago. Whoever was bringing her home had an accident – more cattle on the road. And now she's missing." He bounded up the stairs with Isaac right in behind him. "She was supposed to stay there till I could pick her up. Fuck! Let's head to the ranch and find out what's going on."

"You go on; I'll be there just as soon as I can secure this place." Isaac assured him.

The McCoys were ready for battle. All the brothers rallied. Kane showed up looking shell-shocked. Lilibet meant the world to him. "I've called in reinforcements. Some crazy son of a bitch has got my girl. And it's not Keszey – we've got him." Although his announcement was noted, there was no time to rejoice. "Any word on Nathan?" Before anyone could answer, he looked straight at Cady. "Can you help?"

"I'm sure I can." None of the other family looked impressed. They were communicating with their ranch hands on walkie-talkies and Aron was even handing out loaded rifles. He meant business. Kane had hastily thrown a map on the desk and Cady ran to get her pendulum. On the way back, she pulled Joseph to one side. "I didn't betray you. I would never, ever do anything to harm you. So, when you go out – I'm going with you. Do not leave me. Please?"

He looked torn and confused, but she seemed to get through to him. "I don't know what to think. Go help, Kane." Cady knew she had been dismissed. And although she had already made up her mind that what they had was over – it still hurt like hell.

"I need something of Lilibet's" Kane handed her a tiny locket. He knew the drill. She went to the map and began to concentrate, dangling the amethyst pendulum over the paper. She was upset, so her hand shook. Clutching the gold necklace in her left hand, she focused on Lilibet and the place on the map that Kane had said she had last been seen. Slowly, ever so slowly the pendulum began to swing – left. "She's been taken toward Austin." The words were barely out of her mouth before Kane was out the door.

"Try for Nathan." Jessie was at her elbow. "I don't believe you did anything wrong." She laid down Nathan's pocketknife. "It was something that had belonged to his dad and meant the world to Nathan." Cady put Lilibet's locket aside and picked up the knife. Again she consulted the map, tuning in to the vibrations of the knife. Funny – there was nothing. No movement.

"Nathan is here, on the ranch, somewhere. I can feel him. He's all right." Cady knew that as well as she knew her own mind.

"I'll find him." Noah left with renewed intent.

"There's a storm coming in – we've got to hurry." Joseph looked out the window and watched the lightning flash in the sky. "I'm heading down the south ranch road and try to herd some of the cows back in." The brothers knew from Lance's report where the men were working and Joseph knew where he could do the most good.

"I'm coming with you," Cady wasn't about to give him a chance to say no. But he did anyway.

"I don't think that's a good idea. We don't know what we're up against. It could be dangerous." His words sounded good, but his concern seemed to be more of an excuse than actual worry.

"I can help," she insisted.

"All right," he gave in, not wanting to waste time arguing with her. "Let's go." He put a hand to her back – his touch electric. And she was glad his hand lingered, his fingers caressing. She couldn't stand to think he thought she would deliberately set out to hurt him.

They went to the truck and this was the first time Cady didn't drive. It felt strange to sit in the passenger seat with him behind the wheel. Joseph didn't waste any time; he was anxious to try and set things right, but he didn't gun the truck, there was too big of a chance of hitting a cow or missing a piece of fence that was down. There was some moonlight filtering between the clouds, but he turned his lights on bright. "You watch the right side and I'll watch the left."

"Do you really believe I told Carrie Warner you faked your paralysis?" Cady broke the uncomfortable silence – she couldn't stand the way things were between them. This was worse than the beginning of their relationship when his every comment had seemed prickly and critical.

Joseph shook his head. "Does it really matter?" He threw the words at her. "As far as my life and career go – I'm worse off now than I was sitting in that damn wheelchair. At least there I had my good name and my good reputation.

Now, that's all in tatters." He slowed down as he came upon half a dozen cows marching down the center of the highway. "Damn, just look at this mess. That whole section of fence is down."

Easing off the road, Joseph stopped the truck, slung open the door and started waving his arms and yelling at the cattle, trying to herd them back toward the safety of their pasture. Cady helped, moving several yards away from him and keeping them from heading back into the road. She stumbled slightly – her gait was still uneven. And though they were separated by distance and misunderstandings, Joseph noticed. "Be careful, Cady. Watch your footing. You could get back in the truck, you know. I don't need your help."

But he did need her help, Cady was convinced of that or she never would have stayed where she wasn't wanted. The dream from the night before was fresh in her mind, she wasn't sure it was some dire omen – but she wasn't about to take any chances. Isaac pulled up next to them and immediately got out and began struggling to untangle the wire. "Can you believe this shit?"

"When it rains it pours." As if Joseph's words were a cue, the rain started coming down in sheets. "Did you see that news report that put the nail in my coffin? "Somebody. . ." and he glanced over at Cady who was out of hearing range, "gave Carrie Warner the idea my accident and being a damn cripple was all a made up job to get more money out of my sponsors. Cady says she didn't do it. But I'm damn confused, and don't really know who to believe."

"It wasn't Cady, Joseph. It was Sabrina. She was in the bar this afternoon bragging about it. Carrie had gone to every person she could rake up in town looking for dirt on the McCoy family and Sabrina was glad to make as much trouble for you as she could. You know the truth doesn't mean anything to Aron's ex-wife. . . And that's not all – we caught. . . " A crack of lightning and an explosion of thunder split the night air and cut Isaac's words off before Joseph had a chance to register them.

A huge limb of a sycamore came crashing down on the electrical wires next to a utility pole. The wire snapped and whipped down wildly, and from where Cady was standing, she could see it was going to fall right on Joseph. Time slowed down and everything became crystal clear to Cady. This was it. This was her time to fulfill her destiny – the reason she had been born.

Joseph looked up. He saw the wire falling, sparks dancing around the end of it like fireflies. "No!" Cady screamed and launched herself at him. Horrified, Joseph realized Cady was placing herself in between him and the hot wire. It flailed against her, she stiffened and her whole body seemed to freeze. The wire fell to the ground and writhed with energy like a snake in its death throes. Joseph grabbed for Cady but she collapsed at his feet.

"Isaac! Isaac!" Joseph screamed. "Cady! My God! Isaac call 9-1-1!" How had this happened? The events of the day began running through his mind. He had longed for Cady to come back to him. He had prayed and begged her to come home and when she did, he had rejoiced and welcomed her and offered her the best idea he could think of to insure they could be together. But Cady seemed to have misunderstood his intentions - something had happened. She had acted differently. They had made love, but it had been with a quiet desperation as if she were somehow, saying goodbye. And then when things had gone wrong, he had doubted her. He had doubted Cady who had always given more of herself to him than anyone ever had. He had doubted her. And now – now, she lay at his feet and he couldn't even tell her he was sorry.

Isaac was trembling. "She saved you, Joseph. She saved you." He was pushing buttons and breathing like he had run a marathon. Turning away, he began barking information and directions into the phone. After speaking to the dispatcher, he called Aron and told him to get to them as fast as he could. Looking over at Joseph, he saw his brother kneeling at a woman's side who had just given him everything she had – her life.

"Damn! God, no!" Joseph was out of his mind. "I can't find a pulse." He frantically began administering CPR. "Don't leave me Cady! Please, God. Don't take her from me. I need her. I love her."

Sometimes we don't appreciate things until they are torn from our grasp. And then when faced with the prospect of losing them forever, we realize how very precious they are to us.

Acadia stood at the foot of the large dais. "I can't leave him like that. He needs me," she begged.

"It's time to come home," Master Gabe looked at her sadly. "You can take care of Joseph from here. The great danger has passed. Well done, Acadia. You have been faithful and now you will be rewarded for your courage."

"Please, Master Gabe. I don't want to stay here. I want to go back. There's so much I need to do." How many times had he heard that plea over the years? No one was ever ready to turn loose of the bonds of earth. Sometimes he wondered what he was missing.

"No. You were dreaming of more than you were allowed to have."

"Please. I won't ask for anything more – just let me go back and be near Joseph. Just to know that I exist in the same realm he does will be enough. I promise."

"That is impossible." Master Gabe was sympathetic, but stern.

Acadia hung her head in defeat. She could hear Joseph praying. She could hear him begging her to return. There were even words of love – words he had not whispered to her when they had been together – but she cherished them all the same. A movement near her caused her to look up.

Another being had joined Master Gabe and was telling him something he did not like – she could tell that by his expression. She strained to hear. "She must be allowed to go back."

"Go back?" Gabe almost shouted, then looked guiltily around.

The other individual looked at Acadia and then back at Master Gabe. "No, you are wrong. What Acadia was sent to do – it has only just begun. The great task she was meant to accomplish was not just his salvation – it was bringing his child into the world. A child with both of their unique gifts and talents, a child that is destined to do great good in the world – that is their legacy."

Acadia almost swooned. "A child?"

Master Gabe rapped a large gavel on his podium. "Acadia is blessed. She has been granted great favour. Acadia can have it all."

Issac had taken over the chest compressions and Joseph was giving Cady mouth to mouth. Between breaths, he prayed. "Please, Cady. Don't die. I'm so sorry. I'll do anything. I was wrong, love. Please forgive me." Slamming of doors and sirens were a welcome sound. Isaac moved back so an EMT could get to Cady. Aron and Jacob came running up.

"Joseph – shit, man. What happened?" Aron knelt by Joseph.

"It was a downed electrical wire. She saw it falling toward me and she grabbed it before it could hit me." He grabbed his brother. "She's gone, Aron. I've lost Cady and the last thing she heard me say was that I didn't know whether to believe her or not. Now, Isaac tells me that she was telling the truth. It was Sabrina that made up those lies – not Cady. Never, Cady."

"Stand back." The EMT directed as he put the paddles on Cady's chest.

For the second time that night, waves of electricity passed through her body. The first wave had stopped her heart, but this second surge of power caused her to gasp. She arched her back and the first words out of her mouth were, "The baby. Joseph, have them check the baby."

"Baby?" Joseph stood stock still as they loaded Cady up into the ambulance. Could Cady be pregnant? His earlier run in with Sabrina came to mind. She had seen Cady in the drug store and had referred to him as 'Daddy' when she left. And he had been just nasty enough to her to set her off on another revenge tour.

"Come on; let's follow them to the hospital." Aron led Isaac and Joseph to his truck. Both of them were shook up and he felt like a pile of shit for planting seeds of doubt in Joseph's mind to begin with. Lord, what had he done? While driving, Aron notified his men of their location and where the major break in the fence was located. He was informed that several other ranch owners had rallied and sent their crews to help out. The calvary was on its way. Kane radioed that Henry's nephew had been booked on felony charges - but there was no word about Lilibet.

"Has Noah found Nathan?" Joseph was in shock, but he couldn't forget about his little brother.

"Yea, he was hiding in the hay loft. It seems he was the one that told Carrie about Cady being a witch. And awhile ago, he overheard us talking and felt guilty and ran away. He didn't mean any harm – he's just a little boy." Aron increased his speed as they got out on the highway and away from the ranch. As the truck ate up the miles, he prayed that Joseph's Cady would be all right. He had heard Joseph pleading and professing his love and he knew exactly how he felt. The thought of losing Libby was something he could never bear.

"So Cady had nothing to do with any of it. I knew that. It was just such a blow to hear my good name being shot to smithereens. I overreacted like a rabid dog and bit out at the one person who meant more to me than anything." Joseph lamented.

"Listen," Isaac took control. This was a new role for him, but he had learned something about taking responsibility. He fully intended to make his business a success and come to terms with who he really was. "There's no reason we can't get the ball rolling to repair this mess. All we have to do is phone Beau and Trey Richardson. We can tell them about Sabrina and Carrie and how all this shit came down. They can start putting out the truth and we can phoneZane and Roscoe and check about slapping gag orders on both Carrie and Sabrina. Hell, we might even have a legal case against The Big Scoop because they ran with the story without checking out the validity of the sources." The only thing he didn't bring up was the circumstances of Keszey's arrest – that news could wait until he could figured out how to handle it.

Joseph was grateful – for everything. But right now – all he could think about was getting to his love. As soon as Aron stopped the truck, he was out and standing at the ambulance door. When they took the stretcher out, he couldn't tell if she was breathing or not. "How is she?"

"Let's wait till a doc checks her out, Mr. McCoy. She's been through hell. Not many people survive that much voltage. She's damn lucky."

"How about the baby?" He was frantic to know if he was going to be a father – and if he was, had their baby survived the ordeal.

"Sir, you're going to have to wait until all the tests come back." He didn't have a choice; he entered the hospital, sat with his brothers and waited for someone to come tell him what was going on. Finally, a nurse came to get him.

"You can see her now." He was up, out of his chair and down the hall before she could tell him which way to go. Joseph only had to look in two rooms before he found her. She was lying in the bed, the covers pulled up to her waist and an IV was hooked up, pumping glucose or medicine into her veins.

"Cady?" He rushed to her side. "Cady, can you hear me?"

She opened her eyes and it was like the sun had risen in the east for the first time after the grey days of winter had past. "Yes, I hear you Joseph." She tried to smile at him, but her attempt failed miserably. Tears were leaking from her eyes.

Immediately, Joseph cradled her to him. "Don't cry. God, don't cry. You don't know how sorry I am this happened to you." He showered her face with kisses. "You are so beautiful. I want you, Cady. I want you in my life."

She could feel him tremble. Cady didn't know what to think. This had to be emotional upheaval on his part. "You don't have to say that," she raised her hand and rubbed his back, seeking in some way to comfort him.

"Yes, I do." Joseph framed her face and kissed her eyelids, her cheeks and both corners of her mouth. "I love you with all my heart."

Cady was saved from answering by the doctor. "Good news. I can find no damage to your heart or brain. You seemed to have come through this 'electrifying' situation with flying colors." It was obvious he was trying to be cute. "And the baby – or rather the babies are just fine. I can hear two strong heartbeats and there is no damage to the reproductive organs, whatsoever."

"Twins?" He was blown away! "How far along is she?" Joseph asked before he thought.

Twins! She was as shocked as Joseph. Two babies? But, he was asking how far along she was. Cady stared at him. Did he question whether the babies were his or not?

"Your wife is six weeks pregnant." The doctor seemed pleased with his announcement.

"I'm not his wife." Cady was quick to comment. "Can I go home, now?" Home to her was New Orleans. Her job was finished. Joseph no longer needed her and it was time to leave.

"Yes, most certainly. I'll have the nurse bring down the release papers." Dr. Peters looked uncomfortable and beat a hasty exit after giving Cady a prescription for pre-natal vitamins.

Joseph was on cloud nine. "How long have you known about the babies? And why didn't you tell me?" He played with her fingers, anxious to touch her anywhere he could.

"I didn't know – not until . . ." She stopped. That would sound stupid. She had almost told him she found out while she was dead. "I haven't had a period since weeks before I left New Orleans. My cycle is very irregular, but I don't usually go more than two months without spotting just a little." It was amazing how interesting the painting on the wall was – she focused on it, almost exclusively. It was easier to look at it than to look at Joseph. "I guess a woman just knows," she finished weakly.

"I think it's incredible news, baby."

He picked up her hand and held it. Cady was dying inside – this was just too much. "I'm very happy about the babies. It was a dream I never expected to be fulfilled." So much had happened; Cady hadn't let herself process the miracle of their children. The babies would be a lifesaver for her – she wouldn't be alone. The loss of Joseph would be easier to bear if she had their children to love and care for.

"We'll get you settled at Tebow and then we'll plan a wedding." Isaac and Noah came in on the tail end of his sentence.

"Wedding? Wow! Three brides, this has movie potential." Isaac was in a good mood. He had heard from Roscoe and there wasnews of Avery. He didn't know what it was yet – but his hopes were sky-high that she was safe.

When Joseph had mentioned marriage, Cady had almost bit her tongue. Words that would have meant the world to her just hours before; now seemed to describe a dream that was lost on the wind. "I can't marry you." Cady's words fell into the room like a lead balloon.

"What?" Surely he hadn't heard her right. Cady loved him. She had never said the words – but he had always felt loved. And now they had babies on the way! Things couldn't be more perfect. "Of course, we're going to get married! I love you more than life. Why wouldn't we get married?"

Cady started crying in earnest now. "Please stop. You told me you were to going to ask me a question, and I needed to rehearse saying yes. Do you know what question I expected you to ask me?"

Joseph had the good grace to look guilty.

"I expected a proposal of marriage, Joseph. Instead, you offered me a job. You can't blame me for assuming that the reason you are proposing now is because I'm pregnant. And it's not necessary. You can have as much access to the babies as you want."

"I want total access – 24/7 – with my children and with you." Joseph drug a chair up beside the bed to get as close to her face as possible. He realized he was going to have to plead his case. "These babies are McCoys and I want them and you to have the protection of the McCoy name." There – that was a fine defense if he ever heard one.

Wrong answer. Cady wiped her eyes, but he had a point. She had to think about what was best for their children. "All right. I'll marry you to give the babies your name and I'll locate near you – but I'm not part of the deal. After a decent length of time, we'll divorce and you can go back to your life the way it was before you ever knew me."

"I don't damn well think so." Joseph ground out the words. He wasn't mad at Cady, he was mad at himself for making her feel so unwanted she couldn't even fathom the possibility he wanted her and loved her. How the hell had he fucked up so royally?

"I agree the children should be part of your and your family's life." She was trying to explain. Apparently, Joseph thought she was trying to trick him in some way. "But *I* don't have to be a part of your family – I can exist on the periphery. Don't you see? It will work out just fine."

"The periphery, I don't even know what the hell that word means." Joseph was trying to hold on to his temper – he had no one to blame but himself.

"It means she would have a marginal position. Being on the periphery means that you are 'outside of' or 'not an important part' of something," Noah stated matter of factly.

"Thank you, Mr. Webster." Joseph looked at his brothers. He thought they looked like two pet monkeys – hear no evil and see no evil. "Don't you two have anywhere else to be?"

"I think you need us." Isaac stated flatly. "You aren't doing too well on your own."

"It's simple, really." Cady continued on with her argument as if the others weren't in the room. "The babies can be your family without you making a commitment to me. This will work. You can keep your bachelor lifestyle and I am free to find someone who will marry me because they want to, not because they have to." She was only trying to give him what he wanted – why was he making it so hard?

"Not. In. This. Lifetime, Baby." Joseph literally growled his words. "If you're marrying anybody – you're marrying me. When I nearly lost you – I realized how much you mean to me. I cherish you." To Cady's amazement – Joseph got down on his knees next to the bed. He laid his head on her arm and squeezed her hand so tight, it almost hurt. "I will never be able to explain to you what you mean to mean. You are more than my best friend, Cady. You are part of me – my body craves yours. Making love with you is the most thrilling, perfect experience of my life. Nothing I have ever done in the past can even compare to what I feel for you. When I touch you, it's like I've come home." She glanced over at Noah and Isaac, but Joseph continued, oblivious to his siblings. "I don't want anybody else but you – just you – I love you, Cady. And I knew this before you said anything about a baby."

"He's telling the truth." Isaac said out of the blue. "I was there, Cady. Remember? When you were electrocuted – Joseph almost died, too. He got down on his hands and knees and begged you to live. He declared his love for you over and over."

She couldn't help but feel hopeful. Cady wanted to believe. She was skeptical, after all he was Joseph – and she was just – she was just Cady. Her heart was telling her to grab hold of this magnificent chance at happiness, but her mind was telling her to tread lightly.

But, Joseph wasn't giving up – "Look into my heart. Test me. Give me some type of magical polygraph test. What do you want me to do? How can I prove it to you?" While he was speaking, Noah and Isaac left the room, realizing this was just too private a moment for them to witness. "I'll give up everything." At that moment – as soon as he spoke the words out loud – he realized how true they were. Nothing in his life was more important than Cady. What had happened with Carrie Warner was nothing. The truth would come out – there were medical records and hospital receipts. Beau and Trey would exposeCarrie for the vindictive bitch she was.

"No, no," Cady was adamant. By now, Cady believed every word he was saying. Joseph was pouring his heart out and she was more than ready to place her life and her heart in his hands.

"Yes, I have to make you understand. Cady, nothing I have ever won or achieved comes close to being as important to me as you are. They can take away every trophy, every title – every record I've ever set. They're nothing compared to you. I would trade them all if you'll just say you'll be my wife."

There are rare times in life when you realize the gravity of a moment. What we do with those moments will mean the difference in the path the rest of our lives will take. Cady realized this was one of those moments. Joseph was offering her – everything. And for once in her life, Cady was going to be brave enough to reach out and take what rightfully belonged to her. "Joseph, I am yours," she spoke softly – so softly he had to bend close enough to hear. "I always have been. Our souls have been entwined since the world began. You are the most precious thing in the universe to me. You are my Joseph, you are my everything."

It finally dawned on him what she was saying. Cady was saying 'yes'. He couldn't stand to be apart from her another second. He slid his arms underneath her and picked her up enough that he could slide in the bed with her. "Thank God! Cady, I love you. I love you more than anything in the world." He echoed her sentiment. "Do you hear me, Cady? You are mine. Mine." He sealed their future with a kiss. "Do you know how beautiful you are? How perfect you are?"

"We were meant to be, I think." She laid her head on his shoulder and her hand over his heart. "Even before we met, I knew you were out here – waiting for me to find you." She swallowed – being very careful with her next point. "Joseph, I'm not blind – I know how I look. But my grandmother used to tell me that when I met the man who would really love me I would become beautiful in his eyes and the more he grew to love me, the more beautiful I would become. That's you, Joseph – if I'm beautiful, it is your love that made me so."

And in heaven there was much rejoicing for one who was lost had come home.

Epilogue

Dr. Angel McCoy stood up to accept the award for her work in stem cell research. As she walked up to the podium, her eyes gravitated to where the McCoy clan stood applauding. Her dad, Joseph McCoy, was applauding louder than anyone. Her mom and four sisters seemed equally proud. The only one missing from her immediate family was her twin, and he had been gone for a really, really long time.

"Thank you, ladies and gentleman. It's an honor to be with you tonight. The strides that we've made in stem cell research this past year have been monumental. And I didn't do it alone. All of us working together, made this happen. I would like to thank my family. They inspired me to try things and go farther in my thinking than I ever thought possible. As most of you know, my father was paralyzed once upon a time. Through the love and healing touch of my mother, Cady – he became one of the lucky ones. He walked again. And it was his vision that created the Gabriel McCoy Foundation, named for my twin who we lost far too early. Gabriel was born with a severe paralysis that caused him to pass on just moments after his birth." Angel watched her father hang his head. He had always – for some strange reason –blamed himself for his son's condition. "But his death was not in vain. The McCoy Family stood as one against an enemy – in all of its terrible forms – that has ravaged countless people's lives." She looked at her uncles and their wives and their children. All of her cousins were boys, only her father had been blessed with daughters – five of them. Her Uncle Aron always said that Joseph had been given daughters as a punishment for his playboy lifestyle. Now, Joseph worried incessantly that one of his girls would hook up with a man just like him. As far as Angel was concerned, that wouldn't be a bad thing at all. She adored her father.

"The Scripture says that all things work together for good for those that love the Lord, and the McCoy family firmly believes that. If it hadn't been for my dad's accident – he'd never met my Mom or been healed or had me or my brother and there never would have been a Gabriel McCoy Foundation and we would not have discovered how to rejuvenate and resurrect nerves so that spinal cords could once again become lifelines between the brain and the body that it supports. Miracles do happen, ladies and gentleman, and today we have the proof."

As they watched their daughter accept the Nobel Prize for advancement in medicine, Joseph took Cady's hand. He smiled at her. She was more beautiful today than she had been yesterday and it never ceased to amaze him how beautiful she was. Together, they had created a family and a life together that he wouldn't trade for anything else in the world. As he raised his wife's hand to his lips and kissed it – he wondered who he was kidding. It wasn't him – all the credit went to his beloved Cady. She was a blessing to every person she met. His Cady had The Magic Touch.

ABOUT THE AUTHOR

Sable's hometown will always be New Orleans. She loves the culture of Louisiana and it permeates everything she does. Now, she lives in the big state of Texas and like most southern women, she loves to cook southern food - especially Cajun and Tex-Mex. She also loves to research the supernatural, but shhhh don't tell anyone.

Sable writes romance novels. She lives in New Orleans. She believes that her goal as a writer is to make her readers laugh with joy, cry in sympathy and fan themselves when they read the hot parts - ha!

The worlds she creates in her books are ones where right prevails, love conquers all and holding out for a hero is not an impossible dream.

Visit Sable:
Website: http://www.sablehunter.com
Facebook: https://www.facebook.com/authorsablehunter
Amazon: http://www.amazon.com/author/sablehunter

Hell Yeah! Series Reading Order

Cowboy Heat http://amzn.to/WhY6dw
Cowboy Heat Sweeter Version http://amzn.to/11fiBVQ

Hot on Her Trail http://amzn.to/U3zpT1
Hot on Her Trail Sweeter Version http://amzn.to/19m1WHf

Her Magic Touch http://amzn.to/11b1aw6
Her Magic Touch Sweeter Version http://amzn.to/1byKNL0

A Brown Eyed Handsome Man http://amzn.to/17zmNpY
A Brown Eyed Handsome Man Sweeter Version
http://amzn.to/15oW1k9

Badass http://amzn.to/UsrJJ4
Badass Sweeter Version http://amzn.to/16TqDNX

Burning Love http://amzn.to/15Z4Lyi
Burning Love Sweeter Version http://amzn.to/1iEzOV0

Forget Me Never http://amzn.to/U3PjwK
Forget Me Never Sweeter Version – Coming Soon

I'll See You in My Dreams http://amzn.to/11nsvpg
I'll See You in My Dreams Sweeter Version – Coming Soon

Finding Dandi http://amzn.to/12kK4Kh
Finding Dandi Sweeter Version – Coming Soon

Skye Blue - Coming Soon
I'll Remember You – Coming Soon
Thunderbird – Coming Soon

*Books in the Hell Yeah! Series are grouped by Hell Yeah!, Hell Yeah! Cajun Style AND Hell Yeah! Equalizers

Cookbook
Sable Does It IN The Kitchen http://amzn.to/VAqFo4

Available from Secret Cravings Publishing
TROUBLE - Texas Heat I
My Aliyah - Heart In Chains - Texas Heat II
A Wishing Moon - Moon Magick I
Sweet Evangeline - Moon Magick II
Unchained Melody - Hill Country Heart I
Scarlet Fever – Hill Country Heart II
Bobby Does Dallas - Hill Country Heart III
Five Hearts - Valentine Anthology - A Hot And Spicy Valentine

For more info on Sable's Up Coming Series El Camino Real – Coming Out 2014
Check out Sable's Fan Page on Facebook
http://facebook.com/authorsablehunter

Made in the USA
Middletown, DE
19 April 2015